DAVID DONACHIE was born in Edinburgh in 1944. He has always had an abiding interest in military history, including ancient Rome, the Middle Ages, the British navy of the eighteenth and nineteenth centuries, and the clandestine services during the Second World War. He has more than fifty published novels to his credit, with over a million copies sold. David lives in Deal, the historic English seaport on the border of the English Channel and the North Sea.

## By David Donachie

**THE JOHN PEARCE ADVENTURES**
By the Mast Divided • A Shot Rolling Ship
An Awkward Commission • A Flag of Truce
The Admirals' Game • An Ill Wind
Blown Off Course • Enemies at Every Turn
A Sea of Troubles • A Divided Command
The Devil to Pay • The Perils of Command
A Treacherous Coast • On a Particular Service
A Close Run Thing • HMS *Hazard*
A Troubled Course • Droits of the Crown

**THE CONTRABAND SHORE SERIES**
The Contraband Shore • A Lawless Place • Blood Will Out

**THE NELSON AND EMMA SERIES**
On a Making Tide • Tested by Fate • Breaking the Line

**THE PRIVATEERSMEN SERIES**
The Devil's Own Luck • The Dying Trade • A Hanging Matter
An Element of Chance • The Scent of Betrayal • A Game of Bones

**HISTORICAL THRILLERS**
Every Second Counts

*Originally written as Jack Ludlow*
**THE LAST ROMAN SERIES**
Vengeance • Honour • Triumph

**THE REPUBLIC SERIES**
The Pillars of Rome • The Sword of Revenge • The Gods of War

**THE CONQUEST SERIES**
Mercenaries • Warriors • Conquest

**THE ROADS TO WAR SERIES**
The Burning Sky • A Broken Land • A Bitter Field

**THE CRUSADES SERIES**
Son of Blood • Soldier of Crusade • Prince of Legend
* * *

Hawkwood

A Conquest Novel

# CONQUEST

## David Donachie

McBooks
Press

Essex, Connecticut

## McBooks Press

An imprint of Globe Pequot, the trade division of
The Rowman & Littlefield Publishing Group, Inc.
4501 Forbes Blvd., Ste. 200
Lanham, MD 20706
www.rowman.com

Distributed by NATIONAL BOOK NETWORK

Copyright © 2010 by David Donachie writing as Jack Ludlow
Map of Italy © David Donachie
First published in Great Britain by Allison & Busby in 2010
First McBooks Press edition 2024

British Library Cataloguing in Publication Information available

**Library of Congress Cataloging-in-Publication Data available**

ISBN 978-1-4930-7626-0 (paper : alk. paper)
ISBN 978-1-4930-7627-7 (electronic)

$\infty$™ The paper used in this publication meets the minimum requirements of
American National Standard for Information Sciences—Permanence of Paper for
Printed Library Materials, ANSI/NISO Z39.48-1992.

*To Natalie*
*Who could recruit me*
*anytime!*

# ITALY IN THE 11TH CENTURY

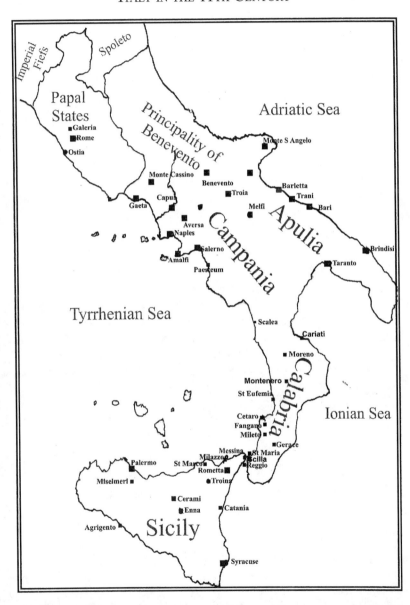

Imperial Fiefs

Spoleto

Papal States

Galeria
Rome
Ostia

Principality of Benevento

Adriatic Sea

Monte S Angelo

Monte Cassino

Benevento

Capua

Troia

Gaeta

Barletta
Trani

Melfi

Bari

Aversa
Naples

Campania

Apulia

Salerno

Amalfi

Paesteum

Brindisi

Taranto

Tyrrhenian Sea

Scalea

Cariati

Moreno

Calabria

Montenero

St Eufemia

Ionian Sea

Cetaro
Fangano
Mileto

Gerace

Messina
Milazzo
St Marco
Rometta
Troina

St Maria
Scilla
Reggio

Palermo

Miselmeri

Cerami
Enna
Catania

Agrigento

Sicily

Syracuse

# PROLOGUE

By the time Roger, the youngest of Tancred de Hauteville's brood, made ready to leave Normandy, the surname of the family was not the obscure appendage it had once been. In twenty years, since the two eldest sons had departed to take mercenary service in Italy, the de Hautevilles had become renowned throughout Christendom: from being obscure knights with nothing but their lances and their fighting ability, they had come to such startling prominence, to serve as an example to all young men who aspired to greatness.

William, known by the soubriquet *Bras de Fer*, had fought his way to land and titles only to die in his prime. In his wake had come his brothers Drogo and Humphrey to both expand the family holdings and elevate the family name. Two more brothers now held valuable fiefs, but if William Iron Arm had led the way, the half-brother who eventually succeeded to his legacy, known to the world by the single soubriquet of the *Guiscard*, had surpassed him.

Styled Count of Apulia, he was as famous for his cunning as his military prowess: Robert de Hauteville dealt on equal terms not only with the temporal power of the papacy, but with the imperial authority of the Holy Roman Empire based in Germany, while being in constant conflict with the Eastern Empire ruled from Constantinople. The lands he now held, from the Apennines to the Adriatic seaboard, had for five centuries been the property of Byzantium and, being valuable, the empire was locked into endless attempts at recovery: Apulia and Calabria were thus cockpits of continual warfare, shifting allegiances, endemic betrayal and ceaseless intrigue.

If Robert *Guiscard* had trouble with the empire in the east he was not spared turmoil in his own backyard: apart from Lombards, Greeks and the native Italians there were other powerful confrère barons south of Rome. No Norman willingly bowed the knee to another and that, on occasions, included his blood relatives. Thus, when the baby of the family made up his mind to head south, it was not by invitation: a brother who shared the name and the family ability as a warrior could be as much of a pest as an asset.

All of those who had preceded Roger had left without comment from their father's liege lord, the Duke of Normandy; it was testimony to how much they had risen that when Roger aired his intentions he was summoned to meet with William the Bastard, an order he would disobey at his peril. Escorted by a party of the family lances, warriors owed in fealty and feudal obligation to the duke, he set out for Falaise, the city his suzerain had chosen as his main residence.

There was, however, one place he was determined to visit, and it was not on the way. It was necessary to bypass Falaise to find the Monastery of St-Evroul-sur-Ouche, while it also required artifice to persuade the noble abbot, Robert de Grantmesnil, that this near-penniless knight was accidentally passing by his door, even more that he should be allowed contact with his half-sister and ward, Judith of Evreux. Roger and she had met the year before at the annual gathering of knights called to render homage to their suzerain. Seven years his junior, she was already a beauty, he was the most handsome of his family; for both, on a mere meeting of eyes, it had been instant mutual attraction.

Only pleading by a distraught Judith melted the relative's initial rebuff: Judith was, after all, a cousin to the duke and the idea of Roger de Hauteville paying suit to such a well-connected beauty was risible – she was destined for a more prosperous hand than his, some great magnate with land, castles and lances. His brother might be Count of Apulia but Roger was a landless nobody. Yet the man was not made of stone and her tears were genuine, so he let her have her fantasy that she could somehow marry for love.

'Italy?' Judith asked, in a near whisper.

They sat in an arbour with a pair of nuns close enough by, placed there to ensure no proprieties were broken, like the touching of hands. Roger, tall, blond and blue-eyed, had been treated by these Brides of Christ like some kind of rabid despoiler and when the two youngsters sat, their chaperones had ensured there was a gap between them of a full arm's length. That was enough for two people enamoured of each other; they sat quietly talking in the way only those who have deep affection for each other can: inconsequential to a listener, heart-searing to the participants.

There was no need to explain the need to go south, given it was a well-worn path for the impoverished knights of Normandy. To prosper at home meant a close connection to the duke, not something a de Hauteville was likely to be granted, given the family history.

'I would have you come with me,' Roger said. 'Allow me to ask the abbot to let you accompany me?'

'As what?'

'As my wife, Judith, what else?'

There was no need to utter a refusal: her crestfallen look was enough. 'I had to beg for this, Roger, a few moments alone, and you know I cannot wed anyone without the permission of Duke William. I am his to give away.'

'Added to that which we had last year our time alone cannot amount to more than half a glass of sand.'

From the church came the sound for which the monastery was famous, the voices of its choir, backed by the musicians her half-brother employed and encouraged. St Evroul was renowned throughout Christendom for this: folk of means travelled long journeys to sit in the chapel and listen to the sweet harmonies, never departing without leaving gifts to an already well-endowed establishment for the sake of their souls.

'It may be all we will ever have. If you go to Italy I may never see you again.'

'I have lances with me.'

She knew what he was saying, and if she had doubts they were assuaged by the determined look in his eye, but Judith also knew that to elope was impossible. Duke William would send men after her and, if caught, she would be ruined, forced to take the veil while Roger would likely spend the rest of his life in a damp and rat-infested oubliette. On her breast she wore a pin surmounted by a freshwater pearl, which she took off and stuck to his blue and white surcoat, moving close enough to have the two nuns on their feet, alarmed at the contact.

'Go south, Roger; become a great man, as I am sure you must, and every time you touch this remember me.'

Judith was gone in a flash: she did not want the man with whom she had fallen in love to see her cry. Roger sat for a while, touching the pearl, then rose slowly and walked, a figure with a bowed head, to join his accompanying lances.

Those steel-tipped lances were for show and he had required the permission of his elder brothers to take them along: once, not long past, they would have been necessary for safety. Duke William had come into his title carrying not only the stain of bastardy, but his own tender years, succeeding aged but seven. He had inherited a province containing numerous powerful vassals unwilling to bow the knee to either his illegitimacy or to his youth, making it a dangerous place to travel, banditry being a brother to rebellion.

During the period in which the de Hautevilles had prospered in Italy, William of Normandy had, with the aid of his uncles, loyal barons and, on more than one occasion, the King of the Franks, fought to first hold on to then subdue his ducal estates. The final battle, fought at Val-ès-Dunes, had cemented his position, allowing William to become master in his own domains. That this was so was immediately obvious to Roger on being greeted by a man secure in his own authority; he had first seen his duke as an easily impressed ten-year-old, when William, only three years his senior, had been invested as a knight by the Frankish king to whom he was nominally a vassal.

The dukedom of Normandy, ceded to the Viking leader Rollo two hundred years previously, was in theory a province of Paris, but being both bellicose and powerful, subsequent dukes had made this a strained relationship, more often one expressed in conflict than alliance. Young and weak, William had needed his powerful neighbour to the east: now, master in his own house, he was more of an equal than a vassal. The Frankish King Henry, sensing his rising strength, was rumoured to be planning to invade Normandy, this time as a mortal enemy.

'It is a time when I need all my fighting men around me.'

'My liege,' Roger replied, 'you have so many that one as insignificant as I will not be missed. Besides, you will have three of my brothers who will rally to your service. They have sworn to remain in Normandy.'

The reference to the number of brothers made the seated William frown, leaving Roger to speculate on the reason: was it that so many of his Norman knights had chosen Italy as the place in which to seek prosperity, or was it the memory of the murder committed by Roger's brother, Serlo, immediately after William had been knighted? Drunk, Serlo had stabbed a potent vassal of the duke, at a time when standing instructions had been issued that no weapons were to be drawn regardless of any perceived slight. Serlo had fled to England to avoid retribution and was still there in the service of the lords of Mercia.

'I should have had all twelve,' William growled, 'though my justice would trim that number by one.'

'I believe, sire, that the reason you do not have all of my family in your service rests with decisions made by your father.'

Surrounded by courtiers it was an unwise remark to make, for they reacted with hissing or horror to what they saw as *lèse-majesté* – odd, since a good half of them would have no idea of the reason Roger had spoken so: the matter to which he referred had happened many years previously. William, alone, might have ignored any allusion to what was an ancient disagreement but he could hardly do so in the presence of so many adherents, some of whom advised him, some of whom protected his person and all of whom would flatter him, such was the way of court life.

'You dare to question the actions of my late father?'

To those three brothers who still lived in the Contentin, as well as many of their contentious neighbours, Roger was known as more diplomatic a person than was the habit of either his own father or his rumbustious siblings. But he was very proud of his name and his lineage, not least of the man he had loved most in the world, his father Tancred, warrior parent to warrior sons and a man who never feared to remind authority they held their power by the consent of those governed, not by force. It was in that memory he spoke.

'No more than he dared to question the motives of mine.'

William shot to his feet, a mistake if he sought to overawe a man a good two hands taller than he. For all his lack of height he had presence, so it was an equal contest, underlined by the even tone in which Roger continued to speak.

'My father asked your father to take my half-brothers into ducal service and he declined for fear of their blood.'

The look of fury had Roger speculating again: Tancred's first wife, Muriella, had been the illegitimate daughter of Richard, this duke's grandfather, so any reference to her could be construed as a reference to that condition of birth, not something to be alluded to in his presence, this again obvious by the vocal disapproval mouthed by his courtiers. But it had undertones some of those would miss, which included the allegation, never wholly laid to rest, that William's father had murdered his own elder brother to gain the title. Tancred de Hauteville, faithful warrior to Duke Richard, had known them both as children and had made no attempt to hide his greater love for the eldest son.

'I have no need to fear your blood, do I?'

The tone was harsh; how easy it would have been to reply in kind, to lay bare before this prince and his arse-lickers that he was no better a man that any of Muriella's sons. Roger might have a different mother but he was part of a family who, proud of their Viking blood, were famed for their temper. Yet he had, and sometimes he wondered if it was a curse, the ability to see where his own abrasive words would lead and to act to avoid it. He thus spoke in an almost emollient voice.

'That is true, My Lord, but if you were to say that I can have no pretensions to your title, I am bound to remind you that my father swore a sacred oath to your grandfather that, by allowing him to marry his daughter, no offspring of that union would aspire to anything other than that already held. I would take it amiss, and I believe be entitled to do so, if any man was to question my father's honour.'

William was checked by that: powerful he might be but there were rules for princes as well as vassals. To go in the direction this man before him was suggesting he might pursue was to open up a can of worms. It did not oblige him to apologise for any imputation of dishonour, but it did mean it would be unwise to labour it.

'Had your father,' Roger continued, 'consented to take my brothers into his service as *familia* knights, as was, I believe, promised to them, they would have laid down their lives to protect both his life and your own, as was their duty. That he refused to do so because he mistrusted their ambition, that he falsely believed they would seek to usurp your position, drove them to mercenary service. I think by their actions and successes they have proved such an act to be a profound mistake.'

That brought forth another hiss from those around them: this fellow was talking to their liege lord like an equal.

'And you?' William demanded.

Roger had him then: he had not set out to trap William of Normandy, reputed by all to be a shrewd statesman and a charismatic leader, but sharp as he was the duke had walked into a snare in which Roger de Hauteville could remind him publicly, before his entire assembled courtiers, that his rank was not much greater than that held by his own family now. He was, and it pleased him to realise it, paying the man back for the insult his father had delivered to old Tancred, loyal and true, all those years ago.

'I am proud most of all of my eldest brother, your namesake, who became Count of Apulia in his own right, a title that has passed on to the present holder, Robert, and it is to him I owe assistance before any other. Not to take service with my own brother would, to me, be a denial of my duty to a loyalty that transcends that which I owe to your house.'

Looking into the face of a man too angry to speak, lest by doing so he would show how much he had been bested, Roger bowed, turned his back, and left, thinking that if his father could see him now, looking down from his place in heaven, where for all his transgressions he must surely reside, he would be smiling.

Roger was not: asking for the hand of Judith of Evreux, a faint hope in any case but one he had been determined to pursue, had died completely with that confrontation.

Preparations for departure had been put in place before the journey to Falaise so Roger had only days back at home before he was ready to leave. Unbeknown to him he performed an act carried out by William Iron Arm twenty years before: he went to the top of the tower to look over the family lands. There had never been enough to satisfy twelve sturdy sons, hence the need to near beg the late duke and, following on from his refusal to take those sons into service, the need to go south to Italy.

All had been born into a world where only by successful combat could the offspring of a petty baron prosper and they had been raised with that in mind. From the top of the tower, stone now in place of the wooden structure William had ascended, Roger could look over the de Hauteville demesne, the small hedged fields, some pasture or directly tilled by family serfs, others let out to tenanted villeins. Hemmed in by trees he could follow the course of the stream where he had first learnt to swim and fish, and to one side of that the open field used as a manège, where he had been taught to ride a pony as a boy, then to handle both horse and weapons as a youth and a man.

It was a contended property: Tancred had been a benign master, seen by some as soft, but he had reminded his sons that the horses they rode, the mail they wore and the weapons they carried came from the toil of these peasants and tenants. If it was a place of tranquillity and security it was still surrounded by trouble, less now than when Roger had been born. At that time the family had been in constant dispute with powerful neighbours who claimed overlordship of the de Hauteville domains, an assertion furiously refuted by his father. That had been laid to rest: this round stone tower on which he stood was proof of that.

Built to replace a motte-and-bailey structure of wood and earth, a proper donjon had been a dream of Tancred for years, a sign of his status, a smack in the eye to those who claimed they held authority over his land. Brothers William and Drogo had sent the funds for the construction, fruits of their successful campaigns, but it was Iron Arm who had persuaded the Duke William to grant permission for its construction – no such structure could be raised without it – by writing to him as an equal in power and prestige.

Not overly emotional, Roger nevertheless felt the tears prick his eyes as he recalled the day of completion. Tancred had been aged then, a shadow of his old warrior self, but still a tall man, grey-haired, grizzled and scarred. He had wept at the sight and also at the loss of his sons to another land, for he knew he would never again clap eyes on those who had gone. That was Tancred: a doughty fighter, a prolific lover who had produced fourteen children with his two wives and yet an honourable husband who had never strayed from his marital bonds, a man passionately proud of his unruly brood.

To Roger, his youngest and very much his favourite, he had been a paragon, entertaining in his storytelling, easily forgiven when he had consumed too much apple wine and became maudlin about his past deeds, a man of fair dealing and strong friendships, that attested to by the number of neighbours who came to any family celebration. How far they had come, those boys of his – even his daughter was married to the Norman Count of Aversa, the greatest power in Campania, while his nephew, raised as another son after his father's death in battle, was now the incumbent bishop of the nearby see of Coutances.

'Can I make him proud?' Roger asked himself, speaking out loud, before looking to the sky and the god he worshipped, who saw all things. 'I ask for no more than to live as he lived, to fight as he fought and to be as honourable as he was in both.'

Looking down to the grey-stone manor house in which he had been raised he saw that his horses were ready, the saddlecloth in the blue and white chequer of his house loaded with his weapons: lance, great broadsword, his suit of chain mail and his helmet, a scene he had witnessed when his brothers had departed, each one swearing an oath to their father on the hilt of their sword the one thing on which Tancred insisted: that, in a world where violence was the norm, no son of his should raise his weapon against a brother.

There was no vow for him: Tancred was long in the ground now and it was different in so many ways. His brothers had left alone and with little: a small amount of coin, salt to trade with in its place, taken from the family pans that lay on the Atlantic shoreline, destined to seek shelter in the pilgrim hospices that lined the route to Rome, to sleep in discomfort and just as often under the stars, heading towards an unknown destination and an even more obscure future.

Not Roger! It was his mother who would weep to see him go, but he would travel as a person of consequence attended by twenty lances, other young sons eager for an Italian adventure, waiting now by the roadway to join him, who would testify to his position. He would send in his name to every great property he passed and that would open the gates. He would be entertained, fed well and given good wine to drink, such was the power of the de Hauteville name. Yet when he got to Italy, albeit he would be given opportunity, the same predicament would face him as faced every one of the Normans who had preceded him.

He must make his own way, carve out his own success, face his travails and overcome them, fight whatever enemies presented themselves and conquer. His name would get him into battle but it was his own sword arm, his own lance and the aid of his own trusty mounts that would raise his name to equal his brothers. Standing on the parapet of that stone donjon, it was as easy to imagine failure as success: there was only one certainty – whichever it was, glory or ignominy, it was not to be found here in the Contentin.

# CHAPTER ONE

Robert *Guiscard*, Count of Apulia, knew that the enemy commander, Argyrus, would be obliged to sortie out at some time: it was his only hope of raising a siege now approaching a year in duration. Brindisi had stout walls that had withstood much in the way of ballista, and many hands to repair any breeches made by the huge, flying stones, so that all his assaults had failed to get the besieging army into the great port city, one of the last of the Byzantine bastions left in Southern Italy; in a lightning sweep the previous year he had taken the other cities of Apulia and Eastern Calabria, leaving the two greatest outposts, Brindisi and the even more formidable Bari, isolated.

But those numerous hands repairing broken stone needed to be fed and the siege had cut off any hope of forage from the surrounding countryside, while hired Venetian galleys blocked off any supplies from the sea. Populous and crowded, Brindisi would be fast approaching the point of mass starvation: the moat and the harbour that bordered the city were already filling up with the bloated, decaying cadavers of the weakest inhabitants: the elderly, the sick and children.

There is a point in an invested city where a good commander must decide whether to feed his horses – necessary for a sortie – or eat them, then distribute the oats needed to keep them healthy to the starving inhabitants: Argyrus was at that point. Delay too long and there was a risk that the citizens, driven by fear and hunger, at a time when there were no more dogs, cats or rats to eat, would take matters into their own hands. Many a leader had waited too long and found himself overthrown, forced to flee or even murdered by those he was tasked to defend, thrown as a corpse from his own walls before the gates were opened to surrender the city.

'I need news,' Argyrus insisted. 'I need to know if any of my stratagems are bearing fruit.'

The men to whom he spoke – his senior subordinates – were also aware of the approaching crisis: they also knew they needed to appear confident before their commander, lest by an expression of doubt they forfeit their own lives, this necessary to destroy any hint of defeatism in the higher echelons of the defence. Argyrus was a man much dependent on spies – he had his informants in the city, some in the *Guiscard*'s camp, yet others dotted around the provinces seeking to stir up trouble in the Norman rear, acting either for gain or from conviction – but getting in and out of the city was difficult: his messengers were being intercepted too easily.

'We will be gifted but one opportunity, so we must make sure it is final in its outcome.'

'We could offer to buy him off, My Lord. Normans are always grasping for gold.'

'Not the one outside our walls! The *Guiscard* seeks power and will not be content with Brindisi. He will have Bari as well if he can. If the imperial court would realise that they would have reinforced me long ago, but there are more fools in Constantinople than wise heads.'

No one would meet the Catapan's eye then: it was not a good idea to question the decisions of the emperor or those who advised him; the dungeons of Constantinople were brimming with those who had dared, no doubt betrayed, as they would be now, by those they trusted. Argyrus had, like his predecessors, never had enough troops to beat the increasing power of the Normans, yet he had kept them at bay for years by intrigue and bribery, provided with gold in abundance. Where that had worked in the past in terms of divide and rule, it was of less use now.

'One day,' Argyrus carped, 'if they are not careful, this count they so disdain will turn up outside their own walls. He seeks the purple and has too much wealth already to be distracted by more. You do not know these de Hautevilles as I do, for I have been close to them. They are of a different breed to their bandit confrères. I saw in William *Bras de Fer* and his brother Drogo...'

That induced a pause and recollection of another failure: it was by intrigue that Argyrus had ensured both those brothers fell to the secret knife. He had tried to do the same to Robert in the early stages of the siege, only to find the man sent to do murder fired bodily and alive over the city walls – an act he was not meant to, nor did he, survive – leaving the instigator unsure of why the attempt had failed.

'They are truly a plague. Kill off one and another rises to take his place, each one more dangerous than the last.'

It was gold Argyrus was relying on now, spread about the provinces to foment revolt in the *Guiscard*'s rear. Not all the Normans of Italy were outside his walls or happy with de Hauteville hegemony; not all of Robert's Apulian subjects were loyal. There were many who might, even if they owed vassalage to the Count of Apulia, see some advantage in revolt. That would draw Robert off and, because he would need to move swiftly, he would have to take with him the men Argyrus feared most, his conroys of mounted Norman warriors, the most feared fighting men in all Christendom.

'Go out into the city,' Argyrus commanded. 'Search for the hoarding of grain and livestock and seize anything you can find.'

'We have done that once already, Lord Argyrus.' The fellow who spoke, one of his senior captains, got a stare that made him feel cold on what was a hot day. Likewise the voice that responded was icy in tone. 'Do it again, there is always more hidden than you can find in one search. If nothing else, let the citizens see we are not close to capitulation. I need more time.'

Robert de Hauteville knew the Byzantine Catapan had spies in his encampment, just as he was sure it would be necessary to employ guile to draw the fellow out. Never comfortable in siege warfare, no Norman was, he was as eager as the leader of the Greeks to get Argyrus and what forces he could muster out into the open. There, superiority in Norman cavalry would count for more than any static assault by his Italian/Lombard levies. Robert's problem was simple: if he knew that he had the advantage in mounted warfare, so did his opponent. He would not emerge to fight Normans, so some excuse must be manufactured to deceive him, and time was no more on his side than it was on that of Argyrus.

The *Guiscard* had his own problems, common to every siege: the constant need to rotate his soldiers out of the immediate vicinity of the walls to avoid the kind of sickness that would decimate his strength; the requirement to forage in a wider area to provide food for men and fodder and oats for his horses, without so weakening his force that he handed over advantage to the defenders. He also had a healthy respect for Argyrus: the fellow was a crafty enemy, the first Lombard ever entrusted by Constantinople to hold high office in the fertile south Italian provinces known as the Langobardian Theme. At one time an ally of the Normans and his fellow Lombards, as well as the titular leader of a Lombard-led revolt against Byzantine rule, he had spectacularly betrayed his race and their cause for personal gain, only to be forced to immediately flee for his life.

Many cursed him for this; his present opponent, who had been a witness at the time to his treachery, saw it as sound common sense. More powerful Lombard princes had been using Argyrus as a figurehead who could be discarded once success had been achieved: the man had seen the sense of looking out for himself while the chance still existed to do so. Yet by his act he had done more than let down his fellow Lombards. The amount of distrust his treachery generated allowed William Iron Arm to take leadership of the revolt, turning it from a Lombard insurrection into a Norman bid for territorial gain, one that had been increasingly successful, as first William, then Drogo and the old misery Humphrey, all now gone to meet their Maker, had expanded Norman rule.

Elevated to the office of Catapan, Argyrus had returned to Apulia and proved a thorn ever since, launching plots and strategies to seek to hold back the Norman tide. Finding their expansion relentless he had even tried an alliance with the papacy, only to see that rebound on him at the decisive Battle of Civitate. On that field the de Hauteville brothers, massively outnumbered, had combined to soundly rout a huge papal army. If there had been genius in the fruits of that victory it had come from Robert, the youngest de Hauteville on the field.

It was he who had seen an opportunity, with the Pope now humiliated, isolated and a Norman prisoner, to turn them from Norman banditti, hated throughout the whole of Italy, into, if not loved overlords, legitimate rulers. With cunning and foresight the *Guiscard* had reasoned that a now defenceless pope, a man with no army who had need of one, had the authority to recognise the titles they had assumed through combat. All they had to do was bow the knee to the man they had defeated and accept him as their suzerain.

In the tangled world in which they lived, a thousand years after the crucifixion, no man could hope to hold a title not given credence by one of the triumvirate of great powers in the Christian world, two temporal, one ecclesiastical: Byzantium, a mortal enemy ripe for dismemberment, was out of the question; the Holy Roman Empire was too Frankish, too disdainful of Norman upstarts, wherever they resided, to reward them with titles unless absolutely obliged to do so. But the papacy, struggling to assert itself and beset by difficulties left over from the time of Charlemagne, had provided the key: the de Hautevilles, thanks to the Pope and his blessing, now stood as equals to any magnate in Christendom. Robert would thank Argyrus once he was captured, just before he hanged him: after all, he must be made to pay for the murders of William and Drogo.

'Has he told you everything he knows yet?' asked Robert, approaching the point where the latest captured messenger seeking a way into Brindisi was slowly spinning, naked, over an open fire pit.

'All he does is pray to God in his screaming, begging his forgiveness as a miserable sinner.'

'A true monk, then?'

'So it seems, My Lord.'

Robert stepped forward to examine the flapping skin, scorched and blackened, that hung from the suspended body, aware of the heightened pork-like smell of his roasting. There was no screaming now, the fellow was long past that, just a low hiss of what he assumed was continued prayer.

'Such an honest man it would be good to spare, so it is a pity he did not speak. It is rare to meet a monk who is not venal, truly a holy person.'

'He is too far gone for life, sire.'

'True,' Robert replied. 'Put him out of his misery.'

His back was turned when the fellow's throat was cut; all he heard was the sound of the heated blood hissing in the coals beneath. He was looking at the walls of Brindisi for the thousandth time, nagged by the thought that he might be forced to raise the siege. The rate of desertions was rising as levies brought here on the promise of plunder lost any certainty of success. He was also aware of the number of eyes upon him, the glare of attention always afforded to the leader of any warlike enterprise, as men sought in his visage a message of the true state of affairs.

If Robert de Hauteville had a fault – many would maintain he had a raft of them – it was that he was not of a trusting nature. Ready to explain any tactical manoeuvre in battle, or to outline the bones of a campaign, he was very guarded in his thinking on his future plans, so open speculation as to alternatives was never discussed. Those he led were told what they needed to know and nothing more. Right now they would have been amazed to see inside his mind: their general was castigating himself, wondering if he should have let that newly expired messenger through.

Men prepared to die rather than reveal what they know had something to tell: those with nothing of value would speak at the first lick of flame, lie to save their lives, so it would appear the man just roasted had been in possession of useful information. Killing him had only been a mercy insomuch as he was already too far gone to interrogate and it was quite possible, given he had as many spies in Brindisi as Argyrus had outside the walls, that he would have found out quicker what that was by letting him proceed rather than instructing his pickets to capture anyone trying to approach the well-defended walls at points where enough destruction had been achieved to allow secret ingress.

Argyrus would want to draw off him and his Norman cavalry; Robert wanted to give the impression of departing without actually doing so, but such a ploy was a tricky thing to manage, given there was not an educated fellow alive unaware of the use of such a tactic since the siege of Troy. He could not go unless his opponent had good cause to believe he was riding to subdue a serious threat and would thus be away for a long time, enough for him to sortie out and inflict a defeat on the remainder of Robert's army. Argyrus was too shrewd: he would not fall for a partial departure; he would have ways of ensuring the Normans were too far off to interfere in his plans.

'Always think your enemy cleverer than you and you will rarely be outfoxed.'

In saying that to himself he was forced to acknowledge the source, his own father Tancred. He recalled how boring he had found the constant repetition of the old man's mantras, usually delivered when he had been drinking. They had never got on and eventually Robert had come to realise that which others had seen more easily: he and Tancred were too much alike to agree on anything. But it would never do to gainsay the old warrior, for his father had seen much and fought in a great many battles. He had campaigned in Normandy, the Frankish kingdoms ruled from Tours and Paris, as well as in Spain against the Moors. He had even sailed to fight in England to put back on the throne that useless Saxon article, King Ethelred.

'What would he least expect you to do, this enemy?' was another of Tancred's sayings spoken out loud, this as a strong northerly wind, common at this time of year, blew across the siege lines sending up spirals of dust and causing the Venetian galleys to jibe on their anchors.

He fears my Norman cavalry, Robert thought, but he is missing one vital fact. The solution came to him fully formed, as such ideas always do, and so swiftly it was a matter of wonder as to why it had lain dormant so long.

'My friend,' he said, quietly addressing a distant enemy, 'you forget, Normans are warriors first and cavalry second.'

Before he had finished that softly uttered statement he was striding towards his tent, shouting for the people he needed, underlings who gathered quickly to hear what their general had to impart. Suspicious as ever, unsure of who was talking Byzantine gold, he felt the need to concoct a story, to say that roasted emissary had betrayed a secret, indeed to make up the kind of revolt Argyrus had been so assiduous in trying to foment, before giving orders for his Norman captains to prepare their *batailles* for an immediate departure, not forgetting to sanction the use of the entire stud of spare mounts.

'There is trouble in Trani, a serious uprising, and we must move with maximum speed, so there is no time to favour our mounts. We must push them hard, not only on the way there, but back as well, lest Argyrus sees a chance to come out and fight.'

'Trani was ever too Greek a city, second only to Bari. We should have torn down their walls when we had the chance.'

These words were uttered by Geoffrey, his older brother, though with a twinkle in his eye: he knew Robert too well to be entirely fooled by what was happening, but held his tongue until those given orders had rushed off to execute them, leaving them alone, not speaking, and softly when he did so, until he was sure there were no servants in earshot.

'So, brother, what is really afoot?'

That produced an immediate frown on the face of the *Guiscard*. He hated to be questioned, while there was also the fact of Geoffrey's greater age, which, if he deferred to Robert in leadership and title could not be gainsaid. The command of the Apulian Normans had come down through the line of de Hauteville brothers: first William, then to Drogo and Humphrey and, on the latter's death Geoffrey had been next in line. But it was clear who the men they led wanted, just as irascible Humphrey, who openly disliked Robert, knew who would hold what had been gained. Robert was popular as well as a brilliant general, and since each in turn had been chosen by acclamation, it became obvious that, put to the men, he would be the one elected.

Geoffrey, who knew his limitations and was happy with the title he held as Count of Loritello, acquiesced in this: he was by far the most good-natured of the brood with an equanimity unusual in a Norman, never mind in the de Hauteville family. The second brother, Mauger, was more typical: he had served longer in Italy than Robert and had not been happy to bow the knee. So he had gone off with a large group of eighty lances, the men he had led for years, to seek his fortune elsewhere. He had just taken the land of a Lombard noble south of Salerno and was now ensconced in his stout castle of Scalea.

'I need to draw Argyrus out.'

'Obviously.'

'Is it obvious?' Robert snapped. 'I see no evidence of anyone doing much thinking other than me.'

'What would be the purpose, Robert, when you are the man who commands?'

'I am open to suggestion.'

Geoffrey actually laughed, which got him a black look. 'Let us leave aside the truth, that you are not and that you are secretive. Tell me what your plans are.'

Even with a man he trusted with his life, Robert hesitated, leaving Geoffrey to wonder what had happened to that bellicose jester who had first arrived from Normandy. Then he had been too open, too free with his opinions, nettling his elders with his denigration of their abilities, not least William, the man who had created opportunity for all. Robert had been banished to the most barren part of Calabria for that attitude and Drogo, equally disapproving, had not brought him back when William died. Only the threat of the combined forces of the Pope, with levies from nearly all of northern Italy, and his alliance with Byzantium, had obliged Humphrey to recall him and he had sent him back to Calabria as soon as he could.

With a glance around to ensure no one could overhear him, Robert, much to his brother's amusement, came close and whispered in his ear.

Watching from the highest point on the walls, having with him a fellow whose eyesight he knew to be exceptional, Argyrus watched as the Normans, two thousand lances, departed in a cloud of dust, heading due north along the coast, marking the addition of the number of spare mounts, which indicated the distance needed to be travelled was great. Those on whom he relied in the countryside to the north, east and south would keep watch and, once they were out of sight would, that night, provided they were sure they had continued on their way, light small beacons on the higher hills to mark their passing.

'You must rest now,' he said to his trusted lookout, 'for you will be needed once darkness falls.'

Then he fell silent, wondering how long he should wait before calling for an assembly of his soldiers. Too soon, with so many spies in the city, and word would leak before the *Guiscard* was gone. But he could not wait too long: opportunity was a fickle thing – it could evaporate in an instant.

# CHAPTER TWO

Surprise was essential for Argyrus and it was a nervous two days while he waited for his chance to strike, a period in which the besiegers had to be kept in the dark about his preparations. It would take time to get his men ready, then they would have to deploy as they issued from the gates of the city to form up outside, that being the moment of maximum danger. He had a limited cavalry screen to protect his levies and keep them from an immediate counter-attack, so the decision to employ them in what might be a suicidal encounter, an all-out charge to pin down his foes, was forced upon him. If the battle were lost they were useless anyway.

Normally foot soldiers took time to deploy and it had to be done in daylight: their level of training precluded any attempt by torchlight. Present his enemy with too much of a chance by their being disordered and the whole enterprise might falter, leaving him weaker than he was now. So they would wait till the first hint of morning light; what they would face could only be a partly known fact – infantry long in the siege lines and thus, he hoped, not ready to do all-out battle.

More important was the lack of the leadership at which the Normans excelled plus their prowess in ensuring that when their *milites* met an enemy army, that force had been badly disrupted and often broken in spirit by the vigorous attacks of their mounted confrères. Vital to his hopes was one factor: they had become so accustomed to Norman support they would wilt for the lack of it, yet whichever way he examined the problems, more ifs surfaced than definite conclusions.

His system of hilltop beacons had seen the Normans pass beyond the point at which they could interfere in the coming battle and, on prior instructions, more fires would be lit if Robert *Guiscard* reappeared. The night before the battle was the worst, and not only for the watch being kept to the north: if Argyrus was a clever and skilled Catapan, he thought himself a far from competent general and thus he was prone to fret. He remembered his first night before a battle, outside the port city of Trani, many years previously, and recalled how calm William Iron Arm had been, just before the assault Argyrus had betrayed and rendered impossible.

Iron Arm had been preparing to lead his Norman warriors onto the walls of the city by means of a wooden siege tower, which meant meeting their enemies in almost single file, one sword against many, surely the most dangerous form of assault in creation. The titular leader of the attack might have been a Lombard but it was really the eldest de Hauteville who was the man in charge. How tranquil he had been, unconcerned that death might come with the morning sun. How different was he, Argyrus, who must now address his troops to put fire in their bellies. It was that last thought that gave him the possible key to inspiration: they needed not fire in their guts, but food.

'Out on the plains before us are storerooms bursting with grain, as well as cattle and sheep on the hoof, an abundance of everything we lack.'

Looking down from the top step of the stairway that led to his citadel, he peered into the torch lit sea of faces, trying to discern the mood.

'I know I can tell you about the need to be brave, to heed your captains, keep your discipline and to do battle with deadly purpose. I can invoke the threat to your hearths, for many of you have wives and children in the city, just as I can say to you who are Greek that beyond those walls are those we call barbarians: the Normans. I do not demean those amongst you who are Italian or Lombard, for you see as well as any the benign nature of imperial rule.'

That set up some murmuring: it was gilding it to say Constantinople was benign, more truthful would be to say it was greedy. As long as the revenues of this great trading port flowed east the empire did not bear down too heavily on its subjects, nor did largesse flow the other way to what was a distant fief. Argyrus knew it was not love of Byzantium that would make the Italians and Lombards fight: it was fear of Norman-led revenge on them and their families. The city had been offered terms a year past and he had turned them down, so Brindisi, by the laws of war, was open to pillage. Once those walls were breached, once the enemy was inside, no one would be safe from rapine or murder.

'And I promise you this. There are, in our midst, many men of wealth, those who have grown rich on the trade of Brindisi, many Greeks who have settled here over the centuries. No doubt these prosperous folk will willingly give up their possessions to be shared once our city is free of the siege. But this I say to you, for

I know they will have secreted away their gold, silver and valuable chattels, their chests of coins, their bezants of gold, concerned to keep at least part of it intact...'

That set off another rippling murmur from the poor people who made up his armed levies: it was they who did the fighting and dying, not the wealthy citizens who bore down on them in times of peace.

'They will not keep them even should they desire to do so. I will undertake a gathering of their hidden goods and there will be, in this very square, a distribution of the spoils, the very thing that those beasts of Normans have come to our walls to steal. Fill your bellies outside the walls from what they have ravaged from the countryside and I will fill your purse from the riches of your city once victory is ours. There will be gold for every one of you.'

The cheering had started before those last words were spoken, a great bellow for a promise Argyrus doubted he could keep: those leading citizens were the very people he needed to hold on to power in this city – without them to carry out his edicts he would be a cipher. But to win this day was the purpose and honesty could go by the board. He waited till the cheering died down, then called forward the priests of his Orthodox faith to bless the enterprise, which they did with incense and incantations over bowed heads and whispered prayers.

Back inside his chamber, on the table, lay a map of the exterior plain on which the city stood, and around it were gathered those who would carry out his plans. Placing an elbow on the table, Argyrus swept his forearm in an arc to emphasise his aims.

'We must sweep them towards the shoreline. With water at their back and the choice to drown or surrender no army can maintain cohesion, all history tells us this. And I want no quarter, every enemy soldier who discards his weapon must die. Any of your troops who give succour must be likewise killed to encourage the soft-hearted. Let them know it is death for them or those they fight and thus there is no choice. I want that seashore red with the blood of those who have dared to challenge the empire. Let it flow out to those Venetian galleys to rot the cables that hold them to the seabed.'

Looking around at those assembled he had no doubt they would be determined. He had few real soldiers but these men were just that, with one notable exception, all servants of the empire come from far-flung places to Italy to fight its battles; if Constantinople would not send him troops, they had sent him men who could command them. They were trained to war and, he had to admit, they had about them that air of calmness he had once seen and so envied in William de Hauteville. Yet his inability not to agonise made him say more; it was Byzantine gold that had made him desert his fellow Lombards and he had never lost faith in the working power of that commodity.

'Be assured, what I said to the levies assembled applies more to you than to them. Win this fight and you will be rich beyond your wildest dreams. Not only will I reward you, so will the emperor. Any citizen of Brindisi with the means to do likewise who fails to be generous to the men who have saved his life and possessions, as well as his family, I will hang from the city walls.'

Looking to the sandglass, now with the last grains running through the neck, he added, 'In one turn of the glass the sun will come up and we will deploy. Go to your men and encourage them, as I have encouraged you. Remember, if our enemies are not asleep when we attack they will not be long from their slumbers, for they will not think to be assaulted so soon after dawn. Go!'

Two dozen fists thudded into leather breastplates as Argyrus received from his captains the salute that had been the right of an imperial general since the time of the Roman legions.

The first hint of grey on the Adriatic skyline saw the great oak and metal-studded gates, oiled to be silent, swung open, the first troops out, the limited force of cavalry, animals led – not ridden – for silence. Out on the plain they mounted up and waited, horses snorting and prancing but held in check. Their task, once the *milities* had exited, was to engage in that wild charge, to pin in their lines the besieging army, to harry them mercilessly and spread alarm and confusion, making an organised defence impossible.

Argyrus was not a general to lead from the front where he feared, being indecisive, he might cause more uncertainty than clarity. He was watching from the highest point of the exterior walls on the landward side of the city, surrounded by those leading citizens he had promised to impoverish, delighted, once the signal was given, by the way his horsemen performed when the order was given to attack.

Nothing was harder to control than cavalry; indeed it was in that which lay the Norman strength. But for what he required this day, a horde of galloping men, yelling and waving their swords, was the very thing, they being insufficient in number to otherwise affect the battle. Behind them the foot soldiers had exited, their captains yelling and using the flats of their weapons to keep them in order, tight cohorts that their Catapan hoped would come up against disorganised bands, hastily assembled, men who would break when presented with their more organised opponents. Cool as was the morning he found he was perspiring, his body jerking involuntarily as he sought to urge on his men.

'Good, good, keep to that line,' he shouted, even if he knew he could not be heard, happy that his captains were doing as he had planned, leading their fighting men in a straight line away from the gates, heading directly inland where they could wheel, hopefully without losing their cohesion, to outflank the enemy at the point of maximum weakness, far from the active siege lines, to roll them up and drive them towards that fatal shore and slaughter.

Agony attends all warfare for a leader; so much can go wrong and so quickly does what looks possible vanish like a chimera, yet for all his fretting and anxiety Argyrus watched with increasing hope as his tactics seemed to unfold in a perfect reproduction of that which he had ordered. Truly, he had caught his enemies unaware. His risk of deploying before the sun was fully up, no doubt a manoeuvre thought to be beyond his poorly trained levies, was paying a huge dividend. His horsemen had suffered much, attacking a vastly more numerous foe, but they had sown the necessary disarray.

Far out from the walls Argyrus could see his foot soldiers, now with the sun on their backs: the uneven ground had spoilt their perfect symmetry, that was to be expected, so it was a heaving mass that began to wheel north towards the main enemy encampment and the tents of their leaders, two crowned by fluttering pennants bearing the blue and white chequer of the de Hautevilles. Robert would be gone, but was his brother Geoffrey still present? Nothing would crown this day more than that a member of the hated family should be taken alive or dead, preferably the former, so that he could make the *Guiscard* crawl for the chance to ransom. A dead body he would return naked and despoiled.

'The day will be ours,' Argyrus cried as his tangled levies hit the even more muddled Lombards and Italians, the *milities* of the Count of Apulia's army. 'They are turning to a rabble, look.'

Eager to watch the cessation of nearly a year of increasing gloom, albeit with even less ability than Argyrus to make sense of what was actually happening, those around him pressed forward to see what was nothing more than a mass of bodies pressing against each other, pikes and other weapons flashing in the morning sun, men in dun-coloured padded tunics, making it hard to tell friend from foe. But if their leader was excited, it behoved them to be the same, until a point came where even the most untutored eye could see that one faction was falling back.

'Look, a de Hauteville banner and the device of Geoffrey of Loritello. Get me a messenger.' A youth came forward to stand before a man now wild-eyed with excitement. 'Go to the leading captains, tell them I will give them all of the ransom for a de Hauteville. Tell them it is an express command, to take him alive.'

Argyrus was back leaning over the parapet as the lad ran off, eagerly pointing out to those around him how favourably the battle was progressing. The news that the Venetian galleys were slipping their anchors and rowing furiously for the shore only added to his glee.

'Let them try to take off *Guiscard*'s army, for they will fail, and if God is truly on our side then they too will suffer the fate as those they seek to embark. We will turn their hulls to cinder and drown every man who dared to ply an oar.'

'They do not give in easily, Catapan,' said one of the men beside him.

That was true; there was no rout and he sought to soothe his own anxiety by allaying that of those around him. 'They are Robert de Hauteville's men and he has trained them, his brothers before him, making them the best foot soldiers in all Italy. But the *Guiscard* is not here to lead them, for I tell you, if he was I would yet be fearful. Thank the Almighty his brother is not half the general he is.'

Having wheeled and committed their entire force, the captains of Brindisi were pressing their opponents back to a point right under the eyes of their leader, so that the line of those engaged ran straight before them. Argyrus fretted that his enemies were retreating in too orderly a manner: he needed a collapse, prayed for a slaughter and swore to heaven above to bring that on.

'God be praised,' he yelled as his wish was granted.

The line of Apulian levies broke and ran, hotly pursued by his own, now jumbled cohorts. Then, inexplicably, they halted, leaving him near to foaming with frustration, which had him running along the walls to shout at them to push on. The sight that stopped him nearly did the same for his heart. It was, without question, the death of his hopes.

In a line, before the beach, stood a serried mass of mailed warriors, obviously Normans by their helmets and tear-shaped shields. In the middle stood the banner of the Count of Apulia and even at a distance, due to his height and build, the *Guiscard* was visible. The men, his retreating army, were not routed, they broke and ran left and right of their confrères and as soon as the ground before the Normans was clear they began a slow and measured advance. Frantically he could see his captains forming their men into a line of defence, beating them again, and hard, with flattened swords, while their best-trained soldiers went to the rear to put a stop to desertion.

All the noise was coming from there: the Normans were advancing in silence, pennants fluttering on their lances, with not even a beating drum to set their pace, as if to underline they needed no sound to control their pace. Behind them, drawn up on the soft sand of the beach, were the galleys that had fetched them ashore, leaving Argyrus to wonder how the *Guiscard* had managed it.

Those beacons he had seen in the night would not have been lit for horses; they would only have been fired when Norman cavalry was seen to have gone by. Yet here they were before him, and worse, they were advancing on troops he knew in his pounding heart would not be able to repel them: the Normans knew how to fight on foot and would not break. The choice for him was simple; to watch the slaughter or to prepare to flee, for he had no illusion of what would happen to him if he fell into the hands of Robert de Hauteville.

The harbour of Brindisi was full of boats that had not set to sea since the imposition of the siege. Yet, in bringing the Normans ashore, the Venetians had opened up an avenue of escape. Turning quickly, he faced those wealthy citizens who had made so much from this port, some leading Greek families that had been here for five centuries. If he had a duty not to fall into the hands of the enemy, and not just for the sake of his skin, surely he had, too, a responsibility to deny to the *Guiscard* as much of the spoils of the city as he could.

'Citizens, the city is lost. The way is clear to get to sea and I must take it and make for Bari.'

'The Normans have not yet won.'

'Then I invite you to stay here and watch them do so. Perhaps the spilling of so much blood will please you as a spectacle.' Argyrus could see how many his words had already affected, the wiser souls: they were moving swiftly away to gather up their treasure and buy or steal a boat. 'If our levies break, those on the gates will close them to keep out the Normans and leave our fellows to die against their own walls. If they stand, they will have a more noble ending to their lives, but an ending it will be.'

'Then, Catapan, send word to them to surrender.'

Argyrus smiled, but it contained no mirth. 'They have one more duty to perform and that is to allow those of us who must flee to do so.'

# CHAPTER THREE

Robert *Guiscard* called a halt to his advance once he had driven the enemy away from what had been his siege lines and encampment: they were now arrayed with their back to their home city, which had already closed its gates against them for fear of what was coming. Looking at the men before him, desperately trying to form some kind of defence, he realised this presented him with another set of problems, though he could congratulate himself on the fact that his plan had worked to perfection. Right now his entire stud of horses was at pasture in and around Monopoli, with enough men left behind to care for them – not least to ensure none were stolen.

The boats in which he and his force had come south overnight, every trading vessel and fishing craft on what was a busy maritime coast, had been sent back and out of sight as soon as they had transferred to the Venetian galleys, lest Argyrus guess that he had returned. The enemy was in less disarray now but they could not stand against his men and they knew it, while what cavalry Argyrus had deployed were either wounded, dead, without horses or riding completely blown mounts.

'Why call a halt?' demanded Geoffrey, breathing heavily and sweating copiously, having run to join him in full chain mail, his standard-bearer at his heels. 'Surely you have them at your mercy?'

'I do,' Robert replied.

If his brother had not posed the question it was in the mind of every man behind him, though few would have dared to voice it. His dilemma hinged on what he was outside Brindisi for, plunder or conquest? For the former it was easy: smash these creatures who stood in his way because they knew they had no choice, then drive to the gates of a city lacking defenders. Those inside would very likely open up, hoping to mitigate what they knew to be coming.

Conquest required a different approach, for, if the *Guiscard* never voiced it, he was intent on being more than that which he was now. The whole Norman intervention in Southern Italy, first as mercenaries, had been generated by a Lombard desire to regain the rule they had once exercised by kicking out Byzantium: the dream had been an independent kingdom. That as a vision was dead, broken on their endemic inability as a race to agree on a leader whom they would all be prepared to see crowned, made worse by a string of treacheries stretching over many decades: they fought and betrayed each other with more resolution than they ever brought to warfare against their common foe.

Could it be a Norman dream? The first Count of Normandy was a Viking raider bought off with the title and land by a Frankish king struggling to contain Norse raids that had bitten so deep into his territories they had frequently threatened Paris. Rollo established a line that might one day aspire to the purple – rumour had it that William the Bastard had designs on the Saxon crown of England: the present holder, his cousin Edward, was childless and, given his piety, likely to remain so. Other Norsemen ruled in

Denmark and Norway. Here in the Mediterranean there existed an even greater prize, a possible Norman-ruled realm and, beyond that, tottering, an empire that had, in the last three hundred years, lost two-thirds of its territories to Islam.

To conquer Constantinople would require every resource available; to massacre the defenders of Brindisi would bring on a satisfying effusion of blood and would lay to rest all the frustrations of the long months of siege. To sack the city would keep happy his own men – they were, no doubt, already imagining what was to come: gold and silver to fill their purse, as much wine as they could consume, women to violate at will, their menfolk slaughtered – and perhaps the children would suffer both. They would amuse themselves roasting babies before their mothers, castrating men and stuffing their genitals into the mouths of their just-raped daughters, in the process creating among those who survived – for there were always somehow survivors – a lasting hatred.

He could tear down the city walls and break apart the harbour moles, sow with salt the fields for leagues around on which the place depended for food and cut down the vines and olive trees, leaving behind him nothing but an empty barren littoral and a bay devoid of life or purpose. It had been done in the past by conquerors of more renown than he, but that would not serve his long-term goal.

'Geoffrey, go forward and ask whoever commands to come and parley.'

His brother had enough of the de Hauteville brains to discern very quickly what Robert was about. 'You will have a riot in your own ranks.'

'Look at the soldiers before you, Geoffrey. Do you see Argyrus?'

'No.'

'So tell me what it is they are going to die for.'

'Their city.'

'A notion they might have advanced behind those stout walls. Out here in the open, where their fate is certain, it is perhaps one they might reconsider.'

'Our men—'

Geoffrey did not get a chance to finish that, as Robert barked, 'Leave the men to me. Are you going to do as I ask or must I seek another envoy?'

'One day, brother, you might ask too much.'

'If it is this day, so be it.'

Such was the *Guiscard*'s height that even Geoffrey had to lift his head to look into his blazing blue eyes. They, on either side of his helmet nose guard, were unblinking, which told him that for all they were blood, this was not a man to challenge. Geoffrey spun away, called to his standard-bearer, and marched forward.

'Now that,' Robert said to himself, feeling pleased at the notion, 'is going to surprise them.'

'My Lord, news has come of many boats exiting the harbour.'

'Don't tell me,' Robert barked as the messenger physically cowered before him. 'Tell those damn Venetians.' The man was already running away from what came next. 'And tell them if any escape it will come from what I pay them to be here.'

The feeling he had entertained, of doing the unexpected, which he always enjoyed, was spoilt by the knowledge that he had failed to instruct the galleys to immediately put back to sea – not that they should have required such a directive, the fools. He was tempted to go to the shore and look out for those trying to escape, suspecting, since Argyrus knew what fate awaited him, that the Catapan would be taking the lead.

But time for that did not exist: Geoffrey was on his way back with a clutch of men around him, an indication that his enemy lacked central direction, and it was pleasing that as soon as they came before him they fell to one knee, bowing their heads – they knew their lives were in his hands, just as he knew that his reputation was such that they would fear immediate decapitation.

'These are the captains entrusted by Argyrus to command his men,' said Geoffrey. 'He did not give anyone rank over another.'

'A fool as general, then, if he's not going to take the field in person.'

'A treacherous toad,' Geoffrey spat. 'I request his head to adorn my walls.'

'Who here is native to the city?' Robert demanded. Only one fellow raised his head to engage his eye, the rest did not respond. 'The rest of you, return to your lines, now, I have no need of you.'

Geoffrey gave that shake of the head a man employs when he wonders what in the name of creation is going on, which caused Robert to smile: if even his brother could not discern his intentions, then that was all to the good.

'Stand.' The fellow obliged, a slight surprise flickering across his face as, close to the *Guiscard*, he understood just how large was this famed warrior. 'Name?'

'Grenel.'

'A Lombard name? You say a native, were you born here?'

'I was.'

'The other captains?'

'Are from many parts of the empire, sent here by the emperor.'

'Then they will pay by mining salt for their loyalty to Constantine. You, however, carry your own fate in your hands.

Succeed in what I am about to ask of you and you will live, fail and I will strip off your skin with red-hot pincers.'

Robert paused to let that sink in, using silence to create tension. 'Go into the city and assemble the citizens as my envoy, then ask them if they want to live or die.' There was a sudden rasp in his voice at he added, 'If the citizens want to see their city burn, to witness every stone thrown down before they themselves are spit-roasted, they will close the gates. If they wish to grant to me the title of overlord they will come out with the keys. Clear?'

'Yes, sire.'

Geoffrey was not sure whether to be impressed or angry. Brindisi had never had any suzerain other than the holder of an imperial title since the time of the Romans. They had been especially difficult as sometime allies in previous revolts, more like a city-state of antiquity, finding it difficult to maintain internal cohesion with their mixed populations, never mind consistent support for insurrection. In truth, they were interested only in their own prosperity, bending with the wind, allies if matters were going well but quick to desert the cause of freedom if Byzantium reacted with force.

'A warning, Grenel! I have to satisfy the men I lead, who have suffered assaulting yonder walls. Much will be asked of the worthies of Brindisi in wealth and a great deal of the lesser citizens in comfort, the womenfolk especially. But what they lose they may be able to recover under my guiding hand, so tell them not to hide their gold or their daughters. Now go.'

The Lombard captain ran off and Robert looked out to sea, where the Venetian galleys were plying their oars at attack speed, in pursuit of the clutch of boats seeking to sail away to safety. He stood between his enemy and his own army, over five thousand men in number beginning to swelter as the sun rose. He needed to convince them that he was right in his approach. That he was about to address them became obvious when a cart was fetched on which he could stand and, ever mindful of their welfare, parties had also been despatched to bring forward what food and drink had not been purloined by the surviving horsemen from Brindisi.

'Eat and drink all of you,' he cried in his stentorian voice, once he was high enough to be seen by all, one which had addressed them many times before, using Greek, the most common language to all assembled. There were Normans too new to his service to understand, but he would just have to trust those longer in Italy to translate for him. 'I want you content and not sour-bellied, and mark this, it is you who do so, not those wretches between Brindisi and us. They must stand and sweat with nothing to ease either throat or stomach.'

Robert watched as that instruction was obeyed, trying to sense their mood, which could best be described as suspicious. Not one of his men, from the captains of his mounted conroys down to the lowest pikeman or crossbowman, was other than wary.

'Now, you all know me to be a devious bastard, do you not?' That got a roar of good-humoured agreement. 'Well, I still am, nor am I about to change.' His arm swept out towards the city walls. 'Over there is a city at our mercy, a place that refused to open its gates when we first appeared before the walls.'

There was nothing good-natured about the shout that statement engendered. It was full of imprecations and promises of blood to be shed and revenge to be exacted. The citizens of Brindisi could hear it and they would be shaking in their sandals.

'So it deserves outright sack, with its citizens, those that survive our wrath, bonded into slavery.' That would not be disputed, Robert knew, and he was not disappointed, waiting till the shouting died down before speaking again. 'But I have offered them their lives and freedom.'

If the reactions had been loud before they were screams now and no longer aimed at the people of Brindisi, they were aimed at him. Robert grinned, deliberately provoking even more abuse, and waited until that expression began to cause doubt among those listening, enough for him to hold up his hands and command silence.

'Now why would a devious bastard like me do that?'

'You want everything for yourself, *Guiscard*?' called a voice.

His response was a loud and carrying laugh. 'You know I am only good for four women at a time, fellow, and there are thousands in there.'

'Then let us at them,' called another.

'No one has answered my question.'

'I will answer it,' shouted Geoffrey.

Robert held out his hand to raise his brother up and Geoffrey, once aboard the cart, turned to face the crowd.

'It is because, not only is my brother a devious bastard, he is greedy too.' The agreement was as loud as all that had gone before. 'He will not be satisfied with just this one port city – he wants Bari and after that the biggest one in the world, Constantinople itself.' He turned to Robert. 'Tell them I am right.'

'Listen, my friends, if I have my way every one of you will leave this place with a full purse and an empty sack between your legs, but the walls will be intact and those fellows cowering behind me will become my soldiers as much as you now are. Up the coast is Bari and one day I must take that, a task greater than this we faced today, for it has stood for five hundred years without being subdued. But more than that, over the Adriatic is Romania, the land ruled by the corrupt arseholes of Byzantium. They have no brains, no balls and no ability to command armies, but I do, as I have commanded you.'

He had them now, he knew that: they were close to silent.

'What they do have is so much wealth that it would buy a thousand Apulias, enough to bury us so we would never see daylight again: gold, jewels – the spoils of seven hundred years of bleeding the fabulous East – and women, think of the women: perfumed creatures just waiting for a proper man to saddle them and show the poor fools what they have been missing with their girly husbands. They have an emperor who is a fool, a man who needs potions and a troupe of naked dancing girls before he can get hard, and even then rumour says he is flabby. Gold, brothers, diamonds and pearls, soft breasts and thighs, and land, masses of land, everything a man could desire.'

Robert had been shouting, he needed to in order to be heard, but he had the ability to make it sound soft by comparison to the bellow he came out with now. 'What they don't have, brothers, is a good enough army to protect it. Me, I have an army that can take it away, every last coin and field.'

Lances and pikes were raised as high as the voices, but Robert knew he had to bring them back to earth, though it took an age to get them to listen.

'You Lombards and Italians of mine, these are the people who have sat on your necks for centuries, bled you dry and kept you from enjoying the fruits of this fertile land.'

'Careful, brother,' hissed Geoffrey, 'for we are not much better.'

That such a remark was true did not make it palatable; if there was one person who could get carried away by the flaming oratory of Robert de Hauteville it was the *Guiscard* himself. His face was alight until Geoffrey said that, but it changed to fury, quickly replaced with concern.

'It won't be easy, brothers, and it will be a long march. You do not have to look far from this place to find those who would stab us in our back ribs, and they must be put in place before we can set foot in Romania.'

'Your fellow Grenel is coming,' Geoffrey said.

Robert looked at him as he approached, the question in his eyes, the answer just a nod that had him addressing his army again. 'Brindisi will surrender to you, and I think so will those poor buggers who came out to fight.' More cheering greeted that. 'I will now go into the city to accept the capitulation. You will make ready to follow me. Brothers, we have a victory.'

'Mostly over simple minds,' Geoffrey remarked, his quiet tone drowned out by loud cheers.

'If there were no simple minds, brother,' Robert growled, 'there would be no cities to conquer. Everyone would stay at home and mind their hearth. Now, do you wish to join me?'

Robert, accompanied by Grenel, his brother and his personal knights, approached the soldiers still locked out of Brindisi by their fellow citizens, walking straight in amongst them in a show of what many people would have called foolhardy behaviour, given they were still fully armed. Yet such was his commanding presence that they fell away from him, as if to remain too close was a foolishly dangerous thing to do. He did not shout, he only spoke so those close by could hear.

'You are going to live, not die, as you have spent the last hours contemplating. But now, I am your lord and master, not Byzantium. It would be fitting if you were to show it.'

There was one, a huge fellow near as tall as Robert, perhaps a fool, perhaps a patriot, who rushed forward seeking to smite with his sword. The *Guiscard* seemed to move with slow grace as he stepped inside the arc of the man's swing to halt his arm. The mighty punch to his upper chest, even if it was padded, was enough to stop him dead, indeed his face and bulging eyes looked as though the blow had blocked his heart. Then Robert de Hauteville was underneath the arm and behind his assailant, the powerful arms encircling the neck. That he broke with seeming ease and a loud crack, the body of the man, now dead, dropping at his feet.

The escort he had brought, Geoffrey included, were standing, swords out, waiting for instruction to begin a massacre, which given they were massively outnumbered was madness. Yet it was a testament to the hold these Normans had on their enemies that no other tried to attack. Glaring at those around him Robert barked, 'I am waiting!'

The first row began to kneel, and like the ripple that spreads out from a pebble thrown into a lake, it extended, until the whole of the enemy army was kneeling.

'Grenel, get those gates open.'

No command was necessary: the huge gates swung apart as he approached and the *Guiscard* entered, to walk in deep shadow between twin lines of cowed citizens, to the old Roman square in which stood the one-time temple, now converted to a church. Before him and the oration platform stood a party of elders with the ceremonial great key of the city on a cushion, held up to him as he came close. Nodding, Robert took it and handed it to his brother, speaking loudly.

'Brindisi needs a great captain to hold it safe for my title. I hereby appoint my brother, Geoffrey, Count of Loritello, captain of the city, port and fortress.' He dropped his voice. 'Take my advice, brother, use this Grenel fellow, who seems honest, but a few chopped-off heads will do more to cement your place than the kind of soft words you normally employ.'

Then he mounted the oration platform and addressed the crowd. Someone must have primed them, for en masse they sank to their knees, which made Robert smile again.

# CHAPTER FOUR

The route to Rome was busy with pilgrims and high clerics, the latter not of the type to suffer discomfort in the hospices and the fabulously wealthy great abbeys. Where previous de Hautevilles were obliged to take accommodation in crowded dormitories, Roger was given an apartment of his own and treated as a valued guest. It was not forgotten that his family had humbled Pope Leo after the Battle of Civitate, nor that they had held him prisoner until they had bled him of favours, but his hosts were men who took a long view: Leo was gone now, Pope Victor was in place and life must continue.

Endowments were sought, which amused Roger given he was a near-penniless knight, but he was treated as a young fellow who might have wealth of his own one day. God's work did not come free, nor could a place in heaven be assured, however well a man thought he had lived. No mere mortal was prepared for the examination of his deeds in a world where death stalked silently and suddenly. Masses must be said for the deceased in case they lingered in Purgatory, unable to enter the Kingdom of Heaven. Thus, a wise man made bequests for the sake of his eternal soul.

Nothing demonstrated Roger's unearned stature, upon his arrival in Rome, more than his invitation to meet the reigning pope. Guards manned the bridge leading to the gates of the Castel St Angelo, for no pontiff was truly safe in the riotous city of Rome. Whoever held the office presided over a fount of wealth and patronage that made it one sought after by a mass of competing interests. Money flowed in to Rome from all over the Christian world and where there were bulging coffers there were those who would do anything to gain control of the keys, so Victor's election had been attended by the usual upheavals.

Invited to sit, Roger did so, seeking to size up his host, reputed to be pious by the standard of the office. 'Your cousin, the Bishop of Coutances, writes to me of events in Normandy and here you are, yet another brother.' The eyes met, with both Pope and visitor maintaining bland expressions as their thoughts ranged over the recent past: there was no love lost between the papacy and the Normans. 'And the Lady Fressenda is married to Richard of Aversa. I take it you will be calling on your sister?'

Roger nodded. 'If there is a message you wish me to take I will happily deliver it.'

'Did you know that Richard has taken upon himself the title of Prince of Capua?'

'No.'

'Deposed the legitimate heir with no reference to Rome, the Western Emperor, or, from what I can gather, the people of the city.'

Robert was a problem to this pope, but Richard of Aversa was a close and permanent nightmare, forever pushing up against the lands that marked the border between the Papal States and Campania.

'Your brother has done nothing to help me curb Richard's excesses. I think Leo, having conferred legitimate nobility on your family, felt he was owed at least that obligation. Who better to contain a Norman than one of his own kind?'

*Norman fight Norman, how that would suit you?* 'I will happily deliver any written messages you care to write, Your Holiness.'

'And perhaps some verbal warnings, gently couched, of course.'

'Naturally,' Roger lied, sure he would do no such thing. 'I am your servant.'

'Then it only remains for me to bless you, my son. I pray to you to kneel.'

Head bowed and listening to the incantation being uttered above him, Roger wondered at the depth of hypocrisy it took to hold papal office. The man now anointing him would probably have happily seen him hanging from his walls rather than let another de Hauteville pass on to the south.

Roger could not avoid Capua. It lay on the Via Appia, still busy with much traffic, the ancient Roman road from the Eternal City to the great port of Brindisi, down which the legions had marched, but it was an accident that, having passed the great monastery of Monte Cassino, he ran into, heading north, half a day later, the impressive retinue of his brother-in-law. Never having met the newly styled Prince of Capua, he would not have known him from Adam, merely standing aside to let pass an important person. But his own sister, every inch the Norman chatelaine and not one to travel by litter, was riding alongside her husband and recognised her little brother immediately.

There were tears, of course, but of joy and surprise, this while

Roger's companions eyed those of the prince, much more numerous and well equipped, with suspicion: being of Norman blood did not induce immediate mutual affection. The introduction, too, was required to be handled with care: Richard of Aversa was a squat fellow, too easy to tower over and he had, in his expression, a guarded look that implied he was unsure if he should be pleased by this sudden addition to the family of which he was part by marriage.

'So you are the last of Tancred's sons?'

'And the most handsome,' Fressenda insisted, which reddened Roger's cheeks.

'I dare say the locals round these parts must thank God that your father has gone to meet his Maker. There's no more room in Italy for his bloodline, it is groaning with his offspring already.'

If that got a terse frown from his sister, Roger felt he did not much like this brother-in-law. The attempt at a jest, accompanied by a crooked smile, was heavy-handed, but it was more than that – almost something in his gut rather than any rational thought. He had to be polite for his sister's sake, but that did not debar a somewhat pointed rejoinder.

'I was privileged to meet the Pope in Rome. At this moment I fear he sees you as more of a cause for divine intervention than me or my brothers.'

'They will elect women to the papal office.'

'They should do that,' Fressenda retorted, with a rather coarse laugh, 'for we would not stand to be troubled by impious creatures like you.'

'You would make a good pope,' her husband said with a wry smile, which did something to soften his battle-scarred face.

Fressenda had aged well, no doubt aided by her position, which kept her from anything menial. A younger version of his mother, she had dark-brown hair dressed with tight curls at the edges, fair unblemished skin, merry eyes and, Roger recalled, a very pointed tongue when aroused.

'It would be a comfortable office to hold, husband, would it not? But I fear I would not pass the ceremony of being carried aloft and exposed.'

Both men smiled at the allusion: every pope since Joan, the only female to hold the post, had been carried bare-arsed over the heads of the cardinals, bishops and abbots to ensure an office the Almighty had reserved for men was never again occupied by a woman, the inspection an obvious indication of gender.

'The sight of your hairy parts would make the cardinals and bishops faint.'

'Only the celibate, of which there are few.'

Roger was not by nature fastidious but reckoned what he was hearing to be coarse, yet he discerned it over the rest of the day was the way these two spoke to each other, a constant spicy banter that carried undertones of endemic dispute. His progress south had been halted: his brother-in-law insisted he and his men travel back to Monte Cassino to witness an amazing event, the nature of which he was not going to divulge – it was to be a surprise. They stopped for the night before ascending to the heights of Monte Cassino, within sight of the white walls and towering buildings of the great monastery on its high hilltop, one of the most holy and famous in Christendom.

It had the misfortune to also be one of the wealthiest, which had made it a prime target for every kind of raid over many hundreds of years. The Saracens had, more than once, burnt parts of buildings and slaughtered those monks who failed to flee, while the Lombards who had ruled Campania, though Christian, were not much better. If the brothers had seen salvation in the arrival of the Normans they had been sadly disappointed there too, something Roger alluded to when he was alone with his sister for the first time.

'If Holy Church will gather to themselves so much wealth they must not be surprised that others wish to take it from them.'

'At the risk of their immortal soul, ' Fressenda replied.

'Do monks not risk eternal damnation for taking vows of poverty, while living lives of luxury?'

'Some are true to their vow.'

'Too many are not.'

'Monte Cassino, at least, may have a secure future.'

'How so?'

'You must wait to find that out, little brother. I have been sworn to secrecy.'

'By your husband?'

'Who else?'

'Are you happy, sister?'

'Content, Roger, and who could not be that when you know how far I have come?'

That was undeniable: the feisty girl who had run around barefoot, had fought her brothers of equal age, foaled horses and delivered lambs and calves while helping to mother him, was now a great lady

'Your husband seems full of himself.'

'Oh, he is immensely proud,' she hissed. 'Too proud sometimes, but I have given him a son and that child makes me satisfied. One day, God willing, he will succeed to his father's titles with our family's blood in his veins.'

'I sense you do not entirely approve of this pride.'

'What I approve and disapprove of Roger is of no moment.' She stopped and looked at the sky, fading to dark with the first sign of stars appearing, now sounding wistful. 'I am but a woman. How many times do I wish I had been born a man?'

'There are enough of us, sister, don't you think, and our father did dote on his daughters.'

'Not as much as he did on you, little brother.'

With that she took his arm and they were into reminiscence, back in the Normandy, with its green, well-watered fields and the high trees they used to climb, barefoot and muddy then, slow to wash and dressed in rough and common wool. Now the cloth on Roger's arm was fine linen and the smell on the air was of the finest perfume.

# CHAPTER FIVE

The first sign that this was to be an unusual day came with the pre-dawn, and the sight of Richard and Fressenda dressed for a ceremony in fine silks and damasks. He wore no mail, only a fine surcoat of red and black, his family colours, over courtier's clothes. Fressenda was clad in silver-trimmed white, topped by a rich red cloak edged with ermine. When they mounted it was not on their normal travelling horses, but on a pair of fine white palfreys, dressed with ornate harness, the saddles worked with elaborate silver decoration gleaming on gold-trimmed saddlecloths, the hooves oiled and polished, both tails and manes plaited.

Roger was obliged by his sister's command to don his own best blue and white surcoat; he could not compete with Richard, but at least he could attempt to look more of a participant, given Fressenda also insisted he ride right behind her and ahead of some of her husband's senior captains, men who had served him for many years, seriously put out to be so surpassed by a person they considered a nobody despite his name.

By the time the party set off, the buildings above them had picked up the rising sun, looking pink and majestic, yet when they came close it was possible to see what looked magnificent at a distance bore the ravages of much destruction, albeit there was much reconstruction going on and the number of Benedictine monks who lined the approaches to the monastery entrance indicated that whatever it had suffered in the past, it was well on the way back to prosperity.

Of all the stories that had come back to Normandy there was one that pertained to this place and it was bloody. A party of Norman knights stopped to pray in the abbey church, leaving outside, as piety demanded, their swords, this at a time when men of their stripe had been ravaging the lands of Monte Cassino. Seeing them vulnerable, the monks and the monastery servants had shut the great doors and locked them inside, ringing the bells to summon from the fields the equally put-upon peasants. Finally allowed out, those knights faced a mob with nothing but knives and died under the blows from their own weapons, an act which triggered a major revolt that took a year to put down.

Yet it was peaceful now: the abbot was there to greet Richard and Roger, who rarely allowed the monkish tribe much credit, had to acknowledge he looked as spiritual as such a person should. His skin had that translucent quality that hints at self-denial and his frame, under simple garments, looked spare, which was telling, given his blood was noble: Abbot Desiderius was a scion of the one-time ruling Lombard house of Benevento. It was Roger's family, specifically Humphrey, who had deposed them.

'My Lord and Lady,' Desiderius cried, coming to stand by Richard's palfrey. 'It is my great honour to welcome you to our simple establishment.'

That word 'simple' jarred: never mind the dimensions of the buildings, the monastery held lands enough to make jealous many a prince, the place had been decorated as if for Easter, with floral chains winding round the wooden scaffolding and the pathway to the abbey church strewn with petals, all clearly designed to impress, that underlined by the raised chair on which Richard was invited to sit. A bowl of warm, scented water was brought forth and the abbot knelt before his guest, removing his soft leather boots so that he could, in an act of humility, wash his noble visitor's feet.

That symbolic act completed and Richard re-shod, Desiderius led the way into the church, followed by both monks and the retinue of Norman knights, there to say Mass, accompanied by chanted plainsong. The interior, too, was decorated, with special stalls set up for their principal guests to pray. Behind them Roger took part with solemn attendance to the ceremony: this was the house of his god, the deity to which he would have to answer for his actions in life when the time came, as it surely would, for death.

They emerged near to noon, for it was a long Mass, to find the courtyard in which they had been received now laid with tables, the numerous servants of the monastery present to feed the famished incumbents and their guests, for they had fasted prior to the Mass. Sat close to the abbot, who ate sparsely, surrounded by men who did not, Roger was finally introduced to Desiderius and it was plain his name registered, for, practised as this divine must be at masking his feelings, his eyebrows were raised appreciably.

From then on he strained to hear what it was Richard of Aversa and Desiderius discussed, catching only snatches: 'Rome must be made to see where its interests lie,' this from the abbot; and Richard intimating more than once that 'Monte Cassino has much to gain if the wise and correct dispensations are made.' Not that Roger could hear what the interests were any more than the dispensations: heads got too close and voices dropped too low to be overheard.

Eventually the abbot rose to speak and reiterate his gratitude that such a noble prince should come to their humble dwelling; it was telling he titled him 'prince', which was responded to with much murmuring and head shaking given it was a purloined title. Richard followed from that, and once he had mouthed the necessary platitudes in praise of God and this house of piety, he came to the true purpose of his presence.

'This blessed endowment, the home of St Benedict, has seen much in the way of hardship. Many times it has been despoiled by the greed of the laity. I, Richard of Capua...' He paused to let that appellation register – not Aversa but Capua – and Roger noticed Desiderius nodding. '...am now the protector of this most holy site. No one will lay a foot upon the soil of this great foundation, uninvited, that does not face my wrath. I pledge that I, and the men I lead, will place their lances, their swords and their lives as a shield to you who have dedicated your lives to God.'

There was a moment while this was digested: was this self-styled prince really saying that the Normans he led, hitherto amongst the worst offenders when it came to ravaging monastery property, were not only to cease to be brigands but, under Richard, to act to protect them against others?

'This I vow!' Richard shouted.

That was answered with immediate acclamation from the throats of over a hundred monks, and with bemused silence from his own followers. Roger could only guess what bargain had been struck, albeit he was sure there was one. When the feasting broke up he took the chance to wander the monastery buildings. He was in the scriptorium, watching the monks work on the illuminated manuscripts for which the abbey was famous, when another approached, and did so in such silence he was momentarily startled when the fellow spoke.

'Sire—'

'Not yet that,' Roger interrupted, 'you give a respect I do not warrant.'

The monk looked peeved, as if the man before him was indulging in unnecessary sophistry. 'The Abbot Desiderius desires to speak with you before you depart.'

'Then why send a messenger? Here I am and he can speak with me as and when he wishes.'

'He would like to speak with you in private. He asks that when his principal guests depart, you remain behind.'

They met in a candlelit chamber, bare of furniture, more a monkish cell than the room of a senior cleric, one of the most important in the Christian hierarchy, for Desiderius, in terms of influence, could outrank a cardinal, given his predecessors had helped to make and unmake popes. Yet Roger was struck by the lack of arrogance in this man: it was rare in the presence of a high cleric to feel any sense of simplicity.

'My son, I am grateful to you. Please be seated.' Once Roger had obliged he found himself fixed by a steady gaze from a pair of grey eyes, the long-fingered hands of the abbot clasped to form a pinnacle before his lips. 'There are certain facts I think it would be of moment to pass on to your brother, the Count of Apulia.'

Roger did not speak: to do so would have been superfluous.

'I think you can advise him that the recent alliance between the papacy and Byzantium, which led to the unfortunate calamity at

Civitate, is unlikely to be renewed in the foreseeable future.'

'I would have thought it dead anyway, if what I have been told is true. Brindisi has fallen and only Bari remains, Byzantium is near to being crushed.'

Desiderius' hands went to his lap and he smiled, a thin affair. 'Then you would be wrong and perhaps disappointed, for there are still siren voices pushing that the alliance be renewed on both sides.'

'My fellow Normans have beaten such a combination once and we can do so again.'

'Such confidence and you not yet blooded.' Roger held his tongue, not sure if he was being guyed. 'It has been the attitude of the Holy See to find the presence of you Normans something they cannot abide, and it must be said you have done nothing to endear yourself to Rome. It is scarce possible for pilgrims to travel in many parts of Benevento without being robbed and left without so much as their garments. The Pope is not alone in seeing you as a pestilence that must be eradicated.'

It was natural for Roger to seek the meaning behind those words: that was in his nature and he was pleased at the slight look of impatience in the abbot's eye when he did not immediately respond or protest. Eventually he knew he must speak but the pause had removed some of the older man's air of superiority.

'And you, do you share this view?'

'We will come to that in a moment, though I would have good cause to. Scarce a day has gone by in the last thirty years that some part of Monte Cassino has not been raided by your confrères. Cattle and sheep stolen, wheat fields trampled, vines cut down, olive trees that saw Roman legionaries pass by destroyed for naught but mischief. For myself, if my family has been dispossessed of its holdings and titles in Benevento then the root cause is the race of which you are a part – indeed, not just the race, but the family.'

'And one ennobled by a reigning pope.'

'After he lost a battle,' Desiderius replied, his tone somewhat sharper; that pleased Roger, he had thrown him a little. 'Pope Leo may have ennobled your brothers but I doubt he took pleasure in the act: he was, after all, little more than a prisoner for two whole years.'

'If Pope Leo was coerced as you imply, he merely made legitimate in the eyes of Christendom a title my brother already held by conquest.'

'A man cannot just take to himself a title.'

'Like the Prince of Capua?'

Now the abbot looked down at his own hands for a moment: clearly he saw the need to compose himself, for matters were not proceeding entirely as he wished. When he looked up again it was with a softer countenance.

'My son, I am not trying to deceive you, much as you may think it in my interests to do so. Perhaps if I speak plain and tell you that I have come to see what others have not, that the notion of pushing you Normans out of Italy is no longer in the interests of this monastery or the Church of which it is part.'

'I may be new to Italy but I think that a task of some magnitude.'

'It could be done, my son, if Byzantium combined with the Western Emperor as well as the Pope. Powerful as you have become, you Normans could not withstand such a combination.'

'Is such an alliance possible?'

'Possible, yes, likely, no, but is it desirable? To many it would be.'

'But not to you?'

'My concern is not for me.' Desiderius waved a bony hand. 'Not even for Monte Cassino.'

'What bargain did you strike with my brother-in-law today?'

'You are sure there was one?' Now it was Roger's turn to smile, which got him, in response, a slow nod. 'This monastery stands on the border between Campania and the Papal States. It is large and rich in holdings, even if it is humble in intention, thus a temptation to anyone with greed in their heart. In itself, to keep that safe would be worth much, but when Richard says he will protect this place he is also saying he will protect that border, something that has never been given as a pledge before. For that, in return, I have promised that I will seek to get the Pope to confirm him as the true and rightful Prince of Capua.'

'Even ignorant as I am, I know Capua is an imperial fief. I cannot see the present emperor, even if he is a child, being too cheered by such a confirmation which denies him his prerogatives.'

Having said that, Roger was slightly thrown by the way Desiderius did not respond. The abbot just looked at him keenly and, in doing so, he forced Roger to think hard and seek a conclusion.

'You wish me to speak to my brother?' That got a nod and nailed an obvious conclusion. 'The Normans combined could protect the Pope against interference by any emperor, man or boy.'

'Even to the way in which we anoint the Vicar of Christ.'

Roger was genuinely surprised. 'You wish to exclude the emperor from papal elections?'

'Enough for now, my son, these are thoughts to pass on to your brother of Apulia, and given he is known to have a sharp mind, I am sure he will see what needs to be seen.'

'Why no papal alliance with Byzantium?'

The answer did not come immediately, which left Roger to wonder how much he was not being told: the man with whom he was conversing was as clever, and perhaps as cunning, as his brother Robert.

'An embassy was sent to Constantinople to discuss certain matters of difference with the Greek Church, celibacy for the priesthood, the place of the Holy Trinity in doctrine and the supremacy of Rome in all matters ecclesiastical. Intended to unite both branches of the faith it has achieved the opposite. The Emperor Constantine might badly want an alliance against you Normans to try and regain the Catapanate but to do that the Eastern Church must bow the knee to Rome in all things. He will not get one for fear of his patriarch and the anger of the people who see their faith threatened. It is not something many eyes see, but I do. I fear that we may be on the edge of an abyss in relations with the Greek Church.'

'Is Rome at fault?'

'My son, in any dispute, both parties are usually at fault.' The abbot stood up to underline the interview was over. 'But when the dust settles someone has triumphed and the blame always lies with the loser. When to travel on south?'

'At first light tomorrow, there is nothing for me here.'

Desiderius made the sign of the cross and blessed his journey.

While Roger made his way south in the company of his brother-in-law, to part company at Capua, the Abbot Desiderius travelled north to Rome to meet with the Pope, who both trusted him and valued his counsel, but more importantly to seek out Hildebrand, ranked as no more than a deacon but the man who ran the affairs of the Church and thus its most powerful voice. He would seek to persuade both that what he had done to protect Monte Cassino was both wise and necessary and that the papacy should adopt the same attitude.

Hildebrand was a churchman with one major aim: to free the process of papal elections from the power of the Holy Roman Emperor as well as the leading aristocratic families of Rome and the scum they controlled. He believed only those anointed as priests and who had risen to high office should choose the man to lead the Christian faithful. Hildebrand was not alone in this: there were many cardinals, bishops and abbots who wished for the same, but the difference between the desire for something and the achieving of the aim was never more stark. The empire had the military power to impose its will and the convocations of the Church did not: the rich Roman aristocrats could pay to put riotous mobs on the streets, which made the city ungovernable. Popes had been more often a prisoner of the Roman mob than ever they had been of the de Hautevilles.

Victor II was not a strong man and, being German, had sought and received imperial approval in his election: he might have wished it otherwise, but he was not one to raise his head above the parapet of the Castel St Angelo or risk his Lateran Palace to fight for it. Being a vacillator he depended on certain advisors to make up his mind, the problem being he was inclined to adopt the view of the last one to which he spoke. Cardinal Ascletin Pierleoni was rich and a powerful voice in the Curia; he was also a man who had harboured for many years a desire for the highest office, only to be thwarted time and again. This he blamed on his Jewish background – his family had converted to Christianity – never once realising that it was the intense dislike his fellows had for him which had barred his passage to the papacy.

Faced with the dilemma presented by Desiderius, Victor had called in both Hildebrand and Ascletin, and was thus presented with diametrically opposing views of how matters should proceed, which was the last thing inclined to settle the mind of a man who was a weathervane. Even if Victor wielded great power and could command such men to bow to his will, he lacked the fibre necessary to impose that authority.

'Give me a hundred lances and I will clear these Norman barbarians out of Italy.'

Ascletin, vain in both appearance and manner, matched those words with a sweeping gesture, as if he were indeed smiting his foes. It was an assertion he had made before, just as he had, many times, cursed the very name of the Normans, never mind their proximity.

'What a pity, Cardinal Ascletin,' Hildebrand replied, 'that you were not at Civitate with Pope Leo and I, to make good on such a boast.'

That these two did not like each other was a given: Ascletin was the scion of a wealthy family and, if he spread enough in bribes one day he might well be pontiff. Hildebrand had started poor and risen in the Church by sheer ability, albeit he had been an aide to Pope Leo; he was clever and far-seeing where Ascletin was narrow-minded and soured by his own ambition. Hildebrand was saved from being tarred with that brush by his own conviction that he was unfit for the highest office.

'Such a boast flies in the face of what is before us,' Desiderius insisted. 'The time when we could easily remove the Normans is long past.'

'If the right combination of force is brought to bear—'

'It never will be, Cardinal Ascletin,' said the Pope, asserting himself for once. 'And do we want to forever depend on an emperor to sort out our inconveniences?'

'Better that than the Normans, Your Holiness. They are more than an inconvenience, they are a plague.'

Hildebrand scoffed. 'They have done no more than others before them. Did not the Ostrogoths conquer Italy and the Lombards in their turn? We must obey Bamberg, for the risk of an imperial army is great, yet we cannot muster a force to defeat anyone, Normans included.'

'Then let the emperor do his duty,' Ascletin insisted.

'Why should he? The empire suffers no ravages from these barbarians, it is us who stands between them who suffer.'

'The Normans do our work,' said Desiderius. 'Every church in every place they conquer is obliged to say Mass by the tenets of Rome, not Constantinople.'

'For which we are much abused,' Victor responded, looking gloomy.

That had been another bone of contention with the patriarch, the way the Normans insisted on such a thing as communion being taken with unleavened bread. It seemed such a small matter here in Rome: in Constantinople it had assumed such great significance it had helped to wreck the embassy sent to seek agreement on matters of more vital import.

'It is not up to Rome to apologise to the Greek Church,' Ascletin barked. 'You, Holy Father, are supreme in matters of doctrine.'

The Pope nodded, though not with much conviction.

Desiderius spoke again. 'I gave my word I would press that Richard of Aversa be elevated to the Principality of Capua. Let us offer the de Hautevilles something similar, the bargain being that they become the protectors of the Holy See and the agents of the Latin Church in an area where the congregations are Greek.'

'A great step fraught with danger.'

'Progress, Your Holiness, demands risk.'

'Well, I for one,' Ascletin barked, 'will never agree to such a course.'

'Then find us protection elsewhere,' Hildebrand replied.

'Capua?' Desiderius demanded.

Victor had to respond: only he could make such a decision. 'Let him style himself prince, and let us see if the emperor responds.'

'Which,' Hildebrand persisted, 'is the last thing we want.'

'Perhaps,' Desiderius suggested, 'an embassy to explain our difficulties and the need to compromise.'

'Who would we send?'

Pope Victor was quick to clutch at that straw, while at the same time ruling himself out. Desiderius, in his turn, reasoned that when the only lifeline was a dead stalk of wheat, it made sense to grasp it.

'Only Hildebrand and Ascletin have the stature,' he said, well aware of the direction in which it would lead.

'They will never listen to me,' Hildebrand replied, in confirmation. 'His council see me as a sworn enemy of his inherited prerogatives.'

'Then it must be I,' boomed Ascletin, with all the pomposity of which he was more than capable. 'And I shall not fear to remind him that he too answers to God!'

'So be it,' concluded a relieved Pope Victor. The problem was far from solved, but it had been put off, which much suited him.

# CHAPTER SIX

The great castle of Melfi, on the border with Campania, was the spiritual home of the Normans of Apulia: this had been their first domicile, taken by subterfuge from Byzantium, a near-impregnable fortress standing on a prominent hill overlooked by the even more impressive mass of Monte Vulture, so high it made a discreet approach to the castle impossible. From their post the sentinels set there to watch could see in all directions and give ample warning of any approaching army.

Holding the castle required few defenders, so high and difficult was the assault, so stout were the walls, and for the rest, William Iron Arm had set the tactic that made investiture fraught with peril. On the one occasion when Byzantium had tried to recapture Melfi, he had, with his Norman warriors, ridden out of the castle to a point from which he could harry the enemy by cutting up their forage parties and raiding their siege lines, forcing the attacker to seek to destroy him before any siege could be instigated. The Catapan who had attempted such an outcome had ended up seeing his army destroyed and himself made a captive.

Any party of armed horsemen was enough to set off the alarm, though in the case of Roger de Hauteville it did not engender a closing of the gates, portcullis or the drawing up of the wooden footbridge. What he found before him, well before he got a proper sight of his destination, was a party double the size of his own, in full mail, blocking his path to the town. He and his men wore no helmets and their lances and mail were still lashed to their packhorses, their destriers unsaddled and led. They represented no threat but it was an indication of Norman caution that they were treated as if they did.

'Roger de Hauteville, come to seek audience with my brother.'

That he spoke in Norman French was sufficient to establish he was of the same race as those before him; his height and colouring – fair of hair, startling blue eyes and a face made florid by too much sun – was enough to underline the truth of the connection.

'Audience?'

There was a haughty air to the way that question was posed, as if he were not believed, which annoyed him and, given his family attributes, to which he was not entirely immune, that high colour on his face reddened even more.

'I question whether you are going to escort me to my brother or merely stand aside and let me pass?'

'I may do neither. I may tell you to wait here while I send a message to Melfi to seek instructions.'

'I am not accustomed to being told anything.'

'And I am not sure if you are who you say you are.'

'I can think of no reason to lie.'

'I, on the other hand, can think of a dozen.'

'And who are you?'

'Ralph de Boeuf, Castellan of Melfi in the service of the Duke of Apulia.'

'My older brother.'

'So you say.'

The reply was sharp. 'If you wish to dispute, I will need time to don my mail.'

Ralph de Boeuf burst out laughing. 'Damn me, you're a de Hauteville all right, always up for a fight. In truth I did not doubt it but it amuses me to see you are the same as the *Guiscard*. Follow me.'

With that he spun his mount and headed for Melfi. Behind him, Roger fetched out his lance and attached to it his pennant of blue and white chequer. He wanted that above his head, wanted those in the castle to have no doubt who was approaching.

Coming close, having ridden through what was a bustling and growing town, Roger was as impressed by Melfi as anyone who had seen the castle before him. Built by the Byzantines to guard their border, it had been designed to deter as much as to protect, the enemy at the time being Lombards backed by a previous and more bellicose Western Emperor. The great corner towers were hexagonal, the curtain wall between them standing over a steep escarpment hard to climb and impossible to use for ballista, thus the place could not be battered into submission at a point away from the main gate.

The causeway that led up to the fortress was steep and that led to an esplanade, at its end a narrow bridge over a deep ditch, which would canalise any attacker into an area of death. On the other side of the bridge was a sturdy portcullis topped by another curtain wall. If the assault could get past, and it could only do so from a battering assault, then they entered the true killing ground between the front and main castle walls. It had never been taken except by trickery and that had only happened once.

Roger and his lances clattered across that bridge and entered a keep full of fighting men at practice, wielding wooden swords as they worked on the various manoeuvres of parry, cut and thrust, employing their shields as a weapon of both defence and attack. On the steps of the great hall stood two of his brothers, men that Roger had not seen for many years.

The first thing he noticed, as he dismounted, was that they were scarred veterans now, not the fresh-faced youths he recalled from the day they departed Hauteville-le-Guichard. Geoffrey he had not seen for a decade past, while his last sight of big, blustering Robert was after the murder committed by Serlo; being present when the knife went in he had likewise been required to flee, not in his case to avoid hanging, but to avoid being shut up in one of Duke William's dungeons.

'Well,' Robert boomed, neither his voice nor his manner entirely approving. 'The sprat of the family has finally come to join us.'

The great hall was full, the table at which the family sat set on a low dais crosswise, with the rest of the tables running down the sides full of Robert's lances, now joined by those of Roger's, and all the way down to his servants below the salt. The noise, echoing off the unadorned walls, was deafening, making the need to talk loudly essential just to be heard. Naturally their conversation at table was of home, though it was plain that if there was a residual hankering for Normandy it did not extend to a return.

'My bones would not take the cold and damp now,' Geoffrey insisted. 'Damn me, they can scarce take service mounted.'

'Would that be a whore or a horse?' Robert demanded, with a braying laugh.

'With the whores you use it would be hard to tell what you were boarding. Half of them would struggle to get into a horse's girth.'

Roger felt a slight discomfort at this ribaldry: he found it difficult to listen to such banter from a brother who he had last sat down to dine with as not much more than a mewling child. Odd that he had felt the same with Fressenda and his brother-in-law, making him wonder if he was, in fact, a prude. Whatever, he decided a change of subject was called for.

'I had audience with Duke William before I left.'

'How is the Bastard?'

'Secure now and thinking of a war with the Franks.' He noticed the faces of his brothers, both of them, close up: the way William's father had treated the family was neither forgiven nor forgotten, even if they had prospered because of his refusals, and news of any comfort in his life was unwelcome. Quickly he changed the subject yet again. 'But tell me about Brindisi.'

No battle is ever fought only once – it is replayed many times. The table, along with the residue of the meal, provided sufficient material to re-fight the engagement, bones stripped bare of meat to show the walls and harbour, bread to denote the disposition of Robert's forces, his manner enough to underline the frustration of a long siege.

'It came down to subterfuge in the end, brother, or we might be sitting there still, while the foul airs decimated our strength.' Robert described his ploy of riding away to draw out Argyrus, well aware as he did so that there were beacons being lit to mark his progress, for he could see them as plainly as his enemy. 'But he forgot the sea, Sprat, and so I had him.'

'How did you navigate all those vessels down the coast?'

It was Geoffrey who replied. 'He had riders on the shore carrying torches, Roger, and he gave each ship's master a catapult.'

Seeing his little brother confused, Robert burst out laughing. 'You cannot see it, can you?' Much as it hurt to confess he did not, Roger had to nod. 'The riders had measured lines which they were instructed to keep as taut as possible.' Robert held up two spread fingers. 'Keep those two flames on the points of the catapults and you have a fair idea how far you are off from the shore.'

'Clever,' Roger acknowledged.

'Not clever,' Robert boomed. 'Brilliant.'

'And Brindisi?'

'The plunder was enormous! God Almighty, these ports are rich and the inhabitants saw quickly which way the wind blew. I doubt the men I led would have had much more fun, bloodshed apart, if we had sacked the place as it deserved. There'll be a raft of Norman bastards come the women's term time.'

'But is it secure?'

Robert shrugged. 'What's to tell? Except the man I left to captain the place is sitting here stuffing his face with goose. If the Byzantines take it back I'll flay him alive.'

'I came to see to my Loritello estates.'

'I think you came for some cool mountain air,' Robert jested, before turning back to Roger. 'Brindisi is in the past, brother. What we need to talk about is the future.'

'Mine?' Roger asked.

'Of course, you don't think I want you sitting around here on your arse like Geoffrey, do you, eating my food and drinking my wine?'

'What would be left, husband, after you had eaten?'

'God in heaven, no man should be checked by his wife!'

Robert growled as he responded to the Lady Alberada, but it was plainly mock anger, not the real thing. They were relatively comfortable in each other's company, not always common in marriage, and it seemed the salacious nature of their previous brotherly talk had no effect on her.

'Now that my mouse has spoken—'

'She is far from a mouse,' Roger jested, 'if she is prepared to gainsay you.'

'Look at the size of her man.'

Alberada was tiny and slim, dark-haired and olive-complexioned, in marked contrast to her huge, florid and golden-haired husband, and it had been an inadvertent thought on introduction to imagine them coupling and the difficulties therein. She looked as though Robert would conjugally crush her.

'Should have heard her when she spawned my daughter, screaming fit to bring down Jericho.'

'She's a big child.'

'She's her father's girl,' Robert boomed, 'even if she has your black hair. But enough of that; when we talk of your future it is to Alberada's part of the world we must go.'

'I heard you wanted to take Bari, then go to Romania and sack Constantinople.'

'In time, Roger, in time, but Calabria first. Bari is the strongest fortress in Apulia and will need a great effort. Besides, I cannot cross the Adriatic until my back is safe.'

'Which it won't be even if you subdue Calabria,' Geoffrey insisted.

It was Alberada who responded to Roger's enquiring look. 'Saracens.'

'I've beaten them before,' Robert insisted, 'and I can do so again.' Then he looked hard at Roger. 'You want something in Italy, little brother, well there's a place there for you.'

'As what?'

Robert's face closed up slightly. 'That we will talk about later. Now, tell me what that papal rogue said to you.'

'Perhaps it would be better we talk in private, brother. What the Pope said is less important than the conversation I had with the Abbot of Monte Cassino.'

It was pleasant to see his elder brother slightly thrown by that.


'Do you trust him?' Robert asked.

Alone now, in a quiet chamber, Robert was speaking softly to avoid waking his child, sleeping close by with her wet nurse.

'It is you who have to worry about trust, Robert, I am a mere messenger, but I have had time to think and what Desiderius says makes sound sense, with the caveat that, if an alliance of all three powers could be raised against you and Richard of Aversa, you must lose.'

'Think on this, Sprat, think of the time it would take to agree such a combination and what the outcome would be. The imperial throne is occupied by a child, but even grown, will a Western Emperor do battle to give Langobardia back to Byzantium? Will Rome raise an army from the duchies of Tuscany and Spoleto to see the churches of Apulia and Calabria once more locked into Greek worship?'

'I think you do not see how much we Normans are hated.'

'Fear not, I know that. No one who takes land and wealth off another is loved, and as for their affection or approval I can do without it. What I am saying is this: even if they could agree to suppress us, their coalition would not hold in the heat of success and would fall apart long before that as the differing aims surfaced. Also, it would demand that Byzantium do the one thing they have failed to do since the first defeat of the last Lombard revolt: send to south Italy an army strong enough not only to help to put us down but to fight the Pope and the Western Empire, in case they tried to hold what they had helped to gain.'

'I suspect you have just summed up the thoughts of the Abbot Desiderius.'

'The other thoughts he might have,' Robert said, 'are these: popes die and so do emperors, and when they do, a policy dies with them. But more important, more likely to give pause, is this. We have not been seriously beaten by anyone for thirty years: the odd small encounter lost, yes, but a major battle, no. We are not so easy to overcome.'

'So you see there might be some merit in what he is suggesting.'

'So far he has suggested nothing, all he has done is air a notion that has no contact with the ground. The Abbot of Monte Cassino is a powerful prelate, but he is not so commanding that he can bring this about on his own. Such a change of policy will need to be accepted by the majority in the Curia, and from what I know of that House of Babel it would be easier to get the Bastard of Falaise to kiss my arse.'

'I sense such a thing would give you pleasure,' Roger replied, smiling.

'He insulted my name and my father. I know old Tancred and I did not always agree—'

'You're wrong, Robert, you never agreed.'

Robert grinned. 'Enough of this, for it is in a distant future. Right now my mind is on Calabria.'

'Tell me.'

'It is wild country, a tough race of people, who gave even Ancient Rome trouble. The first time I went there – William's doing to get me out from under his feet – I ended up nearly eating my stirrup leathers, we were so strapped, but I found a spot to build a castle, before I was required to return. After Civitate I had trouble with Humphrey too, the miserable bugger—'

'Upsetting brothers comes easily to you.'

'Take heed of it,' was the sharp reply. 'I had some success, Roger, but, with Humphrey dying and a succession to see to, I had to leave before I could settle matters in the right way.'

'You gained a wife.'

If Robert saw that as a gain it did not register. 'It's not fertile like Campania or Apulia but it could be better and the trade they do in silks and damasks is of high value.'

'Which is why the Saracens raid so often.'

'When they see we can defeat and destroy them wherever they land they will cease to raid and go elsewhere, there are rich pickings on the western coast.'

'The best way to subdue them, surely, is to take Sicily.'

'You do not want for ambition, brother, but I would not say much for your sense.'

'Are they hard to beat?'

'In Sicily, yes, to them it is home. Byzantium failed to take back the island in brother William's time.'

'And how do you contain them in Calabria?'

'They come only to raid and everyone looks out for their ships. Once the towns have closed their gates they must lay siege, and even if the coastal settlements are not strong, they are robust enough to hold them off until a mounted force can ride to relieve them, especially if they have a leavening of Normans to man their walls. If they move inland they are even more at risk if there are powerful forces that can be gathered to oppose them.'

'That was your policy?'

Robert nodded. 'I showed them it was possible, not that they loved me for it, and I intend to do so again, this time properly. They have a choice: give to me the dues owed to a lord, or see everything they own stolen by the Saracens, and that includes their women and children.'

'And you want me to come with you?'

'I left Geoffrey in Brindisi and I would leave you in Calabria. Together we can properly subdue the whole province, one that Byzantium has never cared much about in any case.'

'For?'

'The future holds many possibilities, you know that.'

'I meant for me.'

Robert responded with a humourless smile. 'Not to please me, then?'

'No.'

'A title?'

'Not enough.'

'What!' Robert yelled, so loud the next sound was that of a wailing baby girl.

'Half the revenues of Calabria if we succeed.'

'Blood is not that thick.'

'Then I go back to Campania. Richard of Aversa will give me employment.'

'Old Tancred would turn in his grave if I denied his favourite child.'

'You care what our father would think? You never stopped arguing with him.'

'Oddly enough, Sprat, I would. Half it is, but you will have to do some hard fighting to get it.'

'Tomorrow, out on that practice ground, I will show you how I can fight.'

'No, Roger, that can wait. Tomorrow we travel to Venosa, to the tomb of your brothers William, Drogo and Humphrey, to pray for their souls.'

# CHAPTER SEVEN

Roger de Hauteville was given the task of subduing the interior of Calabria while the *Guiscard* secured the western coast, where lay the larger settlements and towns, but that went by the board as news came from Apulia of a revolt by some of the Norman barons, supported by disgruntled Lombard nobles who had seen their power destroyed, naturally encouraged by the scheming of Argyrus, now ensconced in Bari. Robert broke his camp and raced back to his most important fiefs with the bulk of his army, leaving Roger to continue to seek to subdue the country with a limited force of cavalry.

It was a tough task: the fighting was hard, the landscape a ribbon of high mountains cut by deep valleys, with low and fertile coastal strips to east and west, warfare that took much out of man and beast – mobile, small-scale engagements with, always, another fief to conquer somewhere on the horizon. The land was at odds with that which provided prosperity, the rough interior parts of Calabria famous for fine cloths, silks and damasks. Started by the Byzantines several centuries previously it had grown into a valuable trade, which made the way the region had been ignored hard to fathom: they had taxed Calabria but, seeing it at the very edge of their imperial possessions, had usually failed to keep it safe from incursions.

In this, Byzantium had followed the old Roman Empire, Calabria Interior being seen as a wild and inhospitable place. Rome settled and civilised the coast but left the locals to their mountains and their feuds. There were few proper castles and no large towns in the interior; instead the Normans were required to subdue numerous hilltop dwellings, which relied on height or scanty walls as protection. Most lords therein were too proud to acquiesce, requiring subjugation and that came down, if they refused entreaties to surrender to the power of the Count of Apulia, to letting them see destroyed, in the valleys below and on which they depended for food, what crops they had planted and what livestock they could not accommodate. That the peasants suffered from this could not be allowed to interfere with the necessity: there were too many objectives and neither enough time, nor force, to adopt any other tactic than slash and burn.

Primary damage tended to be done as soon as their column was sighted, not difficult in such mountainous country: the lord of the demesne would clear anything close to his walls that would provide either shelter or a point from which to mount an attack, usually the huddled dwellings of the poor, casting to the elements those who could not be accommodated within the defences. Thus the first encounter on approaching a fief was usually with disgruntled peasants, forced to seek shelter where they could, and sure they were about to be slaughtered by these mounted barbarians. Given their lack of love for their masters, and finding themselves spared, they often provided Roger with a valuable source of information.

He would be told of the numbers and quality of what men he faced, the level of food stocks and, in some measure, how determined the defenders were to resist. A parley would follow, where Roger would try to persuade the incumbent that he would enjoy a safer and more prosperous future under a powerful magnate like Robert, who could be trusted to keep the Saracens at bay and stop neighbour from warring with neighbour. All he was required to do was to swear fealty and undertake to pay a portion of his revenues – in kind, for coin was scarce – to his new overlord instead of Byzantium; in return he could work his lands and people in peace. For people who trusted no one, often not even their own blood relatives, it was hardly surprising the response was usually a blunt refusal.

'They are a damnable lot, these Calabrians.'

Roger mouthed this while eyeing yet another clutch of dwellings that seemed to merge with the low cloud cover that made humid and uncomfortable the air around him, tumbledown houses surrounding a church and a high-walled manor house, all set next to an ancient near-ruined acropolis, situated at the top of a high hill. It was superfluous to say that to attack it was to risk much.

'I thought the local peasants told you this fellow was Greek?' replied Ralph de Boeuf.

'He is, and so are those who will defend the place, but being Greek makes no difference, they are all forged in the same way. If they did not hate each other so much I think we would be chased out of these mountains in a month.'

'Then thank God they do. They have to be damned to even live in such a place. My legs ache just from looking at it. Imagine living up there with nothing but silkworms for company.'

The one-time Castellan, who had first greeted Roger outside his brother's castle, looked around him at the high wooded hills to both north and south, as well as the rock-filled watercourse that tumbled down the steep ravine at the very base of this latest objective.

'You wish you had stayed in Melfi?' Roger asked.

'I had hoped for plunder and I never ever thought that easy, but this?'

'This is more work than we both imagined. My brother made it sound easy. I should have known.'

'He likes to tell tall tales.'

Roger smiled. 'Do not think such a habit has come with his title. He was like that as a youth – something he got from our father – though I think old Tancred was less given to outright embroidery.'

'Is that another word for lies?'

'It could be.'

'This one might agree to terms.'

'Then this one will be singular, for few have.'

The route through the mountains had been a succession of such obstacles and only a handful had allowed themselves to be persuaded what was proposed made sense. There was really only one other carrot Roger could dangle outside security – to accept his brother as suzerain was to be on the side of right and might – not something extended to those who had to be overcome by force. Their land, if they resisted till the bitter end and drew too much Norman blood, became forfeit, available to be parcelled out as a fief by one of the Count of Apulia's captains.

The only saving grace was the end was not in doubt: there was no chance of a Byzantine force coming to the rescue, unless they were prepared to mount the kind of expedition that left bare the more valuable Eastern possessions where they faced the inroads of the warlike Turks. Previous incursions into Calabria, like that of Robert *Guiscard* years before, had been more in the nature of armed raids than invasions; this time he had arrived with a complete army and a set aim: total subjugation.

'We have been at this longer than we hoped, Roger, and must soon think of quartering for the winter.'

Ralph de Boeuf was right: the task was incomplete but to seek to continue in this high country when autumn faded was not a good idea. There would be snow on the higher ground even this far south and, lower down, the kind of persistent rain that rotted harness, rusted weapons and ruined chain mail. His men were already, after a long spring and summer of fighting, showing signs of strain. The horses, too, were giving indications of decline; they needed to be rested and allowed to grow their coats to ward off the coming cold, not something that could be allowed if they needed to cover long distances and bear on their backs armed fighting men.

'Time to climb up there and talk to this so-called Count of Montenero.'

'That's a grand title for the possession of such a pigsty.'

'It may look better when the sun shines.'


There was a winding roadway up to the heights, more of a cart track and, judging by the many areas of repair, one subject to the elements, especially torrential rain and rock falls. His horse slithered often on the loose stones, head down and weary, entirely matching the mood of its rider, who had to force himself to look eager and martial, knowing he was in view of those to whom he must speak. The clatter of a thrown rock landing in front of him told Roger those behind the walls thought he and his dozen strong escort had come far enough, close enough to be heard if he raised his voice to an undignified shout.

The words had become too familiar, spoken in his far from perfect Greek, addressed to an unseen listener, outlining the power of his brother, soon to be lord of all Calabria, a man who had beaten Byzantium to the east, where they had been strong and committed, and would do so here where they were weak and absent. The truth: that this small fief could not exist in safety alone, so they would be better to peacefully accept the new dispensation and volunteer tribute to the *Guiscard*'s tax collectors than face his wrath for their refusal. Then there would be the invitation to submit, followed by the dire nature of the consequences.

There were rules to this game: they could not throw a lance or fire an arrow to tell Roger they declined, but he was not surprised the reply came as a hail of stones, which made his mount skittish as they rattled all around, one or two ricocheting to strike its forelegs. He had to press hard with his knees and haul on the reins to keep it facing to the front and when he retired it was not far. He needed to dismount and, leaving his horse on a piece of flattish ground, he proceeded to walk the defences and seek out the weak spots at which he might make a breech.

'Will they have enough water to withstand us?'

The question, addressed to one of his escort, was rhetorical and the fellow knew it, so did not reply. If they lacked wells at this height they would have cisterns dug into the rock that held the falling rain and snow melt, enough to last the summer, however hot. For food they would keep within the walls live animals to be slaughtered and, in cool cellars, sacks of grain and peas, so to starve them out was probably impossible, even if he thought the place worth the time it would take, which he did not. The best solution was to give whoever led the defence the chance to surrender with honour. It was not necessary to completely overcome them but to make it plain that the eventual outcome was not in doubt.

Yet up here he was aware the place had attractions not obvious from the base of the hill, having, as it did, a sight down several valleys in all directions. He also suspected on a clear day he would be able to see the coast and the Ionian Sea, though now, on a grey afternoon of hazy mist, the whole melded into one indistinct line. Sharp eyes from a tower at this elevation would be able to oversee much of the surrounding countryside, and with hill beacons it could act as the centre to provide security for a hundred square leagues.

Most of his life, old Tancred had dreamt of having his stone watchtower, a donjon atop the hill at Hauteville-le-Guichard from which to overlook his demesne, to replace what he did own and could afford to maintain for protection, the old structure of wood and mud. That he had achieved it was due to the wealth sent home by his successful sons; Roger, as a boy, had dreamt of owning a stone castle with four corner towers, a keep with a great hall, all surrounded by stout curtain walls.

Many hopes had travelled with him and that childish vision was one, the ultimate mark of success for a Norman warrior, a castle of his own, which flew his own personal standard to tell the world of his possession. Some achieved it through service to a greater being, as fortress captains; few were gifted the chance to build their own, as Robert had done at Monte Fagnano. Yet here was a fine spot for that very thing, one that could hold a permanent garrison. The more he walked, the more he looked over the walls he and his men must overcome, the more vital it seemed he must have possession of the place.

At the base of the hill he could see the bulk of his men and their horses, the latter now unsaddled and tethered, with hay at their feet or being taken in turns to drink at the pool that had formed in the rock-strewn river. They would be useless up here: the ground close to the defences was too steep, and mentally thinking ahead to the possibility of a garrisoned castle, he reasoned there would be a need to build stabling if this was to become a permanent Norman holding. It would be wise to accommodate warriors and mounts down below, so they could move swiftly to meet any threat in the surrounding countryside or on the coast.

'So, no terms?' Ralph de Boeuf asked when Roger outlined his thinking.

'No. We must take the place.'

'Quarter?'

'We will kill what we must, but keep alive what we can.'

'Then we had best get what we need up that damn hill.'

'I will organise the peasants to supply us and when that is complete I want them building fences around the local pasture. If we are going to be here permanently, properly husbanded grassland will be necessary.'

If whoever was overseeing the defence had any doubt about the Norman intention it would have died when he saw them constructing a dry-stone wall set across the track right to the cliff edge, high enough and stout enough to make any attempt to sally out and dislodge them dangerous. They could also see a constant stream of packhorses, as well as their own local peasants, carrying heavy loads up to this encampment: food, skins of water and wine, as well as copious amounts of wood for the fires they would need at night, added to the kind of timber and reeds needed to make shelters to protect them from both sun and rain.

'The one thing they might not have is an abundant supply of weapons, so we want them using those against probing attacks.' He looked around the assembled conroy leaders, all thirty of them, each in command of nine other men. 'We will approach the walls then retire when they respond. I don't want these attacks pressed home, I want them to be coming from different directions, drawing their fire before retiring.'

'If they've got any sense they'll ignore us.'

Roger looked at the man who had spoken, his blue eyes steady but without any rancour: it was good they voiced their concerns, good that they used their brains and experience and did not just blindly follow orders. There were men here who had many years on him as well as a wealth of fighting skill. The lances he had brought from Normandy would follow him regardless but he had worried at the outset of the campaign that those Normans given him by his brother might baulk at having to obey such a young and untried leader. There had been a trace of resentment to begin with but that was now gone: Roger had proved himself able, proved that he was not the leader just because of his bloodline.

'If they do I will be racking my brain for an alternative.'

'Then we are going to be here an eternity,' jested Ralph de Boeuf, to general laughter.

Working in parties of thirty at various points, the tactic was partially successful, depending on the amount of control exercised behind the walls: if the man commanding that section was strong of mind there was little response, if weak then his men let fly with what they had. The result of each probe was reported back to Roger, who then made his dispositions. To fight at night, without mail or shield, gloves or helmets, was risky but necessary, and he led the way, discarding his surcoat – the white could alert the defenders – the sword in his hand sheathed in straw in case it inadvertently struck stone. Scabbards, too, had to be left behind, seen as a possible encumbrance.

Torches lit the ground close to the walls, but they created pools of Stygian darkness not far off. Being strewn with scrub and rocks, it was a place into which the Normans could crawl, on a cloudy night, without being seen, the only sound a hissed curse or two as skin was rasped or bruised by passage through unseen obstacles. That died down as they got into the places they had sought out in daylight, and there they lay, waiting in utter silence, listening. The soft sounds of movement were not long in coming and glimmers of light would illuminate a small area of ground as a shaded lantern was uncovered, while, if the man holding it was careless, they would see what it was he had come out to find, a pike or a lance thrown from too much excitement.

'Now!'

The single cry was followed by a mass of yelling as the Normans raced towards where they had seen those pinpricks of light, swords now ready for battle, seeking out those lantern-holders who panicked enough to show where they were located. It was never going to be conclusive, Roger had never intended it should be, but it had the virtue of showing the defenders the determination their attackers intended to employ to subdue them. At the cost of a succession of cuts and abrasions they managed to kill half a dozen of those who had come out to retrieve their weaponry – their bodies were obvious as soon as the sun rose – and to prevent the rest from succeeding in their task of recovery.

At first light, those Normans not employed in the dark launched a proper attack on a section of the walls, lopping off the ends of the defenders' pikes while avoiding being impaled on the points, while the shields they bore were used to deflect heavy rocks big enough to break a bone. That, too, was only partially successful – in fact it cost Roger more in wounded than it caused harm to the defence, but it had been deliberately targeted at the place where the defence was strongest, on either side of the entry gate.

'They'll think us fools,' de Boeuf said, watching as the attack was repelled.

'I hope so,' Roger replied. 'Sound the recall.'

The horn blew, the Normans fell back as ordered and the garrison cheered.

They hit the walls again that evening, lances probing at the fools who, so eager for success, tried too hard to push the Normans back, then again as soon as the sun rose the next morning, never once at the point Roger had selected for an assault he thought might succeed – part of the defence on the eastern side where the land was reasonably flat. The ladders they would need were taken to that section at night, with torch-bearing Normans haranguing the defenders, while just out of the arc of light they created, their confrères laid the climbing frames in place for the morrow.

It was mid-morning before they moved and much play was made of a third of the Normans marching to the chosen spot, while the stronger contingent once more attempted the gate, this to pin the defence. What could not be seen were the preparations until the attackers lifted up their ladders and ran to the walls, this while the lances at the gate pressed home their assault to keep occupied those with whom they were contesting.

The defences were not high, not more than twice the height of a man, so the ladders were short. But they were also numerous and a surprise, creating a degree of confusion which got many of the Normans, personally led by Roger de Hauteville, onto the walls, there to fight the Greeks on more equal terms. Now defenders began to die, the difference soon apparent between men who lived and trained for war and those forced to partake of it. Yet the Greeks were stalwart and fought back with gusto: ladders were cast down along with the men climbing them. The point of maximum exposure came when any Norman tried to transfer from ladder to wall, at the point when his weapon and shield were not covering his body. Mail was armour against a cutting blow, less so against a determined thrust by a sharp-pointed pike, and good as Roger's men were, several paid the price of the assault with wounds that were deadly.

Standing atop the wall, feet apart but precariously balanced, Roger swung his sword with all his might, the blue and white surcoat now massively stained with blood of those into whose flesh he had cut. Finally he got onto the wooded parapet, to the right and left of him, protecting his flank, two of the young men he had brought from Normandy, all fighting to create a space that would allow their fellow warriors to join them. Once an unbroken line could be formed they would overwhelm the defence by sheer weight of weaponry.

The defence hardened as defenders were brought from other, less threatened parts to hold the endangered section, but that had been anticipated, for behind Roger the men who had been assaulting the gate would be thinning out as instructed to make their way to join him. He needed to get off the parapet and down to ground level, where superior close-battle control would really count and all their numbers could be brought to bear. The fighting became lethal on both sides, narrowed down to what was right in front of each man, whatever side he was on. The Normans had skill and determination, the defenders desperation, but in the end it came down to faith in leadership. Roger led men who knew he would die as readily as they; it was only to be discovered later that those who held the town lacked that vital ingredient. A rumour circulated that their lord was preparing to flee and the defence began to crumble with a suddenness that surprised every Norman, Roger included.

Weapons were cast aside, while men fell to their knees pleading to be spared, those at the very front in vain. The defence was about to disintegrate, but then the leader they thought about to desert them appeared, dressed in a fine helmet, good mail and wearing a multicoloured surcoat. Voice raised, he rallied his broken ranks in a way that, even engaged, Roger found time to admire, and the fighting resumed its deadly pace.

Much as he needed to share his men's travails, Roger was also required to direct the battle. Trust had to be placed in Ralph de Boeuf and his other conroy leaders to carry on the command at the very front, while he himself withdrew to seek an overall view of where the enemy weaknesses might lie. Dry-mouthed and with sweat running down his face – the cloth band he wore under his helmet was drenched – Roger tried to assess each part of the enemy line and he thought he spotted a weak spot right by the walls, where the defenders lacked firm leadership. Pulling back some of his knights he formed a phalanx and struck hard at the very edge of the wall, driving forward with mighty sword blows and equally heavy thrusts with his shield. His opponent was no fool: he saw the increasing danger and led at a rush a portion of his men to defend it.

Thus the two leaders found themselves face to face. The Greek Count of Montenero was not gorgeous now, he had been in close combat and was as bloodily stained as the Norman, and if he was fresher, he lacked Roger de Hauteville's height and reach: the Norman sword swung in a wider arc than his, making it hard for him to get close to landing a blow, and by engaging as he did he had created a situation he would have been well advised to avoid. The men knew their leaders: the contest had become personal, lessening the general melee, and the count was no match for the man he faced.

He fought valiantly, even as it became clear he was outmatched, his sword taking blow after ringing blow as he put up a stout defence, never letting it show that, barring a shock, there could be only one outcome. Swinging hard and continually, his arms and shoulders aching from the continued effort, Roger beat down the man's every effort to best him, wondering why he did not drop back, let fall his sword and beg for succour.

Yet Roger knew why he fought as he did: this was his fief and, in effect, his life. Everything he had of himself and his personal esteem coursed through the blade with which he fought: he had to kill this man before him or die in the attempt, there was no other way with honour. That came when he, tiring also, failed to parry a sweep of Roger's sword and in seeking to recover from that error he left himself exposed. The following blow, the broadsword held high and swung with maximum force, caught the man at the join of his shoulder and neck. It did not decapitate him, the mail cowl under his helmet prevented that, but the blade sunk deep into his neck, forcing his head to cant at an angle, as a fount of bright-red blood spewed from the ruptured arteries and the light died in the man's dark eyes.

Those he had led lost heart, but they had so incensed their Norman opponents by their fortitude that few were spared, so that the hard ground of the interior of Montenero was fed with much blood. Some fought on with the despair which comes from knowing death awaits and it is better to expire fighting than on your knees, falling back until they found themselves under the canopy of that ancient acropolis. It ended there with slaughter and the Norman leader, his chest heaving, leaning on his sword, rasping that combat should cease, aware that for once, he was being ignored.

When it did stop there was no one left to kill and Roger, looking around the stone columns of the ancient building, tried to say that what held them up would make fine foundation stones for his castle: tried but failed – he lacked the breath to make himself heard even by the men right at his side.

# CHAPTER EIGHT

'I have been faithful to my word, Robert, sending you everything I pillaged as well as the revenues I have gathered from those who submitted.'

'Everything? I think not, Sprat.'

'Stop calling me that.'

'I am your liege lord, I can call you what I wish.'

Roger was aware that his brother was uncomfortable, as to his mind so should he be. Famed for his generosity, he had not been that with him, quite the reverse: the revenues sent to Melfi in the last year had stayed there in their entirety.

'I decide who is my liege lord, not you, and as of this moment I am not inclined to acknowledge a man who acts like a common thief.'

'I will not let you address me so,' Robert yelled, his voice echoing off the stones of the great hall. Meant to cow Roger, it signally failed to do so.

'How you are going to stop me, unless you are willing to use your dungeons? I cannot pay my men, damn it, Robert, I can scarce feed them. What happened to the half of the revenues I was promised, all that gold I sent you?'

'It has been used wisely.'

'For what?'

'The needs of my holdings, which are of paramount concern.'

'Your coffers are full to bursting, I'll wager. Is it that you have become a miser?'

'The revenues of the lands I have are mine to do with what I wish…'

'Which clearly does not extend to keeping a solemn promise.'

'Promise? I recall no promise.' The booming voice had mellowed, but it was the sly look that went with it that really annoyed Roger. 'A discussion yes, a proposal and one larded with avarice from you, given you were without prospects lest I grant them to you.'

'Have I not served you well? Half of Calabria accepts you as suzerain.'

'You have served me as you should.'

'Perhaps you fear me, Robert.'

'If you believe that you are a fool.'

'The one thing am I am not is a fool, brother. Pay me what you owe or I will depart your service.'

'Do you think you, of no account, can threaten me?'

'If I am of no account I may as well depart.'

Seething, Roger turned on his heel and left. The next heard sound was of him and his knights riding out of the castle of Melfi. What should have troubled the *Guiscard* more was that accompanying them were Ralph de Boeuf and many of the men Robert had sent with his brother to Calabria.


'I have never known him like this,' Geoffrey said, 'And I have good reason to say those words, for Robert has never been short with me.'

'You are another one,' Roger replied, not without asperity, 'who is going to boast of his liberality, something I am sick of hearing about.'

The remark made Geoffrey frown. 'I beg you take some more wine and calm yourself.'

'How can I be calm? How can you just sit at this table and eat and drink while I am being cheated?'

If Roger had a reputation for being diplomatic it had deserted him in the face of his treatment. He had been fuming since he left Melfi and no amount of hospitality from Geoffrey was going to assuage it. Two years he had spent campaigning in Calabria, sustained by the promise of two things: half the revenues, obviously, plus the promise that Robert would return to complete the conquest of the province once he had settled matters in Apulia. Neither had been kept and Roger had found himself making war with diminishing resources and disgruntled lances, men not being paid that which they were due because everything was being remitted to Melfi. What plunder they acquired from resistant places like Montenero did not last much beyond their desire to celebrate with wine and women. His own purse had been emptied to keep them fighting but that was now bare.

'I am at a loss to know what you think I can do.'

About to bark at Geoffrey, Roger stopped himself: abusing this affable and somewhat ineffectual de Hauteville would do nothing to help him. Geoffrey had Loritello and his captaincy of Brindisi, the latter gifted to him by Robert, the former held from the time of Drogo.

'You may have been too successful, Roger.'

'How can a man be too successful?'

'You do not know Robert as I do,' Geoffrey responded. 'He

does not warm to anyone he feels can match him in the field.'

'He's jealous?' Roger asked.

'Not jealous, but inclined to be made uncomfortable by an ability he perceives might equal his own. He fell out with William, Drogo and Humphrey, though I would add falling out with the latter was too easy.'

'I pose no threat to him.'

Geoffrey sat forward and for once replied with feeling, which led Roger to think he was talking more about himself than the problem being discussed. 'It is for the person who feels threatened to judge such a thing.'

'Will Robert listen to you?' he asked, in a calm voice.

With just a trace of bitterness Geoffrey said, 'He never has before.'

'I need you to advance me some funds.'

That made his brother guarded, though it did not engender an outright refusal. 'I cannot spare much.'

'I don't need much. I am going west and when it comes to food and fodder Robert will provide them whether he likes it or not.'

Good as his word, Roger de Hauteville lived very well off the *Guiscard*'s lands: when his men ate beef it was from his brother's cattle, when his horses downed oats they came from Robert's grain stores. It would have pleased him to know that such theft, when reported back to Melfi, nearly produced an apoplexy.

Roger's stop in Capua was of short duration: although he was made welcome, it was clear that his brother-in-law found his presence either irksome or inconvenient and no intercessions by his sister carried any weight. Richard's relations with the *Guiscard* were fragile, as suited two equally powerful magnates whose interests did not always coincide. They would combine if the Norman position in Italy was threatened, but that did not extend to a deep common purpose and the fear always existed on both sides, in a world where suspicion was rife, that one great Norman fief might combine with outside forces to destroy the other, despite a long-standing commandment that, here in Italy, Normans did not kill Normans.

The Prince of Capua took care to keep his operations to the west of the Apennines, while Robert *Guiscard* made sure none of his lances strayed into his neighbour's bailiwick. If they met at all it was in the papal fief of Benevento, which straddled the mountains and was rich in everything that was of value in their world: field crops, orchard fruit, vines, livestock, fish and timber, as well as all the trades that commanded good payment. Both Norman fiefs had treaty relations with the papacy in the Principality of Benevento; both treated such obligations more in the breech than the observance.

There was also the jealousy of Richard's captains: a de Hauteville was too prominent a personage to be a mere lance, too well connected to be employed as a mere warrior, quite apart from the fact that he had arrived in Capua leading fifty followers. To show them any favour was to upset the delicate balance any leader had with his own key supporters. After a month of well-fed idleness, Roger knew his own men were becoming impatient: like every Norman in Italy, these men served for reward and plunder. It was time to move on.

'To where?' asked Ralph de Boeuf.

'We could offer our swords to Gisulf of Salerno.'

'If we do, we'll soon find ourselves fighting the men we are living with now at odds of a hundred to one.'

There was truth in that: having swallowed Capua, Richard continued to press in on the territories of his one-time nominal suzerain, so squeezing Salerno that the prince could only now say with certainty he ruled in his own city.

'I have also heard that Gisulf is short on sense.'

'Let us travel through that city and see what presents itself.'

The sight of a strong party of Normans riding towards Salerno did not go unnoticed: word of their presence reached the city gates before they did. Prior to that, Roger and his men had sat on a high hill looking at the great bay on which the city sat, one of the premier trading ports of Western Italy, rival to Naples, Amalfi and Gaeta, all of them wealthy, all of them victims over the last five hundred years of internecine Lombard rivalries, expanding and contracting as one fief rose and another diminished. Now they faced the Normans, a bitter pill for Salerno, given it was the duke of that city who had first sought their mercenary aid to fight the Saracens.

'They are accustomed to disquiet,' Ralph observed, his eye following the trace of the exterior walls. 'How long do these Lombards have?'

'How long do we Normans have, Ralph?'

'There's no one to threaten us.'

'God has a way of marking and dealing with hubris.'

'God in heaven, you are dismal.'

Roger smiled. 'I am made thoughtful, Ralph. We have just ridden the same roads that my eldest brothers traversed many times and they are now bones. William's iron arm did not save him from a secret knife, nor did being a doughty fighter spare Drogo the same fate. Sitting here, I feel somehow their presence, more so than at their tomb in Venosa. This is where my family's adventure began.'

'And where yours will end if we don't eat soon.'

Roger nodded, and taking a tight hold of the reins of the mounts he led, he gently kicked with his heels to set his horse in motion.

The de Hauteville name got Roger an immediate audience as well as accommodation in the Castello di Arechi, the towering fortress that overlooked the town, but Gisulf of Salerno did not impress. The prince was too shifty in nature and that trait was marked in both his features and manner. He fidgeted constantly, unbecoming in a nobleman who, whatever his own anxieties, had a need to appear calm before his court, many of whom were present and loud in the way they reacted to his pronouncements, however outlandish. Dark-complexioned, with black hair and eyes, Gisulf looked and acted like a schemer and, given what he had been saying to Roger, one with a tenuous grip on reality. He had already created a great armed host from nothing but his imaginings, and sent it, with Roger at its head, to inflict a terrible defeat on Richard of Aversa.

'I see his head on my city gate,' he cried.

'You speak of a man to whom I am related by marriage, sire.'

Gisulf, slightly hunched and too gaudily dressed for his slight figure, waved an impatient hand: such ties clearly meant nothing. 'And you would be paying back his family for what they did to your own, the treacherous swine.'

Roger wondered at that misinterpretation of the past, which got loud approval from most present: certainly Richard's uncle, Rainulf, had cheated his brothers, but Gisulf's own father had not treated William and Drogo well at all; indeed, if this inelegant prince was a schemer, then it was a parental inheritance. Guaimar, who had sired this fellow, had done his best to play off Rainulf against the de Hautevilles. That he had not succeeded in getting them to kill each other came from an over-reliance on conspiracy rather than a lack of the desire to indulge in such a thing.

While listening with seeming intent to the prince, Roger was taken with one of his advisors, a tall sallow-complexioned fellow in a skullcap, very much older than the rest of the courtiers present, not given, either, to reacting with enthusiasm to their lord's more outlandish suggestions. Indeed, the slight smile that played around his lips hinted at a more realistic grasp of where Gisulf stood in relation to the main enemy, for there were others. Roger's brother, Mauger, from his castle of Scalea, preyed on Gisulf's territories from the south, as much as Richard of Aversa did from the north and west.

'You will dine with me this night, Roger de Hauteville, and we will speak. Plans must be laid, messages sent to Naples and Amalfi to seek alliance – I will not deal with that pile of ordure they call the Duke of Gaeta.' Gisulf stopped both his pacing and fidgeting and fixed Roger with his beady eyes. 'Would a force of Saracen mercenaries be an advantageous idea?'

He spun then to face the tall fellow in the skullcap.

'Ephraim, do we have the funds to pay for such aid?'

'If you sell your plate, sire, yes.'

'Sell my plate? Am I so reduced that I cannot dine off my gold?'

'The man whose head you wish to see on your city gates is an avaricious neighbour.'

Gisulf spun to look at Roger again. 'You see what a robber your Richard is, you see how much I have to give him to have peace? He demands bezants and I must pay.' The cunning look came on now in full force. 'But you will also see what wealth you could gain if he were no longer my bane.'

Having been given an apartment, Roger retired, wondering how long he should stay in this land of fairies and their dreams. Quite apart from any ties to his sister, he was disinclined to do battle with his powerful brother-in-law to advance the cause of a Lombard, especially one who would seek to swindle him, even if he had a chance to succeed, which he most certainly did not. In contemplation of this, he was distracted by the knock at the door of his chamber, opening it to find the man called Ephraim outside.

'I wonder if we may have a private word?' Roger stood back and indicated he should enter, quite naturally looking to ensure he was not armed. Once inside and the door shut, the fellow looked at him and smiled in a friendly way. 'You remind me of your brothers, William and Drogo. It is striking how you all resemble each other.'

'If you had seen my father you would know why.'

'Ah yes, Tancred. He and I did much business, even if we never met.'

'Business?'

'I served as a conduit by which your brothers could send money back to Normandy.'

'You are a Jew?'

'With a name such as mine, could I be otherwise?'

If Ephraim was a Jew he had none of the physical traits associated with his race, barring the sallow complexion: he was tall, well proportioned and the facial features were even and handsome.

'I used to accompany my father to the home of a Jew in Rouen.'

'To whom I remitted your brothers' gifts. I recall some mention of the building of a stone tower as being his heart's desire.'

'He always left that house in Rouen with a smile.'

'Did he get his donjon?'

'He did, but only after William had begged the Duke of Normandy for permission.' Roger, recalling that such a thing had angered his father, was suddenly aware of his lack of manners. 'Please sit, sir. Can I get you some wine?'

'That would be most pleasant. I recall sharing many goblets with William.'

'Not Drogo?'

'Less so Drogo,' Ephraim replied with a wistful look. 'He was, how should I say, more impetuous than William, and although we transacted business it did not extend to conversations regarding his well-being.'

'Why have you come here?' Roger asked, handing over one goblet and sitting down with his own.

The Jew did not reply at once: it was as if he were searching for the right words. 'I must tell you that I am in the service of the Prince of Salerno, as I was in the service of his father. I hold the office of collector of the revenues of the port.' When Roger did not respond Ephraim added, 'You do not see it as strange that a man of my race is entrusted with so valuable an office?'

'I would not see it as likely in Normandy, but this is Italy. Things happen here that are strange to us northerners.'

'Nothing more strange, I wager, than a Lombard prince seeking to engage you in mercenary service against one of your own race? It is, I suggest, a task you should decline.'

'Strange advice for one who serves the prince.'

Ephraim acknowledged that with a nod. 'Good service, as opposed to mere sycophancy, often requires an advisor to impart to his lord unpleasant truths, things he would rather not hear.'

'Yours being?'

'That any attempt to confront Richard of Aversa would result in the complete destruction of his house. Rainulf once turfed his grandfather out of this very Castello di Arechi. Should he persist with his illusions, the same will happen to him. It is advice I have given him often and too many times it has fallen on deaf ears.'

'So you choose to tell me?'

'If you share William's good sense, you will heed what I say. I fear that there is another strain in your bloodline, which I could best describe as that of Drogo.'

Roger grinned: he had grown up hearing of the latter's exploits, the number of fights he had got into with his mercurial temper, added to riotous escapades which did not point to much in the way of good sense. He had also met several of Drogo's bastards and some of the fathers who still cursed his name for debauching their daughters, as well as men who recalled him fondly as a good man with whom to drink and carouse.

'Meaning Drogo would accept?'

'He was, as I said, impetuous, yet maybe I do him a disservice for he was not stupid.' The Jew stood up. 'I have said what I came to say, now it is up to you to decide.'

'Would it surprise you to learn I already have?'

That got no more than a nod, though he was clearly pleased. 'I esteemed William and I am proud to think I was of some use to him while he was alive. Should you have need of my services I would be more than happy to provide what I can.'

'What services would they be?'

'To answer that would require me to be immodest, but if you ask you will find many people able to tell you, though some I am sure will curse me. Let us just say, that if I thought Saracen mercenaries would be advantageous, I have the means to fund such a thing from my own resources.'

'And you would aid me likewise?'

'I sense something in you, so yes.'

'Why?'

'You are right to ask, which shows you share William's sagacity. I saw in your brother a sense of honour not much in evidence in the world I inhabit, and he never gave me cause to doubt it. Humour my poor deluded prince, then seek employment elsewhere, perhaps by repairing your bond with Robert.'

Roger was surprised. 'You know we have parted company?'

'It is my business to know what goes on in my world. Not to do so for one of my race makes life too dangerous.'

Roger did as he was bid: he listened to Gisulf as excessive drink detached him even more from the actuality of his true situation, which was that if Richard of Capua decided one day to take Salerno he might well have the means to do so. It would not be easy, it would require allies and a siege of long duration, for the walls were strong and in good repair, while the sea was open for the supply of food and men.

The only relief was provided by Gisulf's sister and that came from observing their differences as much as their manner. Where he was weedy and narrow of chest, Sichelgaita was huge, as tall as Roger and with a frame and a voice to match, strikingly blond where Gisulf was dark, and she seemed fearless of nature where he portrayed anxiety with his continual twitching, so much so that Roger was wont to wonder if they truly shared the same sire. The last act of his day, when the feasting was done, was to alert Ralph de Boeuf to make ready to leave at first light.

'Where are we going?'

'Away from this madhouse, we shall go on south to Scalea.'

'They might try to stop us leaving.'

'Then you know what we will do if they try.'

De Boeuf grinned. 'I'll get the swords sharpened just in case.'

# CHAPTER NINE

The approach to Scalea was along a rocky shore, leading to a fertile plain hemmed in by hills and mountains, the most striking feature a rock escarpment on which stood the walled town, topped by the outlines of a castle, that replacing an old Byzantine watchtower on a volcanic plug right on the shoreline. With a mind naturally military, Roger could not help but see the strengths of the location, which were many, and its weaknesses, which were few, yet it could be taken: had not Mauger done just that to the previous incumbent, a Lombard vassal of Gisulf?

Stopped by sentinels in the approaches, a messenger had gone ahead to alert the garrison and, of course, the suzerain and soon Roger saw a lance bearing a pennant of the same blue and white chequer that adorned his own. A space apart, both brothers dismounted to approach each other; Roger was welcome anyway, but when his elder brother found out he had fallen out with Robert, he was hugged by a beaming sibling unsurprised by what had brought him to this place.

'The weasel dunned you,' Mauger hooted. 'That does not surprise me.'

The soubriquet *Guiscard* might mean cunning to those who esteemed Robert, to those who hated him, and there were many, the secondary meaning, weasel, was the more accurate. Mauger was still smarting from the way Robert had taken over from Humphrey. He saw himself as the equal of any of his brothers, and having been longer in Italy he felt the title of Count of Apulia should have devolved to him

'Geoffrey insists he is generous by nature, that the way he has treated me is an aberration, and so does every other Norman to whom I talk, though he did wonder that Robert might be made cautious by my successes.'

They were in Mauger's apartments now, in the newly completed main tower, hung with tapestries and the heads of wild beasts, the furnishings well made, the carpets Eastern in their design and the wine, as well as the food, local and excellent. The horses of Roger and his lances had been put out to good pasture, while the riders were being well looked after, no doubt swapping tales of home with their Norman confrères.

'He is a thief, Roger,' his brother maintained, 'and as for Geoffrey, all he ever does is kiss Robert's arse so he can hang on to his titles. If our father had not made us vow never to raise a weapon against each other I would have been sorely tempted to dispose of that swine.'

The ability to keep a straight face in receipt of hyperbole was a gift Roger needed now. Mauger was a big man but he had none of the sheer physicality of Robert, the breadth of shoulder and the leonine head. Robert also had a presence, which, much as he was angry with him, bespoke of a great leader. Mauger would certainly be able to command men, but did such ability extend to the leadership of complex armies on difficult campaigns?

Observing one brother and recalling the other, he knew precisely why Humphrey had named as his successor the brother he actively distrusted – not that he was prone, it seemed, to gift much in the way of affection to any of his siblings. Roger remembered Humphrey as beetle-browed, sour, humourless, cruel to men and animals and the one, as a child, he tended to avoid. Added to that, Tancred had little time for him.

'That is a vow I never took,' Roger finally replied.

That brought forth a keen look, as if Mauger were thinking that Roger could do that which he had forsworn, but the fact he had not knelt before Tancred to swear to that oath counted for nothing. Roger would never raise arms against any of his brothers, never seek to draw their blood: it had been his father's wish and for him that was a command.

'Well, you are here now so we must find you something to do, but before that you must tell me what you learnt in Salerno.' Mauger grinned like a mischievous child. 'Did that popinjay Gisulf curse me?'

'I have to tell you, Mauger, that he did not even mention you.' It was the wrong thing to say, a dent to his pride, immediately obvious as the smile disappeared to be replaced by a childlike scowl. Realising he had made a gaffe, Roger said quickly, 'He is too taken with the inroads of Richard of Capua to worry about any of our family.'

'Is he, by damn? Then I shall have to show him that he has more to care about than that impostor.'

That required equal prudence when it came to a reaction: Mauger was lord of a small fief, even if it was a valuable one, and perhaps a hundred knights. Richard was a master of great estates and counted his lances in the thousand. Even on such short acquaintance he was beginning to discern that it was not just physicality that had denied Mauger Apulia: such pronouncements indicated a want of common sense and an inability to accept his own limitations.

'We shall raid together, Roger,' Mauger said, leaning forward, 'and show Gisulf what we are made of. You will also be pleased to know that from my fief we can steal as much from Robert as we can from Salerno. In truth, that gives me greater pleasure.'

'I doubt we can steal as much as he owes me.'

'We can try, brother,' Mauger boomed.

That they did, riding out on raid after raid, side by side with half their available lances, never too far or too long away to be in danger of reprisals by any force large enough to stop them, secure in the knowledge that the men left behind would keep safe that already held. Certainly they met resistance, but in the lands of Gisulf of Salerno it was by small bands of Lombard warriors who, if they fought at all, left their bones on the field of conflict.

With Normans it was more a case of a parley, a realisation by those they encountered, individual conroys owing allegiance to the *Guiscard*, that a spillage of blood for what could not be prevented was unwise. Harsh words would be spoken, threats of retaliation would be issued, some of the plunder would be given up, but each side would withdraw without a fight: the unwritten rule applied – Normans did not, if it could be avoided, kill Normans.

Usually they would return to Scalea with their plunder intact: lowing cattle, bleating sheep, donkeys and packhorses loaded with wine, grain and olive oil, some of which would be passed on locally to traders, or if Mauger was feeling generous, as gifts to his subjects. The rest was traded with the other ports and cities that lined the coast, even, an irony, with Salerno itself.

That summer and autumn were good and profitable, though raiding had to be put in abeyance during the winter, resumed as soon as the buds began to open, with Mauger now raiding deeper and deeper into the territories of his neighbours – expeditions that lasted a month, spreading fear and mayhem to Gisulf and Robert's subjects seemingly unchecked. The day they found themselves, eighty lances, facing a Salernian force ten times their number, came as a shock, that being close to everything the Prince of Salerno could muster.

'Now Gisulf knows I am here and a threat,' Mauger cried, waving his sword.

These words were, Roger surmised, meant for his ears, Mauger seeking to make the best of what had to be seen as a tactical error. He was in command, he had brought them to this place on a raid that had over-extended the time away from safety, without taking the precautions necessary to ensure that any force sent to interdict them could not get between them and their base, this despite gentle reminders from his younger brother that to come such a distance, without leaving small parties behind to warn of a threat to their rear, was unwise.

'I think we are going to have to fight them,' Roger said.

'Of course we must fight them,' his brother replied, while he searched the surrounding landscape for a way to avoid that very thing.

Whoever had chosen the spot had done well. Between them and the sea, distant and hidden by high hills, lay a river in full spate, too ferocious to cross, even on horseback. Inland was thick forest running up steep hills leaving only two options, to move forward and fight or seek to retire and find a way round. That would require them to first of all abandon that which they had pillaged.

Even accepting that as a necessity, and it would be hard, the most pressing problem was the condition of their horses.

They had been active for forty days, rarely with enough rest to keep them at peak. A horse ridden continuously, sometimes pushed harder than was wise, soon lost fitness. They were far from being blown, but in an attempted flight they would have to push them to the limit with no certainty that they could avoid battle. If they could not, they would be forced to fight at an even greater disadvantage than that they faced now. Despite such concerns it was clear Mauger preferred that course.

'They lack the will, these Lombards, for the kind of pursuit we will force upon them. They will tire before we will.'

'They had the will, brother, to seek us out and get behind us and we have no idea if this is all that we face. There could be more to our rear.'

'Gisulf could never raise more than this?'

'That would depend,' Roger replied grimly, remembering the words spoken in Gisulf's council chamber, 'on how much he is prepared to spend.'

A small group detached themselves from their enemies and rode forward, clearly intent on talking, leaving Mauger to ruminate on what Roger had implied: soldiers could be bought and the notion just voiced affected his brother, who had not yet considered a possibility that should have come to him at once. The last thing that would serve the men he led was indecision, and right now Roger realised, which was worrying, that Mauger was unclear as to what to do. He was good company, generous with the proceeds of that which they had jointly plundered. Roger's men were as content as he with the state of their purse and, as part of the garrison of the castle, they had also enjoyed the privileges that gave them in the town, not least with the women they had taken as concubines.

Roger had also fallen into a kind of happy stupor: he was well fed, had a local girl of tender years to keep warm his bed, who had just produced for him a lusty son called Jordan, as well as a group of uncomplaining personal followers and a decent amount of gold in a locked coffer. But it was not what he had come to Italy for, to be no more than a brigand: his ambition was to emulate the best of his siblings.

Odd that he should be suddenly back in that arbour with Judith of Evreux, thinking of the words he had left unsaid, of his desire to make so much of himself that no man, or no duke, could deny him her hand in marriage. What would she think to see him now? These thoughts ran through his mind in the time it took the party to get close enough to speak, and he pulled his mount back a few paces to let them know he was not the man to address.

'You speak Greek?'

The voice from under the metal helmet was brusque, with Roger straining to see if he could recognise the speaker, perhaps one of those courtiers who had attended on Gisulf, but all he had to go on was the unfriendly eyes.

'I speak better Latin,' Mauger replied.

'Then in Latin I demand you surrender yourself.'

'You come to confer with only one message?'

'I do not come to confer. I require you to dismount, move away from your horses and put your weapons in a heap where they are plain to see. Then you will be bound in chains and taken by us to Salerno.'

'On foot?' asked Roger.

'Yes, Roger de Hauteville.'

'You know me?'

'Enough to name you, as I also know that I am addressing the usurper of Scalea.'

'Usurper!' Mauger thundered.

His brother knew what that meant: he had taken Scalea from a Lombard, a one-time inferior lord to Gisulf, so if he capitulated on this field he would be surrendering the fief as well. Yet Mauger did not respond: wondering what his brother was waiting for, Roger spoke, almost out of a sense of impatience.

'High words for someone who has yet to see us as his to command,' Roger said. 'Remember we are Normans.'

'You are thieving scum who will make redress to my master when your brother of Apulia pays to get you out of a dungeon.'

'And the men we lead?'

'We have oars in galleys and chains to bind them, or perhaps we will sell them to the Saracens to dig salt.'

Roger laughed: he did not feel like it, in fact he was deeply concerned, but it would never do to show this Lombard the truth. 'Go back to your men and be prepared to see their blood stain the ground over which you have ridden.'

'The blood will be yours.'

'Tell them,' Roger said, carrying on as if the Lombard had not spoken, 'that if they do not stand aside every one of them will die, there will be no quarter. Then see if they still want to fight us.'

The Lombard looked at Mauger. 'Is that your answer?'

The pause was too long: he should have responded immediately, for not to do so was to yield ascendancy. Roger wanted to shout but he dare not.

'It is,' Mauger said eventually.

'So be it.'

The Lombard spun his horse and, with his escort, rode back to join his men. Looking at his back, Roger thought him a fool: you do not threaten warriors with a life as a galley slave if you want them to put up their weapons. Most men would rather face death than that.

'What do you think, Roger, fight or run?'

'Fight, brother, there is no choice. We either do so now or when we are weaker. Will you permit me to speak to our men?'

'Of course.'

Not a thing I would grant to another, Roger thought, as he spun his mount and rode to where the men sat. As a raiding party they were on their ordinary riding horses; the destriers, which they would have liked for such a confrontation, were happily at pasture outside Scalea. But these horses were well trained, every Norman mount was. They might not be as stalwart in battle as the sturdy battle-chargers but they would perform well with what he had in mind. It was with some disquiet that he realised he was thinking as the man in command, even more disturbing was that Mauger had already gifted him that role.

He had an idea, based on the certain knowledge that the men they faced did not have the discipline of those he was about to address; it was a risk, but then so was all war. Standing in his stirrups he told them clearly what he wanted, based on the very obvious fact that they would have to initiate any action. The plan accepted that for their enemy, standing on the defensive, given they were between the Normans and home, was the right thing to do. They had to be tempted out of their certainties.

Everything unnecessary had to be abandoned before they could proceed: it was not just cattle and laden donkeys; each knight had saddlebags containing that which had been stolen and was portable. Roger had them empty those onto the ground, reluctantly at first, until he told them they would end up in the salt mines of Sicily if they did not. Never afraid to raid an Orthodox church, one of which existed in every settlement, the discarded items included plate, chalices and, to the shame of the despoiler, an odd crucifix. The whole, along with donkeys tethered and hobbled, was left in a high heap where his enemies, once the Normans were no longer blocking the sight, could see it.

The force he split into two unequal parts, the first and largest to attack as an unbroken line to mask the smaller body behind, which he hoped his opponent would see as a reserve waiting to exploit any success. Mauger led the initial attack, Roger with the lesser group, a tight knot of lances and, in the main, his own men, bringing up the rear. That the Salernian line would hold he took as an absolute: the man in command must have enough confidence in those he led to so deploy them: if he did not he was a fool, and Roger had no intention of treating him as such.

Cantering forward, Mauger met a wall of lances as he and his warriors engaged, which led to much fruitless jabbing on both sides, with the occasional thrown lance causing a man to fall. Had Roger been leading the defending force he would have been well pleased: the men of Scalea appeared to be blunting themselves on his line, but he hoped the fellow would not observe that the reserve force had moved to the right, to the point at which the defenders' line met the riverbank.

A horn blew and the most telling aspects of Norman ability, their close battlefield control, showed itself. The whole of Mauger's attacking force ceased combat and moved speedily to their left, exposing the riverbank before engaging again. Roger's lances, with hooves in the very water's edge, hit the gap they created at some speed, not charging, but at a fast and controlled canter, taking by surprise men who had raised their own weapons only to find they suddenly had enemies right in amongst them.

As soon as they showed a sign of weakening, not breaking but yielding ground, the horn blew a different set of notes, and Mauger's force disengaged for a second time and fell back slightly, preparatory to a move to their right. Roger, now in the thick of battle, his lance already deeply embedded in an opponent, was slashing with his sword at any neck that presented itself, part of a tight wedge of men forcing their way through the enemy crust, with the tumbling river on one side sending up a ferocious spray.

Relieved of pressure on the main front, the enemy right did what came naturally: they moved forward to keep contact with the retreating Normans, when what their commander required them to do was to reinforce his now struggling left. His horns were blowing but to no effect, or to be more truthful he was watching his left begin to fall back while his right wing was moving forward, creating what Roger had sought to achieve, a swinging door, his sole aim to create a large enough avenue through which they could get on the safer side of their enemies: if he was going to run, and they would have to, it was best to have a clear route to home and safety.

Even then it was risky: if the Salernians kept their discipline and contact, the Normans would end up fighting, outnumbered, with a river at their back, never a happy prospect. But that heap of booty, the clutch of heavily laden donkeys and the pile of treasure was now visible and tempting. Once a few had detached themselves to get hold of the plunder, the rest were damned if they were going to lose out on the spoils. Still fighting, praying his ploy was working, Roger knew only that he had the first sight of clear ground to his front: his conroys had broken through. Behind him the whole Norman contingent was now at his back, while the cohesion their enemy was falling apart as greed took over from obligation.

Once he had space to manoeuvre, Roger attacked the now exposed enemy flank, fighting to keep them on the defensive, the men coming through to his rear not running, but in a display of discipline and comradely cohesion, extending the assaults across the floor of the battle area. The blown signal to disengage was given by Mauger, in a better position than his brother to see it was time to depart, not that it was clean. They had to fight as well as retire, that made possible by the diminishing number of their enemies who were intent on killing instead of acquiring booty.

The next five days were hellish: the enemy commander got his men back into formation to pursue, which led to a succession of rearguard foot-bound fights, stalemates necessary to get both men and mounts some respite, furious and bloody engagements in which Mauger and Roger lost as many men as they had on the field of proper battle. Finally they reached the defendable defiles that led to Scalea and, seeing what his losses would be if he dared continue, their opponent, whose troops and horses had also suffered much, called off the pursuit and retired.

# CHAPTER TEN

'Gisulf must have had help from Robert. The prick of Salerno would never have dared move otherwise.'

Mauger had been making the same point for the whole of the summer, every time he had a bit too much to drink, so Roger's response was a weary nod. They had not stopped raiding: Gisulf could not keep a force in the field, but it had been more constrained and a lot less profitable, indeed just enough to keep the men they led content. If Mauger was bitter he was not unhappy, but it was not enough for his younger brother: in truth Roger was bored as much as frustrated, something which he took out on his opponents when they trained in the sand-covered manè`ge Mauger had set up for the purpose.

These were, if anything, the key to the Normans' success, a notion imported from their homeland. For the mass of their opponents fighting was a case of being levied to do so, only their leaders trained with any application for war. Every Norman lance did so: if they were not engaged in battle they were practising their skills daily, either on foot, with mock wooden swords, or on horseback with padded sword and tipped lance, individually or in their conroy. This basic unit of ten would then train with their confrères in larger formations so that everyone responded to the same commands in the same way right up to and including a ducal host.

To watch them in those enclosures was to understand why other armies feared them, especially on horseback. Normans never indulged in a frenzied charge, instead, mounted on their short, heavily muscled destriers, they went into battle at a fast canter and in an unbroken line. Other cavalry could not be constrained – a horse will run flat out if given a chance, especially in the presence of others. The trick was not to get a horse to run but to teach it when to run, at what pace and to keep in line with its fellows; in this the Normans were exemplary. Single combat they also practised: their horse-borne advance was designed to break an enemy line so that their enemies could be cut down or forced to flee.

Mock battle was not pain free: when they fought each other there were bruises to tend and many a cut to be stitched. Men occasionally lost their lives, more from finding themselves under horse hooves than any action of their fellows, yet this was where Roger was getting out of hand. Certainly the most potent fighter, the tallest, broadest, strongest and most skilful, it would have behoved him to hold back; dissatisfaction with his present way of living honed his aggression.

When a message came from the *Guiscard* asking him to meet with him in Calabria, with a promise he would be repaid every gold *solidus* he was owed, he was more than ready to break the monotony, while those he trained with, the men who suffered from his anger – rarely his own lances – were happy at the prospect he might depart. It was Mauger who was most disgruntled.

'He will cheat you again.'

'He needs our aid, there is a rebellion in Calabria and he dare not turn his back on Apulia with Argyrus up to his tricks. Nor will he trust just anyone to take it back. Robert is strong for blood; he will not give command to any of his captains to do what must be done so he must call on his family. Come with me, make your peace and we can both prosper.'

'Never.'

There was a temptation, then, to tell Mauger that which Roger knew and he would not accept. It was only the power of the Count of Apulia and Richard of Aversa that kept him safe: without those two magnates pressing on the lands of Gisulf, even a useless article like that prince could muster enough force to crush the Normans of Scalea. True, Robert might have granted Gisulf permission to curtail their activities, but would he have seen one of his family harmed? Roger doubted that: if he and Mauger had been taken the previous spring they would have been handed over to Robert and no doubt faced the humiliation of having to show gratitude.

'I think Robert would gift you more than Scalea if you fight at his side, Mauger. There are a dozen Byzantine strongholds still in Calabria waiting to be conquered.'

That childlike scowl Roger had come to know so well reappeared. 'So you are about to desert me?'

'I am about to find out what it is one of my brothers has to say and first, before I listen to a word, he will have to pass over what he owes me. Then, I suspect he will have a proposal that involves Calabria. If he needs help I am prepared to give it, but the price for that aid will be a high one.'

'I will never bend the knee to Robert and you know why. He stole my title.'

'Then let him give you another, more worthy of your name.'

'No!'

'Can I go with your blessing, without bad feeling between us?'

'I cannot stop you leaving, nor would I try, but when you depart you must do so for good.'

'You would force me to choose?'

'I must.'

There was pain in the farewells: Roger had his bastard Jordan on his saddle bow but the mother of the child had to be left behind, though with funds to buy both land and a dowry to attract a husband. Friendships had been formed that required to be broken but that was the way of the warrior, by their very nature tending to be rootless.

'Still smarting is he?' demanded Robert, in his customary booming voice. 'He calls me a weasel when he should look to himself.'

In late summer, at Morano, high in the Calabrian mountains, it was cool. Down on the plains it was not it was baking in a season known for heat at any time, but one that had seen no rain for months. The crops had withered in the drought, so, lacking food and encouraged by the Basilan monks and Greek priests who ran the local churches, who persuaded the peasants they were experiencing divine retribution for casting off their loyalty to Constantinople, the people had revolted.

In truth the peasants were being led by vassals who, seeing no income from their fiefs and being raided for what they did have by bands of men loyal to Byzantium, were disinclined to pay the dues owed to Robert *Guiscard*: it was those nobles who had egged on the priests to stir up the peasants, but the result was the same. The revenues of Calabria had dried up, as much as the irrigation ditches and the rivers that fed them, and that could not be allowed to continue.

'I can give you as many lances as you need, Roger.'

'And what else?'

The response was angry and loud. 'I have already gifted you a dozen talents of gold, what more do you want?'

The anger was a stunt: Robert was well aware he would have to give more, but he wanted to drive a hard bargain and one that suited him, something he could not be allowed to do.

'They were not a gift, they were my due and I am now waiting to see what you will offer for my lance and my sword to get you out of a sorry mess of your own creation.'

'I have become divine and I control the burning sun,' Robert scoffed. 'Perhaps if I dance the rains will come.'

'You have borne heavily on this province, Robert, too heavily perhaps. Now you need me to pacify it and I will only do that for a just reward.'

'Make a demand, then.'

'No! You have in your mind a price to pay, so offer it and stop wasting my time.' Roger indicated the sweltering plains, easily visible below, the rippling heat haze obvious even from this elevation. 'Matters are not going to improve down there and you are not going to get as much as a bronze *follis* from those who are hoarding their coin until it is pacified.'

Looking at his older brother, big, blond, red-faced and wearing a look of fury, Roger wondered how long it would be before the dam of that anger burst. Tancred might have made Robert swear never to use a weapon against a brother but that did not extend to fisticuffs. Robert was capable of a mighty buffet round the ears and he had seen him administer a few, so he kept his distance:

fighting Robert with lance and sword was just possible – wrestling or boxing with him was not.

The sudden roaring laugh that emerged, the throwing back of the head and the holding out of the arms was typical Robert – it was in his nature to go from fury to humour in an instant, leaving the recipient unsure if either emotion was sincere. The men he had brought with him as escort, who had been frowning at Roger, were now grinning at him, partly, he suspected, from relief: with a mercurial master it was not often they knew what was coming next.

'My God, Sprat, you have grown,' he roared. 'It can't be from residing with Mauger, that ditherer. There are castles out there, and towns, needing to be reminded to whom they owe their fealty. Take them back for me and you can have as title any one of them you like, letters patent and your gonfalons from my own hand.'

'The revenues?'

'Yours to keep for ten years.'

It was a generous offer: Roger was being given permission to depose the existing lords of the fiefs in revolt and become the overlord himself – better than what he had gained in the past, really only one fief and one self-built fortress. The previous campaign, still incomplete, had been about money and who was suzerain: to whom did these lords owe their taxes, Byzantium or the Count of Apulia? This would be about taking lands and titles from the intransigent for personal gain, a much more alluring prospect.

'What do you say, brother, do I have your support?'

Roger hesitated, suspecting that such generosity was prompted by a revolt that was more serious than he knew, one which would be that much harder not only to contain but to put down in a way that would last. The cause was starvation: desperate people would fight in a reckless way, which might mean a campaign of more than one year. He could have fires breaking out sporadically behind him as he passed onto another rebellious vassal. Would he have to kill so many who tilled the fields as to render the region a continuing desert?

'Let me think on it.'

The humour evaporated as quickly as it appeared. 'You mean you might say no?'

Roger grinned. 'I might, but not on an empty stomach.'

It was while eating and drinking – there was no shortage of food in the well-watered mountains – that Roger saw a possible solution. The question which had troubled him was how to separate the peasants from the lords they had toiled for all their lives, to whom they had a loyalty that often transcended good sense: there were good landowners but more were not, most exploited them to the hilt. Certainly he could massacre the peasants in their thousands: untrained levies wielding pikes could not stand against proper warriors, exposing those overlords, many of whom had probably eaten well while their serfs starved. But within that lay the seeds of future revolt: the sons of the dead would harbour a deeper hatred than their sires, a dangerous legacy in a land as yet not wholly conquered.

'Robert, I accept.'

His brother, gnawing on half a sheep's leg, replied in a voice muffled by mutton, 'I never thought you would refuse.'

'I want five hundred of your best lances here within the month. Ralph de Boeuf will see to their mustering.'

'And you?'

'I must go to the coast and take a boat.'

'To where?'

Roger just grinned and tapped the side of his nose.

\* \* \*

The journey to Salerno was made by sea for one very simple reason: it was too risky for a de Hauteville to travel alone by land, especially carrying gold. On arrival he ordered the captain of his boat to anchor out in the bay, staying aboard and sending a message ashore, waiting with some impatience until Kasa Ephraim came out to answer his request for a secret meeting. It was odd, given his office of collector of the port, how uncomfortable the Jew looked in a boat: he had all the appearance of a man only secure on land and that did not relent when he made it from rowing boat to the deck of the ship. Leading him into the little cabin, an arm ready to catch him should he stumble, Roger was not surprised when the man refused a drink.

'I fear if it went to my stomach,' he replied, sitting down with alacrity, 'it would not stay there.'

'I like the sea,' Roger replied. 'The journey here was most pleasant.'

Ephraim looked at him as if he were mad, but his voice did not betray that when he spoke. 'There are few who could tempt me to take to the water, but your message did intrigue me.'

'No one knows you are here?'

'No, the men who brought me out to you are smugglers who know they would face being stoned by the mob if they betrayed me. So, how can I, a trader, put down a revolt in Calabria?'

'A revolt triggered by famine.'

'Yes.'

'Help me feed them.'

For all his discomfort, Ephraim, after a brief moment, smiled. Roger had suspected the man to be shrewd; that expression proved it, for he required no explanation of what was far from obvious. Roger had deduced the only way to assuage famine and bring peace, instead of soaking the parched earth with blood, was to feed the hungry. The lord who saved their hearths and children would have their gratitude for ever, instead of generations of enmity.

'When I saw you as clever, I was not mistaken.'

'Grain, shiploads of it, to buy, as well as seed for the spring planting.'

'The cost will be immense.'

'I have gold but nowhere near enough.'

'So you require me to provide more?'

'At a proper rate of interest. My brother Robert has promised me land and titles, and the revenues of Calabria will be mine for a whole decade, so I know I can reimburse you whatever the cost.'

'For a Norman you are acting in an unusual manner.'

Roger's response betrayed his impatience. 'Can it be done?'

Hands on his lap, the Jew sat silently, thinking, his eyes lowered and Roger waiting anxiously: this he could not do without help, money and lots of it, the only other source of that being Robert. But the price his brother would extract for such aid would be too high; he certainly would not give it for nothing, regardless of how sensible the notion, and Roger could not fault him for that. You did not get to be and stay a great magnate without certain abilities and habits of character, and extracting the best from any negotiation was as central to that as the ability to fight and win.

Ephraim lifted his head and spoke in an even tone, surprising given what he had to say.

'I have often found that in commerce a man must speculate, and sometimes profit must be put aside for a long-term aim. I said before I saw William in you, but it may be that you will surpass him in wisdom.'

'A tall order,' Roger replied.

'I will support you and for mere repayment of that which I advance plus any interest I have to pay on borrowings.'

'No interest on the principal, which has to be your own?'

'My interest is long term. I think by aiding you I will prosper mightily in the future. Now, if you will be so kind, let us find a place on land where we can transact the finer points of that which you seek. I have a villa at Paestum, which is on the shoreline to the south. I will proceed there this very evening, and so shall you to meet on the morrow. Tell whoever sails your boat to question the fishermen as to where to land.'

Not even an extremely wealthy Jew could transact that which Roger needed, but he had what the supplicant did not, good credit with other rich individuals: Kasa Ephraim could buy on the promise of future payment and on terms few people could command. It was not just flour and seed that was required: bread might be a staple but it needed to be supported by other commodities. Vegetables, fruit, cuttings for olives and vines and the stocks necessary to restart herds of livestock – goats in the main, for they were hardy – as well as the more delicate sheep and cattle.

Roger had to locate a place to land all that had been purchased, then to find a means to distribute it to the best advantage. He chose a small landing stage at Cetaro, not far from the *Guiscard*'s fief at Fagnano, that one-time hilltop monastery now a formidable castle large enough to house the men Robert provided. That the news spread quickly of food to be had was unsurprising, but Roger did not want the starving to come to him, he wanted to go to them.

That their lords shut their gates to a Norman host, even in the midst of famine, did not surprise him, but he had with him Lombards capable of building small ballista, not required to batter walls, but to fire the loaves of bread he had baked, always from a point at which the wind would carry the smell over the ramparts. To a garrison, already hungry, and to one pressed into resistance, it was a more telling military tactic than any battering ram applied to the gates.

Just enough bread would be catapulted in to remind the defenders of what they were lacking, and when such men looked at those who commanded them to resist, most with full bellies, the will to support their overlords evaporated. The sensible, who realised their people would not fight for their title, opened their gates and sought forgiveness, readily granted provided payment was made for what had previously been withheld. Some did not, and such was the fear their people had of their revenge, the walls had to be stormed and those inside put to the sword, innocent and guilty alike, the news allowed to spread that this was the choice: surrender and you will live, eat and prosper, in time, with re-sown fields and fresh livestock, or resist and die, for no quarter would ever be given.

The speed of re-conquest surprised even Roger: many lords came in to swear allegiance and hand over the contents of their coffers, or more often their plate, this so that the lands they owned could be returned to what they had been, while the man to whom they swore eternal peace and friendship was able to ship to the coast enough wealth to reimburse Kasa Ephraim for the credit he had provided.

At every place taken Roger had a Mass said to thank God for blessing his purpose. Insisting on the Latin rite might have unsettled the laity – it infuriated the Greek clergy, but their protests were ignored, and, as if to show that what they preached was inferior, no sooner had the provinces been returned to fealty than the heavens formed heavy black clouds and the rains came to turn a land of brown grass and hillside forest fires back to fertility.

Content, free of his obligations to the Jew, Roger sent back the lances Robert had provided, laden with plunder taken from those towns that had resisted. At the head of his own men, equally burdened, Roger collected Jordan and rode to his own fief of Montenero to find that even in the midst of famine they had continued to build, his subjects praising him to the skies for the food he had sent from the coast, one of his first acts on landing. The first two towers of his fortress, built from the stones of that ancient acropolis, were up and occupied, the blocks for the curtain walls and the other two towers being quarried nearby.

With full bellies and great praise for their lord and master, the Mass that was said in a church now occupied by a priest from Normandy, obviously in Latin, was the sweetest of all.

# CHAPTER ELEVEN

There was still much to be done, several Byzantine strongholds to subdue, the most important being the main city of Reggio, but now Robert *Guiscard* was content to see Roger as his trusted lieutenant, who could be left in command while he saw to matters in his other fiefs, where rebellion, instigated and financed from Bari, was endemic. That the Apulian Greeks were unhappy to be ruled by Normans was only to be expected: they had enjoyed privileges under Byzantium denied to the other races in the Catapanate. The Italian indigenes consisted of tribes that could trace their origins back to the old Roman Empire and they were like any people: they hated whoever taxed them from wherever they originated. They had to be stirred to insurrection, a task readily undertaken by the priests of the Orthodox persuasion to which most of them belonged.

The main problem was the Lombards, who had never shown much in the way of cohesion in the past, their leaders continually manoeuvring for personal advantage. There had been exceptions, paragons who had got them to act in concert, Melus, the father of Argyrus, being one. If he was a sainted figure to the notion of

Lombard independence, he had one flaw for which they would never forgive him: it was Melus who had brought the Normans into Apulia as mercenaries to aid the revolt he led.

Driven from power, they seemed more willing to combine and act in concert with the three other elements in Robert's fiefs: the aforementioned Greeks and Italians, plus any Norman baron dissatisfied with the dispensations of his titular overlord. With the latter, the mere appearance of the *Guiscard* was enough to bring them to heel – they were rebellious only in his absence and easily mollified by small concessions. It was a question oft posed but one that lacked a clear answer: how was he to so engage the others in his rule as to stop these endemic uprisings, which kept dragging him away from Calabria. To take Bari was one answer, but one he was wise to shy away from, given it was near impregnable.

'You should have married a Lombard,' Roger said, 'and produced sons.'

'Alberada has given me a daughter and Bohemund. He is big enough to be a whole family. I think, one day, I may have to strain my neck to meet his eye.'

'Which means he will always be seen as a Norman. With a Lombard mother you could have claimed to represent them and demanded they be loyal to your heir.'

They were gazing at the walls of Cariati, a Byzantine stronghold outside of which he and Robert had been positioned for months. There was no point in discussing the tactics required to take the place: that as a subject was exhausted.

'I should have wed a woman of greater girth in the hips, brother, who would have given me the same number of sons as my father.'

Roger felt a slight reddening of the cheeks then – had he not thought on, as well as been amused by, the image of the two of them in congress? Apparently bearing Bohemund had nearly killed tiny Alberada, the boy a credit to his sire's dimensions, not his mother's. It was rumoured to have caused such damage as to render any chance of her bearing more children impossible, but that was a secondary consideration: it was again revolt which was troubling Robert. Trani, outside Bari the most Greek port city in his domains, had become the seat of Lombard-inspired rebellion. Robert was promising to cast down the walls and silt up the harbour.

'Winter is coming, brother. If you were to ask my advice—'

Robert growled. 'That is always welcome, you know that.'

That got him a jaundiced look: he did listen to Roger, but only after a long and tedious argument, though it had to be said dissension on tactics was rare – the *Guiscard* was a superb soldier whose only fault, apart from his being close-mouthed, was a degree of impatience, that, Roger suspected, brought on by the frustration of never having security at his back.

'I think we should suspend our efforts to take this place and concentrate on just keeping the garrison bottled up. You know yourself it is unwise to keep men in siege lines too long. Let me rotate them in and out while you go back to Apulia, hang a few Lombards and perhaps give some comfort to your ailing wife.'

'I doubt she'd welcome my comfort,' Robert growled.

Unbeknown to Roger, that casual remark of his, a joke about Robert needing a Lombard wife, was to have long-term consequences. Unbeknown to either brother, matters were moving elsewhere that would have a profound effect on the future.

Cardinal Ascletin, always the self-centred fool, was doubly stupid not to realise that anything he got up to in Bamberg would quickly be known in Rome: a long-time opponent of imperial interference in papal elections, Ascletin did a complete volte-face when he actually met the child-emperor Henry. On the journey north he had reviewed his prospects of becoming pope. His family had invested huge amounts of Pierleoni money in getting him to his present eminence; had he not had a bishopric before he was aged twenty and his cardinal's red hat soon after?

The whole scheme had been designed to raise the family profile so that they stood in equal importance to the other great Roman aristocrats, cliques who schemed to get elected to the fabulously lucrative office of pontiff, by fair means, or more often foul, numerous members of their clan. This allowed them to distribute to their relatives the many wealthy benefices in the papal gift. Why could not the Pierleoni, or more pointedly he, do the same? Yet Ascletin reasoned, in a rare bout of self-criticism, that he might never see himself elected due to his own personal unpopularity, a situation naturally ascribed to things other than his own mendacious character.

'As you know, sire, there are many voices raised in the Curia to question your rights in these matters.'

'Hildebrand?'

The ten-year-old spat that name, before looking to ensure he had the right of it, happy when he saw his counsellors nodding. Not yet of an age to command such men, older and wiser than he, Henry prided himself that once told of what to say, he had the ability to deliver it with proper imperial *gravitas*.

'Hildebrand is indeed the loudest voice in condemnation of the imperial prerogative and the office he holds gives him great sway.'

'Backed by the likes of the Abbot Desiderius.'

'Unfortunately true, sire.'

Even the most partisan supporter of imperial rights would have had to acknowledge it was unfortunate to name the abbot: when it came to personal probity and lack of ambition Desiderius was a paragon; the papacy, come an election, was his for the asking, no one would oppose him, but he had made it plain it was an office he neither wanted nor was it one he would accept.

'And you, Cardinal Ascletin,' Henry demanded, in his high and piping child's voice, 'where do you stand on my rights?'

That was tricky: given his often very vocal objections to imperial interference, he was not seen in Bamberg as a friend, something in his introspections regarding his own future he had concluded must be reversed. His first reaction was to temporise.

'It is, sire, as you know, a vexed question.'

'Not to the heir of Charlemagne.'

'Quite, but more of a problem stems from the way the leading families of Rome interfere in such matters.'

That was a fine piece of sophistry: the Pierleoni, while not of the front rank, were a leading Roman family and had started a few riots in their time, bribing the scum of Rome to cause mayhem for family advantage. That they had not done so with the frequency or violence of their competitors, given to deposing elected popes and installing their own candidates, was not much of an excuse. Too many times this young fellow's predecessors had been obliged to descend on Rome to restore order, often to depose a usurping pope and needing to rescue the true incumbent, besieged by some paid-for mob.

'Do you have an answer to that?'

Henry suddenly looked his age: having spoken without thinking he looked nervously again to those advisors to see if he had done right, not helped by the fact that they were split in their opinion, evident by their contrasting expressions. Some saw it as right to nail a difficulty, others were less convinced the bald illustration of a truth was the way to deal with such matters. Yet the reply was smooth: if Ascletin was a selfish man who allowed that trait to cloud his sense, he was also a polished politician.

'It has often been mooted, sire, that an imperial force kept close to Rome would serve to keep the most troublesome elements of the slums in check.'

'Not something any pope in my memory would countenance.' The man who spoke, Robert of Lorraine and Count of Milan, maternal uncle to the emperor, was the most powerful imperial vassal present; certainly potent enough to speak without permission, though he observed the conventions. 'Forgive me, sire, for speaking out, but popes in the past have seen that as even more excessive imperial interference.'

Ascletin replied before the young Henry could. 'Then it may require a pope to be elected who does not object to such a presence.'

There are, in certain exchanges, times when words are superfluous and this was one. No one spoke to underline that which was evident in what Ascletin had said and in the steady gaze which accompanied it: that he was putting himself forward for such a role. Elected to the Holy See he would not object to an imperial garrison close to Rome. Henry might be young, but he was as quick as any to see the point.

'Perhaps we may speak in private, Cardinal Ascletin, with my most intimate counsellors, and ponder on the whole problem.'

Robert de Hauteville and Alberada were generally comfortable in each other's company, it could even be said they were friends, despite their often barbed public banter. What was rare was for Robert to talk with her on matters pertaining to his title and it was clear, in the way he was doing so, he was moving towards some telling point which made him uncomfortable, so much so that he was being irascible with Bohemund – unusual since he doted on the boy – who was busily crawling around upsetting whatever he could.

'Damn the child,' he barked, as the toddler dragged a cloth from a table, taking with it a fruit bowl and a pewter jug half full of wine. 'Get his nurse in here, I am trying to talk with you.'

Alberada raised her head from her embroidery. 'Singular in itself, husband; I am more accustomed to your shouting.'

There was truth in that, for he was given to bellowing, indeed to have Robert in her private apartment when it was daylight outside, was abnormal: he was a nocturnal visitor and one, though she would never admit it, she had come to dread. The child crawling around was a delight and a true rascal, but had been far from that on arrival. Physical relations with Robert might produce another child of the same size and she was sure such a thing would kill her.

She called for the nurse and observed the way she picked the boy up, straining to do so: at only a year and a half he was the size of a four-year-old and strong in his resistance. Once alone, her husband recommenced his grousing, now damning Lombards as the most fractious of his subjects, then cursing a string of lesser Norman barons who took Argyrus's gold, men who would be eating their harness if it were not for his generosity. Alberada was only half listening, that was until he alluded to the fact they were second cousins. The way he did so obliged her to concentrate, as she began to see the drift of his remarks.

'The consanguinity troubles you, husband?'

'Of course it troubles me, woman. It could be seen as impious, given it falls within the prohibited degree. I wonder if I am cursed because of it.'

'Not a thing that has hitherto raised any concern.'

That was sharply delivered and recalled the way they had come to be married. Robert de Hauteville was not one to woo a potential bride: instead, having decided the time had come that he should have one, he had browbeaten her nephew, Girard, into acquiescence. She was indeed a second cousin to the de Hautevilles through Tancred's second wife, while her nephew was a mercenary who had been granted his title and fief by William Iron Arm, to whom he had been a faithful captain.

It was Drogo who had arranged the nuptials, seeking to both endow his brother and calm his unruly behaviour by marriage. Wealthy Girard of Buonalbergo had been left in no doubt that if he wanted to keep his fief he had best surrender his aunt – nephew Girard was older and her guardian, such was the confusion of generations – this, of course, accompanied by a demand for the proper dowry. In short, it had been a marriage for money, not affection and, as was common, having been accepted by both parties as such, they had set about making the best they could of the arrangement.

'Perhaps if Girard had not been so wealthy this concern would have surfaced sooner.'

Slightly embarrassed, Robert took refuge in loud bluster. 'It has come to me now!'

'Why?'

His wife found herself now looking into a face suffused with anxiety, which she suspected was false. 'Such a marriage risks our souls, Alberada. We could pay in the fires of hell for what we have done here on earth, do you not realise that?'

She did not look up, lest, in her eyes, Robert observed she knew his claim to piety to be a convenience: it always was with the race to which she belonged; this she knew, being the daughter of a Norman knight. Her father had been no exception and neither was the nephew who had given her away: Norman men would invoke God to suit their purpose and forget his existence for the same reason. Certainly her husband attended Mass daily and confessed, but he was not truly constrained by the tenets of Christ, he was driven by the need to succeed as a warrior, the craving to extend his power and the necessity of being seen in the eyes of his men as a great leader.

Robert stood up suddenly. 'I must tell you again it troubles me greatly and I must think upon it.'

'If there is a special part of hell for apostates and double-dealers then surely Ascletin will end up there.'

'You cannot be sure what you are being told is true, Hildebrand.'

The deacon looked at Pope Victor as though he had lost his senses, wondering why it was that feeble men seemed to fill the office more than those of purpose. The truth was, of course, that strong candidates to the papacy tended to have powerful enemies. God knew, even if he had never aimed for elevation himself, he had enough of them: priests, bishops, cardinals and the aristocrats of Rome, to name just a few. He doubted the child-emperor Henry would accept that he had the utmost respect for the office he held. Hildebrand just could not agree that the election of a pontiff was anybody's business but that of those ordained in the faith: the laity, however powerful, had no business to interfere.

'Hildebrand is right, Your Holiness, I'm afraid,' said Desiderius, the other advisor present. 'Ascletin can only have reversed his position for his own ambition. If it is a sin to be that way, it is not one in which he is alone in transgressing.'

The abbot said that in his habitual calm manner – he being a man who rarely, if ever, raised his voice – which also irritated Hildebrand, who was as likely to be short with the saintly as with the ineffectual, and that was made doubly so by the way Desiderius smiled at him, able to see his mood and be amused by it.

'You can stop grinning like some gargoyle,' he snapped.

That produced a laugh, which was not likely to lighten Hildebrand's mood, given he had just used the soubriquet by which he was known to those who hated him and, it had to be said, by some who esteemed his sagacity. Squat, ugly and beetle-browed, his face too often reflected his passions which, given it was not of surpassing comeliness, only served to underline his lack of physical beauty.

Pope Victor spoke again. 'The question is this. Will Ascletin contrive to succeed me, and if he does, will he be a tool of the emperor or a true son of the Church and hold to his commitment to end imperial interference?'

It was unbecoming to shout at a pope, even more so to ask him if he was a fool, but Hildebrand was not constrained by that. If Ascletin was to be elected because of imperial support then there must be a price to pay and that would rebound to the detriment of Holy Church. This tirade led not only to a moody silence and, on Victor's part, to his own questioning whether he should seek the advice of others, but also a deep desire to change the subject.

This led to a discussion of the bitter exchanges between Rome and Constantinople over the various bones of contention: celibacy of the clergy, areas of doctrine relating to the Holy Ghost and, not least, the way the Normans in Apulia and Calabria were still inducing the local populations away from their adherence to the Orthodox creed by insisting Masses be said in the Latin rite.

'To be ignored, Your Holiness,' Hildebrand insisted. 'Let the patriarch do as Rome instructs. He ranks as an archbishop and no more. We have disputed with Constantinople many times in the past and I daresay this, like other disagreements, will be resolved by acquiescence.'

'It may be unpleasant to consider,' said Desiderius, 'but consider it we must. What can Ascletin have promised Henry and his council that would gain him imperial support?'

Pope Victor's face registered his discomfort at being brought back to that which he wished to avoid. There was selfishness in this: much as he cared for the future of the Church, what these two close advisors wanted to discuss would only happen after he had gone to meet the Almighty. It was a matter on which he could have no influence, so he changed the subject again.

'I have had a communication from the Count of Apulia, asking if he can be granted an annulment of his marriage to Alberada of Buonalbergo on the grounds of consanguinity.'

The Pope was greeted with silence then, this being a situation where morality and doctrine tended to clash with the more temporal needs of the Church, and such matters required careful consideration before any answer could be given, even a verbal opinion, which was hardly binding.

'To what purpose?' asked Hildebrand finally.

'He does not say.'

'What does he say?'

'That they are cousins,' Victor replied, 'that they fall within the prohibited degree of consanguinity and that he feels their union is impious.'

'Something,' Desiderius ventured, 'it might have been proper to consider before their nuptials and the birth of his two children.'

That remark left the trio deep in thought. An annulment was not out of the question, especially where the rules for such things had been breeched, as in this case they clearly had, but if doctrine impinged, politics had a greater influence. Robert *Guiscard* would pay handsomely for such a service and he, being powerful was a man it would be unwise to gainsay. He might be a vassal of Rome but he was, in truth, too mighty a warrior to pay any attention to strictures from his nominal suzerain; he was more likely, if rebuffed, to send his lances raiding into the Papal States and, if angered enough, he might appear at the gates of the Holy City itself.

'It is for you to decide, Your Holiness.'

Hildebrand gave Pope Victor a direct look that implied, in no uncertain terms, he wanted no part of such a judgement. A look at the Abbot of Monte Cassino produced no enlightenment either; if the poor pontiff had been uncomfortable discussing Ascletin and his manoeuvres, he had changed the subject to one which was even more troubling. Truly, he was thinking, being pope was nothing but a sea of troubles.

Nothing blighted the papacy as much as the fact that a man coming to the office of pontiff was rarely in the first flush of youth, in a world where death was relentless in the way it stalked mankind. Reform of the kind Hildebrand favoured had been proposed before and it was not always a combination of political forces that stymied it. Just as often it was mortality, a fact which kept alive the hopes of the powerful Roman families: they might be out of power but God – or was it the Devil? – had a way of altering matters to their advantage.

Pope Victor was ill, something he had managed to hide from his two closest advisors, a lingering sickness of the kind that allowed him to carry out the functions of his office if not too taxed. One of the acts he continually put off was to write the papal bull granting the *Guiscard* his annulment. It would never do for a pope to be seen to be indulging in haste: if God was eternal so was the pace of pontifical decision-making. In keeping his infirmity a secret he sought only to make life easy for himself: that he created more trouble for those he held in high esteem was inadvertent. He died while the most powerful members of the Curia who supported him, Hildebrand included, were out of Rome.

Well versed in the intricacies of Roman politics, Ascletin, newly returned from Bamberg, moved quickly, making alliances where none had previously existed by promising to share the spoils of his office with those families who might oppose him. They, knowing speed was of the essence and unable to impose their own candidate – matters had to be concluded before the likes of Hildebrand appeared back on the Vatican Hill – agreed to his elevation: within days of Victor's death, Ascletin was proclaimed as Pope Benedict the Tenth.

Those who had voted against the new pope hurriedly left Rome, for if Ascletin was a bonehead he was popular with the mob he bribed with low-value coinage, meaning their persons were not safe. They travelled north to meet Hildebrand and their gathering was grim; in times past the only hope of redress was an appeal to the Holy Roman Emperor. That the present incumbent was a child mattered less than the power of the office.

Yet that was unpalatable for the very simple reason it once more abrogated to the reigning emperor the right to confirm a pope or deny him his elevation; yet again the papacy was caught between the empire and the corrupt Roman families, and to side with one or the other was to set back the process of reform by decades. Hildebrand would have none of it: first they must elect a true pope, and then seek the means to depose the man they considered false.

With much ceremony the Bishop of Florence was elected as Nicholas the Second. To deal with the antipope there was one other force to whom they could appeal, and one the newly elected Ascletin was known to hate and was determined to crush – the Normans. If the assembled divines were fearful of the consequences of such an act, they were more fearful of Hildebrand, the man on whom Nicholas depended and who forced the measure through, finally persuaded that, if needs required it, he must sup with the Norman devil.

Abbot Desiderius was tasked to sound out Richard of Capua. He saw, as quickly as would any other Norman baron, yet another step in the long march towards legitimacy in this part of the world was being taken. He immediately marched north with three hundred of his best knights, forcing Ascletin to flee. Pursued to the walled town of Galeria, he was besieged there, able to watch from its battlements the nature of those he had wanted to destroy.

All the devastation came from these Normans: Richard was unrestrained in the way he let his knights ravage the countryside around Galeria– growing crops were burnt, as was the next season's seed, vines and olive trees cut down, with any peasant who sought to stop this despoliation hanged from what trees were left standing. Yet Galeria resisted and beat off many attacks on its walls until starvation forced them to surrender. Ascletin was publicly unfrocked, then dragged back to Rome where he was shut away in the crypt of a church, never again to see the light of day.

If the mobs of Rome were sullen when Nicholas arrived to take up his duties, they were not stupid: they rarely saw Normans this far north in numbers but they knew their reputation, while the aristocrats of Rome were left in no doubt by Richard of Capua that if they acted against the new dispensation, they would pay with their own blood.

# CHAPTER TWELVE

'You would make our children bastards, Robert?'

Alberada's voice was low and bitter. In her lap she had the reply from Rome, granting her husband that which he had requested, a papal bull annulling their union, one of the first acts committed by the new Pope Nicholas on the advice of Hildebrand, who saw, like Desiderius, that a counterbalance was needed against Richard of Capua.

'There is no answer to this, is there?'

He could not look at her. 'It is final.'

'Your son will want for an inheritance.'

That stung enough to make Robert turn round and glare. 'Do you think I would abandon Bohemund? I do this so he will have more, not less.'

Alberada had known this might be coming, even if she had not been asked to agree: you could not send such a communication to Rome without word of its contents leaking out and that had induced mixed feelings. If she had hated Robert it would have come as a blessing, her children's future apart. Did she esteem him enough to fight for her place? Over the months in which it had taken the Pope to decide, Alberada had thought not, and while she was saddened by the way this had come about, she was of Norman blood and knew the reasons why: if her marriage had not been dynastic, this manoeuvre of her husband's was wholly so.

'You will be free to marry again, woman.'

That protestation almost implied she was being unreasonable, that she was failing to see the needs of his title. Never discussed with her, that too was no secret: Robert was not content with what he now held, nor was he happy with the need to continually put down rebellion. He wanted to extend his domains and for that he needed an army drawn from the entire population of Apulia, and given the Lombards were the most fractious, the obvious answer was an alliance which would allow him to demand their loyalty.

'Who is to be my unfortunate replacement?'

'Unfortunate!' he bellowed.

That engendered a mischievous smile. 'It pleases me that I can still make you angry.'

The response to that was gentle. 'Alberada, it is not dislike that prompts this.'

'No, but I would like to know who it is to be.'

'I have decided on Sichelgaita of Salerno. No Lombard family has a lineage to match hers.'


'Never!'

Stomping around his council chamber, Gisulf of Salerno was near to foaming at the mouth. The notion that his sister should wed Robert *Guiscard* had sent him into a frenzy: if he hated Normans, Richard of Capua most of all, Robert de Hauteville came a close second. Yet he dared not look into the faces of those who were gathered to advise him, for in their eyes he would have seen that they thought he had no choice. To refuse was to threaten his very existence: that they did not speak said more about the capricious nature of their prince than it did about their intelligence.

Under pressure from the Normans for years, there had been a small flicker of hope that Gisulf's fortunes might improve during the brief papal tenure of Ascletin. They had engaged in correspondence about ways to rid Italy of what both saw as a plague. That had gone into reverse with the election of Nicholas – things were even worse now that his greatest enemy had become the main support of the new pontiff.

Kasa Ephraim rarely spoke at such gatherings, preferring to give his advice in private, a privilege he was granted on a regular basis given he had discreet business to transact. Part of his task as controller of the port was the management of smuggling and, being a pragmatic fellow who knew it could not be stopped, he sought to keep it in check and profit from it. He allowed himself to be bribed by those seeking to avoid the mandatory custom dues, threw to the mob those who sought to cheat him and through this provided for Gisulf, as he had for his late father, a source of secret revenue that never showed up in the tally books of the official treasurer.

Neither parent or successor had ever discovered how much the Jew made from the arrangement, but that which he provided was sufficient to endow them with that most necessary thing for a ruler, secret funds he could use for his own purposes: private reward for those close to him, the ability to pay spies to report on those he doubted he could trust, both Lombard and Norman. Given such sources, surely he must have had wind of the coming of this proposal, or was he wasting his monies on nothing but secret pleasure?

'Sire,' Ephraim said. 'You must see there is advantage in accepting this application and much danger in refusal.'

That got him a suspicious look: the Jew transacted business with the Normans, indeed he had done so before the arrival of William de Hauteville: if it was not common knowledge that he had aided Roger in the Calabrian famine it was suspected. For all that, Ephraim had a sound reputation: he might transact business for many but he held to his bond with each. What was told to him by those he dealt with in secret stayed locked in his bosom and any advice he gave was likewise held in trust.

As a man engaged in trade, in a febrile world where the fortunes of any ruler could change overnight, and likewise that of any merchant, knowledge was the key to both security and success. The Jew, through his many contacts and business dealings, knew more than most, indeed had knowledge of what was happening outside the confines of the part of the world in which he lived. His confrères, thanks to the great diaspora, resided in many places and they, like he, were eager correspondents.

'Is there advantage for you?' Gisulf demanded.

'Have no doubt, sire, when I offer you a view it is your interests I hold close and those of Salerno, which is my home. A marital alliance with the Count of Apulia will deal a blow to the increased influence of Capua.'

'There is no guarantee of that.'

'There will be if you make it a condition of the marriage.'

Gisulf's father would have needed no telling, but then Guaimar would never have allowed Salerno to sink so low that protection would be needed. If he had been a far-from-perfect prince he had at least always seen ways to protect himself, never falling in to the trap of trusting anyone with the future of his patrimony. He had played Rainulf off against William de Hauteville; here was a chance to do the same with the successors to those two Normans.

Aware he was being eyed by the other courtiers with some mistrust, and not least by Gisulf himself, he was tempted to tell them of his motives. At the centre of the Jew's concerns lay the security of himself and his family, and if that was common then few faced so many threats as those of his race. He had been loyal to Salerno in the past and would continue to be so: he would not betray his prince as long as his prince did not betray him.

He had discerned before others, long before they held their present land and titles, the Normans were likely to become the dominant power in South Italy and that the Lombards were too fractious to contain them, while both the Eastern and Western Empires were too distant to put a brake on their expansion. He had watched the increasing impotence of all three as the fortunes of the Normans rose. The crisis had come at the Battle of Civitate: that was the moment when the pendulum swung decisively, when the Pope's massive host, supported by levies from Germany and allied to Byzantium, had been soundly beaten and the pontiff made a virtual prisoner. If that combination could not stop the Normans, no one could.

In a world where authority relied on military ability and racial cohesion, the Lombards, unsupported by outside assistance, could not stand against the likes of the *Guiscard* or Richard of Capua; the question for Salerno was not how to avoid being swallowed up by one or the other, but the need to find a way to choose who would, in the future, be the most benign conqueror.

Richard of Capua would swallow Salerno and, of necessity, to assert his legitimacy, he would need to snuff out Gisulf's line. With the men under his command given to rapine, the level of destruction could be total. Robert de Hauteville as a brother-in-law might also seek to take over the port city, but with a Lombard wife and perhaps children with the blood of Salerno in their veins, the likelihood of the city being razed to the ground, of the gutters running with the blood of the inhabitants, was lessened. Quite possibly he would leave Gisulf or his heirs in place, asking only to be acknowledged as suzerain. Yet how do you tell a prince, and a purblind one, he is doomed, that he must choose the lesser of two evils? Kasa Ephraim suspected only a false promise would serve.

'With this marriage, the *Guiscard* becomes your ally against Capua and perhaps, in time, one who will help you recover the lands that robber upstart has stolen from you since the death of your father.'

Watching Gisulf think was like watching an infant pile wooden bricks, a slow deliberate affair that took no cognisance of the instability of the final result. In private discussions he had posited the notion of several alliances, not just with the papacy – with Byzantium or the Saracens of Sicily, as well – all to rid himself of the Normans, each idea foundering on the fact that once on his soil these putative allies would, like those very same Normans who had come as mercenaries, never leave without they be forced to.

As he had listened to these fantasies he had been privy to Gisulf's imaginings. The Jew suspected, at this moment, the prince was conjuring up great armies, with this time Robert de Hauteville bowing to him as the superior general, astounded by his skill in routing his enemies. That gleam in his eye was one Ephraim recognised – he had seen the same look in the eye of the prince's father as he contemplated the chance of becoming the ruler of the whole of South Italy: that the son of Guaimar should harbour such dreams was not a surprise; that he thought them achievable bordered on madness.

'You think the *Guiscard* would march against a fellow Norman?'

'Sire, at some time they must either come into conflict or one must bow the knee to the other. Such a thing is inevitable.'

Richard of Capua and the Count of Apulia had a relationship that waxed and waned as circumstances demanded. But two such powerful patrimonies could not forever stay at peace – it could happen tomorrow or it might be decades distant. For now it was a telling carrot to a vacillating prince.

'The *Guiscard* will demand a dowry.'

'You surely intend that your sister should be married, sire. Whoever she weds would seek a dowry.'

'I shall demand of him that he puts his brother of Scalea in his place. Do you think he will agree to that?'

'He was willing to gift you a free hand before, sire. There is no love lost between those two brothers and the Count of Apulia lost as much from his raids as you did.'

'Then why, if he does not love him,' Gisulf demanded, 'does he just not kill Mauger?'

It would do no good to explain the vow each of the brothers had taken with their father: a man like Gisulf would not understand.

'He will not do that, sire, but he will, I am sure, oblige you by curtailing him.'

That Robert did, and swiftly, but not just for Gisulf: Mauger had led Roger astray and it was therefore a pleasure to descend on Scalea and accept his surrender, for he could not stand out against the massive force Robert brought to bear. He and his men were stripped of their gains, the gold they had acquired shipped to Salerno, with Robert insisting on an increase in the dowry so that it stayed there for no time at all.

Mauger was obliged to swear allegiance to his brother and to keep the peace, to cease his raiding and be satisfied with the revenues of the fief he was allowed to keep. A promise he swore in Holy Church and one he had no intention of keeping: let Robert depart, let things settle down, and he could go back to his old ways. The suggestion that he might attend the wedding was brushed aside with contempt.

Roger had to attend – the siege of Reggio, now that the other bastions like Cariati had surrendered, would have to wait, and if he felt Alberada, a lady he had come to like, had been treated badly he could also see the future needs of his brother demanded it be done. At some time he too must marry, and like Robert the notion of attraction would have nothing to do with the choice: he would seek a bride who enhanced his position, probably one of his brother's wealthier vassals. Sichelgaita was coming with a huge dowry, not that such a thing stopped him and Ralph de Boeuf amusing themselves with the notion of the two giants coupling.

'It's like two ends of the gamut,' Ralph said as they rode into the still-growing town of Melfi. 'First a mouse to be crushed and ripped by childbearing, and now a wife bigger than his destrier.'

'And as fearless, Ralph. Their wedding night will draw blood lest we pad the walls of the bedchamber.'

'You have sat close to her, Roger, is she actually bigger than Robert?'

'Nearly, and she's as broad in the shoulder. All I can say is there is no dowry large enough to persuade me that the risk of deflowering her is worth it.'

They rode into the keep of Melfi to find a beaming Robert awaiting them. The ribbing, which always attended a bridegroom, began almost as soon as the two brothers had embraced, yet Roger was surprised by Robert's reaction: while the words he used were sharp, the grin on his face as he led him into the great chamber took any sting out of them.

'I will make you laugh on the other side of your face, brother.'

'It's your bride you have to pleasure, not me. I take it she is here?'

'She is, and so is the Norman divine who will carry out the ceremony. Someone very special has come to do the honours.'

'And who would that be?'

'I hope you may recognise him.' Robert pointed straight ahead. 'There he is.'

Looking towards the end of the semi-crowded hall and following the pointed finger, Roger could make out a dim figure, for there were no candles lit at this time of day and the embrasures, meant to be defended, were narrow. There was something vaguely familiar about him, but it was not so obvious that Roger could name him.

'Have you fetched from Normandy our cousin of Montbray?'

'It is not Bishop Geoffrey, yet it is a fellow I hazard you will greet with greater joy.'

'There would be few men who could claim that,' Roger insisted.

'My dear Abbot, pray let my brother see you more clearly,' Robert called, his voice echoing and turning other heads.

The figure moved closer and Roger could see his clerical garments, as befitted the title his brother had just used, but it was only when he got really close that he was recognised, for it was a face Roger had not seen since that fateful trip to Falaise many years previously.

'Grantmesnil?'

The head before him bowed in acknowledgement and Roger's heart skipped a beat as he posed the obvious question. 'Judith?'

'Is with your brother's future wife.'

'Why are you here?'

It was a lame question and one which, whatever the answer, did not signify: the only thing that mattered was the proximity of Judith of Evreux, if you put aside Roger's pounding heart.

'He has fallen foul of the Bastard,' Robert boomed, 'just as we de Hautevilles have in the past, which would make him a friend if he was not a blessed addition to our estates in any case.'

'Do I have your permission to talk with her?' Roger asked.

He was moving before Grantmesnil could finish saying yes, with a very amused Robert shouting after him that he should behave himself.

'I'll get no more jests about my nuptials from him, will I, de Boeuf?'

Courtesy demanded that Roger greet Sichelgaita first, and also that he ask after her brother, the Prince of Salerno, but his eyes were not on her as she replied and nor did he hear the words in which she dismissed the polite enquiry: she and Gisulf did not have much in common, in fact it was doubtful if they had anything shared.

'Would it be permitted for me to greet the other lady present?'

'Sweet Judith,' Sichelgaita responded, in her slightly braying way, her eyebrows knotted on her rather unbecoming face. 'You know of each other?'

'I had the good fortune to make the lady's acquaintance in Normandy.'

The look on his face must have made obvious the undercurrents of that, for Sichelgaita gave a hoot that was more guffaw than laugh and one in its tenor that would not have shamed her husband-to-be. Her whole frame, and it was a big one, shook with amusement and she looked at Judith, demure, with her head bowed.

'You wish to take her away from me?'

'For a short while, yes.'

Roger stepped forward and took the end of Judith's fingers, feeling a sensation run up his arm, one he likened to that which he occasionally got from a touched piece of rubbed velvet, though in this instance he had no desire to snatch his hand away and shake it. She raised her head to look at him and he saw that if she was older there was no diminution in her beauty, quite the reverse: where there had been some puppy fat there were now clean and definite lines, while the eyes, blue and direct, were as becoming as ever.

'You are more lovely to look at than even my memory allowed me.' The maidenly blush was entrancing. 'I hope, battle scarred as I now am, I do not displease you?'

That had Judith looking keenly at his face, which was in truth bearing marks that had not been there at St Evroul. The way she suddenly touched one, where a sword tip had very slightly sliced his cheek, was like being fingered by something divine and the spell it created was only broken by the booming laugh that came from behind him.

'I pray God my husband does not behave like this. What a couple of milksops.' The shove in Roger's back was close, in force, to the last time a horse had head butted him. 'Go on, you fool, kiss the woman.'

Having had to grab Judith to prevent knocking her over, complying with that demand was almost a requirement. They got some time alone eventually, when Roger could listen to what had brought her to Italy, nothing less, as described, than the tyranny of William the Bastard, who now ruled Normandy with a rod of iron and was as rapacious as any despot could be. He had demanded Judith marry one of his followers, a man her brother thought unsuitable. That refusal was followed by an order to hand over the portable treasures of St Evroul, and Grantmesnil had rejected that too, which was tantamount to his asking to be slung into a dungeon for life. The only option was to flee.

'All the musicians the abbots had gathered over many years and those sweet-voiced monks were scattered.'

'I cannot believe you stayed unwed.'

The answer was delivered from under lowered eyebrows. 'I hope it makes you happy.'

'It makes me delirious, Judith, but, of course, I must speak with your brother and guardian.'

'Would it please you if I say I hope he consents?'

Roger laughed out loud. 'I cannot see how he can disagree. I am no bare-buttocked knight now, Judith, I am lord of many fiefs and I say to you I will be more than just Roger de Hauteville very soon, as soon as I can get my brother to keep some of his promises.'

'Your station matters not, Roger.'

'Not to you, but your brother, the abbot, will take a different view.'

Which he did, but all was well: Abbot de Grantmesnil had just been told by Count Robert of Apulia that he was to be endowed with the means to found a new Benedictine abbey, along with extensive lands, near Nicastro in Calabria, where he was charged with recreating the traditions of St Evroul in both music and singing. To refuse to allow Judith to marry his brother would have been ingratitude indeed, especially when Robert boomed his reasons.

'That's one in the eye for the Bastard of Falaise! Get me a scribe now, I want to write to the swine.'

That the permission to marry immediately was withheld by his own brother mattered not: Robert wanted nothing to overshadow his wedding to Sichelgaita and what a sight they created entering the rebuilt church in Venosa, where, passing the bones of his late brothers, Robert led his bride-to-be to the altar. Matching his height and so fair as to be near white-haired, a looming Amazon even in fine silks, they took their vows with due solemnity before emerging to partake of an open-air feast, surrounded by thousands of Robert's knights, many themselves with wives of Lombard descent.

The time came for the newly-weds to retire, accompanied by much behind-the-hand sniggering, ribald joking and predictions of imminent bloodshed, for many thought Robert, lusty and strong as he was, would meet his match in Sichelgaita. They were, of course, followed and eavesdropped upon, the listeners gratified to hear much shouting and screaming, though even the most malicious had to admit they appeared to be sounds of deep pleasure, not conflict.

Roger, in the company of Judith and her half-brother, departed the next day, to journey back to Calabria, and he and Judith, with Jordan in attendance, were married in the church of Mileto, the town Roger had chosen as his future residence, the ceremony accompanied by music and singing arranged by his new brother-in-law, who had decided that he would henceforth be the abbot of a Benedictine monastery dedicated to the memory of St Eufemia.

# CHAPTER THIRTEEN

'Pope Nicholas is coming south to hold a synod at your castle at Melfi and he asks, most humbly, that you attend.'

'To what purpose?' demanded a bemused Robert *Guiscard*.

The envoy was surprised to be so questioned. 'I cannot read the mind of the pontiff.'

Now outside the walls of Reggio, the last Byzantine bastion in Western Calabria, Robert was reluctant to once more be dragged away from campaigning. That Roger was competent to press home the siege was not in doubt, but following on from Robert's wedding and, on his previous return to the region, the mere sight of his banner had brought about the surrender of the last three inland bastions held by the Greeks. Yet Reggio, the old Roman city and a capital to Byzantine Calabria, was proving a tough nut to crack, for to lose this was, to the Eastern Empire, to lose their last foothold in this part of Italy.

'You cannot refuse such a summons,' Roger suggested.

'Yes I can,' Robert growled, his brow furrowed. 'I cannot leave here now.'

'Before you do something foolish, brother, I think there is someone you should meet.'

Roger asked that one of his brother's attendants take care of the papal envoy, to get him out of the way, then sent another to his own tent to fetch his visitor, refusing to respond to Robert's querulous enquiries as to what he was about. When Kasa Ephraim entered his tent he looked even more confused, doubly so when introduced.

'What can a Jew tell me that I do not already know?'

'There is not enough time in my life to allow for an answer,' Roger replied, a remark which earned him a jaundiced look.

'I have heard of you, Ephraim.'

That barked greeting from the *Guiscard* had no effect on Kasa Ephraim, who had on his face a bland look: if asked, he would have replied he had been insulted too many times, from his childhood to the present, for the perceived failings of his race, to ever feel the need to respond to irate behaviour.

'I was an admirer of your brother William,' he said.

'Oh, it was mutual, Jew,' Robert replied. 'He mentioned you to me more than once and said you gave him sage counsel. Is that what you have come here to do for me?'

'He came at my invitation,' Roger interrupted, 'and I would be obliged if you would treat him as you would any invited guest.'

'I suspect he came in the hope of profiting from our seizure of Reggio.'

'If my presence offends you then I will leave,' Ephraim replied.

'No, stay,' Roger insisted. 'Tell my brother what has happened in Rome.'

Ephraim nodded before looking directly at his brother. 'You will know of Richard of Capua's intervention in the deposing of the false pope?'

'I do.'

'Yet you will not know that the new Pope Nicholas, urged on by Archdeacon Hildebrand—'

'Archdeacon?'

'He has been elevated to that rank.'

'Why not make him a cardinal?'

'Hildebrand runs the papal office, if not the Pope himself. He is more powerful than any cardinal.'

'So?'

'Pope Nicholas, no doubt at Hildebrand's bidding, called a synod at the Lateran and promulgated a bull on future papal elections, which takes scant notice of the privileges of either the Roman aristocracy or of the imperial claim of approval, though the emperor is to be consulted.'

'Does that mean anything?' demanded Robert. "Consulted'.'

'A courtesy is what it means, a piece of verbal flummery to sow confusion and buy time.'

'Time to...?'

'From now on it is intended that it should be the sole right of the leading dignitaries of the Church to elect a pope.'

Robert rounded on his brother. 'You must have known of this, so why did you not tell me?'

'I only found out before you summoned me to hear that papal envoy.'

'I came from Capua, where the news of this was received just before my departure. It surprises me, yet it shows how important the needs of the pontiff are, that this envoy of his has arrived here so swiftly.'

'You can fathom what this means, Robert.'

The answer was so obvious it did not need to be spoken: with a child on the throne in Bamberg, thus lessening the chance of an army imposing his will, a chance had come to detach the papacy from imperial control. Richard of Capua had so recently, with a fraction of his lances, helped depose the papal choice of the Roman aristocracy. The decision of that synod at the Lateran could only hold if Rome could count on the same armed force and someone, probably Hildebrand, was shrewd enough to see that to solely rely on the Prince of Capua was unsound. To be truly secure they needed the *Guiscard* as well. No wonder his annulment had come through with such alacrity following on from the elevation of Nicholas: he was being wooed.

'And what, Jew, is this pope prepared to offer me?'

'More than you could possibly ask for.'

And so it proved: Pope Nicholas invested not only Richard of Capua with a legitimate title of prince, he created Robert *Guiscard* Duke of Apulia, Calabria and Sicily. That his right to do so was very dubious – the two mainland provinces were Byzantine and Capua was held to be an imperial fief, while Sicily was Saracen – was not allowed to interfere with the ceremony, nor with the aim, articulated by Archdeacon Hildebrand rather than the Pope himself, that it was now the duty of these newly elevated magnates to spread the faith as practised by Rome.

Kneeling, both Robert *Guiscard* and Richard of Capua swore to uphold the papacy against anyone who would threaten either its lands or the pontiff's prerogatives, to acknowledge whoever was pope as their liege lord and to protect his person. More than the battle at Civitate, this changed the whole nature of power south of Rome. It also offered the Normans protection from the only authority which could raise a combined force against them of a size they could not overcome: the fear for these mercenaries had always been that alliance between Rome and Constantinople which had led to Civitate, or another with the might of the Holy Roman Empire; both threats were now dead!

An open-air Mass was said and a sermon preached, one that had only one real message from this new pope to the thousands of knights attending. 'It is our Christian duty to uphold the power of my office. I also command you to purge Sicily of the infidel and spread the word of God.'

Kasa Ephraim, a witness to the ceremonies in Melfi, was not the only person present to ask which god, nor did he, far-sighted as he was, realise that this pope had just initiated a movement which, over the next two centuries, would dominate the world in which they lived and spill rivers of blood – a crusade to take back from Islam lands that had once been Christian.

The problem for the *Guiscard* was concentration: he returned to Calabria after the investiture to resume his final attempts to subdue the region by taking Reggio. A settlement of note since early antiquity and an important commercial centre of what had once been Magna Graecia, it was the key to trade with the fertile island of Sicily – the Saracens might be at religious and political odds with their neighbours across the water but that did not interfere with commerce. So important was Reggio to the exchange of goods that it, of all the cities in Calabria, had suffered least from their raiding.

Yet no sooner had the new duke invested the city than he was once more called away to face a Byzantine army that had landed on the Adriatic shore at Bari, leaving his brother in command. Over the winter, Roger accomplished something never before attempted by the Normans themselves: the building of ballista with which to attack the walls, a tactic they had hitherto relied on the Lombards to provide. But to just sit around watching carpenters and metalworkers toil was anathema, so he mounted a small raid on the Sicilian shore with fifty knights, only to find he and his lances facing the garrison of Messina, which led to a hasty re-embarkation.

Nevertheless, he saw it as valuable in the way it identified the core problem, one that had faced Byzantium in the aborted invasion in which his brothers William and Drogo had taken part: the need for a Saracen ally. Any thoughts of a return to the island had to be put to one side when Robert returned: Reggio had to be taken.

'God forgive me,' Robert said, crossing himself with a mailed glove, 'but I love what we are about to do.'

Roger de Hauteville could see that his elder brother's eyes gleamed with the prospect of a fight: had he been equine he would have been champing at his bit, snorting and pawing the ground. To their rear stood lines of dismounted Norman knights and ahead, not more than two hundred paces distant, lay the walls of Reggio, now being pounded by the stones from Roger's mangonels. If it was an inaccurate mode of fire, it was a telling one, with those hitting the flat curtain wall gouging great chunks out of the masonry and the odd lucky boulder flying high enough to take out not only the top of the wall but the men defending it as well.

Yet it was the equipment which completed the elements of this assault that would most worry the defenders: two huge siege towers high enough to overcome the height of the defences, and a wheeled, metal-tipped battering ram, which would soon be pounding into the central gates, which the mangonels would seek to set alight with fire pots full of inflammable materials.

'They may accept your terms at this sight.'

'No,' Robert replied. 'They will fight until they can fight no more.'

'And when it falls you will truly be Duke of Calabria. Our late brothers should be witness to this.'

Such a remark got a growl from Robert: he was not comfortable when reminded of how much he owed to those who had preceded him, while Roger was mindful that neither of them would be here if it were not for William Iron Arm. Those remarks of Geoffrey's regarding Robert's disinclination to abide comparison had, over time, been seen by Roger as a sound appreciation. It was the seat of any disagreement between them, for sometimes Robert saw in his younger brother a rival, not an ally, and no amount of reassurance seemed to be able to shake that concern. But such distractions were not allowed to interfere with the need to concentrate the ballista fire, for it was easy to see that in one spot the destruction was greater than anywhere else.

'Time for fire pots,' Robert said.

'Not yet, we should stick to rocks and move their aim,' Roger insisted, once he had pointed out the obvious fact that at one place the walls showed a telling crack.

'That will take time.'

'Better to waste time, Robert, than blood.'

It was, of course, the *Guiscard*'s decision: he was the man in command, ready to personally lead his men towards the gates under a hail of crossbow bolts, and it was obvious that his impatience was having an effect on his thinking, or was it his reputation? He was a great leader of men and one whose personal example was inspirational: even Normans fought better under his banner than that of others, though Roger was close to matching that, but sometimes it seemed Robert was too proud of that standing.

'No one will think the worse of you for a little delay, and if we can effect a breech then Reggio is lost.'

'Half a glass of sand, brother, no more.'

Roger was gone before Robert finished speaking, hurrying through the lines of warriors to those working the four ballista, one set of men toiling, stripped to the waist and sweating, to load the great stones into the baskets hauled down by a windlass to contain them. They were not wheeled, and of necessity the bases were heavy, so levering three of them so they were all aimed at the same spot was the hardest work of all, this while Roger sought to persuade his master stonemasons to have a care in their choice of projectiles so they were a similar shape and weight.

The first balls were hitting the walls by the time he returned to stand by his brother, who responded to their effect with no more than a nod: they were doing damage, striking close to and very occasionally right on the spot where the first crack had appeared. It was clear that above the point no defenders remained – they too were aware of the possibility of an imminent collapse. Not that such a thing promised easy access: if the wall did crumble it would be into a heap of masonry difficult to traverse.

Part of Robert's misgivings was that delay tended to sap the will of attackers more than defenders, and good as they were the Normans were not immune to such a loss of morale. Any good commander had an ear for what was being said in the ranks of the men behind him, even if it was indistinct. He would know that there was thirst: no man ever did battle with a wetted throat, and then there would be the warriors who thought their skills equal to his own, no doubt grousing that he had lost the use of the rising sun to blind his enemies.

The men atop the towers, his best fighters in one-to-one combat, would be wondering when the great machine on which they were perched would move to take them to the deadliest form of combat – the need to get down the dropped front ramp, exposing them to immediate and close crossbow fire if their own archers, atop them, could not suppress it. They had to fight their way onto heavily defended walls where they would be outnumbered until some of their fellows, in full mail and impeded by sword and shield, could make their way up the internal ladders to their aid, this while the defenders did everything in their power to set the towers alight.

The portion of wall went with a rumbling that spread across the glacis before them, half of it tumbling into the deep protective ditch, the rest into an untidy heap sending a great cloud of dust billowing over the landscape. Robert's sword was up before the sound had died away and those on the ropes began to haul forward the siege towers. To their fore, parties of *milites* advanced, planks held above their heads, accompanied by nimble boys too young to fight, clearing away any stones that might halt the progress of the rough-hewn wheels, others with water butts to douse the fireballs flying in their direction. To their rear came a solid mass of Norman warriors, shields held high to keep away crossbow bolts, swords ready to slice human flesh as soon as it presented itself.

Clay fire pots flew over the heads of the men pushing forward the battering ram, many falling short of the gates, others flying too high, only a few doing what they were supposed to and spreading flames up and down the thick oak. The aim was not to set the gates alight – the wood was too solid and too seasoned to do anything other than smoulder – but dense smoke from that made it difficult for anyone right above the gates to breathe and seriously hampered their ability to interfere with the efforts of those beneath them. The ram was already moving at speed, the band tasked to protect their heads running alongside, bearing the thick thatched and wetted canopy designed to nullify such defensive ploys as boiling oil and pitch.

The yelling from the walls, designed to induce courage in the defence as much as fear in the assault, rose to a mighty pitch, met by silence from those coming to do battle: well versed in war, these men were not about to waste their puff – or render even drier their throats – by shouting: that they would reserve until engaged. So there was no sound from the attackers until the ram crashed into the join of the gates which, no doubt buttressed at the rear with timber baulks, did not move a fraction. The chances of breaking them down were slim: the value of the effort lay in the way it committed the fellow commanding the defence to keep men occupied in seeking to prevent it, while behind the gate he must have force enough to repel success, for if the gate did go and the assault was not repulsed, the city would be lost.

The men bearing the roughly hewn planks dropped into the ditch and sought to get them set to bear the weight, which would allow the siege towers to be rammed hard against the walls. Robert had redirected his own assault to that breech in the walls, leaving Roger to lead the tower support parties. The first tower reached the bridged ditch, but those now pushing it instead of pulling had not followed correctly the directions of the man guiding them and one of the wheels at the very fore missed the edge of the laid boards.

It began to tip to one side, slowly and majestically, though not silently, for many a scream came from those up top, most fearsome those crossbowmen at the very apex, there to suppress the defence. The men below would see nothing but would know they were in great danger as the floor below their feet began to tilt. Mentally Roger was with them, knowing each would be dropping their weapons to seek some kind of handhold they could use to break the inevitable contact with the ground. But he could not dwell on their fate – the second tower was successful, crashing into the walls and the ramp, fitted with deadly spikes, dropped on the heads of those defenders too stupid to get clear.

It was time to run hard: the defence was split, not into three as had been hoped, but divided between protecting that breech and fighting off the assault from the siege tower. Roger was perspiring and sucking in air: climbing a ladder fully armed was no easy matter but speed was of the essence: only twenty knights had been accommodated on the tower – too much weight made it immovable – and they would now be fighting to get onto the parapet, massively outnumbered by defenders who had been gifted ample time to identify the spot where they would arrive, a place to which even a half-brained commander would send some of his best fighters.

The rest would be in that breech, ready to sell their blood at a high price to keep Reggio from sack. Robert led his men onto the rubble, slithering and sliding as he sought to climb to where he could partake of the fighting he so loved. Now he was yelling, waving his sword, that great bellow egging on those with him, their responding cries soon drowned out by the sound of clashing metal as sword and shields were employed in close battle. Robert had a man close on either side of him, his shield used to protect the right-hand side of his left neighbour, he benefiting from the same for the man on his right as he swung the great weapon, destroying both shields and flesh before him.

Roger emerged onto the top of the tower to find the knights he had come to help being driven backwards, so numerous were the enemies they faced. Instinctively he knew they would be tiring: wielding a heavy weapon without a moment of respite wearied even the most puissant warrior. Hearing his shout that they should disengage, they broke off contact quickly, surprising their opponents, and slipped through the line of knights who had come up to stand behind them – they immediately moving forward to take their comrades' place in battle, fresh arms against those also tiring from combat. The result was immediate, the defenders falling back under the relentless pressure and, within moments, Roger and his knights were over the wall and on the parapet, splitting up to carry the battle forward in both directions, seeking by hard blows to knock those they faced off this platform, to fall with bone-breaking screams onto the cobbled streets below.

In the breech, all Robert could taste was dust; he knew he had lost men to the thrusts of pikes and lances, but the line had closed as quickly as a gap appeared, while those in support dragged away the wounded so they, too, could come up to take their place. The *Guiscard*'s sword was lopping off more weapon heads than human ones and, identified by his blue and white surcoat, he knew he had become the prime target of the defence: kill him and the assault would falter. Such a thing was to be expected, so he did not mind any more than the bruises he knew he would discover when he stripped off his mail, as well as the odd bleeding wound he could now feel.

But by trying to kill him his enemies were making a fatal mistake: the men he led might not have his outstanding skill but they were superb warriors who knew how to press on their opponents without his personal leadership. They began to drive back the defenders on either side of those determined to kill the *Guiscard*, creating the one thing that doomed them, a small salient of the over-committed who, so busy with what lay to their front, could not at the same time keep safe their flanks, now being pressed upon by the Normans. The men before Robert de Hauteville began to die, and in doing so created a fissure in the whole defending line, and that, just like the wall itself had done so recently, began to crumble.

Roger and his knights had possession of their section of the wall and ladders were being fetched up to provide a means to get the lightly armed *milities* down to the narrow roadway that ran to the rear of the walls, this while the crossbowmen sought to suppress the fire of enemy bolts from the windows of the high buildings that lay close to the parapet. The task of the knights was to push back the defenders beyond the stairways by which they had come up to man the defence, so they, too, could pour down and begin to fight their way into the city.

The point at which those seeking to beat off an assault realise they are losing is not something an attacker can easily calculate: an easing of effort, the look in an opponent's eye that says he is not secure to either side and indicates he wants to disengage. Roger de Hauteville was sure it was something you could smell, a definite odour of spreading fear and he was sniffing that now, unaware that his brother had led his men through the breech in the walls and was now fighting his way down the narrow street that led to the gates, while behind him the thousands of men he led were pouring through and spreading out in all directions.

Robert knew the defenders were mixed: certainly there were proper soldiers, the men of the Byzantine garrison, but in the main they would be citizens drummed into service, many with a passion to defend their homes, others more fearful of losing their lives. The time of decision would come when those whose profession was arms, and especially the man who commanded them, knew the battle was lost, that his enemies were as likely to be behind as in front of him, at which point the commander would call upon his men to fall back and seek out a place they could defend.

The collapse was sudden, as the conscripted citizens found they no longer had amongst them the men of the garrison: they ran for their homes, casting aside their weapons to leave a line of Norman knights, led by both Robert and Roger, chests heaving, surcoats and swords stained with blood and caked in dust, too weary to cheer and far too worn out to pursue; that was left to the levies the *Guiscard* had raised in both Apulia and Calabria, many of whom had not even had to fight.

Yet there were enough Normans with breath left to do what Robert required: to find the leading citizens and get them to surrender the city before the whole place was set alight and his army became so uncontrollable that they would begin the kind of blind, drunken massacre that would leave few of the people of Reggio alive.

Clean and splendidly mounted, just ahead of Roger and the rest of his captains, Robert de Hauteville rode down the magnificent avenue lined with colonnaded villas that had stood since Roman times, interspersed with one-time pagan temples now dedicated as places of Christian worship. With them came the Latin priests from the north, to take over those churches and dedicate them to the Roman rite, displacing the Greeks who had held them for centuries; from this day, Calabria would be a part of the Church of Rome.

The Byzantine garrison, those professionals who had survived the battle for Reggio, had retreated to the fortress of Scilla on a high and rocky headland. They did not stay there long, they took ship and sailed away, no doubt heading east to tell the emperor that he had lost the last portion of what had been a province of Byzantium since the time of Justinian.

# CHAPTER FOURTEEN

To always play second string would occasion frustration in the most benevolent breast and it was a feeling to which Roger de Hauteville was not immune. The *Guiscard* having returned to Apulia, once more leaving Roger in Calabria, did nothing to assuage the desire to achieve something on his own. The province was not at peace: there were sporadic outbreaks of violence which had to be contained, but they were things that could be safely left to the individual captains manning the castles so recently taken from Byzantium; in short, there was nothing by which Roger could distinguish himself, as he had in the famine.

Residing at Mileto, enjoying the company of his wife and two recently born daughters, he was at the same time taking a hand in the education of Jordan, now old enough to ride a pony. That he existed at all, Judith accepted with equanimity and treated him in every way as if he were her own. The boy, every inch a de Hauteville, with his red-gold hair, blue eyes and unusual size, was taught in the same manner as his grandsire had educated his father, to both ride and care for his mount, and he did so alongside the warriors his father led. Thus, daily, he was surrounded by their example as they practised endlessly for war.

Jordan was an engaging child, loved by Judith for his cheerful nature, tender with his two infant siblings, yet also enough of a scamp to be something of a mascot to his father's lances, not a group of men renowned for tenderness. Many had sons of their own, born to their concubines, for few underwent any kind of ceremony, so Jordan had children of his own age and race to play at the games that such boys do: mock imitation of the battles in which their sires had fought, activities he was often dragged away from to partake of the one thing he did not enjoy, the need to learn to read, write and reckon figures from monks appointed by his stepmother.

Roger insisted upon this, as had Tancred with his own sons, he being aware of the shortcomings a lack of lettering brought to the most puissant warrior, given he was one of the ignorant. Jordan heard from his father the same words Roger recalled being drummed into him: that he would be at the mercy of lesser beings if he depended on them to read and write his letters as well as calculate the value of his holdings and monies owed, the latter being that which had exercised Tancred most.

'How many times,' he would growl, 'have I been cheated out of my due by some snivelling, tonsured clerk?'

The old warrior saw monks and priests as shirkers who worked little and ate well, slippery men unsafe to leave unattended in the company of women. The exception had been his nephew, Geoffrey of Montbray.

'One day you may meet my cousin, who is an important bishop now, but he began as no more than the family priest. He was a proper Norman, mind, not like these timid Italian priests, just as capable with the sword as the epistle. It was he who taught your oldest uncles, William and Drogo, and I doubt they would have enjoyed as much success as they did if they had not had those skills. Even Robert, troublesome as he was, owes much of the success to those teachings.'

'He did not teach you?'

'He was too elevated by the time I was born, but your grandfather always engaged a priest for his church who undertook the task, so when you pull that face, on being told to attend to your lessons, be aware it is one I know well, it being one I used to employ myself. It never managed to release me from the obligation to learn and it will not do so for you!'

Roger valued highly the time he spent alone with Jordan, teaching him to ride and fight with a lightweight wooden sword, to strike a hanging target as he rode past at a fast canter with his tiny lance, but it was not always mounted education or mock combat with a parent who occasionally allowed himself to be bested: the stable and paddock were just as important and Jordan had drummed into him the many other things he needed to know.

'The time may come when, like me, affairs take you away from dealing with your own animals, but until then this pony and the horses that will surely follow are yours to see to. Feed them, groom them, care for them when they are ill, for you cannot get to a field of battle without them, nor can you fight without a destrier to carry you to your enemies and stay steady in the face of the noise of fighting men and the clash of weapons.'

It was drummed into Jordan that a horse could not ride all day: to do so would render it useless. Equines needed a lot of water but they must not be allowed to drink before fast work, likewise they should be kept from munching pasture, which they would do naturally wherever they found any. They required oats and hay, were fond of root vegetables, but these should be used as rewards. Their bedding had to be changed daily if they were in stalls, the paddocks to be regularly cleaned of dung if they were out in the fields, though the peasants seeking fertiliser usually saw to that.

In hot weather and on campaign their coats needed to be kept short to reduce sweating, and once stopped for the night hooves had to picked and oiled, nostrils and anus cleaned as well, ears checked, the coat brushed till it gleamed, with a careful eye kept out for any sores, abrasions or skin parasites – things which must be treated quickly. If they showed signs of wishing to fight they must be allowed to do so, for horses had their own hierarchy. Training for war must be continuous, a constant search for equine perfection, work which extended to the harness and brasses of the reins and bridle, to saddlecloths and saddles which would crack if not attended to.

And he also was taught he was a warrior in the making, that the horses he rode would sometimes sicken and die or be so wounded in battle that their throats must be cut, a task that could not be left to another, and when there was no food to eat and he was starving, a hazard on campaign, then the meal of last resort was the animals he rode and led.

'Care for them before you look to yourself, form a bond so they obey and look to you, but do not love them too much, for one day it may be your task to take their life.'

He was not being raised to toil in the fields, that was a task for others, the less fortunate of God's children, but the other lesson passed down from Tancred was that no man could have the equipment to fight without the toil of those in mean occupations and that to despise them was foolhardy.

'And remember, Jordan, God sees everything, every petty act

and every noble one, and even if the priest absolves you it is your Maker you will one day face and he will ask you to account for that which you did. It has been my purpose to act so that I can do that with calm, and I expect and hope you will do likewise.'

'My Lord, you have a visitor.' The look of distaste on the servant's face, come to deliver this message, was explained by his next words. 'He is a Saracen.'

Stinking of the stable and the manège, Roger went to wash before proceeding to meet the man he now knew to be Ibn-al-Tinnah, one of the three warring emirs of Sicily: the followers of the Prophet were noted for their personal cleanliness, part of their firm religious code, so he was disinclined to meet the fellow in any other condition than one which matched it. On the way to his privy chamber, he passed many an eye seeking some indication of what this surprise visitation portended, looks that exactly matched his own curiosity.

Al-Tinnah spoke Greek, the language of his Christian subjects, so, there being no need for anyone to translate, the two conversed alone. The emir was a small man, so Roger's first act was to invite him to sit, a courtesy he saw as wise for another reason: constantly in conflict with his neighbours, he would not have travelled all the way to Mileto unless he was seeking help of some kind, and, although the information from the island was imprecise, Roger knew he had recently suffered some serious reverses against Ibn-al-Hawas, one of his fellow emirs; it was thus a moment of some promise.

'Al-Hawas is, of course, a coward who makes war on women.'

That piece of deceit had to be treated with diplomacy: if anyone made war on women it was al-Tinnah – the cause of the present quarrel was over al-Hawas's sister, whom, to cement a peace treaty, al-Tinnah had first married and then tried to kill by ordering a slave to open her veins. This made her flee back to her brother's formidable mountain-top fortress of Enna. Enraged at the refusal to hand her back, al-Tinnah had marched to Enna intending to besiege it, only to be soundly trounced when his enemy emerged to do battle. Now he was struggling to hold on to his own lands along the eastern coast. Thus a marriage designed to create peace between rival emirs had achieved the exact opposite.

'I will not disguise from you, Lord Roger, that the beast threatens me, or that I have come here to seek your aid in throwing him back.'

'I am not at liberty to act at will, Ibn-al Tinnah, you must know that.'

The Saracen responded to that ploy with the same level of tact as Roger had shown to his previous untruths: Robert de Hauteville might be Roger's titular overlord but they both knew he could do what he wanted, for if he could not, al-Tinnah would have ridden on to Melfi. Roger was itching to go to Sicily anyway; he was merely prevaricating to see what this emir was prepared to offer for military aid.

'There cannot be peace on my island with the three most powerful emirs in constant disagreement, nor is there any hope that one will see the wisdom of another being superior in power and prestige. I have the mind to command loyalty but not the means to impose my will.'

*An opinion not shared by those who are your equals*, Roger thought, but he said nothing, silence in negotiation being a vital tool: a man speaking will give away more than one who is mute, yet the knowing smile that Ibn-al-Tinnah produced was slightly disconcerting, implying the ploy was not working.

'Lord Roger, I think I know how your mind will work, so let me save us both much tilting at shadows when I say that, having conquered Calabria, the next thing you Normans will seek is to take Sicily.'

'Have you come to warn me against it?'

'No, I have come to encourage you to act.'

Roger did not react, while aware of how hard he had to struggle to avoid doing so. To invade the island without support, as he had already found out, was hazardous and probably doomed, but with the aid of an emir...

'I could ask you to ally yourself to my cause, Lord Roger, but I am not a fool. You will not fight just to keep me in my palace.'

'I might if paid enough.'

'You would say that, swear on Allah perhaps, but it is not a vow you would keep, whatever the agreed price.'

'You seem very sure how we Normans will behave and me in particular.'

That reply was less sensitive, yet his visitor was speaking the truth. Roger needed a toehold in Sicily: enough defendable land to establish a presence, a secure base that could be protected by a Norman castle, somewhere to land in numbers and in safety at a time of his own choosing, an enclave that could be reinforced quickly if threatened. The trick was to get onto the island for long enough to make that happen, and he suspected it could only be achieved with the aforesaid Saracen ally. Would that be something welcome to such a person or his cause in the long term?

The chronicles of previous invasions, including those of antiquity, proved that Sicily was a hard island to conquer, which would have been attested to, if they could speak, by Attic Greeks, Phoenicians, the Carthaginians who had contested with Rome and lastly the Byzantines who had retaken Sicily five hundred years before. It had subsequently been lost to Islam. His eldest brothers had partaken of the last attempt at Byzantine recovery, which had faltered on the arrogance of the general in command. But the one fact that had come down through Roger's own blood relatives was this: Sicily could only be invaded with an indigenous ally like the man now sitting before him.

The emirs were continually at loggerheads and petty rulers existed by the dozen, many in small fiefs, but in truth only a trio of them counted, the great landholders who garnered huge wealth from an extremely fertile island. Ibn-al-Tinnah was Lord of Catania and the province that took its name from the port city. Sicily was like Southern Italy in its disquiet and it shared one other trait: the rulers of the greater provinces were as untrustworthy as their contemporaries across the Straits of Messina.

'So, Lord Roger,' al-Tinnah continued, 'let me propose something more tempting, nothing less than the island of Sicily as a Norman possession. Your brother has been given a ducal title that has no meaning. I am saying it could be made real.'

That such an offer was astounding was an understatement: it was nothing less than fabulous, so much so that it was unlikely to be true.

'You are now thinking I am lying, that I wish your aid only to repudiate it as soon as my enemy has been driven off.'

'That makes sense.'

'So, Lord Roger, would be your agreeing to aid me for no reward, when in truth you would like to cut out a piece of the island for your own purpose.'

Roger, tired of maintaining a rigid expression and given any subterfuge was wasted, burst out laughing. 'I think you had best tell me what it is you want and what you are prepared to sacrifice. What comes after can be left to the future.'

'I need Norman lances to defeat al-Hawas and for that I undertake to aid you in securing a foothold on the island. Then, when you are ready for a full campaign, I will join you and help you to take all of Sicily, as long as Duke Robert allows me to remain on my land and keep my possessions as his vassal.'

'You offer a great deal, perhaps too much.'

'When a man risks losing not only his land but his head, it would be foolish to offer too little.'

It was not al-Tinnah's to give – Sicily would have to be taken by force – but that mattered not and Roger listened as the emir outlined his thinking, immediately disabusing the Saracen of the notion that Norman lances could land in Catania and seek battle with al-Hawas: Roger lacked the strength to do other than contain him there. But with the Emir of Enna absent there was nothing to stop anyone from raiding his possessions on the northern coast and that was, Roger insisted, where they should go. If successful enough, it would achieve what was necessary by forcing al-Hawas to abandon his Catanian campaign.

'It may not be all we can do to help you,' Roger added, 'but it answers your immediate concerns and, for the future, we can carve out an enclave from which my brother can attack your rivals.'

Al-Tinnah was less than pleased, however he had no choice but to accept: his position was obviously too weak to do otherwise, for if it were not, he would not have come to Mileto. Roger suggested that Cape Faro, which was right opposite the fortress and port of Scilla, would be a good place to land adding his concomitant thought: that further along the coast lay the peninsula of Milazzo, a narrow neck of land, easy to protect where it joined with the mainland and also a prime spot to build a castle to act as a base for future Norman operations. The question however remained: given what he could muster in lances, should he go?

'Lord Roger, I have offered you all that I can. I need a speedy response.'

Sensing the desperation in that request, Roger stood suddenly. 'Please wait here.'

Striding out of the chamber, his mind was in a whirl: it had been obvious that his brother would turn to Sicily at some time, had he not been given the ducal title, which he would want to make good, and no doubt he would engage Roger to aid him as he had here in Calabria. Yet any campaign on the island would be to enforce Robert's claims, so once more Roger would be at the mercy of his generosity, and he had already proved that when it came to his younger brother, that quality for which the *Guiscard* was famous could be in short supply.

Here was a chance to strike out early and to be in a position to demand a due reward for what he achieved: that toehold would be his and the price of its use was one he could dictate. He could not take Sicily on his own: that would require everything in the way of force Robert could bring to bear, but with the aid of Ibn-al-Tinnah he could establish a claim too great to refute, nothing less than a Sicilian fief as the springboard for a full invasion. Frustrated enough when unwed, he now had a wife and children to consider, an estate that demanded he assert himself: he required bread from Robert, not crumbs, and here was an opportunity that might never come again.

'Serlo, to me.'

That command, bellowed from the door to the great hall, echoing round the walls, had his nephew, only months arrived from Normandy, running to hear what was afoot. A promising youth, he had soon become Roger's close aide.

'Uncle?'

'Messengers are to be sent to Ralph de Boeuf. He is to gather up every knight he can muster, as well as foot soldiers, and make for Scilla – another to Reggio to tell Geoffrey Ridel I need transports sent there for some four hundred men, half mounted. Your next task, once that is done, is to prepare our lances and *milities* for immediate departure.'

The youngster, dark-haired like his sire, grinned at his uncle. 'Where are we going?'

'Sicily, Serlo, where else?'

Geoffrey de Ridel was not only an able commander: being from the port of Honfleur he was at home on water and thus a good choice to act as master mariner. Ships had to be commandeered from Reggio, their lower decks fitted with temporary stalls for the mounts, three for each lance: it might be a short crossing but it could also be a choppy one. As usual, getting horses onto ships was fraught with problems. If there was an animal more suspicious than the equine, Roger had never met one. They hated anything unfamiliar, and a long wooden ramp leading to a moving deck in a less than perfectly protected harbour, really no more than a hook of a jetty, was just that.

Few went willingly, many had to be hooded, others given something in their feed to sedate them, with the very worst hoisted aboard on slings. Ridel had waited until he knew the wind and seas to be right before loading took place: he did not want to be stuck at the quayside overseeing a floating stable, not that such a precaution stopped the animals from kicking out at the wooden stalls and pissing and shitting all over the lower decks as soon as they were installed, with the ship's owners wailing that they would never again be fit for cargo.

Roger left early, in full daylight, boarding a small sailing vessel that would transport him across the straits at their narrowest point, large enough to carry his closest companions, Serlo plus twenty knights and enough wood, kindling and oil for what they needed, their weapons well hidden and their mail covered by common clothing: boats from both shores were out in the good fishing ground and any sight of armed men might be reported ashore. Their destination was a long sandy shore leading to a flat and barren plain, with mountains to the south dominated by the snow-covered and smoking peak of Etna.

The remainder of the lances, after a Mass said on the quayside, weighed in darkness, with a messenger sent to light a beacon built on the promontory of Scilla. The night chosen was clear, without a moon, but showing enough starlight to satisfy de Ridel, the water was choppy, as it often was in this narrow channel, and flowing quite fast, but a southerly wind kept them from being carried too far down and away from Cape Faro, this while each man struggled below decks to keep his animals calm.

Three stacks of wood had been built at intervals on the open beach and Roger looked towards Scilla, seeking the sign to tell him his men had sailed. When he saw that lit beacon, he ordered his own fires ignited to act as a guide to the ships, which stood off till first light before anchoring close to the shore. Lines were then used from the beach to haul them in till their keels touched sand, their ramps once lowered ending in shallow water, the ship rising to re-float freely as the equine cargo was discharged.

The beach was soon a mass of men and mounts and, given surprise was the key to their endeavour, the column of lances quickly headed inland, making for Milazzo, the first major town on the northern coast, traversing a landscape as fertile as any the Normans had ever seen. The next weeks were, with no force of any note to stop them, the very best they could be, culminating in the taking and sacking of Milazzo, that followed by a raid inland to so ravage the lands around Rometta that the formidable fortress town, denuded of a garrison by the Emir al-Hawas, opened its gates to avoid destruction.

The booty from both towns was massive but it was matched by what they took from the countryside: there were cattle and sheep to steal, amphora of oil and wine to load aboard purloined donkeys, manor houses to raze to the ground and precious objects to appropriate from the Orthodox churches they encountered; so much, indeed, that it was necessary to return to Cape Faro, where the ships were still anchored, so that this abundant plunder could be shipped back to Reggio.

That such a course of action disappointed al-Tinnah was obvious: he knew only continuous pressure would distract an enemy who would soon hear that this Norman incursion had ceased. Roger had his own concerns but they had to be put aside for the sake of keeping happy his men: the Milazzo peninsula, and any notion of beginning to fortify it for the future invasion, would have to wait.

# CHAPTER FIFTEEN

The Normans, herding before them sheep and cattle, drawing behind their own laden packhorses plus numerous beasts of burden, once they emerged from the trees that shielded the beach at Cape Faro, were presented with a very different sight to that which they had left a month before. The sea was not blue but grey now, reflecting the clouds under which it lay. The water was no longer choppy but angry, with white-crested waves rushing up the beach, driven by a wind strong enough to direct stinging sand into their faces, this while the ships which they needed to load pulled hard on their anchors as they rose and fell on the swell. They could not load in this.

'Well,' Roger called, 'we shall not want for food and wine. Set up camp.'

The land on which they settled was a narrow strip between the sea and an inland lake, so fresh water, without which they could not have stayed, was plentiful. Trees surrounded that lake and wood-cutting parties immediately went to work, this while the livestock was herded into an area that could be turned into paddocks with long cut branches, others used to make horse lines for the mounts, still more timber employed to fill the pit fires on which the food for the soldiers would be roasted.

Few orders were required for this, either with or without animals: it was common work for an army on campaign, a daily ritual eased by the fact that the weather, if windy, was dry, while they had plentiful supplies of everything they needed, which was not always the case. Travelling with a minimum of baggage, there were no tents for the leaders, and since the few houses and fishermen's hovels that had existed in the vicinity had been burnt down the day they landed, Roger and his captains would, like their men, sleep under brushwood cover, as would a still-disgruntled Ibn-al-Tinnah.

Before that he had to boat out to Geoffrey Ridel and get some assessment of how long the weather would remain foul. A rowed boat on an angry sea presented nothing unusual for Roger: as a boy he had fished and swum off the Normandy coast, and when it came to white and disturbed water nothing he was experiencing now could compare with the kind of waves which broke on that shore. Likewise he was comfortable on the bucking and dipping deck.

'If we are to be here long I will have to forage for feed. The sheep and cattle need it, as do our mounts.'

'If you are asking me to tell you how long this will last,' Ridel replied, 'you may guess, for that is all I can do. It could abate tomorrow or it could be a week.'

'The ships' captains must have some notion of the time of year.'

'This might be the inland sea, Roger, but it is no different to what we knew as boys and young men, subject to any number of winds, north, south, east and west, and they change in a blink of your eye. We may get a tempest from Africa or the Levant just as bad, and in this narrow channel it becomes ten times worse. Be patient and wait for a good wind to take us back across the straits.'

The morning brought no respite, obliging Roger to send out parties to forage, more as a precaution against continued bad weather than a pressing need. A cautious commander, he also sent out individual scouts to ensure that no force was approaching of a size that could pose a threat; the opinion of an impatient al-Tinnah, that such a thing was unnecessary, he politely squashed.

'Al-Hawas must know what we have been doing. Protecting his own land might be of more importance to him than ravaging yours.'

The emir made a gesture meant to imply that no Norman could comprehend the true situation. 'It is my body he wants, my severed head on a pike. He thinks me still in Catania and nothing will tempt him away from that prize.'

'Unless he knows you are with us.'

That was said to end the discussion, not because Roger thought it true and, since it was one of the emir's times for prayers, he suggested he ask Allah to grant him a calm sea. This again raised in the eyes of his ally a frown of disapproval of the tactics being employed, which, in his opinion, leant more towards mere banditry than a proper pursuit of any long-term aim.

You cannot hide several hundred men for very long, especially when many are mounted, before the smell they create begins to carry on the wind: not a farmyard stench, but one with its own particular composition of human and animal waste mixed with wood smoke and cooked food. It was a stink with which every Norman lance was familiar, so when one of Roger's scouting pairs picked up a faint trace they first checked their own position to that of their confrères camped at Cape Faro. A wetted, held-up finger indicated it was not from that source: the wind was from the wrong direction.

It took a sharp appreciation to then dismount and hide the
mounts in a copse, with only one of the pair, careful to use what
cover he could, heading unarmed and on foot, in the direction from
which he thought it came, in the end climbing a tree to get sight
of the mass of soldiers encamped behind the nearest set of hills
close to the shore. Seeing they were making no attempt to move,
the man stayed where he was until dusk and the point at which
they knelt to perform their evening prayers, carefully seeking to
establish their number before creeping back to join his companion.
Getting back to their own camp presented little difficulty: the light
from the Norman fires was reflected on the clouds.

'Some seven hundred, I would say, only a third of that mounted.
They doused their fires before dark to stay hidden but I saw no
sign they were preparing to move.'

Roger, looking out at the still-angry sea, was troubled that
such a force, greater in numbers than his own, had appeared and
he had no idea from where. They had also got so close that they
could attack at will, but why had they not done so? Had they
tracked him from Rometta? Had they come from the south, sent
by al-Hawas? Were they an advance guard or the whole threat?
Whatever the answer was made no difference, they were clearly
enemies and they had to be dealt with.

'Serlo, gather half of the lances and get ready to leave before
first light.'

In the glow from the fire around which he and his captains
stood it was possible to see a stiffening among them: this was
nothing but family partiality – was not this nephew too young
and inexperienced to be preferred over the more tried and tested?
Roger ignored it: there was not a man present who would not
have favoured one of his own if the circumstances allowed – it

was the Norman way, and one from which he had benefited from the moment he had arrived in Italy. Serlo was a de Hauteville; here was a chance for him to win his spurs.

'No stars, so you will have to use the wind to guide you till the sun begins to rise. I want you to the west of this threat and prepared for battle. Find some high ground and look out for the rest of us, for we will break camp to move against them at grey dawn. Attack as soon as you see our pennants and seek to get behind them. With luck they will be surprised and panic.'

Suspecting his own camp to be under scrutiny, the preparations for the morrow had to be made with subtlety: Serlo had his party form up under the trees, conroy by conroy, weapons and harness hidden out of sight, with no trace of haste, before the horses were led to where they could be saddled out of view. Finally the whole force marched away from the camp on foot, the horses led to lessen the noise of their hooves.

The rest of Roger's lances quietly made their preparations, checking weapons and ensuring that all that was needed was close to where it was required for a quick departure. This showed another part of that endless Norman training, the ability to harness their mounts, arm themselves and move out at speed, a set of actions which, when executed, clearly impressed Ibn-al-Tinnah, a fellow somewhat subdued since his own appreciation of the situation had been shown to be false. The foot soldiers, camped apart from the mounted men, were the last to be alerted, not being trusted to avoid showing their activities as they scuttled around the campfires.

Serlo was in position by the time Roger broke camp and he had the enemy in view, so was thus able to see the hurried way in which they readied to confront the approaching threat. Again a tree was employed to give height to a lookout, eyes peeled for the first fluttering pennant. The increasing light allowed Serlo to assess the ground before him, the entrance to the valley in which the enemy camp was situated. He had his instructions, but he also was well aware of the trust placed in him: he was expected to act as he saw fit. Thus, he led his men out to where they would be in plain view prior to the time agreed, gratified to see what had been hasty but ordered preparation for battle turn into alarm.

Nor did he delay in his attack, trusting those under his command to form up on the move, so what the enemy first saw as a ragged assemblage of horsemen coming towards them at a fast canter soon turned into a regular formation, the points of their lowered lances dull under the still-scudding clouds. The blowing of the horn, the way that line turned south, told whoever was in command that this attack was aiming for the rear of his position. He had been busy forming up his soldiers to face the oncoming assault coming from Cape Faro.

Nothing collapses more quickly in confusion than discipline, and the troubles of the enemy general were confounded by the need to take the crest of the northern hill before it was barred to him by Roger's cavalry, while at the same time seeking to direct enough of his men to cover the flank exposed by Serlo; in the end he achieved neither, and before he had properly deployed he was under attack from the front, with an echelon of disciplined horsemen threatening his rear.

Roger's lances, having heard Serlo's horn, sped to the hill crest, arriving just before their opponents, not to halt but to use the slope to increase the effect of contact, their lance points slicing into the opposing cavalry and stopping dead their uphill advance. Lances embedded, their swords were out and employed, the Normans using the gaps created by the shock of their initial charge to get amongst their opponents, great blades flashing down on weak human flesh in a battle arena where the greater height and weight of their Viking heritage, added to their professional ability, counted – doubly so since most of those who opposed them lacked much in the way of fighting skill.

Serlo was driving his lances into the softer flank and rear, if anything killing more than Roger's men. His uncle, surrounded by his personal knights, was made visible both by his size and the damage he was meting out to anyone who came within range of his weapon, on this occasion an axe, which spurred his nephew on to prove himself equal. That nearly led to his undoing as he found himself surrounded and fighting for his life, lacking a personal following dedicated to keeping alive his person.

How Roger saw his plight while himself hacking with his axe and, at the same time deflecting blows with his shield, Serlo did not know. All he did discern, through the sweat dripping into his eyes, was Roger's near presence at the head of a phalanx of knights, cutting their way through to him. Wounds he had already suffered, but mortal danger threatened: even a deflected pike can deliver a telling blow and he was aware of one coming, aimed to take him under his sword arm, while he was locked in combat, with a mounted enemy blow. He could do nothing to deflect it.

The arm holding that pike seemed to split in two, before the weapon and the hand and forearm holding it fell to the ground, and there beside him was his Uncle Roger, magnificent in his yelling frenzy, slashing at everything within the range of the axe. The men who had forced their way through with him surrounded Serlo in such a tight circle he was left with no one to fight and, breathing heavily, aware of his injuries if not the pain which would come later, he realised that the enemy soldiers were trying to seek mercy, and mostly failing. Roger's foot soldiers, his levies from Calabria, were amongst them now and they had suffered much from the Saracens of Sicily, making murderous revenge inevitable.

When the killing ended there were barely enough of the enemy alive to tell Roger de Hauteville they had come from Messina, further questioning revealing they constituted the entire garrison. They had planned to wait until he was loading his booty, when the Normans would be dismounted and disorganised, to attack him and drive him and his men to drown in the sea. Having failed in that, they unwittingly dangled before Roger's eyes a prize he could barely have dreamt of, one greater by far than any enclave on the Milazzo peninsula.

'Count the bodies in this field, Emir al-Tinnah. That means Messina is now undefended.'

'We do not have the numbers for a siege, Lord Roger.'

'We may not need one. The population is mainly Greek. Without Saracens to man their walls and threaten to cut their gizzards the citizens may open their gates to fellow Christians. A mere demonstration of force might be enough to gift us entry.'

The emir was on the horns of a dilemma: what Roger was saying was true, but he needed these Normans ravaging the lands of his enemy. If Roger de Hauteville occupied Messina he would stay there and ensure it was made too formidable for even the strongest Saracen force to retake it: anything else would go by the board, this while Roger was trying to imagine the face of his brother when told that his sibling had possession of the second greatest city on the island.

'My friend,' he said, with an expression he hoped conveyed his sincerity. 'We have nothing to lose. The weather is still against us and I swear to you, even if Messina opens its gates, my men and

I will go back to ravaging the possessions of al-Hawas.'

There was no choice but to accede, even if the emir did not believe what was being said: he was not in command, the leader was Roger de Hauteville and his goodwill was more important than any other consideration. Leaving a bloody, corpse-filled battlefield to the ravages of scavenging peasants, with a proud, bruised and bandaged Serlo at his side, Roger led his band south, which brought them outside one of the many gates of Messina, a mere four leagues in distance.

Roger rode forward under a truce flag, leading the few survivors of his recent battle with halters round their necks, to demand a parley with the leading citizens, some of whom were already on the battlements. Immediately they refused to come out to open ground to talk, forcing Roger to make his offer with a craned neck.

'You see before you what remains of those tasked to defend you, so you are at the mercy of myself and those I bring with me. Open your gates and not a hair on the head of anyone in Messina will be harmed. Deny me what I ask and I will burn your houses to the ground and make dust of the bones of everyone who resides within your walls.'

Expecting they would seek time to talk amongst themselves, Roger was surprised by the speed and the brusque nature of the response, which was in Greek, immediate and negative from a greybeard, probably an elder of the city, who first stated that he knew of the Normans and their habits of rapine and plunder, insisted he did not believe what he was being told, then concluded with the words, 'Do your worst.'

'You have no notion of what my worst is.'

'Hear this, barbarian,' the old man called. 'Many have tried to take our city and have left their blood in the dust of the fields around it. You will do the same, for you do not have the means to stay outside our walls for the time it will take to starve us into submission, a thing even an ignorant like you must know requires a fleet of ships that would block our access to the sea.'

'I will send for those, never fear.'

The old man just laughed, which induced the same in those who stood with him. Such a response made Roger's blood boil. His bluff was being called and in the most insulting way possible, which could not but diminish him in the eyes of the men he led. If he was noted for his sound common sense, this was one occasion when that gift deserted him: his bloodline was the stronger.

'Then defend your walls.'

As a force to mount such an assault, Roger had pitifully few men, less than four hundred in total after the losses, albeit they were small, in his recent battle. Added to such constraint was the lack of enthusiasm from anyone other than his own nephew as to the chances of success. Hurriedly made scaling ladders were all they could manage to assault stout walls and Roger's assertion of little in the way of defence was met amongst his fellow Normans with ill-disguised scepticism. Yet no man refused, their leader might be right and the Calabrian levies, fired with anti-Sicilian bloodlust, were too ignorant to make sense of what they faced.

The attack, launched at dawn the next day, was not a fiasco because of poor execution, it was rendered foolhardy by the sheer tenacity of the defenders who, if they were untrained, had fire in their bellies. Time and again the Normans got their ladders against the walls, with hardy fighters clambering to the top, and just as often the task of those seeking to follow was to break the fall of the repulsed warriors in the hope of saving their bones.

Roger did at least manage to get his feet on the parapet, only to find himself assailed by dozens of frenzied citizens, who seemed to care little how many of them died to force him to withdraw, lucky to get a foothold on his ladder and keep enough distance between himself and those trying to kill him to allow an ignominious retreat. The Calabrians fared even worse, leaving scores of their number twitching and dying at the base of the walls and forcing the man in command to call off the assault.

For Roger the humiliation of this reverse was total and there was no one close to him, seeing his mood, who had the temerity to tell him the attack should never have been launched in the first place: the thunderous look and the mood that went with it indicated to advance such an opinion was a sure way to die. Before him, as he stood out of crossbow range, he surveyed a scene of tangled bodies and smashed scaling ladders, this while horns blew from the parapets to crow the victory of those within the walls.

His request that he be allowed to collect his wounded was denied: they could expire where they lay and if they did not then the city had knives in plenty to slit their gizzards, adding they would not be buried and no prayers would be said for their souls. Let the vultures and the carrion crows cleanse their bones, for there they would lie to warn any other invader of the fate that awaited them. Roger raised his sword before his eyes, as a makeshift cross, then uttered a promise that sounded very like a curse.

'One day, Messina, I will make your women keen for the death of their men and their boy children, and that before I send every one of those wailing creatures to the slave markets of Africa.'

Sheathing his weapon he gave the orders that would take them back to Cape Faro, a journey made with none of the joy and anticipation of the outward leg, and it was a mood not cheered by the sight of the shore and the angry waters off the cape. They still could not load the ships.

# CHAPTER SIXTEEN

The gloom of such a reverse was bad enough; what followed was worse. The citizens of Messina, fired by their success and in their thousands, issued from their walls to pursue their foes, and it was only a lack of coordination that prevented them from sweeping what remained of Roger's band into the sea. It took every lance he had to bring their attack to a halt and that was only made possible by the narrow neck of land that lay between Lake Faro and the sea.

'They do not know how to fight.' Serlo insisted, now with even more wounds than hitherto.

Roger, bruised himself, was reluctant to answer his nephew, for to do so would only underline the depth of his miscalculation. If he had ever questioned the sense of the word 'hubris' he knew what it meant now. He had allowed his own ambitions to cloud his judgement and the men he led were being called to account for his folly.

'Think on their numbers, Serlo,' he replied, indicating a landscape full of humanity. 'And our losses.'

'Leaders?'

'At times such as these, men of the right kind come to the fore.'

'Then they will pay a high price for their hopes.'

Every city, if it wished to stay unconquered, made sure its citizens had access to arms, swords and pikes, as well as some ability to use them. He had massacred the trained soldiers who had abandoned the protection of their walls but this he faced now was of a different order. They lacked the skill of the Normans but skill would not overcome odds of a hundred to one. Roger had lost half his strength, not all killed, but enough so wounded as to be unfit for battle, while everyone else was carrying injuries and that took no account of their shattered morale.

If he wished to hold here he would be required to split them in two, sending an equal number to the north of Lake Faro where another neck of land lay between fresh water and the shore, this while his opponents, once they had fully deployed, would have the power of decision about from which area to launch an assault. Time was against him: contained on this exposed cape, if he had ample food for his men he did not have enough for his horses. Without horses he could not launch the counter-attacks that would keep these people at bay, and on foot he lacked the numbers, especially given his split force, to form enough of a defence to secure the integrity of his encampment.

No one else was backing Serlo in his bellicosity; they were silent and that included a miserable Ibn-al-Tinnah: this was a time when a leader needed to make a decision. If Roger sought advice it would do more to diminish him than raise him in the eyes of those he led. What remained of his Italian levies – not many for they had, numerically, suffered most at the walls of Messina – would do as they were told. His lances, if he so commanded, would die where they stood rather than retreat and he would fall with them, being too proud of their reputation to lay down their arms, asking only that they be shriven before the end to facilitate their entry into paradise.

'We might pay a higher price, and for what?' Roger smiled, indicating it was not a question requiring an answer.

'We cannot run away,' his nephew insisted.

'That is a fine sentiment in a lad your age, but if you look you will see it is not one many of your confrères share.' Roger turned to the man he trusted most, who would take over command if he fell. 'Ralph?'

'We must run, with our tails between our legs, Roger, you know that as I do. A bloody end is the only other outcome.'

'Which you would face?'

'If I must.'

'Ibn-al-Tinnah?'

'I love Allah as much as you, Lord Roger, but I am in no rush to meet him.'

If they were going to depart, it would need to be near empty-handed. Occupied with fending off attacks, they could not load their plunder, even if the sea were akin to a millpond, and they would never get their horses away. Added to that they would have to sacrifice the narrowness of the approaches to the north and south and seek to defend themselves on an open beach, possibly a recipe for disaster.

'Send word to Ridel to bring in every boat he has and get the remaining Calabrian levies aboard first. In the meantime they must be put to slaughtering the livestock. The horses we will leave till last. Ralph, I want a sentinel at the northern approach, I need to know if the enemy get there in strength. Tell him to look out for a beacon of smoke as a sign to rejoin us and advise him to be swift when he does so.' Looking around the assembled faces, he added, 'We are not going to get away easily. Some of us are going to leave our bones on the beach. I suggest it would be a good time to make your peace with God.'

Fatalism is an essential quality in a warrior: the more he has been exposed to death the less he will consider it. Every lance Roger led knew the words he spoke to be the truth but it interfered not at all in what they now did, the only point of disagreement being that some of his knights would have left the Calabrians to die or used them to gain Norman time. Roger would not abandon them, his Christian soul would not permit it, but he also thought like a ruler: leave those men and he would struggle to raise more when the time came to return to Sicily as well as the gates of Messina. That was a vow he had not made lightly!

Stopping those levies panicking proved difficult and, an added difficulty, many were landsmen and feared the sea, happy to board a ship from a jetty but terrified of doing so from an open boat. Further trouble came from the open nature of his actions – it could not be hidden from his foes and they did what he anticipated, launched an immediate attack on his too-thin lines. He lost a dozen knights in driving them back, albeit with much slaughter, during what had to be his last use of his horses.

Having achieved a breathing space, he broke off the battle and retired to the beach through a landscape saturated with the blood of sheep, cows, donkeys and the packhorses, ground which was also littered with that which the latter had carried, fighting to keep his own mount's head in the right direction as it was spooked by the overpowering smell of blood. On the sand, his knights dismounted and each man saw to his own animal, before forming a tight arc behind their carcasses, weapons at the ready for the inevitable assault, the only positive being that the wind had finally begun to ease, the sea state calming with it.

Their enemies came on buoyed by their fury and the Norman retreat, while to the rear of the defenders the boats plied back and forth with their human cargo. To the pile of equine corpses was added a multitude of the human variety as the menfolk of Messina, many fired up by an excess of drink, flung themselves at the gore-spattered Norman line. Weary arms could not be allowed respite and swords were swung with deadly effect, Roger losing track of the number of men he had decapitated.

While fighting he had to oversee the collapse of the defence, shrinking his perimeter as boats came in to take off his knights in parties of twenty. The concomitant of that was obvious: those remaining, already massively outnumbered, faced an increased threat, yet if anything aided them it was too much desperation on the part of those attacking: each mad-eyed assailant wanted a kill, wanted to be able to say they had, by their own hand, slain a Norman barbarian. Also, in such close-quarter fighting their lack of professional skill was most exposed, frenzy in a fight not always being an asset; it can be a liability.

The second-to-last withdrawal did not make for the ships: taking advantage of the less-troubled water they took station in the shallows, with men over the side to seaward to keep them level so the remainder could stand to aid the final evacuation. Roger, at the head of his own personal conroy, was now up to his knees in water, the waves coming in bubbling white caps to run up the beach, before hissing back down suffused with a deep red colour. At his command, instead of backing away, Roger, called for a swift advance, summoning from both himself and his men their last vestiges of strength.

Surprised, the citizens of Messina fell back. Roger's next shouted a command to break off fighting and run, which, given they were soon in deep water, was more a hope than an actuality. There was no elegance in boarding those boats either: it was dive in bodily and hope that those who had stayed to aid them could keep at bay those rushing to achieve their kill. Nor were those manning the oars willing to die; the sailors had their oars biting the water in desperation, so the last seeming part of Roger's Sicilian adventure ended with him as a humiliated heap in the bottom of the boat, lying on the sword and shield he had thrown in before him, with water dripping off his body where he had spent a few moments submerged, spitting salt water out of his mouth.

Some of the attackers were foolish enough to follow too far: it is hard to fight on land, impossible with water lapping your chest, and they faced Normans who had been gifted time to recover their breath. So much of their blood was expended that the waves going ashore were as red as those receding; others, with nothing but death facing them, resorted to yelling imprecations, while wiser heads looked for lances to throw after the retreating boats.

Struggling to his knees, Roger looked at the bodies on the beach as well as those floating in the pink spume, saddened to see how many more of his own men he had lost, until, within a short time, he was being hauled up onto the deck of Ridel's ship, a hive of furious activity as men pulled on ropes to hoist the great square sail while every warrior brought aboard had been sent to the windlass to get the ship over its anchor. Roger felt relieved to be off that shore, though he was wondering why, instead of looking pleased, Ridel was looking grim. A finger pointed to the south, to the great hook of the bay that housed the harbour of Messina, showed him the reason.

'Galleys,' Ridel growled.

The long, low ships, ten in number, with huge sweeping oars dipping and rising rhythmically, were heading straight for Roger's little fleet, come out because the weather had moderated enough for them to be employed. Even if he could not see, Roger knew the decks would be crowded with the seafarers of Messina, bound just by their trade to be hardy individuals and, in waters much affected by piracy, probably more accustomed to fighting than those he had already faced.

'Can we outrun them?'

'No, Roger, we cannot. We are going to have to engage them just to get on a course to Scilla.'

That destination soon changed with the wind, which swung into the north, bringing blue skies for the first time in a week, making a southerly course the best point of sailing for Ridel's ships, obliging him, taking account of both wind and current, to head for Reggio, which had the advantage of a properly defended harbour as opposed to just a jetty. Ridel's primary task was to get his little fleet into some kind of order, a defensive huddle around his own vessel that, even untidy, would make it difficult for any galley to single one of them out, which did little to allay the threat; it took time and such a delay allowed their opponents to close the gap to a dangerous degree.

Now fully under way, with their enemies swinging to pursue, it was possible to calculate the odds and they were not favourable. The current was moving in the same direction as the wind was driving the sails but that mattered little, given it favoured the galleys as well, making rowing that much easier. Soon the first crossbow bolts were hissing across the intervening water, many dropping short but others thudding into shields under which the

Normans sheltered; the Calabrians had taken to hiding behind the thick bulwarks.

If such salvoes lessened as the supply of bolts diminished, it was not a cue for a respite as the galleys manoeuvred round the sailing ships in an attempt to ram them. Close to, it was obvious they were crowded with eager enemies, and if curses and shaken fists had been thunderbolts they would have been doomed there and then. Time and again the galleys used their greater manoeuvrability to suddenly swing round, their reinforced prows aiming straight for the side of one of the huddled fleet.

Fortunately the sailors who manned Roger's vessels were as well versed in avoiding pirates as those in pursuit. Time after time, with a swift shift of the single great sail, or by letting it fly, often accompanied by a heave on the stern sweep, the masters avoided a crunching, disabling collision, yet proximity exposed the fighting men on deck to thrown lances, something else they could not reply to: their lances were embedded in the human remains that lined the shore of Cape Faro.

'They cannot keep rowing at this pace,' shouted Geoffrey de Ridel. 'They must cease soon.'

'Now would be soon enough.'

Roger's reply was given as he tried to extract an embedded lance from his shield. All around his men were gathering up like weapons, which they would need to repel more attacks.

'Damn them,' Ridel shouted a second time, 'they are changing to sail.'

The reason required little explanation: with mountains on both sides of the straits acting like a funnel the wind was increasing in strength, which allowed the sleek galleys to ship their oars. That alone added to the danger: the projecting oars had kept the enemy away from the actual side of the fleeing vessels. That would no longer be the case: now they would range right alongside and seek, by their greater numbers, to board.

'Get those weasels on their feet,' Roger yelled, knowing no one would need to be told of whom he was speaking. Newly acquired lances were used to poke the cowering Calabrians and get them into order, this while spare sailors produced knives and axes with which to cut away any grappling hooks that attached to the ship's side; that they would come they had no doubt. At the same time Roger was conscious of the need to watch out for what was happening on the other vessels and it was soon apparent one was falling behind.

What happened then, albeit slowly, reminded Roger of the activities of a pack of wolves, animals who lived off weakened prey. The galley sails began to flap, allowing the vessels to fall away for a moment until the mass of the Norman fleet was past them, only to immediately make their canvas taut again, their great steering sweeps employed to bring round their bows to aim for the straggler, the sail being clewed up and oars reappearing so they could close in.

'Ridel,' Roger yelled, pointing to the labouring vessel.

'I know, but unless you want to lose us all we must leave them to defend themselves.'

'No!'

The eyes of the two Normans locked, creating a contest of authority: if Roger de Hauteville was the leader of this expedition Ridel was the man who held the command on water.

'Every vessel would have to slow to that pace,' Ridel insisted, 'and the more time we are at sea the more we risk. Those galleys have the advantage in men and you have just seen how easily they can change from sail to oars.'

'We must risk it.'

The pause was short enough to tell Roger that his sailing master disagreed, but he did then pick up a speaking trumpet and yell orders that carried to the other ships, this while his own sail was eased to slow their rate of sailing. Soon the straggler was back in the huddle, but it was clear the act of salvation would add much time to their bid to reach safety.

There had to be a central directing mind on those galleys, given their tactics changed speedily. They formed up one behind the other, a manoeuvre which took time, but not a concern to them, given they were not short of that commodity. Also, smoke began to rise from their decks, clear indication that if they could not take their enemies they would be content to set them alight with catapulted fire pots. Then the lead vessel, once more employing oars, began its attack, this time the prow aimed at the gap between Roger's ship and the one just ahead.

'They are going to try and cut us out.'

Roger was at a loss to know how to counter this – luckily Ridel was not. He called the ship ahead to slow and increased his own speed, so closing the gap that the galley entering it risked being trapped, which would leave it, near stationary and isolated, at just as much of a risk as any of the Norman fleet. This being noted, the approaching prow swung towards the stern, to the now greater gap behind. The master of that vessel was too sluggish to react, failing to tighten his canvas and increase his rate of sailing and, worse for him, the second galley in line swung even more to get astern of her.

Ridel was close beside Roger now, wanting no more shouted disputes, whispering his opinion. The only way to aid what was about to be a stricken vessel was to come about, something which the whole fleet would be obliged to do, a manoeuvre so dangerous they might all end up being lost. He could see, in Roger's face, how he was struggling for a way to overrule him, when the first of the catapulted fire pots came flying towards them. Hitting the deck the clay smashed, sending flaming wads in all directions.

There was no time to think of rescue: fire was the ultimate fear of every sailor, the means by which a ship could be utterly and speedily destroyed. Every hand needed to sail the ship, the only people who could bring aid to their threatened consort, were now engaged in trying to save their own vessel and they were shouting to every soldier aboard to help them. The master, guessing what was coming, had seen fit to fetch up and wet some spare canvas and this was now thrown on the multiple fires, aided by every bucket on the ship being used to fetch aboard seawater.

Almost alone at the stern, Roger de Hauteville watched as two galleys closed in on the ship behind, one crossing the bow so close to him he could reach their deck with a cast lance, the other disappearing behind the stern. They sent no fire into a ship they were intent on taking and lines snaked out with grappling irons to fix their prey and lash it to their sides, too many to cut, men pouring across the divide even before they were pulled close, to face a small knot of a dozen Norman warriors lined up to oppose them.

The result was swift and bloody: his men went down, taking many with them, but under such an assault they were soon surrounded. He could no longer see them, and hardened warrior as he was, Roger felt the prick of tears for men who had survived so much only to fall now, wondering, as he rubbed his eyes, if some of that emotion was brought on by self-pity.

Ridel's response was immediate: trumpet in hand, nearly

drowned out by the cheering coming from the vessel taken, he called on every ship to close up to him so they were practically able to touch each other over the divide. Taking their lives in their hands, Normans from the inner vessels leapt onto the outer decks, there to form a line formidable enough, they hoped, to get them safely home. It was nip and tuck, fighting fires, attempts to board, avoiding lances thrown and the remains of the crossbow bolts, thrown swords and even rocks from the ballast, Roger and his men had to fight all the way to the harbour entrance of Reggio. Only then did the galleys of Messina give up and only then could it be considered that in only losing one vessel they had got off very lightly.

# CHAPTER SEVENTEEN

The *Guiscard* was outside the walls of Bari when he heard of Roger's Sicilian debacle, completing a ferocious but successful year-long campaign to recover Apulia, fighting against a Byzantine army that had not only retaken several important coastal cities but had also besieged Melfi, mostly due to the fact that if Argyrus had held the titular command, he had been wise enough to defer to the professional general sent from Constantinople to aid him.

Having relieved his own castle he had taken back the cities one by one, his army swelling as he gained success after success, yet he was only back where he had started, holding most of Apulia but unable to finally eradicate the forces of the Eastern Empire as he had in Calabria; he might have to do the same thing all over again, if not this year, then at some time in the not-too-distant future. Argyrus was still busy plotting, and such was his skill that no one could ever guess from where the next threat would come.

Yet there had been a subtle shift during this campaign: what had helped save the *Guiscard*'s position, especially in the relief of Melfi, was the way many of the Lombards had rallied in numbers to his cause, though he was unsure why. Was it because they thought him less of an evil than Byzantium, or was it that he had not only married a Lombard princess, but that she had borne him a son and heir?

Probably more important was that Sichelgaita was at his side as often as her condition would allow, as commanding a presence as he with her golden hair and telling stature. Just as significant was their relationship, obviously a contented one. Robert had found in Sichelgaita a soulmate who was as capable of being as coarse as he – nothing amused her more than a bedcover-lifting fart – while she had a laugh to shake the stone walls of a castle; Jericho would have fallen to her with one good jest: refreshing after the delicacy of Alberada.

Even with Lombards to aid him, Bari, into which the enemy army had retired, still held out and the region would never be at peace while the city remained in Greek hands. Yet Robert could see no way to take it, standing, as it did, on a long, narrow promontory sticking out into the Adriatic, with massive sea walls difficult to attack, which left only one place open to a land assault: the easily defended wall and great gate that cut off the peninsula from the mainland. To attack that was to seek success at its strongest point, not only in the height and formidable nature of the walls, but also in the sheer number of men that would be committed to holding it.

'Starvation is out of the question, brother,' Robert said, 'even if you block up the water gates the city walls extend to the seaward side and they can be supplied from there, so that's a problem best put aside.'

These ruminations were being imparted to a still-chastened

Roger, who had endured much ribbing for his Sicilian fiasco. With Apulia subdued, in possession of an intact and successful army, and with many months remaining of the campaigning season, Robert had left enough of his foot soldiers behind to mask Bari and keep Argyrus quiet, then marched his lances straight to Reggio, insisting that, given the aid of Ibn-al-Tinnah, conditions were still favourable for an assault on the island, this time a proper invasion.

'Do you trust him?' Robert suddenly demanded, moving from his gloom regarding Bari, back to Sicily – hardly surprising given the two brothers were standing on a hill overlooking the Straits of Messina and the long shoreline opposite, backed by mountains, the snow-capped peak of a smoking Mount Etna clear as a backdrop.

'I think he will betray us as soon as he feels he has nothing to fear from Ibn-al-Hawas. He showed no indication to stay with our cause after Cape Faro, did he? He scurried back to Catania.'

'He is safe there now; it is we who have to worry about al-Hawas.'

That emir had abandoned his Catania campaign as soon as he heard of the arrival of Robert's army, being no fool. Such a powerful Norman host posed a grave threat to the likes of Messina, and if a port and city of that size fell to them, then even his city of Enna, far distant in the interior mountain fastness, would not be safe, while in the lands Roger had already ravaged he would struggle to hold on at all. Al-Hawas had gathered up ships to patrol the shoreline around Cape Faro all the way to the Milazzo peninsula, where he expected them to land. Roger, for one, was full of caution.

'For now al-Tinnah is on our side,' Robert insisted, overriding his brother's concerns. 'That might not continue, and all history tells us that to invade Sicily without an ally is doomed, so we must make use of him and damn the difficulties.'

'Nothing would please me more than to go back,' Roger growled, still smarting from the rebuff of Messina, 'but not to Cape Faro. An opposed landing there could be as bloody as our forced retreat, and we can hardly sail an entire army of two thousand lances over the Straits without being observed.'

'So you have an alternative?'

'Let us go in waves, say of a tenth of number, from one of the small ports, and choose a more constrained landing place where we will not be expected. There is a tiny bay I came across just a couple of leagues south of Messina—'

'Came across?'

'I have sailed the Sicily coast these last weeks in order to get to know it properly. After what happened...' Roger did not finish that sentence: he did not have to. 'It's big enough to land a couple of hundred knights at a time. The crossing is some four leagues by my reckoning.'

'Defendable?'

'Backed by high hills with only one narrow ravine leading inland. Twenty knights could hold it and it has an underground stream running down one side to provide fresh water. It's perfect.'

'Do we want to be that close to Messina, brother? That is where al-Hawas is strongest. Further south is al-Tinnah's land where we can come ashore without interference.'

'And go where, Robert? Clamber up Etna to warm our feet at the crater? If we are to invade and stay we need to find and defeat our enemies quickly, as well as a place that can support a fortress we can reinforce at will.'

'Like Milazzo?'

Roger flushed to be reminded he had abandoned a perfectly good location for that very thing for what appeared to be nothing but avarice. To return to Milazzo by land, with al-Hawas and every man he could muster standing between them and it, would be difficult and risky, even more so by sea.

'Catania is a port,' Robert insisted.

'And one we can use as long as al-Tinnah is our ally. But it obliges us to make a long march north to fight. Next you will be telling me that's something you wish to avoid. You should trust me on this, brother.'

'You think yourself cleverer than me, Roger?'

Roger responded with a wry smile. 'I don't suspect, brother, I know.'

'As an answer that is not very bright given what I have and you do not.'

'It is the only answer you will believe.'

'I am not persuaded your plan is sound.'

'Then, with power, you have lost your insight.'

'To think I named my son after you,' Robert replied, his face flushed with anger. 'When was the last time I boxed your ears?'

'The last time I was too small to fight back.'

Robert stood up and so did Roger, still the smaller of the two, though not by much and, for a moment, it looked as if a blow would be struck, without any certainty as to who would be the first or the winner, for there would certainly be more to follow. Suddenly Robert burst out laughing again, encouraging his brother to reiterate his arguments.

'Let me show you the bay I have in mind. When you see what I am talking about I am sure you will agree. If you do not, well it is your army to command.'

'Ships?'

'Arranged already,' Roger replied, adding quickly, 'subject to your approval.'

'To sail from where?'

'St Maria del Faro, halfway between Reggio and Scilla, and if we go in the numbers I suggest it is big enough for the quantity of vessels we will need.'

Robert walked forward, looking once more at the island over the narrow waters. 'You have been here for a long time, so I am going to bow to your greater knowledge. But pick a good saint's day, Sprat, I want as much of God's grace on my side as I can get.'

Roger de Hauteville, after a Mass said on the quayside, weighed in darkness aboard just a dozen ships, leading an advance guard of two hundred and fifty lances. There was no moon in this part of May, but with a clear sky they had ample starlight by which to steer, and this on calm waters. The crossing was swift and trouble free, so that he had no difficulty in landing his men off his lead ship before first light, their immediate task to take and hold the approaches. As soon as that was achieved, he disembarked the rest of his command and sent the ships back. Serlo was sent inland to scout ahead and returned to say he had sighted a huge baggage train heading for Messina.

Should Roger investigate? The landing ground must be held secure for what would follow and his arrangement was to await his brother's contingent at the very least, and probably the whole Norman host. The baggage train lacked armed protection, but there might be forces close by to protect it, strong enough to threaten their landing place. If there were, he needed to know what level of threat they might portend and how far off they lay.

In truth and in his heart Roger knew he was looking for an excuse to act on his own and the Fates had gifted him one: common sense dictated he intercept a baggage train, which was probably resupplying al-Hawas. He left thirty men to hold the ravine, knowing, if need be, he could retire through them in haste, then set off inland with the remainder of his lances. Serlo's slow-moving mule-and-camel train, all of a league in length, was easily caught. A party was sent to cut off their progress and another to the rear to stop them running for home.

'Save the beasts,' Roger commanded.

'And the drovers?'

'We cannot risk news of our presence to be spread around the countryside.'

There was no need to underline the meaning of that: they attacked and, in a short and bloody engagement, slaughtered every man leading a mule or a camel, then spent a longer time rounding up their charges, they having fled. Fortunately a laden beast will not run far, and once they were gathered and examined Roger was surprised by the amount of booty they had just taken: not only food, but several panniers carrying gold, all transported back to the beach, which took the remainder of the day, by which time the next contingent of lances had come in.

Buoyed by easy success and leaving on the beach his booty, Roger set off again at first light, this time at the head of five hundred knights, riding through the rolling hills that led to Messina, surprised at the speed with which they were allowed to proceed, slowed from a canter only when they were required to walk their mounts up the steeper sides of the valleys through which they travelled. Finally at the top of a wooded hill, Messina lay before them, still formidable; yet peering at the parapets they could see no soldiers, not even a skeleton guard, and there was no sign of any of the forces al-Hawas would have mustered camped outside.

'Where in the name of God are they?' Serlo asked, as, screened by trees to keep out of sight, he, Roger and Ralph de Boeuf, for the second time in three months, surveyed the pale walls of the city, looking deceptively soft and pink in the sunlight. 'We have not seen so much as a piquet on the way here.'

'Perhaps the earth has swallowed al-Hawas up,' Ralph said, 'he being an infidel.'

It looked as if he might be right: the fields between where they sat and the city, ripe with wheat rippling in the soft sea breeze, were almost devoid of any human life and certainly bare of any military presence. The gates were open and a small trickle of traffic entered and exited through them with no hint of any kind of alarm. It was so pastoral, obviously not one of those inhabitants knew the Normans were even close by.

Roger replied softly. 'Much as I think God is ever on our side, I do not believe in miracles.'

'Then what?' Ralph asked.

Roger thought a long time before answering. 'Al-Hawas is expecting us to land at Cape Faro or the northern shoreline. Maybe he has placed every available man there to stop us, knowing he will be forewarned when our fleet sets sail.'

He then pointed out the waters of the straits, the Italian mainland visible as a hazy blue line, devoid of shipping if you excluded fishing boats. 'There is not a galley in sight, which means he is not even patrolling the waters off the harbour.'

'Then he has made an error,' Serlo hooted. 'Once Robert's ashore we will have him.'

'It is not unknown,' Roger replied, with some feeling, 'for military leaders to make mistakes, and I for one will not make any rash judgements.'

Roger had been chastened by his previous failure and he was not alone. Yet, Ralph de Boeuf, the man who had served with him for years, was positive. 'You have a chance here to wipe out a stain and one that will not last. Robert will already have sailed.'

Roger answered in a grim tone. 'I have had my pride broken once on those walls, Ralph. Besides, as soon as we are sighted, messengers will be sent north to alert al-Hawas.'

'Roger, you cannot allow one reverse to blind you to such an opportunity.'

'Uncle,' Serlo protested, 'we must at least try.'

Looking over his shoulder, Roger observed what he had with him: five hundred lances, at present resting in the cool of the woods, standing by their mounts to deny them grazing in case they were needed to make a speedy retreat. This force exceeded that with which he had tried to take Messina before, and there were still fifteen hundred more men to come. What gave him pause was that, in his mind's eye, he could see the image of the bodies he had so recently left below those parapets.

Badly as he wanted to redeem his reputation, it was not that which decided him to proceed. Even if he did nothing he could not avoid the news being carried to the city that there were enemies outside the city walls; he had been lucky up till now to outrun any of those who must have spotted his lances. But when messengers rushed north, it would likely throw al-Hawas into a panic and one in which he might compound his already faulty dispositions. Unsure of what he faced the Saracen might hesitate and give time for the whole Norman force to invest or bypass Messina.

Whatever course was taken the city would be isolated and cut off from immediate support. In time it would fall and he would be vindicated, his vow fulfilled.

'Serlo, get our men ready. Ralph, ride back to the landing beach. When Robert sets foot ashore tell him he is not to delay but to come on with every man he can get astride a horse.'

Seeing the disappointment in de Boeuf's face, Roger added, 'It has to be someone of enough standing so he will believe what he is being told is true.'

'Which does not provide much comfort.'


Roger's lances exited the trees as one continuous line, spread across the wheat fields through which they rode, trampling the corn that ran to the shoreline. At their rear, Roger had his men bring forward their other mounts to the forest edge so that they would be visible, hoping that, from a distance, it would appear as an even greater number waiting to attack. There was no rush to his advance: it was carried out at a walk and he himself made no effort to move forward separately as if seeking to parley. If there were any fighting men in Messina, he wanted them to flee for the safety of their Saracen army before the gates were slammed shut. Thus would the place be more vulnerable later.

'They must know,' he explained to his nephew, 'Robert's whole army is about to descend on Sicily and they will be acquainted with his reputation. Like al-Hawas they will be surprised to see us here, approaching from the south. News travels, and much as it pains me to admit it, I am using my brother's reputation as a weapon. I want them to think he is close by, to think he will be around their walls before the people they depend on to keep us out can get back to their aid, so they risk being locked in to face a soldier who has taken more walled towns than anyone in Christendom.'

Roger called upon his horns to blast a command, and his long line of lances broke into a trot.

By the time Ralph de Boeuf got back to the landing bay the light was fading, Robert had arrived and was ashore, bellowing loud orders. Though he was pleased by the news of no substantial forces lying between him and Messina, he was less so by Roger's unexpected absence, and utterly disinclined to warm to his brother's notion of an immediate siege with an enemy army still in the field. Basic good sense said the right tactic was to first defeat al-Hawas.

'If Roger sees any sign of al-Hawas,' de Boeuf insisted, 'he will send word to tell us. Messina looks totally undefended.'

'I seem to recall it was totally undefended the last time you saw it and look what happened then. Now, help me get my lances ashore so we can get them marching to where they need to be, facing the enemy's main force.'

'You will have to bypass Messina anyway.'

'Where,' Robert growled, 'I had better be joined by a brother who was supposed to await my arrival before undertaking anything.'

Disembarkation took most of the day and they could not march at night, so it was dawn on the third morning before they set off, Robert hoping that if al-Hawas had made his dispositions as Roger outlined he could not move any quicker. He led his army through fields of growing wheat mixed with vineyards, and lemon and orange groves. No one working in the cool of the morning lingered at the sight of these strangely clad horsemen who rode by in what seemed like an endless stream.

As Robert rode through the same line of trees that had hidden his brother previously, the shore on which Messina stood came into sight, but there was no sign of Roger, no tethered horses and a view of the plain showed only where the crops had been crushed by his advance hooves; in the shimmering heat of the middle of the day it looked as if he too had been swallowed up.

'Damn Roger, where is he?'

'He must have bypassed the town to seek out al-Hawas,' Ralph de Boeuf said.

The reply was an angry shout. 'He should have waited!'

Those who surrounded the *Guiscard*, his senior captains, de Boeuf included, watched him in silence as he surveyed the deserted landscape before him, leading up to those pinkish walls and, even from here, the dark blob of the now firmly closed gates. For all his barking about Roger, Robert knew him to be a good soldier and he would not just dismiss any of his suggestions: to do so out of pique was foolish.

His companions guessed Robert would be working out where to place his siege lines, wondering about supplies of wood, water and forage, also how to thwart his enemies who must surely be on their way south to meet him, added to the problem of how to do battle with al-Hawas while instituting a siege, in no way forgetting the alternative, which was to seek out the Saracens and defeat them first. Such ruminations were a commonplace for a leader like the *Guiscard*, who knew as well as anyone that even carefully laid plans rarely survived the first point of combat.

'Keep the army in the shade until the sun has softened a touch,' Robert commanded, finally, his next words nailing his decision. 'While I go forward and offer Messina terms.'

Reposing scant confidence in what he was about to do and not yet having made up his mind about his next course of action, Robert de Hauteville called for his standard-bearer, his herald and his personal knights. He then rode forward with panache, magnificently mounted, clad in his blue and white surcoat, under a banner bearing the devices of his titles, his head crowned with a helmet that had long since ceased to be plain metal, but now was gold-decorated so that he could be seen to be what he was, a rich and powerful duke, come to claim that with which the Pope had enfeoffed him.

The walls seemed deserted, it was as if no one had stayed behind in the place, ridiculous given this was one of the most populous settlements on the island. Nodding to his herald, the man rode forward and began to shout up at the point above the gate.

'The most noble Robert, by the grace of God, Duke of Apulia, Calabria and Sicily, does hereby call upon the citizens of Messina to open their gates to their rightful suzerain, on pain of dire penalties should this claim be denied. The laws of war are plain: surrender and open your gates and all will be spared in peace and prosperity. Fail to do so and you will face the wrath of your liege lord and none, down to the meanest creature, will be spared a bloody death.'

No reply came, no one spoke, which had the herald looking back at his master, wondering what to do. A long silence was finally broken by a creaking sound, as slowly one of the great oak gates, studded with metal, swung open and Roger walked out.

'Do forgive me, brother,' he said, 'but I was at my place of easement.'

The laughter broke out slowly but rose quickly to roars of amusement as Roger's lances stood up from where they had been hiding behind the parapet, to look down on a far-from-smiling *Guiscard*.

'You made me go through that farrago because you were having a shit!' he cried.

'I was going to invite you into my city of Messina, Robert,' Roger gloated, 'but if you are going to adopt that tone maybe I will force you to take it after all.' When his brother looked set to explode, Roger added softly, 'Let me have my joke, Robert; after all, you have Messina without a drop of blood being spilt. I have assembled the elders before the cathedral. They are waiting to meet, greet and do homage to their new suzerain.'

'They did not even try to resist. Al-Hawas stripped the city of every able-bodied man and I suspect they thought him already defeated, so, with a Norman army at their gates, their position was hopeless. I rode up, demanded entry, and the Greeks opened the gates to prostrate themselves before me, while the Muslims fled. I let my men loot what they abandoned.'

Following on from his triumphant entry, and the ceremonial acceptance of his title, both brothers repaired to a palace that had accommodated governors from as far back as Ancient Rome. Looking over one of the best harbours in the Mediterranean, port to a city that could not be taken without the aid of a powerful blockading fleet, Robert was full to bursting with exhilaration: he had come to beat an enemy army, to clear the coast so that he might be able to build a defensible castle and this changed everything. The only problem he had was his determination not to show either pleasure or gratitude.

'You know what this means, Robert?'

'Oh yes, brother, we are here to stay now. There is a not a force on the island sufficient to push us out of Messina when I have done with fortifying it.'

Roger waited for the words, 'Thanks to you.' He waited in vain.

# CHAPTER EIGHTEEN

Ibn-al-Hawas, on hearing of the fall of the city, fled to the west, taking his army and the Muslims of Messina with him, so the immediate threat was gone. Much as Robert wanted to meet and defeat him the pursuit must wait – the first task was to make his new port city impregnable: for all it was strong it had been taken more than once in the past, and the *Guiscard* knew that if he was ever to conquer Sicily then this was a foothold he could not afford to lose. Whatever happened out in the field, if he had Messina to retire to and a strong enough garrison to hold it, he was secure.

The men he led were horse-trained warriors but they were also builders and soon they were toiling in the heat on the walls and towers, or supervising the locals in the digging of a great ditch to surround the walls, one that could be breached to let in the sea and create a deep moat, rendering ten times more difficult any future assault. The harbour was easier to secure, being in a deep bay with a narrow access, which in time of trouble could be sealed off by an underwater boom of chain-linked logs. To leave a sufficient garrison to back up these measures was to diminish his strength, yet that was a price he knew he must pay.

Roger oversaw as much of this work as his brother, still wondering at the way he was behaving: nothing was allowed to hint at a split in their relationship, yet he could sense an underlying lack of trust, as if, in acting as he had, even in being successful in taking the city, he had somehow created doubts regarding his judgement; or was it his ambition? At other times he would berate himself for being oversensitive: Robert was mercurial in his moods, always had been, growling or bellowing angrily at one moment, booming with laughter in a twinkling.

Ibn-al-Tinnah soon appeared, singing Norman praises, offering that which he had previously promised, not in the least bit abashed at the way he had so quickly detached himself from Roger after the debacle at Cape Faro. In fact, while polite, al-Tinnah paid him little heed: the Saracen emir had come to see the new power in the land, the only man who could protect him from his enemies – Robert *Guiscard*.

Watching his brother in conversation with a man he knew he mistrusted was instructive: nothing of that was allowed to surface for, like Messina, Robert needed al-Tinnah. He held the eastern seaboard of Sicily and protected the city from the south and was also a source of essential supplies: weapons, very necessary replacement horses and even, if he could be persuaded, foot soldiers. Was Robert treating his own brother in the same manner, keeping him close but hiding a lack of faith in him?

'Ibn-al-Hawas you must destroy,' the Emir averred, in a theatrical and passionate manner, unnecessary histrionics with a calculator like Robert. 'You will have no peace while he lives.'

'And you also, Ibn-al-Tinnah.'

'I acknowledge your wisdom, Duke Robert, but kill him and there is no other power with the means to oppose us. We can take

Palermo, which will give you rule of the whole island.'

Much time had already been spent with al-Tinnah, he explaining the complexities of Sicilian politics, a lot of it known but both brothers more than willing to admit to ignorance. The capital of the island and the greatest city was Palermo, a distant object in the west, with many an obstacle in between, and while al-Tinnah painted a picture of great and easy conquests, both de Hautevilles, without communicating, were independently assessing their situation in a more realistic fashion and homing in on one very pertinent fact: the Saracens were numerous and they were not.

Such knowledge did not daunt them: Normans rarely fought a battle in which they were not outnumbered, but the sheer ratio, as well as the difficulties that must be overcome, like the terrain itself, was sobering. There was one point of agreement: despite the distance and what lay in between, Ibn-al-Hawas, now in his fortress of Enna, had to be their first objective: to allow him to come to them was too risky. Al-Tinnah would join them at Rometta, then concentrate on harrying those areas he and Roger had raided months before. His task was to keep the Normans supplied and protect their northern flank.

Down to a thousand lances, with some local support and levies from Calabria just fetched across the straits, they set off fr m Messina, heading into the first of the endless mountain ranges that defined the island. Rometta, standing on a volcanic plug, which had risen sheer from the surrounding foothills, was a formidable objective that had troubled many an invader in the past. Roger and al-Tinnah had secured it previously, having been welcomed as liberators, but with al-Hawas back in his own lands, Robert anticipated a siege. It came as a pleasant surprise to find the

Muslim castellan al-Tinnah had left in command had remained faithful to his overlord, so they were able to enter the citadel without a fight.

Robert immediately ordered a Mass to be said in the Greek church – the population was overwhelmingly of that race – though with his own Latin priests officiating, for it seemed once more that God had blessed his cause. He was now safe in the fortress that protected the passes that led to Messina, rendering his base even more secure. Later he and Roger walked the ramparts over which their brothers William and Drogo had fought twenty years before, seeking to take Rometta as mercenaries of Byzantium. It had been a bloody fight then, they knew, and few had seen the place finally fall without the scars of ferocious combat.

'Enna will not be easy like this, Robert,' Roger said. 'I am told it stands even higher.'

'Then it would be best we get there quickly, before it becomes an even harder nut to crack.'

'The Saracen governor?'

That raised a tricky problem. Robert wanted to leave behind a Norman contingent on the grounds he had to protect his line of retreat, when in reality they were a garrison of what he now considered to be a fortress he, not al-Tinnah, held.

'It will be a test of the emir's truthfulness, Roger. If he objects we will know he plans to play us false once we have dealt with al-Hawas.'

'I would not send him north, brother, I would keep him close.'

'But, Roger, it is not your decision.'

That sharp reminder broke the mood and Roger walked away, muttering that he would get his men ready to depart, while wondering if he should beard his brother and demand of him what doubts he harboured. Part of the problem, he knew, stemmed from his own nature: he was not a natural subordinate but a leader in his own right, while Robert was not one to allow his domination to be challenged in any way. That he did not understand Roger had no desire to issue such a challenge mattered less than what he believed and would not discuss. It would have to be resolved but this was not the time: they had a campaign to finish and one that was going to spill much blood.

Al-Tinnah parted company, leading his forces north. Robert marched west, driving his cavalry hard, pushing on ahead of his foot soldiers, moving out of the fertile Greek-populated valleys and on to the high central Sicilian plateau, aiming for Centuripe, the next fortified place on his route to Enna, the whole journey dominated by the towering presence of Mount Etna, the snow-capped volcano spewing smoke by day and glowing red at night, as if to warn anyone close by that they were but mere mortals in the presence of a greater power.

Up till now the local populations, mainly Greek and Christian, had seen him as a liberator from Saracen hegemony. Once in the high hills, the people were either Muslim or the kind of indigenes who had been here since the time of the Phoenicians, hostile to Saracen and Norman alike. Thus care had to be taken with his lines of communication, further weakening a strength already depleted by what he had left behind at Rometta.

Centuripe, like every other Sicilian township, was set on a high hill and dominated by its citadel, this a fortress on a conical outcrop so steep it was near impossible to assault. The Normans needed the garrison to surrender, but whoever was in command, a vassal of al-Hawas, was wise enough to discern that this walled

town was not the main target for these invaders. He refused to
even parley, forcing Robert to call off what was in any case a
half-hearted attempt to invest it. Yet Centuripe could not be just
left on his line of march so he shifted that to the east and took
the less formidable town of Paternò, detaching even more of his
limited strength to garrison that. Given there was no sign of the
great army al-Hawas was reputed to have gathered to oppose him,
a further thrust brought him eventually to the plains below Enna,
the most fearsome fortress in Sicily.

'God save us if we don't win here,' groaned Serlo de Hauteville,
looking up at the fortress, standing high above what was already
an elevated plateau. 'Any Mass said will be a requiem.'

Enna was in a position that could not have been improved
upon: nature had already set it apart. The town was clustered
along an elevated, impressive table, while at the highest end stood
the castle, the only approach along the narrow ridge of the walled
town, the other three sides of the escarpment falling away into the
valley.

'His army is not in there,' Robert barked, 'and it is they we
have to beat.'

Roger spoke to support Serlo. 'If it is anything like the size of
the rumours we have heard it would be wise to choose our ground
to fight.'

'I will not attack them,' Robert replied, just as angry with him,
'and before you point it out, we cannot just sit here either, we
must get them to attack us. Serlo, this is something you will enjoy:
get out there, find them, and prick them until they can stand it
no longer.'

'And me?' Roger asked.

'You, brother, have got to help me choose where we are going to bring them to battle.' Then he pointed up, as if to the sky. 'And once we have scattered them, how we will besiege that damned fortress.'

It was well away from Robert's ears that Roger voiced his opinion to Serlo. 'He is praying for divine intervention when he talks about taking Enna.'

'The Saracens took it from Byzantium. It is not impossible.'

'They took it after a two-year siege by sending men crawling up the main sewer through decades of shit and that, you can guarantee, has now been blocked off. They will have strengthened the place since, as would we.'

'Are you saying we cannot take it, Uncle?'

'Not with what we have, Serlo. We need a more secure rear and thousands more *milites* just to seal it off, as well as to mount the kind of repeated assaults that will be needed to wear down the defenders.'

Serlo nodded. 'What about Robert's plan to pester the forces outside?'

'It's not only sound, it's essential. All al-Hawas has to do is sit still. It is we who will get weak, not he.'

'You did not say this when you had the opportunity.'

Roger wondered how to reply to that, then it occurred that Serlo might be young but he was no fool. 'Do I need to say why?'

That got him a grin. 'No, Uncle, you do not.'

'Robert has favoured you as I did. Make good use of it.'

That Serlo did over the following days. Having located the Saracen host he first established where they were strong, around the main command tents, then where they were weak, on the flanks. His probing attacks were just that, sorties designed to annoy and spread panic, to force the enemy to be alert at all times, for if they were not they would find a fast-moving Norman band inside their lines, slashing and cutting at often unprotected flesh.

Stronger cohorts were moved out to stop these raids, weakening the main concentration, so his final incursion was launched there when the leaders were in their tents at their evening meal. Using the swiftest mounts as well as the terrain, Serlo seemed to appear from nowhere, driving through the central camp roadway. If a flashing sword or swinging axe was not used to kill or maim, then it served just as well to cut the guy ropes and bring the canvas down about the leaders' ears, the dent to their pride doing more to rouse them to action than any number of their followers being killed or maimed.

The horns blew the following morning, the sound faint but clear in the warm air. Robert soon had sentinels riding in from their outposts to tell him that the whole host was on the march, heading straight for his position. In anticipation, the orders had already been given: Roger was on the right flank with a hundred and fifty knights, Serlo on the left with the same number and for once the *Guiscard* was clear that they should act as they saw fit. He commanded six hundred lances and the eight hundred *milities*.

'Serlo puts our enemies at seven thousand in number, with at least fifteen hundred horses. Those, if the Saracens act as they usually do, we will have to face first.' Seeing the look in many an eye, for Robert had never fought a Saracen army, he added, 'Today I will follow the advice of my brother William, who did battle with these men many times in his life. Do not be troubled by the numbers, for they are but levies, poorly trained. The horsemen are the elite; kill them and the exposed fellows on foot will break at the first sight of our advance.'

Faint now, they could hear the drumbeats setting the pace of those coming to fight them, a deep timbre that seemed to resound within their hollow bellies, for, not yet shriven, they had not broken their overnight fast. Quickly the priests moved to their allotted places, calling on these bands of warriors to kneel, captains at the front, each with his sword before his eyes as a makeshift cross.

Each man now looked to his own soul and his own sins, seeking forgiveness for much transgression, while the priests moved amongst them, dispensing the body and blood of Christ crucified. Cleansed of sin they could eat a hasty breakfast, then see to the horses on which they would fight, the sturdy destriers, fed early so they would have well digested their oats. Now they were tied with their heads on a short halter that ensured they could not graze.

Having chosen the crest of a hill they saw their enemies debouching over the opposite rise, each eye keen in examination. Robert had deliberately waited so that his deployment would be visible: he wanted the enemy to see how disciplined were his men, desired they should observe the orderly way they formed their lines. In the centre, under his personal command, he drew up his lances in three lines of two hundred men but kept them still, as the sun rose to fully light the valley in which the contest would be decided.

Aware that al-Hawas was not leading his army in person, and close enough to the fortress of Enna to be overlooked, Robert guessed the emir would be watching from the ramparts, no doubt praying to Allah for a victory this day. He would see the mass in the centre and the way the other de Hautevilles had taken up their positions and spread out in a single line to deny his men the chance to outflank the main Norman force, puny in number when he gazed upon his own army, now all visible and covering the ground so it had disappeared from view.

Robert wondered if he might be invited to parley, with the offer that he could withdraw peacefully. When no sign came he was pleased: al-Hawas wanted to see him crushed and, if he had passed on such a command to his captains, it might make them rash. Right now there was no evidence of that: they were stationary, if you discounted the flurries of activity designed to get them into reasonable order.

'Look at us, Ibn-al-Hawas,' he said softly to himself, 'and see what it is you would dearly love to command.'

There was movement in his ranks, but it was slight, as horses were troubled by their neighbours and the men astride them were obliged to use a sharp tug to keep their heads facing to the front. Robert surmised he would have to initiate any action and he did not want his enemies to deploy in peace. He ordered the horns blown and the first line of two hundred lances, under his personal command, moved forward. No directive was needed for the second line to move, which it did when the requisite gap had opened up, a manoeuvre repeated by the third line. The ragged mass of foot soldiers, pikemen in the main, stood their ground, something obvious to those in the fortress, but hidden from those to the front. Had they seen it they might have wondered why.

Trotting forward Robert's men rapidly closed the gap and, though the odd horseman broke the Saracen ranks while many had trouble keeping their horses still, the enemy line seemed solid. There was no horn for Robert's next command, merely the dipping of his ducal banner and, as if on some kind of parade, all three of his mounted lines spun round and began to trot away from their foes.

Horses, even well-trained mounts, are excitable; men wound up for battle and a possible death are likewise taut so it took few of the Saracen cavalry to break ranks, either through their own excitement or a disinclination for the remainder to keep their horses under control. Once one horse began to race it was very hard to stop the others from doing likewise, and the more that broke ranks the harder it became for the mass. The ground beneath the Norman hooves began to tremble as, in ragged groups, the Saracens began to charge, each horse and rider seemingly determined to be the first to engage, and within no time at all the whole of the enemy cavalry was in motion.

Robert's banner dipped again bringing round his lines to once more face their foes. That completed, the blowing horn set the lances into a canter. To the watching eye it must have seemed like the first line would be swept away by the now hurtling enemy. Did al-Hawas see how close these Normans were to each other, understand that, with each knee nearly touching that of his nearest confrère, the Normans presented an unbreakable line of sharp-tipped lances aimed forward and held in arms that had the power to keep them there even when struck?

The two groups clashed, one screaming, the other silent. When the Saracens struck Robert's line it seemed, given their pace, not only should it break, the edges must be overlapped to surround him. Ripple it certainly did, for the Normans faced a furious attack and it was impossible for the strongest knight to avoid recoiling when either a rider or his horse became impaled on their lance point. Within moments it was sword and axe work as men hacked at each other, the figure of Robert *Guiscard* prominent and murderous in his action.

The instruction to break was not his to give; that came from Ralph de Boeuf, commanding the second line and as soon as his horns blew, Robert and his men disengaged and moved away to the right and left, fighting to get clear, only just in time. De Boeuf's men now struck the disordered enemy with their fresh line of lances, riders who were not charging now but milling about in an unruly mass, which cost them dear. Yet soon the engagement became a repeat melee, requiring replication of what had gone before when Robert, having taken command of the third line, ordered de Boeuf to break off his attack.

Roger and Serlo de Hauteville seemed of one brain in the way and the time at which they moved, both coming forward, as disciplined as their confrères, to take the Saracens in flank and drive them towards an ever more crowded centre. As the mass increased, fewer and fewer of the enemy could properly deploy their weapons, leaving those at the perimeter exposed and outnumbered, the greatest aid to their survival being the bodies of men and mounts either dead or writhing beneath the hooves of those fighting.

Whoever commanded the army of al-Hawas, knowing his cavalry were in difficulties, ordered a general advance to aid them, but by the time they came up, the first Norman warriors had broken through to confront them, this compounded by the men led by Serlo and Roger having come round the flanks to the enemy rear. Behind the still-fighting Normans Robert's *milities* too had come forward and were either piking their enemies or slashing at the horses' fetlocks with knives to bring the rider down, those same weapons employed to kill, their task to ensure the mounted Saracens could take no more part in the battle.

Without commands, the conroys facing the enemy foot soldiers had formed a single line and were once more cantering forward to engage across the whole field of battle, their swords and axes, already dripping blood, ready for more work – Roger on one end and Serlo on the other. The sight made the untrained bands hesitate, which was fatal to their endeavour, for the Normans hit them like a tidal wave, rolling them back onto their fellows. Brave men commanded them and tried to effect a rally but to do so was to be identified and singled out for a swift death. As they went down so did any cohesion, and what started as a slight retreat soon turned into a rout.

There was no order in the Norman line now: it was each man riding as fast as his tired horse would carry him, to employ a swinging weapon upon the fleeing necks and backs of the men who had come so confidently to fight them. Behind them came Robert's levies to ensure that anyone who fell was quickly despatched, so that when they crested the opposite mound the field behind was littered with dead bodies, few of them Normans.

At their centre, covered from head to foot in blood, as was his horse, now with its head lowered and its flanks bellowing to suck in air, stood Robert de Hauteville and he turned to look up at the ramparts of Enna. He could not see Ibn-al-Hawas but he guessed him to be there, just as he knew the Saracen emir would have him in view. Taking his banner from the herald who bore it into battle at his side, he raised and pointed it at the fortress as if to say, 'These men have died and you will be next.'

# CHAPTER NINETEEN

A month later the whole Norman army could see that for what it was, idle boasting. Though great honour could warm the breast of every lance he led, they had not been able to prevent the bulk of the defeated army from retiring into the town and castle. Given such a defence, taking the outworks that protected the town would be hard enough, never mind the fortress, and it was as plain as a pikestaff that the attacking army was dangerously overexposed, far from a secure base as well as suffering in the heat of high summer.

There was to their rear no easily defendable stronghold to which they could retire, no source of men to replace the losses they suffered, more from disease than in battle. The land around Enna, standing as it did on a high rocky plateau, was not fertile as it was in valleys and coastal plains, while to top all that, Robert seriously lacked the kind of strength and equipment needed to take one of the most formidable bastions in Sicily.

Attempts to bring Ibn-al-Hawas to a parley by burning his fiefs produced no results either. From his high elevation he could see how many manor houses and watermills the Normans could burn, how much light could be generated by glowing night-time fields of smouldering crops. If many of his subjects, in order to appease the invaders, came to the Duke of Apulia with tribute and offers of allegiance, Robert knew them to be only as strong as his presence; once he had departed they would renege.

Relations with Roger wilted in the debilitating heat: if Robert could not admit they were static to no purpose, Roger could. After much squabbling the younger de Hautevilles were sent to foray beyond the confines of Enna. Roger and Serlo rode out at the head of three hundred lances and raided all the way south to Agrigento, plundering in lands that had not seen conflict for decades. They were thus, on their return, laden with spoils and it did nothing for Robert's temper to have them distribute enough booty to satisfy his whole army, given such generosity only underlined the uselessness of what he was about.

Added to this was the news from Apulia, sent by Sichelgaita, of the Byzantines he had chased into Bari preparing to sally forth and set his home province alight once more, that accompanied by an urgent request that he return. Stubborn, unwilling to admit to the truth, increasingly short with a brother who hinted it was long past time to go, even the great *Guiscard* had to admit a check to his ambitions. The leaves had begun to fall, winter was the coming season and if he had been ill-equipped to campaign up till now, here, in high country, his lack of resources would be compounded by increasingly inclement weather.

'We leave in darkness,' he told his grim-faced captains, his eyes fixed on Roger for any sign of a gloat, he too wise to show any such emotion. 'I do not want to hear in my ears the cheers from the walls of men we have beaten in battle.'

Doubly galling was the very simple truth: he could not hold

on to what he had taken either in lands or strongholds. This was, Roger's contingent apart, an army he had brought from Apulia. Too many of his lances, with wives, children and landholdings to consider, hankered for a return. Even if they retired in good order and their enemies were too wary to trouble them, the Normans had to bypass and abandon places they had fought hard to subdue. Close to Enna, the locals were jubilant to see the Normans depart, not so once they left the high inland plateau and entered territory mainly Christian and Greek.

Sure that Ibn-al-Hawas would take advantage of the retreat they were strong in their persuasion, offering land and comforts in exchange for protection to the more itinerant knights, those with nothing in either Calabria or Apulia, a chance to settle and prosper. Robert was not about to abandon Rometta, which protected Messina from the south-west, but he was persuaded the northern coastal route was vulnerable. Thus he gave permission for fifty knights to stay and make their home in a town with a broken-down citadel, standing atop a mound from which they could see well to the west and which gave them sight of the northern shoreline, naming it San Marco in honour of his god. When he and the remainder of his army moved on, it was to the sound of hammers on rock, as those he left behind began to construct a proper Norman castle.

'We have learnt much, Robert.'

That got Roger a basilisk stare as his brother took a harder grip of the ratted rope he was holding, part of the rigging of the ship taking them back to Reggio. Over the stern they watched Messina diminish, becoming an indistinct line of white buildings on a long green shore. That, at least, was safe, with a strong garrison commanded by Serlo de Hauteville, made up of men who knew that whatever they had in Apulia could not be matched by what they could gain in Sicily. There would be ships plying in the other direction soon, bringing over their families.

'We have learnt that the Saracens do not know how to fight Normans,' Robert replied.

'They may not repeat the mistakes of Enna.'

Nor, Roger was thinking, would his brother repeat the error of trying to subdue an island like Sicily in one campaign.

'They will, brother, never fear. No one learns lessons after one defeat. Even the Byzantines have still not learnt.'

'A little time out of the saddle will be welcome.'

Robert responded with a humourless laugh. 'I will exchange a wearied arse for a troubled brain.'

That acknowledged what he was returning to, not just domestic harmony in his wife and child but the needs of his title: fractious barons, endless jealousy-inspired claims for preferment, the doing down of a neighbour or rival and the problem, yet unsolved, of Bari and the machinations of Argyrus. What he was not about to mention was how to deal with Roger himself, and it showed in Robert's ire when Roger brought the subject to the fore.

'You have Calabria,' Robert growled.

'I have oversight of your holdings in Calabria, brother. Outside of Mileto and a couple of other fiefs I have nothing, not even a title.'

'Such a thing is naught but adornment.'

'Which is why you are so proud to be addressed as a duke.'

'Have I not earned it?'

'I could ask you the same question.'

'You will get your rewards, Roger, never fear.'

'When?'

That sharp demand got a typical response, barked as Robert moved away from an interrogation he found uncomfortable. 'When I am good and ready.'

The parting was amiable enough; it could hardly be otherwise with Judith present. Robert admired her as a true Norman wife and a beauty with it, uncomplaining to see her man away at war, a creator of domestic bliss when he returned, as ready to breed as the most fecund mare – there was a new male child called Geoffrey.

The *Guiscard* would never admit that Judith stirred memories of his own childhood. The first child of Tancred's second wife, he had been raised with more love than Fressenda *mère* allotted to those of his half-brothers she had inherited from the deceased Muriella. Also, at Mileto, there were none of those troubles of which he had been so aware aboard ship, that is, if you excluded how to deal with a brother who was every bit as good a soldier and administrator as he, a man who might need to be curbed lest ambition sour his soul.

'We have yet to discuss a new campaign in Sicily, Robert.'

'As I have yet to decide what to do. I cannot move lest Apulia is at peace.'

'Will it ever be that?'

'If you have a plan that will give me Bari then tell me, brother, for outside a ten-year siege I have none.'

Robert was still smarting from what he saw as a rebuff, a hard thing to take for a warrior accustomed to, when it came to major combats, unbridled success in the field. Roger was aware that what advice he had proffered – not a great deal, but mostly to say they could not take Enna – being proved right in the end, was not a thing of fond memory.

'Perhaps when I come to Melfi we can talk of it then?'

'In the spring,' Robert barked, as he swung his leg over his mount. With a nod he was gone, his *familia* knights following in his wake, the banner of his dukedom flying stiff in the wind.


'He is a fine child, Judith,' Roger said, taking her hand and looking into the crib containing his newly born son. His other hand was in that crib, a finger strongly gripped by the gurgling infant.

'He is your heir.'

That obliged him to look at Judith, on his face a wry smile. 'I must speak with Jordan.'

'He requires that you do.'

'He has spoken with you?'

'He has been sullen with me, which is not in his nature.'

'It may be in his age, Judith. Manhood is not far off, as you can see in the eruptions on his face.'

'Given the way he lusts after the serving wenches he might make you a grandfather before they disappear.'

'I never thought to come to this, to be like my own father, dispensing advice.'

'With Jordan you need to show love.'

'Surely he knows how much of that I have for him.'

'No, Roger, he does not.'

Being awkward with a growing son is a rite of passage for all fathers, and it is only when facing it themselves they realise the misery through which they put their own sires. Showing affection to a girl child was easy, only made awkward by signs of womanhood. With a son it was not possible to easily be tactile. To treat Jordan like a man would sound false, to act as if he were still a child would cause anger. Roger took refuge in that parental standby, an enquiry about progress in something the boy cared about.

'Let me show you,' Jordan said, 'for to boast of prowess is immodest.'

That was a pleasing response, from a spot-covered youth, gangly in his frame now, but ready to fill out and become a man of the formidable proportions that were part of his bloodline. They made their way to the paddocks to fetch out his horses, then to the manège where he could demonstrate his prowess with both mounts and weapons. Roger had been proud of many things in his life, sometimes he had checked in himself the sin of excess, but watching his bastard boy perform those manoeuvres he knew so well, and seeing the accomplishment with which he carried them out, his heart swelled.

'Acceptable, no more,' he said, holding the head of a sweating destrier. Jordan looked crestfallen to receive no more than those three words; that made Roger laugh, which in turn made Jordan angry. 'Do not seek praise, my boy, for I have learnt that those who give it too freely are rarely sincere.'

'I want to come with you next year.'

'With me?'

'On campaign.'

'You are sure there will be one?'

'There is always a campaign,' Jordan insisted.

Thinking back to his own youth, when, due to Tancred's determination to stand aside from the turmoil of Duke William's succession, there had been no such thing as a campaign, only neighbourly quarrels, it caused Roger to wonder at the life he and his kind now led. There was no pessimistic direction to that thought, he had been raised to be a warrior and was happy in the role. Yet there was just a hint of a hankering for a more peaceful life, one in which he could watch his children grow and see to the husbandry of his fiefs that soon followed by the thought that he would go mad in such an existence.

What to say to Jordan, who was, at thirteen summers, really too young for war? He should say no, say that he must wait, but here was a chance to show him how much regard he had, show him that the arrival of Geoffrey, which would deprive him of any chance of inheritance, did nothing to dent his father's feelings.

'I had a mind to suggest it, Jordan; after all, the sooner you set about carving out your own patrimony the better.'

'For which I had looked to you, Father.'

'Never fear, Jordan. If you are half the de Hauteville my brothers were you will end up a duke.'

'Is that what you will be?'

'Perhaps,' Roger replied, but he did not elaborate, given the question took him back to his relations with Robert. 'But I have a charge for you. Geoffrey is your brother, he will need your hand to guide him. Swear to me now that in all things you will be his friend and guardian.'

Christmastide was hardly over when he felt that such a piece of advice would have been welcome to Robert, who was, once more, holding back on the monies promised to meet Roger's responsibilities in Calabria, added to a demand that he remit even more. It was not one that Roger could accept and, added to previous frustrations, it brought about a sharp response.

He reminded his brother of the services he had rendered, of the promises he had received, as yet unfulfilled, as well as the fact that he was now not some bare-arsed bachelor but a married man, a father with a household to support and a wife who deserved to live in a manner befitting her station. The closing words were a warning of the risk of a final breech, that if Robert did not meet his legitimate claims, he would have no recourse but to resort to a decision by arms; the reply was not long in coming.

'No mention of all those titles and fiefs I was to be granted, plus a threat that should I fail to comply he will come personally to chastise me.'

'Why are you smiling?' asked Ralph de Boeuf.

'What else would you have me do?' Roger replied, waving the parchment on which Robert had written his demand. 'I have no intention of giving in to this.'

'You think he does not mean it?'

'No, he will mean it, but it is the why that interests me, given I am the only brother Robert treats in this way. Geoffrey he indulges and Mauger he ignores.'

'He has no fear of either of them.'

'What has he got to fear from me?'

Roger was being disingenuous, yet Ralph de Boeuf tapped his forehead anyway. 'You are at least his equal up here. Was it not the Jew who said he saw William in you? Well, Robert may see that too.'

'I would never challenge him.'

'You don't have to, given he is challenging you! You were right at Enna and he was wrong, something known to every lance he leads. The *Guiscard* wants you to acknowledge he is your superior in every way, he wants you tugging your forelock like some peasant, and he would truly be happy if you did it in front of his entire army.'

'That I will never do.'

'Then you must dispute with him.'

'Should blood be spilt for a brotherly squabble?'

'There's not a man you lead, and I am one of them, who would respect you if you did as Robert wants. So I suggest that word be sent out for every lance we command to gather here.'

'Will that be enough?'

'Roger, you have no notion of how much you are loved in Calabria since the famine. There is not a town that will open its gates to the *Guiscard* without he has to use force, unless you command they do so. You may move around at will and our men will be welcomed and fed. You can attack your brother wherever he is and wound him, even if he has superior force; you do not have to do battle with him but to wear him down. His numbers will be a burden to him, not an asset, for he must forage where you have no need.'

De Boeuf sat back from the table at which they sat. 'I do not know why I am telling you all this, given you already know it better than me.'

'Knowing it does not make it palatable,' Roger replied grimly. 'He will besiege Mileto, for certain.'

'Then it is best we are not here when he does so.'


'Robert will not harm me, or our children,' Judith insisted. 'He is not some beast.'

'I know, but I have no idea how far he might go in his jealousies. If he storms Mileto all of you are at risk, not from Robert but the men he leads, who will be drunk with the passion of combat, as well as too much wine. It is a thing I have seen often and it is not pleasant.'

'You forget I am a Norman.'

Roger grinned. 'How could I, Judith?'

'Then as a Norman I will hold our castle of Mileto.'

'You're asking me to desert you?'

'No. I am saying you should do as you intend, stay outside the walls where you are too great a threat to ignore. Is that not what William did at Melfi?'

'You are the second person to mention William this day, and the same person gave me similar advice regarding not being trapped here.'

'Then he is a wise judge.'

Roger laughed. 'Whatever happened to that sweet girl I knew in Normandy?'

Judith came close, stood on her toes and kissed his cheek. 'She grew up to become an Amazon. I will send the children to my brother at St Eufemia. Robert will respect a foundation he himself funded, but when he comes outside these walls of ours he will be obliged to parley with me, and when he demands surrender, if you leave me enough lances, I will refuse him.'

Deep in his heart, Roger felt it would be impossible for Robert to harm Judith, for all his irascibility he was not like that and, even if he growled about his bloodline he had respect for his siblings and their offspring.

'Very well, Judith, you will be the Chatelaine of Mileto, and no doubt troubadours will compose songs of praise to you. I must take Jordan with me – I promised.'

'He is too young, Roger, and he will seek to prove he is not.'

'I will look after him, never fear.'

'Can you win against Robert?'

'No, but I can make him pay too high a price for what is, after all, nothing but his pride.'

'When will you leave?' Judith asked.

'On the morrow. Robert is no fool, he will suspect I will not give in to his demands so he will already be on the way. I doubt his message was sent before he was ready to depart.'

'One more night, then?' she said, an unmistakable timbre in her voice.

Roger grinned as he held her close. 'No warrior should go into combat unshriven, it is seen as impious.'

'If you are not impious this night, husband, it is not Robert you will have to answer to, but me!'

Roger, at the head of his personal knights, plus those who had already responded to his call to arms, rode out of Mileto the next morning, with Jordan at his side. Behind him other lances lined the parapets as the gate swung shut, the portcullis came down and the drawbridge over the moat was lifted. This being a fortress designed and built by the man now departing, it would not be easy to take.

# CHAPTER TWENTY

Robert was outside Mileto within ten days, proving that Roger had been right – he had departed Melfi at the same time as his message, looking a proud figure as he rode up to the gates to demand both entry and submission, genuinely surprised when Judith of Evreux was the person who answered him, his first reaction a declaration that he did not parley with women. That rebounded on him as Judith nodded and disappeared, leaving him fuming with impatience until he had his herald call her back.

'Where is my rebellious brother?'

'Raising lances to fight his duplicitous one, among folk who love him and despise you.'

'I demand he appears before me and recants.'

'Demand away, Robert,' Judith replied, 'but you are not talking to your lackeys now.'

'He owes me fealty.'

'You owe him gratitude and more besides.'

'Let down the portcullis, drop the drawbridge and open the gates, Judith, to my castle of Mileto.'

'The gates to MY husband's castle will remain closed to you until you repent.'

The yell that engendered was loud enough to make stone tremble. 'Repent! I am the Duke of Apulia.'

'And you are a mean-spirited scoundrel.'

'If you were a man, Judith—'

'How I wish to God I was, Robert, to knock you off that magnificent horse you are riding. You're so puffed up with pride I would need no more than a feather.'

'You know the price of a refusal?'

'I do. Your men will die trying to overcome these walls.'

'Judith,' Robert said, sounding emollient, 'I know you to be brave as you are beautiful, but I sense that if you are speaking to me Roger is not within the walls. I think I know my brother well enough to be sure he would not hide behind your shift. Very well, he has gone elsewhere and, rest assured, I will find him. So what you are about is an empty gesture. Open the gates and allow me entry. No harm will come to you or yours, I give you my word.'

'Is that the same word that promised my husband the revenues of Calabria for ten years, promised him titles, or is it the word of a man so consumed with jealousy for a wiser head and stronger arm, a man who does not have to bribe his lances to be loved?'

'You're trying my patience, Judith.'

'How can that be, Robert, you have none.'

'Open the damn gates,' he bellowed.

The barrel that appeared over the walls must have been thrown by two very sturdy fellows, for it cleared the moat to land in front of Robert's mount, which reared in fright. It burst open, spewing a foul-smelling eruption of brown liquid, which managed to spatter both the Duke of Apulia and the chequered caparison on his horse.

'That, Robert, is the night soil of Mileto, the piss and shit of the town. Rank as it is, it smells sweeter than your blandishments.'

Furious, Robert pulled on his reins and swung round his horse, departing with no dignity at all, a furious pace he maintained until he got to his tent, jumping off to enter, demanding to be brought hot water and fresh garments, not that such needs stopped him from shouting commands.

'Send men out to find my brother, scour the land. By God I'll dip his head in a bucket of shit for what his wife just did.'

'The siege, sire?'

'Siege!' he yelled, as he tore off his surcoat and his fine cambric shirt, showing a body of rippling muscles and numerous deep scars. 'You want me to make war on my brother's wife?'

Two servants brought in a large tub of water, warm enough to produce wisps of steam. Robert's head went straight in and stayed there, while those he trusted to lead his men stood and watched. Eventually the great leonine head came out again, dripping water, his hair turned a flaming red by being soaked.

'Set up the siege lines and make it look as if we plan an assault. If Roger intends to fight me that will draw him to us.' Looking into the blank faces before him, he was moved to shout once more. 'What are you waiting for?'

One captain was braver than the rest, Grenel, the Greek from Brindisi, who had taken wholeheartedly to service, trusted to lead a *bataille* of Robert's pikemen.

'My Lord,' he said, 'it would help us to know your purpose.'

The look that got was enough to freeze Etna, yet it took no genius to see the same question was in every mind, for none of the others would look at him. He had come here to make his brother grovel, not to draw de Hauteville blood. That others might die to achieve that was, to Robert, a price worth paying, yet to be open about that would not elevate him in the eyes of these men and he needed their respect. Besides, the *Guiscard* was never too open about his thinking.

'It is enough that you do as I bid you to do.'

'Of course, My Lord.'

'Then do so, all of you.'

Unbeknown to Robert, the sortie had already been discussed by his Norman captains, who knew they were on was an errand driven by conceit rather than good sense. These men knew his brother as well as they knew their duke and had fought alongside him, not that such a thing alone would have stopped them from killing him if so ordered: their loyalty and any hope of advancement, to a castle or even a fief, lay with the man who led them. Yet they knew Robert would never harm Roger, so if they were to risk death or injury, and to be asked to inflict the same on their conroys, it had to be in a cause in which they believed and this one was not.

'Best find him,' Grenel said forcibly. He might be Greek but he shared the same thoughts as his Norman contemporaries. 'And make a dumb show of preparing to attack. The sooner the two of them are face to face and Roger bows the knee the sooner we can go home.'

'Perhaps, when Sichelgaita arrives, she will be able to talk some sense into him,' said one captain.

Robert had his wife and child on the way, though not obliging them to keep to the furious pace he had set in the hope of trapping Roger.

'Are you mad?' another captain replied. 'She's more of a warrior than he is!'

Throughout the day, riders were sent out in all directions, watched from the battlements by Judith. Likewise she saw the preparations for an assault on the walls where she stood: ladders being cut and assembled, the sound of the stone wheel sharpening swords, axes and lance points. Roger would come as soon as he heard his brother was outside Mileto: he was not a man to see others die to save his pride and that was doubly the case when it came to her. That she wished he would desist, that it was not expected by the men he had left behind, who would face what was to come with their accustomed equanimity, counted for nothing.

She turned to face those lances, who were awaiting her orders, as well as the men stood around the great metal cauldron with a pile of faggots at its base.

'Light the fires. Let's get that oil bubbling enough to strip skin.'

The problem for Roger was simple: he was too obvious, given his height, build and colouring, to move around unnoticed, that compounded if he rode at the head of over three hundred lances, displaying as his banner the family blue and white chequer. The second difficulty was that Robert had twice that number of men, and if he was going to induce a stand-off in which matters could be discussed, if not settled, his preferred aim, he needed more warriors – not necessarily cavalry, but in sufficient numbers to induce Robert to talk rather than fight.

Encamped in the mountains above and to the east of Mileto, with ample wood, water and fodder, Roger was sure, if he could bring that about, he had the means to talk Robert out of his foolishness, unaware that his brother was working on the same principle but seeking the opposite outcome. For all Roger was popular, many had not rallied to his banner as quickly as he wished, leaving him only one choice: a personal plea for their aid.

'There are thirty lances guarding the coast at Gerace.'

'Which is ten leagues from here,' complained Ralph de Boeuf.

Roger put his arm round Jordan's shoulder. 'Ten leagues would not trouble you, my boy, would it?'

'Never, Papa.'

'Then you will accompany me.'

'And the rest of us?'

'Stay here, Ralph, there are none of Robert's conroys this side of Mileto.'

'Take an escort, Roger.'

'And wear men out to no purpose? What need do I have of an escort when I have Jordan at my side?'

Ralph de Boeuf's expression showed he knew that to be rubbish, but Jordan was beaming, his face so flushed with pride his juvenile spots looked like fire coals. Told to prepare, he rushed off to get their mounts ready, his bright blond hair flying, followed by the admiring eyes of his father.

'I swear he has grown half a hand since we left Mileto.'

'Which makes him just as easy to mark as you. Be careful, Roger, remember your brother is no dimwit.'

Roger was right, there were none of Robert's conroys east of the central mountains. What there were, however, were numerous individual riders seeking news of his whereabouts, and even if he avoided towns, he was every inch the Norman knight, while Jordan had an innocence and a pride that meant if he was asked, out of Roger's earshot, with whom he rode, he was only too happy to tell the enquirer not only his father's name and title, but where they were headed and why. Pushing their mounts, it was only a day's ride to the walled town of Gerace, full of Greeks and one which had suffered much in the famine, happy to welcome the man they saw as their liege lord and saviour.

Normans cared for their horses when they must: Roger and Jordan walked their mounts a third of every league. The fellow informed of their presence and destination had no such consideration. He rode his horse till it nearly dropped, then commandeered another that got him swiftly back to Robert's encampment. Few grains of sand made it through the neck of the glass before the Duke of Apulia was mounted and on his way with a hundred lances, driving his mounts with the same lack of regard. It was only by the greatest good fortune and a whisker of a wooded hillside that he missed Roger and Jordan, who had spent a whole day and night in Gerace, and were now riding back to their mountain retreat with half the men of the garrison, the rest pledged to follow.

Robert's lances were spotted thundering towards the walls and even if they had not known his identity they would have slammed shut their gates. Nothing they subsequently learnt was inclined to alter such thinking: to these Greeks the *Guiscard* was remembered as a ravaging brigand, for Gerace had met him before. He had not been a duke then, nothing more than a thief, one feared by the citizens of this part of Calabria for the destruction he had wrought.

'You know me and you know what I will do if you do not open your gates.'

'We do know you too well, weasel,' a voice cried. 'May the Devil take you!'

'I am your duke.'

'We are loyal to Roger of Mileto.'

'Which I will burn and when I have I shall come to Gerace and do the same.'

'The children of the men you slaughtered before await you, pig.'

It was a futile exchange: he had no idea if Roger was in Gerace – with just a boy alongside him he would be mad to show himself – and no way of forcing entry with the forces he had to find out, as obvious to those hurling insults as it was to him. Previously he had taken Gerace in a lightning raid which had left the inhabitants, undefended by Byzantium, no time to bar his entry. Blood had been spilt, but that was to be as expected as was the violation of the women – it was a Greek town owing allegiance to Constantinople and he was a Norman seeking plunder. There had been much of that, too, but what he also recalled was the name of one citizen who welcomed him. It was time for a touch of the famous *Guiscard* cunning.

Having set up camp far enough away so his fires could not be seen, Robert posted sentinels around the town with instructions to ensure his brother did not sneak away. Having divested himself of his surcoat and mail, with a cowled cloak over his body and head, crouched to minimise his height, he made his way back to the town, sure that folk would be slipping in and out, going about their various errands. He was right: the carts that had come in from the country before he was sighted were sneaking out to return to their outlying farms and it took little effort to creep along the unlit wall and dash through the gap, hidden from those guarding the gate on the other side of a cart.

Memory helped him find the home of the man he thought

most likely to help him, a Bulgar named Brogo, and a man who so hated the Byzantine killers of his people that he had secretly helped Robert to identify those citizens of the town likely to have hidden wealth – a betrayal for which he had been well rewarded, his secondary pleasure being in watching them tortured to reveal their hiding places. Fifteen years is a long time and Brogo had aged much, yet he could not fail to recognise a man of the height and build of the *Guiscard*, nor did he hesitate to drag him from under the lantern outside his doorway and into his hovel.

'Lord Robert, how I longed to see you come again.' The man was slobbering over his hand in the most embarrassing fashion, yet Robert knew he must indulge him. 'I hate the Greeks and I hoped once more you would come to strip them of their gold.'

Robert wanted to say, recalling what he had plundered here, there had been precious little gold. But he held his tongue on that: there was only one question to which he required an answer.

'Is my brother still in Gerace?'

'No, My Lord, he left this morning before the sun was high.'

The string of curses that induced, in Norman French, might have been incomprehensible to Brogo but he knew what they portended in a man much given to anger. 'I have wasted my time, friend, I must away and pursue him.'

'Wait, My Lord, do you not intend to take Gerace again?'

In a room with enough candles to see reasonably well, Robert looked at unsavoury Brogo, a thick-necked, round-faced creature who perspired constantly, with misshapen features, broken teeth and breath that would have halted a camel. He had made money from Robert before and it took no great imagination to see that he saw in this visit a chance to repeat his good fortune.

'You cannot depart now, it is not safe.'

'The gates are in use, Brogo,' Robert growled, 'how do you think I got here?'

'They will not be so now, all who needed to leave will have done so. But at first light, when the country folk want to come back, as long as your men are not close—'

'They will not be.'

'Then wait till then, Lord Roger, and perhaps you will allow me to offer you food, humble fare to a man of your wealth, but you cannot have already eaten.'

In truth, Robert was sharp set, having ridden hard and consumed little and, even accustomed to hard service, he was weary. The prospect of a seat at a table and food, risky as it was to be sat here in an enemy town, was too tempting to resist. He threw back his cowl and nodded.

'Very well, Brogo.'

'If you would pay, I could buy food more to your liking.'

The odour of the place was enough to tell the *Guiscard* this was no house of plenty, more likely an abode where rotten vegetables were the staple fare. In his absence this man had not prospered, no doubt because, if he hated the Greeks of Gerace, they were not fond of him. Some coin from Robert's purse produced a shout that brought into view a much younger woman, Brogo's wife, a dark-skinned creature introduced as Melita. Another shout brought forth an ageing servant so thin and rickety he looked as though he was half starved, he given the coins and sent out to buy meat and wine.

Robert paid no attention to the way the servant's lacklustre eyes were fixed on him: the fellow being in a dreamlike state, his only reaction the notion of such a household having a servant at all. Having lost interest in the fellow before he slipped out of the door,

Robert was left to listen to a litany of oleaginous flattery mingled with an equally heartfelt damnation of the Greeks who had, in times past, slaughtered his race as they would a flock of diseased chickens. Robert was only half paying attention, so it was he who first heard the rumble outside the door that led to the street.

Brogo, who had been talking too much to pick up the sound, was stopped by the look of dread in Melita's black eyes. By the time his jaw dropped it was no longer a rumble but the noise of a yelling mob, their voices echoing off the stone walls of the narrow alleyway, which had Brogo running to slip the wooden bar across his front entrance.

'Where is your servant?' Robert demanded; the look that received gave full answer. 'Is he Greek?'

The pounding at the door had Brogo grab Robert's arm and propelled him, big as he was, towards the back of the hovel, the man's wife following, gabbling about their being betrayed. The exit they used was like a trapdoor and Robert had to struggle to squeeze through, with Brogo insisting he should make for the gate and seek to force his way clear, leaving a clear impression: this Bulgar did not want to be anywhere near the *Guiscard* now, he wanted him out of his sight.

'My wife and I must go to the church and seek sanctuary. Go, Lord Robert, and may God look after you.'

Half dragging Melita, Brogo scurried away. Robert, given little choice, followed, his head high and his step firm, eventually losing sight of the pair and left to follow as best he could by the noise of their echoing footsteps, while in the background he could hear the increasing sound of yelling and screaming: clearly the size of the mob had increased. Emerging at the end of an alley to look out on the main town square, with the church as always the dominating structure, he saw Brogo and his wife; he also saw that some of the wiser heads in the mob, sensing their quarry would flee, had made for the square to seek them out, filling the space with torchlight.

Melita tripped on the rough cobblestones of the square, losing her grip on Brogo's hand. He looked at her briefly, then at the mob now debouching onto the square, many armed, and decided to try and save his own skin. Running for the church doors, stumbling up the steps, he nearly made it, getting only one blow on the closed doors to seek sanctuary before the first club struck him down, the precursor of many. Brogo disappeared under a hail of staves and fists; if he was screaming it was drowned out by the imprecations of those intent on his murder.

Another crowd cornered Melita, dragging her by the hair and ripping at her clothes until eventually she was naked, her wild black eyes, in the torchlight, full of fear. As many women made up the mob that surrounded her as men, and as they screamed and spat invective, Robert heard the words that damned her as a witch and a whore. By now those battering Brogo had done their worst and moved away from his broken, blood-soaked cadaver, that somehow bringing to the crowd a degree of hush. Then they parted and that skeletal servant was in plain view, slobbering the words that nailed him as the cause of their gathering. His damnation was rambling, but this was a fellow who had witnessed the previous plundering of the town. He had recognised Robert and raised the alarm, firing up their passions by telling the town of the nature of this Bulgar traitor and his whore of a wife.

'Let her die for that which she lived, the slut,' a woman yelled, a cry taken up by many. From somewhere appeared a pointed stake, standing upright before Melita, like a high fence post, and hands took her and raised her over their head and its point. She screamed in terror at what she knew was coming and squealed in pain as those holding her let her down onto the point, before exerting every ounce of their strength to impale her, satisfied that the point which had entered her vagina erupted out of her ribcage, spewing out bone and gore.

Robert, sensing escape was now impossible, stepped out of his alleyway to let himself be seen, making those who had been holding the stake on which the now writhing and dying Melita was impaled turn to face him. In the growling and shouting this produced he could make out the words of damnation, along with a litany of his past crimes, so, stepping further forward he held up his hand and in a loud voice commanded silence: it was a tribute to the presence he possessed that it worked.

'People of Gerace, you have me in your power.'

That brought forth howls of agreement and required him to raise his voice.

'And no doubt you are set on revenge for what you say are my crimes?' It took an even louder shout to add, 'But hold a moment and consider.' He opened his cloak to reveal he had no sword and also used the moment of curiosity created to remove and throw down his knife. 'Having me at your mercy will tempt you to an error, for if you kill me, what then do you think will happen?'

He could see in the movement of the crowd that men of better dress and stature were pushing to the fore, elders, holding up their hands to induce calm in their fellow citizens, while behind them there were soldiers by their garb and Normans.

'There would be pleasure in your revenge, but with that comes a price. I have a hundred lances outside your walls, five times that number at Mileto and thousands more in Apulia. Do not, for your own well-being, let your passions rule your heads. Nor would I beg you to forget that I am your liege lord – that Gerace, as did every town in Calabria, swore to obey me.'

He raised one hand to the heavens. 'God is watching us now, you and I, and he will observe the breaking of your solemn oath. The men I command will have his blessing to deal with those who sever it, and would it not shame you to slaughter as a mob a single soul who means you no harm, but seeks only his brother? Kill me, if you cannot contain your bile, but know it is a sin that God, and my confrères, will avenge.'

Robert did not have to say they would all die: they knew it, and such a threat was enough to make them sullen and silent, until a commanding voice spoke, the same one which had damned him from above the gate.

'Take the duke to my house, and not a hair on his head to be hurt.'

# CHAPTER TWENTY-ONE

The gathering of the leading citizens soon turned into a babble of competing notions of what to do next: if fortune had favoured them in the gift of the body of Robert de Hauteville the Devil had cursed them equally. Some wished to just set him free in the hope that in his gratitude there would be no price to pay, others were firm of the opinion that the *Guiscard* could not be trusted: he would burn Gerace out of pure malice. The sky grew light and the arguments continued, this while outside the walls, at Norman camp, it had become obvious that their leader was missing and, since he had not left unobserved, even if Robert had not told anyone where he was going, it took no great gift of imagination to discern his destination.

One of the Norman lances still in Gerace, Odo de Viviers, who had been making preparations to join Roger, witness to the disagreements of the town and mightily fed up with them, slipped out to tell his confrères what had happened. He, at least, had a clear sight of one fact: Gerace, where he had made his home and had a wife and children, could not keep so puissant a lord as the *Guiscard*; even to hold him too long was to invite total destruction. Robert, or his men, would kill every living thing down to the last cat regardless of how he was finally treated.

That continuing, unresolved discussion was brought to an abrupt end when the elders were informed that there were Normans outside their gates seeking parley. If they wondered at how quickly these warriors had found out about their prisoner it made little difference: they could not give him up for fear of immediate reprisals and they could not keep him for the same reason. Assurances that no such thing would happen were dismissed. As one elder put it succinctly to Robert's most senior subordinate, 'Such decisions are not yours to make, fellow.'

Dire warnings about what would occur should Robert be harmed changed nothing: those voices that wanted him hung from the walls were fatalists who suspected that they had done enough to be sure of bloody retribution so they might as well rid the world of a human devil before they, too, went to meet their Maker. Men who thought themselves more sage in counsel argued the opposite. Odo de Viviers, still outside the walls, was succinct in his advice to Robert's captains.

'It is an impasse and one only Roger can resolve.'

'What are you saying?' more than one voice demanded.

'I am saying that Roger is much loved in Gerace. I am saying if he asks for Robert's freedom, and assures them there will be no reprisals for his confinement, they will let him go.'

'The *Guiscard* will flay us alive if we beg his brother.'

'His brother will roast you over a spit if you don't,' Odo barked. 'Who do you think will be Duke of Apulia if Robert dies?'

There was no need to elaborate: on coming into his title of Count of Apulia, Robert had put aside any claim by Abelard, the young son of Humphrey, just as Richard of Aversa had ignored any claim by his Uncle Rainulf's bastard child, Hermann. Roger would do the same to his baby namesake – he would have no choice: to avoid doing so would fracture the Norman presence in Italy, which depended on strong leaders in both Apulia and Campania.

'Will you tell us where he is camped?' one fellow said finally.

'Better than that, I will take you there.'


Sichelgaita turned up outside Mileto to find her husband gone, though tents had been sent ahead to accommodate her and her son in great comfort. On learning of how Robert had been rebuffed and by whom, she fell into gales of laughter, so loud, that baby Roger cried with fear and had to be calmed by a nurse. Once she had regained some composure she called for her horse, while that same nurse was told to make little Roger ready.

'Where are you planning to go, Lady?' asked the man Robert had left in command.

'I am going to call upon Judith of Evreux.'

'Lady, Mileto is under siege.'

That got the fellow a cold stare. Certainly Sichelgaita had observed much marching to and fro when she arrived, had watched the lances at their practice, had seen the ladders ready for an assault as well as woodcutters working on the baulks that would make up the base of a siege tower. But Sichelgaita was far from a fool, she was clear-headed and mightily interested in military matters; in fact, it was one of the bonds that united her and Robert: he could discuss with her things he normally kept to himself.

'Get a pannier for my child and when my sister-in-law admits me to Mileto, which she will certainly do, no one of you is to take advantage of my entry.'

Few people had the commanding presence of the *Guiscard*:

Sichelgaita was one of them. Within a short time she was trotting towards the gates, baby Roger in one pannier at her side, the other filled with fruits and sweetmeats. She stopped before the drawbridge to find Judith already on the walls.

'I have come to show you my baby, Judith.'

'It would give me great pleasure to see him, sister.'

'Then let me enter.' Judith hesitated, as was proper. 'Under flag of parley.'

The creaking sound began as the double defence of the gates was removed, continuing as one great oak door swung open, allowing Sichelgaita to enter – the postern was too small. Judith was there to greet her, standing on her toes to peer into the pannier at the now sleeping child.

'Take him, Judith, I sense you are more gentle with children than I.'

Not long after, they were inside Judith's private apartments, chatting away like old friends while Roger's daughters billed and cooed over their cousin. Judith, cradling baby Roger, was decorous both in appearance and manner; not even the kindest observer would gift that to Sichelgaita: she was loud, clumsy and raucous in her humour, roaring with mirth when her sister-in-law repeated the words she had used to her husband, even more tickled by the notion of him being covered in shit.

'They are both fools, Judith,' Sichelgaita said. 'Too proud to admit they are wrong.'

'I am bound to say, and not just in support of my spouse, that Robert is most at fault.'

Sichelgaita frowned, as if not in full agreement. 'You do not see him as he truly is, Judith, you only see the bellowing man who gives of no doubts. But those he has, I assure you, and you are holding one that troubles him. What if he falls when his heir is of such tender years?'

'Bohemund?'

'Has been made bastard, Judith! Roger is Robert's true son. I daresay Bohemund's father will care for him, but my child, if the Good Lord spares him and his sire, will live to one day be Duke of Apulia.'

'Why have you come, Sichelgaita?'

The blond eyebrows on her wide face lifted in surprise. 'Why, to see you, Judith, to talk to you of this nonsense between our husbands.'

'You feel they should be at peace with each other?'

'You, surely, do not believe they are at war?'

Looking down at the slumbering child in her lap, Judith was aware of the true reason Sichelgaita had come. She wanted harmony between the husbands for the sake of the child and she wanted from Roger an assurance that, should the *Guiscard* expire, he would act as true guardian to his namesake and not as a usurper. Odd: she had thought of her sister-in-law as more manly than was proper, but the birth of her child had brought to the fore the true nature of her gender and such a thought was touching.

'I am sure you have nothing to fear, Sichelgaita. The Good Lord will surely bless such a comely infant with a long and happy life.'

Their smiling eyes locked: Sichelgaita could not bring herself to ask for that which she had come, Judith's help in gaining an assurance from Roger, and besides, much as Judith loved her husband and was sure he loved her, no words of hers would alter what he felt he needed to do in the event of his brother being killed or dying.

'It may be a good notion, Judith, to go now and pray for such an outcome.'

'Let us do that.'


'If you were to ask me, Father, I would suggest that what the people of Gerace did to that woman would be best visited on your brother.'

Roger did not lose his temper, nor did he look Ralph de Boeuf or any of Robert's men in the eye. Instead he beckoned to Jordan and led him outside the manor house he was using as his temporary home. Only then did his anger show, though he took care not to raise his voice as he admonished him.

'Never say that about one of your name, Jordan. If your grandfather were here and heard you he would have booted you round the encampment. You are a de Hauteville, think and act like one. Never even dream of spilling the blood of your family. Now return with me inside, and make out what you said was a jest.'

Back inside, he looked at the fellow come to plead. 'You want me to rescue him?'

'Yes.'

'I doubt the folk of Gerace will harm him.'

'There are those who might, Roger, young firebrands and the like, as well as those who lost their fathers to him years ago.'

'Am I permitted to speak?' asked Ralph de Boeuf. 'You cannot even contemplate leaving them in his hands, Roger, and you know it.'

Roger smiled. 'A period of confinement might temper his pride.'

'It is more likely to fire his irritation, and having been on the end of that only God knows where it will lead.'

In truth, much as he was deriving great pleasure from what had occurred, Roger knew he had no alternative; he would have laughed out loud if it had not been so unseemly. To leave Robert was too risky: if Jordan in his youth could be so foolish so could his contemporaries in Gerace. Good sense was not often gifted to the young, nor any thought for consequence.

'Odo, go ahead. Ask the elders of Gerace to meet me outside the town under my personal safe conduct.'

'Shall I tell them anything?'

'Yes, tell them I am far from pleased. No, tell them you could not face any more of my fury.'

Robert, confined to a small chamber, was chafing at the bit, wondering what the hell was going on: surely these peasants could not be foolish enough to keep him confined? Not that he was in discomfort: he had been well fed, had slept on a decent bed and looked hard at anyone who entered, they being terrified before doing so and more so when they departed. If he had been told that his was a name they used to frighten their children, he would have been pleased.

'Terrified' was the word that would have equally applied to those on the way to meet with Roger, given Odo had not been gentle in his delivery. Much as they respected the younger brother, there was not one among them inclined to repose unbridled faith in a barbarian Norman, a race given to much passion, and bloody-minded with it, even if some lived amongst them. Greeks regarded such people as ruffians, with none of the subtle philosophy of their betters: they acted like spoilt brats instead of mature adults.

Roger's hard look when they came before him did nothing to soften their anxieties and that deepened when he tongue-lashed them for holding his brother captive, though they were pleased that none of the *Guiscard*'s own lances appeared to be present. 'Did you send to me to tell me, as it was your duty to do? No, one of your number with more sense, he being a Norman, was the one who saw what must be done.'

'We were troubled as to what course to take, Lord Roger.'

'Your course was simple,' he yelled. 'Your duty was to hand the Duke of Apulia over to me.'

'Which we will happily do now,' cried one elder, relieved to be shot of a burden with which he did not want to have to deal.

'Then take me to him now.'

Roger deliberately set a firm pace, obliging these elders to move faster than their natural gait, so they were breathless and stumbling by the time they made the main square before the now open church. No evidence of the previous bloody murder was apparent – that had been washed clean – but a messenger of more puff had rushed ahead so that Robert was on one side of the square when Roger entered from the other, followed by Jordan and Ralph de Boeuf. The youngster glared at Robert; Ralph could not help but smile.

'Well, Robert, I see you have made a fool of yourself.'

'It gives me pleasure to greet a brother who has outshone me in that. I need hardly mention your first incursion into Sicily.'

'Then it is a family trait as I told you at Enna.'

All around them stood the citizens of Gerace, wondering what was going to happen. Would the Lord Roger take this opportunity to slay his brother and if he did, how would that rebound on their town? That it made sense did not make it welcome: they were in dispute and even in such a backwater it was known what the younger of the brothers would stand to inherit – the whole of the *Guiscard*'s holdings.

'What a family we are, brother.'

'There is not a soul in Christendom who does not rate us remarkable for what we have gained, given what we had, which was nothing when we started out from the Contentin.'

'And here I have you in my power, not something to which I'm accustomed. What would Tancred say I should do?'

'I think Tancred would remind you of a vow I took and you did not.'

'And what would you do if the positions were reversed?'

Robert actually laughed. 'Why, Sprat, I'd box your ears.'

With the exception of Ralph de Boeuf, who was sure he knew what was coming, not a jaw was not dropped by what happened next. Without another word the two de Hautevilles moved towards each other and, gleefully, they threw their arms around each other in an embrace later described as like that between Benjamin and Joseph of biblical fame.

'Don't call me Sprat,' Roger said.

'What in God's name am I to call you if not that?'

Robert had pushed his brother back to arm's length before Roger replied, still in high humour. 'I can think of one or two titles that might suit.'

Robert responded with the kind of laugh that shook rafters. 'Come to think of it, Sprat, so can I.'

'No harm to come to Gerace?'

'None, Roger, they have not harmed anything bar my conceit.'

'Which would not suffer from the odd wound.' The pause was short before Roger asked, 'And me?'

'Everything you are owed, I give you my word.'

'There is a church there,' Roger said, jerking his head. 'Would it trouble you to know I would be happier to hear you swear that before God?'

'Lead on.'

Arm in arm, the pair walked towards the church, disappearing into its cool interior where, kneeling Robert de Hauteville swore to respect every promise he had ever made his brother.

'And now, Robert, I invite you back to *my* castle of Mileto, where we will have a feast of celebration and talk of future matters, not least how we are going to divide the revenues of Calabria, so that when the Devil visits your bedchamber, you are not tempted to renege.'

Sichelgaita was back in her tent when the horns blew to signal the return of her husband. As soon as she was outside it was obvious that Roger was with him and, given he was riding by his side, no captive. Close to the castle Roger peeled off with his knights and rode to the rapidly opening gates, there to be welcomed by a beaming Judith. Given the numbers to be entertained, the feast had to be held in the open and since it took time to prepare, Judith had the chance to send for musicians and singers from her half-brother's Abbey of St Eufemia.

That time also allowed her to talk to Roger about Sichelgaita's unspoken anxieties, and if she was troubled by his silence in response, at least she had a good idea of what prompted it. Naturally Robert and his wife had forsaken their tents and moved into Mileto, so the uncle had an opportunity to gaze into the crib of his nephew. Anyone watching would have worried at the way he failed to smile, indeed what they saw was a frown, for Roger de Hauteville was thinking that, should this dilemma ever be faced, he could not do that which he knew he was about to be asked.

Most of the time was spent with Robert, haggling over how to divide the revenues of the province, no easy matter since each fief had a different value and trading them off to find a balance was a nightmare. Finally they compromised by dividing every one equally: each would hold half the land and each would collect and keep half the revenues. Neither thought it anything other than a dog's breakfast, but it answered what was quite obvious: their continuing and deep mutual suspicion.

More harmonious were their discussions of what to do about the future, with Roger persuading a not-too-hard-to-sway Robert that Sicily should be a priority and that their next campaign was one which must be properly plotted to not only invade but hold whatever they conquered.

'And then,' Robert said, 'there is Bari.'

'I will not begin to advise you on that, brother, my priority is Sicily.'

'There is something I must ask of you, Roger, Sichelgaita insists on it.'

Knowing what was coming, Roger's reply was guarded. 'And you do not?'

'Yes.'

'Your son?'

'You guessed.'

'That would not be difficult.'

'I must tell you that in marrying Sichelgaita I have gained a great deal.' Seeing Roger begin to smile, he snapped, 'No jests about her size, please! I would also say that her having given birth to what is seen as a Lombard prince has eased my life.'

'I cannot give you or Sichelgaita a guarantee, Robert, you know that.'

'Sadly, I do, but I would ask you to give me your solemn oath to do your best for the boy. If we Normans stand to lose everything we have gained in Italy, no child, even my son, is worth such a price.'

'I would never harm him.'

'That I take for granted. He might be seen as a Lombard prince but his name is the same as yours, but if you can allow him to inherit, I would ask that you do so and guard against others who might challenge his right.'

From what Roger knew, if his namesake had anything to fear it was from Bohemund, who, if reports had any truth, looked likely to grow up the image in size of his father. The same might apply to his Geoffrey and Jordan. Inheritance was fraught with peril regardless of the level of power; was it not an oft-told tale that one Duke of Normandy had murdered his own brother to gain the title? The future could not be seen, but an answer was required and he gave the only one he could.

'If I live, brother, which is in God's hands.'

'Are we not all in that?' Robert sighed. 'Do I have your word?'

'If I can, I will.'

'Thank you.'

'That, Robert, is the first time I think you have ever said those words to me.'

'Cherish them,' Robert barked, 'it could be the last. Now to the great hall where your wife is waiting, as is mine, along with all your knights and the Abbot of St Eufemia, to bless what I am about to do.'

'Which is?'

'To give you that title you so hanker after, brother.'

'Which will be?'

'Count of Sicily, Roger, what else?'

# CHAPTER TWENTY-TWO

To Roger the time spent arguing with Robert was time wasted and nothing proved such a truth more than the news that the Ibn-al-Tinnah had been ambushed, his forces soundly beaten and he himself assassinated. Worse, the Norman garrison of Troina, which, like Rometta barred the route to Messina, had abandoned the castle for fear of what would come next. The Saracens loyal to al-Tinnah had fled the town in their entirety.

Within days Roger was on his way with three hundred knights, this time taking not only Jordan but also Judith – Geoffrey, now weaned, being left with a nurse. Judith was happy to go whatever the reason, much preferring to be with her husband than to be stuck in Mileto; Roger wanted her not just for her company, which he missed when they were parted, but to show the Sicilians he was committed enough to the conquest of the island to settle there.

There was no delay at Messina: Roger and his lances rode straight to the stout fortress right in the shadow of Mount Etna, the most forward stronghold of the late al-Tinnah, surprised and delighted to find that no attempt had been made to take what was a castle devoid of a proper defence, proof that Ibn-al-Hawas had not yet recovered from the drubbing Robert had inflicted upon his army below Enna. Slowly he rode into the lower part of Troina, which rose through narrow streets to the upper town and the castle, expecting to be greeted as a saviour, nonplussed by the lack of zeal shown by the locals: indeed they seemed sullen.

That was not something to which he could give much thought: this was to be his base for future operations into Saracen territory and an inspection of the fortification showed repairs were necessary. Once they had been completed and a suitable set of rooms made good for Judith, he detached thirty knights to guard the place and rode off with Jordan to seek out his enemies.

Had he stopped to enquire, Roger would have seen more than a surly population. All Greeks now, they had begun to think the Normans worse than the Saracen overlords who preceded them, more abrupt in their manner and too free with both the wine and the local women. Then there was the way they enforced their Roman rites in the church ceremonies, that causing more resentment than their unseemly behaviour. No sooner had Roger disappeared than the plotting started and he had not been gone a week by the time the first uprising broke out, signalled by the sudden disappearance from the castle of every one of the Greek servants, including the women who had attended Judith.

That first disturbance, a riot in the streets, was quickly brought under control, but was not, as his men thought, trouble snuffed out. Like one of those smouldering forest fires that plagued the surrounding hills in high summer, problems broke out sporadically and it began, with the help of Orthodox priests, to form into a proper rebellion, until the garrison of Troina had a full-scale revolt on their hands. The target of the insurgents was simple and would have been telling had they succeeded: the Greeks would capture

Judith and use her to bargain with the Count of Sicily. Let him take his garrison, let him leave them in peace and his wife would be spared.

Sudden as it was, they had underestimated those with whom they must deal: the knights left behind were Roger's own conroys, some of whom had come with him from Normandy, and his wife was of the same race – for her to show fear, for her to even think of discussing terms, was anathema. Neither were the knights guarding her content to be constrained: they sallied out to meet the rebellion head-on, fighting in the constricted streets and even narrower alleys, constantly needing to defend their rear as much as their front, determined not to be driven inexorably back towards the castle. More tellingly they got away a mounted messenger to tell their leader what was happening.

The numbers seemed too great to contest and were growing: it was as if every Greek in Troina were now fighting, men in the hundreds and getting more numerous by the day, making it increasingly difficult for the garrison to hold the upper town to keep the citadel safe. Operating as conroys, constantly attacking instead of waiting for the Greek assaults, they kept their enemies guessing as to where they would appear next and in what number, driving them downhill time and again.

Roger, besieging the nearby town of Nicosia, left as soon as he heard the news and flogged his horses half to death to get back to Troina, storming into the town and driving a wedge through the Greeks until he could join up with the men he had left behind, now sorely depleted and with every one of them carrying wounds, his first call to reassure his wife that, despite the loss of a third of the garrison, all was now well.

'You are safe, Judith.'

'I was not afraid, husband, do not ever think that I was.'

That got her a bear hug that lifted her bodily and he spun her round. 'No, you would not be, but I need to leave you again. I must go out and assess the difficulties we face.'

His attempt to depart was stopped by a strong pull. 'Go, but do not stay away too long. I have missed you.'

'Not as much, my love, as I have missed you.'

'I look forward to testing that,' she breathed.

'Damn you, woman, let me be till I am done with my work.'

'Father?'

Jordan was in the doorway, looking anxious; if he had overheard that uxorious exchange he showed no sign of being abashed. It was something he had witnessed before and a fact much remarked on in the world in which they lived, Roger de Hauteville loved his wife and she demonstrably returned his feelings in equal measure.

'I have been out in the lower part of the town.'

'What!'

'I went in disguise.'

Looking at his blond hair, Roger was angry. 'You would need soot to hide your race.'

'We do not just face Greeks. There are Saracens flooding into the lower sections. I think they have come to make common cause.'

Roger was out of the chamber immediately, Jordan at his heels, for this was, if true, very serious. His plan had been to wait until the morrow, then issue an ultimatum to the inhabitants, to come back to their allegiance or face his wrath, a telling threat given his numbers. But if his opponents were more numerous than he thought, such a warning might be wasted. As he exited the castle gate half a dozen men fell in behind him, following as he strode through the rapidly darkening streets, feeling as he did so the chill in the evening air.

It was as well he had that escort for, at every turn, he found his way blocked by mobs of armed men, as many Saracens as Greeks, an oddity since there was little love lost between them, which led to an unpleasant conclusion based on that sullenness he had experienced on first arrival: much as they despised each other they hated the Normans more.

Such a combination had another troubling facet: with both Greeks and Saracens against him, it indicated the whole country around Troina was hostile, which meant he was cut off from Messina and assistance. The option did exist to fight his way out and he knew, even if he sustained losses, he would succeed, but that meant the abandonment of Troina and that he could not countenance.

'We are going to stay and we are going to wear them down,' he said to his men assembled. 'Everybody out and barricade the streets leading to the citadel, we must hold them away from the walls.'

'Surely they are strong enough?' Jordan asked.

That got the youngster a look from the more experienced knights: you did not question such commands in the situation in which they found themselves, even from someone as understanding as Roger – you obeyed them.

'A lesson, Jordan,' Roger replied gently. 'In this kind of situation never let locals near your walls and always worry that one will betray you to your enemies if besieged. We have built on what was here before us and the Saracens built on what was here before them. If there is a secret way into this castle, or some flaw in the defence, who would know it best?'

'Those who live by its side?'

'And have done for generations. I have known boys climb cliffs to supposedly impregnable fortresses that would defeat the most puissant warrior. Why? Because they know the way, knowledge handed down from father to son and brother to brother. So, we will keep them behind barricades, which has the added advantage of forcing them to fight us in small numbers. On the concourse before the gates, we could be overwhelmed. Only if those barricades fail must we rely on the castle walls.'

They worked hard into the dark and through the night, fighting often to repel those who wished to contest their placements, incurring wounds but inflicting more. Carts were overturned, houses stripped of their timbers, even their doors pressed into service, anything used that would serve to block an approach, creating a barrier that could be defended. Roger, meanwhile, was in the storerooms, to assess the state of their provender. That done, and he satisfied they could hold out for a long time, he finally retired to bed. Judith, despite the hour, was waiting for him.

'We are trapped, Judith.'

This was said as she lay in the crook of his arm, both of them in a blissful state of post-coital well-being.

'Surely men will come from Messina to help?'

'In time, and always with the caveat they are not occupied elsewhere. But they will not risk Messina to save Troina.'

Kissing his chest she murmured. 'There are worse things, husband, than being besieged with you.'

'Don't let my men hear you say that.'


The first snow came within a week, having long blanketed the higher slopes of Mount Etna, the volcano smoking and rumbling angrily in the near distance as if peace were impossible. No more did studded boots ring on cobbles; now they moved silently about on a bed of soft white powder. Men sat round blazing fires fed by the ample wood store of the castle above the smoking chimneys of the lower town. If the snow masked the noise of boots it also hid the preparations for any attack, which were launched often, with the Greeks, aided by an increasing number of Saracens, probing for weakness, so that every day involved a raft of small conflicts, with Roger's men rushing from one hot spot to another to keep them at bay, action that took a steady toll on his numbers.

Roger had his sources of information: not all the Greeks were happy with rebellion: many had prospered from a Norman presence, wine shop owners and the like. So he knew the numbers he faced and their composition, though that brought him scant comfort. News having spread, every Saracen for leagues around had come to aid the Greek cause, contingents arriving also from the surrounding towns, which explained how his enemies were able to keep up their pressure, launching sorties at varying points to keep him and his defenders off balance.

It was when that stopped, after the first four weeks, that Roger really began to fret, for it indicated that those keeping them confined had decided to settle for a different outcome, starving him out. He launched attacks, moving aside barricades to raid the lower town and slaughter those he found there, as well as stealing their stores. It was hard and dangerous fighting in which men died and were wounded, and too often Roger found he needed to restrain his overenthusiastic son, who seemed intent on getting himself killed or maimed. Jordan was filling out by the day, turning into a fully grown man before his eyes, still seeking to impress his father, unwilling, despite constant repetition, to accept it was unnecessary.

They started to eat their horses before Christmastide, two

months into the siege, and in his daily examination of the
storerooms Roger was bleakly aware of what was needed to feed
his remaining fighting men, over two hundred in number, plus the
wounded, anything they managed to plunder a drop in an ocean
of consumption. No sign had come of any kind of relief, and
while he could speculate endlessly on the reasons for that, it was
pointless: if it came it came, if it did not and this cordon around
his castle was maintained, he was going to be in serious difficulty,
which made him curse the fact that he had brought Judith to this
place.

That was not a regret shared by his lances; they saw her as a
talisman. Judith tended the sick and spoke with them all and what
she did not know about their families and how they came to be in
Sicily she soon learnt. If food was scarce, she insisted by rotation
that, conroy by conroy, her husband's knights should eat at high
table in the great hall to underline their shared difficulty. If Roger
was in love with her, by the time it came to celebrate the birth
date of Jesus Christ, so were half the garrison.

The high hills in which Troina stood were now in the grip of
deep winter, the whole landscape blindingly white, the air crisp in
the day if the sun shone, freezing when cloudy and at night. It was
some comfort to Roger to know that, sentinels keeping watch on
the barricades aside, he and his lances were in reasonable comfort.
His tactic of launching surprise raids, which he kept up night after
night, burdened his besiegers more than it weighed on him: he
had professional fighting men, those they attacked were not good
in a sharp combat, meaning they had to keep greater numbers
in position to ward off his raids than he employed to undertake
them.

Yet there was the gnawing worry of where it was all going to lead, a feeling that grew as week followed week. The Greeks and Saracens had access to the countryside and supplies, which, even in the midst of winter, gave them meat to eat and wood to burn, this while he was running short on both. By the third month the horses were gone and the garrison was eating their oats, the stores of hay long gone onto the fires that kept them warm. Every building inside his barricades had been stripped of timber and they were now knocking out roofs to get at the beams and still there was no sign that his plight had registered in Messina.

One tactic he initiated seemed to be paying dividends, his instruction that if those of his enemies opposite his barricades lit a fire it should be a signal for an immediate assault. If they were going to confine him and his men let them do so cold: it took time for the Greeks and Saracens to realise this, but come to the sense of it they did and, each night, they huddled in their defences, often while snow fell around them, which was at least warmer than a clear and frosty night.

'They are drinking wine to ward off the chill,' Jordan said.

This information was imparted through chattering teeth. He had been out, in the snow, now melting off his discarded cloak, on one of his daredevil escapades, which he continued in spite of a direct instruction to desist, and he was now trying, at what were feeble flames, to get the blood flowing through his frozen frame. Roger, angry with the continued insubordination, could not help but notice the drawn nature of his son's face, which was not brought on by fatigue but by lack of food. It was the same with all of his lances, the sick now added to the wounded and that included the man he relied on most, a fever-stricken Ralph de Boeuf; he had cut the rations but it took no genius to work out that they were running out of the means to stay alive. If something did not break soon, he would be obliged to surrender.

'The Greeks, yes,' he agreed, pulling his fur cloak tighter round his frame, 'but Islam forbids its sons to drink wine.'

'Why do you never believe what I say, Father?' Jordan asked brusquely.

It was an unaccustomed tone from his son and Roger was about to react as he thought he should, only to realise that it was induced as much by hunger as anger at him.

'Do I not?'

'No. And you diminish me in front of others every time I speak.'

'You cannot fault me, surely, for trying to teach you what you need to know.'

'I can fault you for doing so in public.'

'If I do so, it is for your own good,' Roger barked, his patience with being corrected evaporating.

'Then,' Jordan responded, equally sharp, 'for your own good, go out and see if what I have just told you is the truth.'

Roger's hand was raised but he did not strike, partly because Jordan showed no sign of seeking to avoid the coming blow. Instead he stood. 'Get your cloak back on and show me.'

Out on the concourse before the castle it was like daylight, with the full moon high in the sky reflecting off the deep snow. Roger stopped to talk to a party of his men coming back from their short duty as sentinels – no one could stay out too long – and established that all was quiet from where they had come.

'Apart from the singing,' one said.

'Singing?' Roger demanded.

'More chanting,' another replied, 'I think to keep up their spirits.'

'It's good to know they are so low.' Roger regretted that as soon as he said it, for in the eyes of the man he was speaking to lay clear evidence that they all knew of their situation: they too were low in spirits. 'Go inside, get warm.'

'Sire, I have forgotten what warm is like.'

'How long do we have, Father?' Jordan asked in a soft voice as they parted company with the sentinels.

'It will be time when you can play a tune on your ribs,' Roger replied in a determined tone. 'And we are not there yet.'

But the thought nagged at him, as he walked ahead of his son: surrender was not more than a week away.

The soft chanting he heard as soon as he joined the men who had just relieved those to whom he had spoken, heavily cloaked, flapping their arms to stay warm, who had learnt weeks before this moment that to touch your sword blade with an ungloved hand was to lose your skin.

'How long has this been going on?' Roger asked.

'A few days.'

'Jordan says they are drinking wine, even the Saracens.'

'Lucky them,' the fellow responded.

The Normans had run out of that first and been forced to part with anything they had managed to plunder to pay those willing to smuggle a few skins into them; rough as it was it assuaged their anxieties. It was from that source, in a broken-down house with a connecting cellar to the other side of the barricades, he discovered the truth of what Jordan was telling him. Of all the garrison, he had the most with which to trade and he used the contact to seek news, always negative, of any form of relief coming his way. When he tried to bargain for some wine, he found the price had gone up and the quality, never high, had plummeted.

'Saracens are drinking it by the tun barrel now,' his contact whispered. 'Their imams have given them absolution for the sin. Can't get enough now they've found out what a pleasure there is in the grape.'

'By the tun barrel?'

'And the rest. Taking more and more each day and hauling skins out with 'em on guard.'

Later, wandering through the now cavern-like storerooms, which months before had been full to bursting, Roger mulled over how to use this information. Time was not running out, it was gone. Something had to be done, yet he was in a worse position now than he had been originally. When first besieged, breaking out would have been bloody, but a goodly number of Normans could have got out of Troina town and, mounted, they would have got away. Now, with men weakened by hunger and no horses, he would have to fight his way out on foot, leaving those like Ralph who could not do battle, against odds he could not calculate, and to what? Countryside in the grip of winter and one in which, unfriendly and dangerous, they could all die.

Over the next few days he could see, in every eye that met his, men resigned to their fate. The only person not so affected was Judith, locked in her self-imposed concerns for the sick and infirm, she being the only one with whom he could openly share his concerns. Her response was to gently drag him to his knees and tell him to pray, tell him that God had got him to his title and only God would save them all. If he prayed with her, and he did, it was with less conviction than she exhibited.

Hunger that woke him in the night, a griping in his stomach that making sleep impossible, got him up and out into the cold air, under a black sky, with no moon and some cloud. He had avoided middle-of-the-night visits to his outposts, which might imply he did not trust his captains to keep alert their men, but he went round them this time and what struck him by the time he had reached the third barricade was the utter silence. There was no soft singing or chanting from the other side of the kind he had heard before.

Unbuckling his sword, Roger took out his knife and, ordering those on duty to be ready to catch him, he climbed to the top of the barricade and stood in what should have been plain view. Nothing happened, so gingerly he crept down the opposite side, not easy on a roughly constructed barrier, all the while conscious he was making noises that, in his ears, sounded like thunderclaps. Still there was no response and it was with one foot on the ground that he heard the first of the gentle snoring.

Just then the clouds parted enough to show a mass of stars, giving him light to see the huddled sleepers resting against the barricade. The snoring was very evident now; the whole lot of them were asleep and each had either in his hand or at his side an empty wineskin. He could not shout, that risked waking them, so, just as cautiously, he climbed back to the top and called softly to his men to take off their swords and join him, sending one fellow back to the castle to rouse out every man now sleeping.

Back down again, with both feet on the ground, Roger helped his men negotiate their descent, urging silence until they were lined up, knives at the ready, each one marking a slumbering enemy. Their throats were cut, quickly and, if you set aside the gurgling of slashed jugulars, silently, the smell of their blood mixing with the odour of their bodies, neither as strong as that of stale, vinegary wine.

It was a long night as, one by one, Roger's men took each barricade, only very rarely leaving a sentinel alive and, if they woke and fled, which they did, found themselves running into parties of

Normans at their back, men who had circled round soundlessly through deserted, snow-covered streets, to take them in the rear. Before dawn, Roger had got down to the lower town with his whole strength, to take in their beds and slay the men who had trapped him for so long. Troina was his again when the sun rose.

The revenge was awful, but it needed to be: Greeks suffered much, but the Saracens who had come to kill him and his men and who had survived the night, died to a man, the snow in the gutters washed away by their warm blood. He crucified the Orthodox priests and burnt at the stake the elders of the town, for these men had sworn fealty to the cause of Ibn-al-Tinnah and had betrayed their oath.

'Let it be known throughout this island,' he said, to those he spared. 'I am the Count of Sicily and your liege lord. Break your bond to me and this you have witnessed will be the result.'

The triumph of retaking the town was followed, naturally, by a great feast, and the still sullen, if chastened Greeks of Troina – there was not a Saracen left – were obliged to witness their restored lords and masters roast and eat oxen and consume as much wine as had led to their victory. Yet the Normans were becalmed without their greatest asset, horses and mobility. Roger's first task was to speed back to Calabria to find replacements, leaving Judith in charge of Troina.

She played her part, touring the outposts each night to ensure that all was well, as the snows began to melt and spring came in the shadow of belching Etna. Roger was back within two months with a full complement of mounts, leading Serlo, foot soldiers and more lances, though not of sufficient numbers to replace his losses. The conquest of Sicily could continue, albeit with a much-depleted force: the retaking of Troina had cost Roger dear.

# CHAPTER TWENTY-THREE

'Take and hold, take and hold,' was the mantra oft repeated by Roger de Hauteville, yet it remained just that: words, not an achievement. He never had the numbers he needed to keep the ground on which he won contest after contest, endless skirmishes with bodies of Saracens of a varying size, but never an army – they seemed intent on avoiding battle. Two years had passed since his first incursion and still he could not claim to hold even the land between Troina and Messina. He raided out from the former taking much booty but also learning of developments, which boded ill for the future.

The death of Ibn-al-Tinnah had removed the major obstacle to Saracen cohesion and they now began to cooperate in order to fight him. While he had been besieged in Troina reinforcements even came in from North Africa, led by the two oldest sons of the reigning sultan, each with an army of several thousand men. Appeals to Robert for aid fell on deaf ears: he had his own problems in Apulia, more now with rebellious Norman barons and Greeks than Lombards. The only reinforcements Roger could muster were a few hundred Calabrians and a small body of crossbowmen.

Successes he had: he won every fight in which he became engaged. Troina's storerooms were again full to bursting and in order to draw his enemies on he moved his base some three leagues further north-west to a small walled town called Cerami, standing on a river of the same name, it having several advantages over Troina. Surrounded by high hills, it gave him a good view of the valley approaches by which he thought his enemies would come and in this he was proved correct. The Saracen host were finally approaching to give him the battle he so wanted and he knew it long before they threatened his position. He also knew the size, which, given the ground they covered, was close to being incalculable. The Normans were accustomed to being outnumbered, but this seemed to be of a different order of magnitude: if the reports he had were true, he was facing, with an army of some six hundred, including *milities,* some fifteen thousand men!

Only a third of his force were lances, yet the thought of retreat never entered Roger's head: whatever the odds he would fight them here, on ground he had chosen, with Cerami at his back and the river before him, sure that those who had done battle with the Normans before would have learnt nothing, while the men from North Africa, probably the bulk of his opponents, had never met warriors like those he led. Besides, numbers did not confer skill and in some cases they could be a liability. Notions had been voiced that he should retire to Troina and allow them to break themselves on its walls, but Roger had no desire to be besieged again. He did want to hold Cerami, so when news came that a large force had been detached to work round his flank and occupy the town he sent Serlo and Jordan to prevent it.

His nephew had been promising, now he was more than that and he was also Jordan's hero. Like any de Hauteville, Serlo led from the front and fought with a panache that few could match, adding to that a clear tactical brain and the ability to hold in close control those he commanded, this proved in the confines of Cerami. Faced with several thousand Saracens and in command of only fifty knights, he drove them out street by street, then routed them in the open, before disengaging to rush back to aid his uncle. What he saw then, cresting the hills on the opposite bank of the narrow river was enough to daunt the most stalwart knight.

The whole landscape was covered in men, horses, donkeys and camels, the dust they were kicking up on their march like a sandstorm. Facing them, on an upslope across the river, stood Roger's tiny host, his lances on foot, their horses well to the rear and his contingents of *milities* holding the flanks which, luckily, were protected by ground so broken as to be near impassable even to infantry. It looked to Serlo as if their confrères would be swept aside.

'How many are there?' Jordan gasped.

Serlo laughed, to spread relief. 'Not enough, cousin, not enough.'

Instead of coming on, and a sign that for all their numbers they lacked confidence, the enemy army stopped and began to make camp, an action which took hours, so numerous were they. Jordan had been sent to ask his father what he wanted Serlo to do. The answer he brought back was stay where they stood and when dawn arrived to be mounted. Night fell over so many campfires that the clouds, orange in colour, gave off enough light to see a face clearly, sound travelling easily to carry the cries of the imams calling their faithful to prayer.

Roger had his men sleep and waited till grey dawn to call upon his priest to bless them. The sound of their murmured prayers did not match the calling of the imams, nor did they make any noise as, confessed, they took the host. In each mind, Roger's included, there would be an image of a loving wife, or perhaps a concubine for whom they had regard, a mother, a child or maybe just the green fields and high hedgerows of Normandy. Few had any certainty that they would survive this day, but by the time the sun was on their backs, every man was sure he had God's blessing and was ready, if he was required to, to meet his Maker with a sin-free soul.

Their enemies had likewise stirred with the sun, a bustling mass of bodies, the Sicilians clad in garments of all colours to denote their various emirs, the North Africans easy to detect, they being dressed in all-covering black. Roger was more interested in seeking out the princes who led them, Ali and Ayub, sons of the Zirid sultan who ruled the old Roman provinces on the southern Mediterranean shore. Like Ibn-al-Hawas they were identified by the imperious way they rode to and fro on their splendid mounts, along the front of their levies, who cheered them as they passed, and that cemented another thought: Robert had beaten Al-Hawas at Enna; the two sons of a sultan might have richer blood than those they led, but that did not make them good leaders in war.

They, peering back, would have seen what looked like a silver thread running across the landscape, a thin line of mailed knights, with their teardrop shields and polished conical helmets. Perhaps they would have laughed to see so feeble a presence, pointed to the rabble on either flank, before them rows of embedded pikes, there to impale any horseman foolish enough to charge their lines, backed by a few crossbowmen. Whatever, it would seem to them that to sweep aside a single ribbon of Normans would be simple; their pike- and bowmen could be slaughtered later. Trumpets blew, the cheering rose, and the leading elements of the Saracen army began to wade the river, forming into one massive, deep column, aimed straight at the blue and white shield of the Count of Sicily.

'They don't seem much interested in Serlo,' Ralph de Boeuf said, long fully recovered.

There was no alarm in his voice: it was merely a statement of what he and Roger could see, the Saracens were detaching no men to protect their flank against Serlo and his mounted lances. Their tactic, if it could be graced with such a name, was to be an all-out frontal assault.

'They aim to brush us aside,' Roger replied.

Ralph actually laughed. 'Can they not spot a wall when they see one?'

'God be with you, Ralph,' Roger said, at the point where he could see the determination in the eyes of the Saracen front rank.

'He is with us all,' Ralph replied, 'but note it, the men who lead this host are not with them.'

'They lead from the rear.'

'A collection of farts, then?' Ralph joked.

Roger still had the opportunity to stand before his lances and give a rousing speech, but this was not a time in which rhetoric would be appropriate. Every man he led knew that they had one simple task, to stand firm in their line or to die.

'Shields and lances,' he said, without much raising his voice.

That was answered down his line: seventy Normans strong on either side of their leader, like a ripple, as shields came up and lances were lowered to form a solid wall of steel, and each man checked his other weapons – axes and knives – were to hand.

Following on from a shout of '*Allah Akbar*', the men before them rushed forward to do battle, their voices rising into a terrifying roar. A wise general puts his best fighting men in his front line and even the divided command of the Saracens had taken that elementary course, so the fiercest combat of the day was at the very outset of the battle. Roger's line was hard pressed, swaying back and forth like rippling waters as they were pressed back in some sections.

Yet the line never fractured: if a man fell it contracted a fraction, and those under pressure knew they had to regain the few footsteps of ground surrendered to hold the cohesion of the whole, fighting with extra ferocity to do so. The leading elements of the Saracens had died on Norman lances and they were either now wrenched out of mailed hands by falling bodies or useless without their metal tips. The positions were thus reversed: it was now the Normans fighting off lance points with swords and axes, yet those seeking to kill them had great difficulty in controlling what they did, so great was the press behind them.

Roger had chosen his field of battle well; he knew the enemy he was going to face would vastly outnumber him, just as he suspected with such superiority they could not resist the temptation to attack – even if it was mooted in a divided command, the wise head who gainsaid such a course would risk ridicule. For all their numbers the Saracens could only deploy so many in the constricted killing zone he had imposed on them and he being on an upslope meant the elements to the rear had no idea what was going on in front of them, while those at the front arrived before him short on breath.

Buoyed up by the prospect of a kill and glory, they pressured the leading fighters onto the Norman line, denying them the ability to manoeuvre in their individual combats, for that was what it became: one Norman fighting at best two Saracens, never any more, levies doing battle with men who trained every day in individual combat. After the first rush those coming on had another obstacle, the bodies of those either already slain or writhing with wounds too serious to allow them to crawl away. They died, too, crushed as their fellows clambered over them to get at the defence, the new assailants slithering and slipping either on their uneven flesh or the huge quantities of blood that flowed into the muddy trampled ground.

Wisdom would have had the Saracens call off the attack and regroup; that was not present and the fools in command let their suffering cohorts continue to press. Now the quality of the men the Normans faced was falling as each successive wave suffered wounds and death, while having to clamber over an increasing wall of bodies just to get at their enemies. Roger could see, like every one of his confrères, the fear in the eyes of the men he was now fighting. What was driving them on now was not zeal but the weight of their fellows on their backs.

A man afraid to die in battle is at greater risk than one who fears it not, the pile of dead a rampart over which it was becoming harder and harder to climb. Roger ordered his men to undertake that, so from a position of height, once they had steadied their footholds, they could inflict terrible punishment on Saracens now cowering in fear from the sweeping blows, yet they could not escape their fate. They were not cheering now but wailing, some stupidly falling to their knees in the hope of being spared, losing their hands as well as the heads they put them to in supplication.

How they managed to keep fighting and killing would cause Roger's men to wonder long after Cerami, but the answer was simple. First it was a discipline drummed into them from childhood, next the fear of letting down the men alongside, members of your own conroy, added to that arms that had a strength and endurance lacking in their opponents. Finally it was the certain knowledge that to relax in battle, even for a blink of an eye, was to risk immediate ruin not only for yourself, but also for the whole number of your confrères.

So they fought on with throats so dry that to swallow was painful, with eyes full of stinging sweat and faces covered with spouted blood and sliced gore, slithering on the ground that was now a morass from bright-red irrigation, wondering how, at every swing of the arm, the strength was still there to lift their weapons, yet it was.

The Saracens were now still, not advancing, debarred from falling back by those following on, crowded, unsighted and less enthusiastic. Now rippling along the lines were cries of betrayal, not bravery or paeans to the Prophet. That was the point at which Serlo attacked; he had been waiting, watching anxiously, fearful that his uncle's line would fracture, intent on sacrificing his own lances to secure enough of a breathing space for them either to reform or retreat, lost in wonder at the way the line held. Jordan had been all for moving sooner: it was his father who stood to forfeit his life and the youngster had needed to be near-physically restrained.

Given his head now, Roger's bastard son outdid his hero in the ardour of his attack. For once, Serlo sought not to hold a firm line, the accustomed Norman way. With the insight given to few who command men he knew that shock was the most important contribution he could deliver on a flank of confused Saracens, who still thought the men they were pushing forward were winning, not dying. Added to that, the enemy command had so filled the field with foot soldiers that what cavalry they had could not contest with him: they were blocked off.

On the hill opposite Roger de Hauteville, the trio who led the Saracens could see what was happening, could see their aim of brushing these pests aside had not only failed but was beginning to crumble, which presaged disaster. Later Roger heard reports of their disputes, two brothers accusing each other of stupidity, then both turning on Ibn-al-Hawas to charge him with leading them into a trap. Only one of them needed to show leadership, to force his way to the front to where their soldiers were being slaughtered and effect a retreat in which they could regroup: the battle was not lost – they still massively outnumbered the Normans.

Possible it might have been, but they disputed too long. The ripple of despair began to spread through the mass of the Saracen army, now not much more than a swirling, leaderless mob, for anyone of authority had died quickly. The terror of those still expiring on Norman swords swept back to the rear elements and they began to panic. Allah might promise them all sorts of pleasures in heaven, but life was suddenly sweeter; they began to fall back to the river, and as the pressure eased at the front they disengaged and began to run.

Now the stress was reversed: those fleeing first were not doing so quickly enough for men who had seen too much death. It was fatal to delay, to even think of slowing the pace of flight, for to do so was to be trampled to death by the more desperate, to slip in the water of the river was to drown, for the crush did not permit a chance to get back to your feet, and to compound that came Serlo's riders, pushing a wedge into the mass, cutting right and left, hacking off limbs and heads, slicing into bodies with no one man seeming to have a peck of the courage needed to stand and fight them.

Roger and his men could not pursue: they were on their knees with exhaustion, every one saying a hissed prayer to his god for their deliverance, looking before them at a wall of bleeding cadavers, and when they raised their eyes, at a field carpeted with bodies, beyond that a mass of their enemies struggling to get across the river and away into the hills where they thought they might find sanctuary. Well ahead of them rode their leaders, galloping to safety on those mounts on which they had so proudly displayed themselves earlier that day.

Serlo and his men were in pursuit, but there were simply too many fleeing Saracens in the way to make that a reality, and besides, their horses were destriers, not of the long-galloping breed. But they did, once over the brow of the opposite mound, come upon a tented camp of such magnificence it brought them to a halt. Stood in a clear piece of ground – those they had passed on their swifter mounts, which were still running, gave them a wide berth – they looked around them.

'Jordan,' Serlo shouted, 'your father will be weary, but tell him to come and cast his eye over this. I swear the sight will banish his fatigue!'

'Who can put a value on this?' Roger said, as he looked over the booty the camp of the emirs contained, the accrued wealth of several hundred years of Saracen rule in Sicily, no doubt gathered to match the magnificence of that which the sultan's sons had brought from Africa.

There were chests of gold coins, finely decorated dress armour, magnificent saddles and harness, valuable plates off which these rich Saracens ate, and ornate weapons, knives and swords in jewel-encrusted sheaths, with handles of gold and silver, studded with gems, never designed to cause harm. There were fine-bred horses that had failed to break their tethers, others that had, needing to be rounded up and fetched back, as well as dozens of camels.

The stores of the army they captured too – flocks of sheep, great tents full of grain, enough fodder to keep the Norman horses for a month – and that took no account of what Roger's *milities*, who had taken practically no part in the battle, were now stripping from the bodies that littered the field. Any not yet dead had their throats cut immediately.

'Tomorrow,' Roger said, 'when we are rested, we go into the hills into which the Saracens have fled. Every one you find is to be killed. I do not want to have to face them again.'

'There will be more, Roger,' Ralph de Boeuf sighed.

'I know, but they will not be the same fellows if we do what we must. Now, call forward the priests, we must say a Mass to thank God for so blessing our arms this day.'

Their prayers were loud this time, words of gratitude that swelled up to the heavens for this victory. All knew they had won a great fight; Roger, Serlo and Ralph de Boeuf had the wit to see they had achieved much more. In amongst their prayers of thanks were other thoughts – that now the Saracens were no longer on the offensive: they had been too soundly thrashed. Troina was safe, Messina was doubly so. What they had now taken to the east of Cerami they most definitely held.

The people of Rome stared in wonder at the quartet of beautifully decorated camels as they were led through the streets towards the Lateran Palace. They had seen camels before, but not of such groomed quality, and many an eye was looking hard at their accoutrements, trying to value the gold and silver of the harness and saddlery as well as what their huge gilded pannier might contain. Forewarned, the new pope, Alexander, flanked by his closest advisor, Archdeacon Hildebrand, was ready to receive this gift, though mystified as to from where it came.

The well-dressed and handsome youth who spoke for its delivery introduced himself as Jordan de Hauteville and let it be known that these magnificent animals and what they carried were a gift from his father, the Count of Sicily, to Holy Church, for he knew, without doubt, such a victory as Cerami could not have been possible without divine assistance. The men he had brought with him unloaded and carried into a private chamber the two heavy panniers which, when opened, revealed a fortune in gifts that had even a pontiff, accustomed to magnificence, gasp with pleasure.

'And for this, your father asks for what?' said Hildebrand, his gargoyle face full of suspicion. In his experience such gifts did not come without a price attached.

'Nothing,' Jordan said, 'but the further blessing of the Church on his enterprise against the infidel.'

'How did you come by this, my son?' asked Alexander, in a softer tone.

The story took time, so much that the Pope and his archdeacon required chairs to ease their legs, for Jordan, proud of his family, was not content to relate merely the bare facts. He made it a saga, embellishing every act by Count Roger and his Uncle Serlo, though careful when he came to his own actions to sound modest. Before the battle a comely youth had been seen on a white horse, bearing a fluttering banner of a red cross on a white background. He had ridden the field of battle, then seemed to ascend to heaven, so they knew it to be the presence of Saint George himself, come to bless the arms, and each man was inspired. At the conclusion of his tale, Alexander looked at Hildebrand, whose eyes were alight.

'He does God's work, Your Holiness,' Hildebrand barked. 'Too long has Islam lorded over lands once Christian.'

'You have spoken of it often,' Alexander replied, with an expression and a tone that implied Hildebrand might have laboured the point too heavily. 'And you know I share your hope to see such possessions once more under the jurisdiction of my Church.'

'Then let Sicily be the place first brought back to the one true faith. Let us bless Count Roger and charge him with the task of clearing Islam out of that accursed island. Let him be a soldier for Christ, and those he leads likewise.'

Alexander nodded but did not speak, yet when Jordan left Rome, he did so with a papal banner, which henceforth he was told should lead Count Roger's men into battle, only one of two in existence, the other leading the Christian knights fighting the Moors in Iberia. He also left with a papal bull granting indulgence to all those who fell in battle against the infidel – so to die was now to gain immediate entry into heaven.

'Let the infidel see,' Alexander said to Jordan as the clergy assembled to send Jordan on his way, 'that Christ comes upon them in vengeance; let them see that salvation lies in repenting their foul creed.'

# CHAPTER TWENTY-FOUR

'One more campaign, Robert, to take Palermo, with everything we can both muster, and Sicily will be ours.'

'Do not put too much faith in Alexander's banner, brother,' Robert replied.

That was not a statement to respond to: when it came to religious piety both brothers played fast and loose with devotion – God was praised when victory blessed their arms or needs, as in the recent news of the death of Argyrus, but not when predicaments arose.

'Sicily? Do I have your support?'

'Let me think on it.'

Roger smiled: that was as good as a yes.

Ever the restless warrior, they were mounted and on their way within the week, taking every lance Robert could muster, picking up foot soldiers on the way, crossing to Messina, then riding on to the west to join Serlo, stopping only at Troina so that they could spend time with Judith.

'You know, Judith,' Robert said, 'you have never apologised to me for the words you lambasted me with at Mileto.'

She replied with slight smile. 'I never thought to say sorry for speaking the truth, Robert. You are a rogue and you know it.'

'God in heaven,' he growled. 'I'd rather face the Saracens than your tongue.'

'And so you should: they you will beat.'

He laughed loud enough to fill the great hall. There was still something of the old Robert in that breast.

A night of conjugal bliss was all Roger was allowed. When battle beckoned, the *Guiscard* moved swiftly to meet it and, ignoring any obstacle on his flanks, he made straight for the Conca d'Oro, the range of hills that circled and overlooked Palermo, and therein lay his first problem. He could make no movement, attempt no manoeuvre, without being observed from the watchtowers on those heights, so that his numbers were known down to the last sutler long before he even set up camp.

That, by accident, led to a disaster: the Normans pitched their tents on a plateau infested with tarantulas and they soon emerged from their nests to sting every piece of flesh presented, producing a range of reactions which made the Normans sure they were suffering from a divine plague. Many found breathing difficult, others collapsed without knowing why they were so afflicted, others were spared, the very least effect a dose of severe, rank-smelling and continuous flatulence that made them fear the corruption of their gut. From being a force full of martial spirit, it had the effect of spreading a deepening gloom and a feeling this campaign was cursed.

Nothing that happened subsequently raised the mood: once Robert had fought his way through the mountains to the walls, Palermo was too formidable to capture with the forces he had. Not unlike Bari, they had to stand outside and watch ship after ship come and go without in any way being able to interfere: they could neither storm the city nor could they starve it out. To this dejected encampment came word of a request from Duke William of Normandy for lances to join him in invading England; with the prospect of booty elsewhere a trickle of lances began to leave and take the road home.

'I hope the bastard drowns,' was Robert's view, but that changed nothing. After fruitless months with his army diminishing and those left behind dispirited, the *Guiscard* decided that being away from Apulia for so long was unwise, so he raised the siege and headed home. Roger returned to Troina and Judith.

That departure left Roger in a quandary: the recriminations from Cerami ensured his enemies remained divided but he could not muster force enough to press home the advantage. All he could do was raid, plunder and retire, for even the forces that could contest with him melted away as soon as he appeared, more interested in fighting their rival emirs or the North African princes. He moved his base closer to Palermo in the hope that opportunity would present itself; what he got for four whole campaigning seasons was deepening frustration and he could get no aid from his beleaguered brother.

If Roger had trouble, Robert had more. In his absence a revolt had been raised by three of his own nephews. Abelard, son of Humphrey, set aside from his father's inheritance, might have just cause to rebel; the two brothers, Geoffrey and Robert, sons of his half-sister Beatrix, did so from frustration at being treated disdainfully by their uncle. The real progenitor was Joscelin, Lord of Molfetta, a knight whom the *Guiscard* had raised to prominence by his own hand. Fed with Byzantine gold, Joscelin had led the younger men astray and, given they were de Hautevilles, many had been attracted to their banner for the revolt to be easily contained; in truth, it was so serious the Duke of Apulia realised, as soon as he landed back in Calabria, he risked being overthrown.

His presence stiffened the resolve of the waverers and he had some success in checking his nephews, but once more Byzantium was ready to interfere, sending to Apulia a force of Varangians, a kind of imperial Praetorian Guard of Viking stock. They came out of Bari as the shock troops of the forces led by a new Catapan called Bisanzio, pushing Robert back – he was fighting on several fronts against his nephews – taking back Brindisi and Taranto, the situation so bad the *Guiscard* was close to swallowing his pride and calling on both Roger and his brother Mauger to come to his aid.

For all his successes with the fearsome axemen of Kiev Rus as his vanguard, Bisanzio could not gain a convincing victory any more than Robert de Hauteville, nor could Joscelin of Molfetta force a conclusion, so the campaign fell into stalemate, leaving those who had stayed to serve with Robert wondering if they would not have been better off going home: the Bastard of Falaise had won a great battle on the south coast of England, had killed King Harold Godwinson and was now in London and claiming the crown.

But time had worked for the sons of Tancred before and it did so now: in a battle between the Saracens, a decision was finally achieved with the defeat and death of Ibn-al-Hawas by the Zirid forces of Prince Ayub. The sultan's son then claimed overlordship of all Sicily, and with no one strong enough to contest him, he was acclaimed Emir of Agrigento, Enna and, most importantly, of Palermo: Sicily now had one ruler, Roger had a single enemy to fight and one who was eager to do battle with the Normans and kick them out for good.

In Apulia Robert benefited from a combination of factors: first the death of the Emperor Constantine Ducas left his widow Eudoxia in power, but the growing threat of the Seljuk Turks – pushing up the Tigris and Euphrates from Baghdad – meant the empire needed not only a man on the throne but a fighting soldier, one able to halt the inexorable Turkish advance which was beginning to threaten Constantinople itself. Eudoxia quickly wed a Cappadocian general called Romanus Diogenes and the new emperor's priorities were firmly fixed on the east: Apulia could go hang; not only did he withdraw the Varangians, he stripped Bari of a goodly portion of its garrison.

Without support, Robert *Guiscard*'s enemies were subdued one by one. Joscelin fled to Durazzo, Abelard threw himself on his uncle's mercy, while the youngest son of Beatrix was quick to follow. Brindisi and Taranto were abandoned by Byzantium; holding Bari was much more vital. The last to hold out, and he did so for months, was nephew Geoffrey, for he had a stout and difficult-to-take fortress. It required Robert to be cunning: he bribed one of Geoffrey's captains with the promise of a fief of his own on condition he opened the gates of the castle. This he did and the place was taken: the revolt was crushed.

Free at last to leave Apulia, Robert rode to Mileto to meet with Roger, taking with him his natural son, Bohemund. It was amusing to watch Jordan and Bohemund eyeing each other – both well-built young men now and, with all the de Hauteville height and muscle, like two alley cats suspiciously strutting round each other. There was sadness, too, for it was clear Roger's son Geoffrey was afflicted with leprosy. Prayers were the only hope of a cure and much gold had been expended for Masses to be said in the Calabrian monasteries, with pleas sent to Rome as well, for no child so diseased could hope to succeed to his father's titles. And, naturally, they talked of their various difficulties, not least Robert's in Apulia.

'The reason your barons are always rising against you is a lack of real war. Bring them to Sicily and let them take out their dissatisfaction on the Saracens.'

Robert was not persuaded, he had his sights set on Bari, now with a much-reduced garrison, albeit he still lacked a plan to take the place, and as Roger pressed him he became more and more irascible. It seemed as if his temper matched the greying of his hair, with him becoming less malleable with age. That his own relatives should take up arms against him had been wounding, and if Roger could see they might have just cause for discontent, his brother could not. There was no point in asking him why he treated his own blood relatives with less generosity than he showed his other followers. At least he had been avuncular enough to spare their lives, merely stripping them of part of their fiefs.

'I should have hung them from a tree, the ingrates,' Robert growled.

'And have father turn in his grave?'

'Sometimes I think he is watching me, Roger, wagging that damned finger of his.'

'Is that why you spared your nephews, Robert, because of our father?'

'They are naught but foolish boys. It was Joscelin I really wanted, but that bastard was too much of a coward to face me.'

'You would have hanged him?'

'Yes.'

'Then he was no fool to flee.'

'He's in Durazzo now, plotting something, I guarantee.'

'Another Argyrus, perhaps?'

Robert nodded with some sadness: it was as if he missed the now departed Argyrus. 'When one schemer dies another rises to take his place, but by damn I am glad he is not still in Bari.'

'Can you take it?'

'I have to try, Roger. Apulia is more united now than ever.'

Roger could not resist a jibe. 'Like Calabria.'

'Must you ever bring that up?'

'Bari,' Roger replied; there was no point in bearding his brother, reminding him that it was he who had pacified Calabria. Also it was less troublesome a province.

'Byzantium is locked in battle with the Turks, the garrison of Bari reduced and I do not see it being reinforced. Romanus Diogenes does not have the soldiers to fight in the east and the west at the same time.'

'Remember Byzantine gold, Robert. They have the means to buy more.'

'Then they'd best spend it quick, for I will be outside their walls in a month.'

'While I go back to Sicily.'

'Roger,' the *Guiscard* said, leaning forward. 'I am still your liege lord, am I not?'

Knowing what was coming did not mean Roger could not respond. 'Yes.'

'If I call upon you to come to my aid at Bari I expect you to do so, whatever is happening in Sicily.'

'I will come, brother, but if your need is so great, I would expect you to call on Mauger first.'

'I'll be damned if I will.'

'Think of our Tancred's wagging finger, Robert. How is it you can forgive your nephews yet leave your own brother out in the cold?'

'He would not come.'

'He will if you ask him.'

'He will if I promise him reward.'

'Then do so, and rest assured, if he is there, I will come when called and for nothing but the glory of seeing you ride through Bari, the same way you rode through Reggio.'

Back on Sicilian soil, Roger knew his Saracen enemy was growing stronger as he imposed his island-wide authority, yet as he imparted to anyone who would listen, they had nothing to fear from an enemy they had beaten more than once.

'What does it matter if they have a change of leader? They are not warriors as we are warriors. This Emir Ayub, is he a better leader now than he was at Cerami? Let them gather, and when they do we shall march to meet them.'

But Ayub was cautious: he marched forward and withdrew, trying to lure a too-clever enemy into a trap, while Roger was patient. The time would come and he had what he needed: when he did commit to battle it would be on a ground of his choosing.

Robert was outside Bari, examining walls he had looked at a hundred times, his mind going back to endless sieges, from Trani under William Iron Arm – so many he was not sure he could name them all. Some he had taken by storm, others by starvation, a few by guile and he knew the latter would be needed here. Bohemund was eager to hear the tale of every one, but it was when relating his ploy at Brindisi that Robert had the first inkling of an idea.

Those watching from the walls, content to stay within when the *Guiscard* was close by, saw him pull on his reins, turn his mount, and, banner flowing on the sea breeze and his knights around him, ride away. The Greeks could pride themselves that once more they had seen off the Norman barbarian. They were safe with their stout walls facing the land and the sea at their back.

'Bohemund, we are going to become sailors.'

It was a command that surprised everyone and did not go down well with many: his lances were not happy on water, but Robert was adamant that, if Bari depended on the sea for its security, then Normans must match them in that to breech its defences. Objections that fighting at sea was a skill long in the learning fell on deaf ears: Robert would have none of it.

'You fight on land, you fight on a deck, where is the difference? Does a cast lance not kill over water, does a sweeping blade not cut flesh for the salt?' He had been brought up within easy reach of the shores of the Contentin, had learnt to fish and swim in waters that froze to the marrow. 'Damn me, what I would not give for a Normandy oyster now.'

This was said so often *Guiscard*'s men began to yawn; if they disliked the sea, they hated his enthusiasm and his japes even more. It was as if the years had fallen away, as if he was once again that jest-playing buffoon who had so annoyed William and Drogo. He played pranks that had his men ending up in the water where, if they floundered, they were encouraged to learn to swim. Did he ever stop laughing in these months of preparation? No one who recalled the time thought so: the only peace they had was when he was absent on other errands related to his plan.

All were speculating on what that plan could be, but if the jolly Robert had resurfaced, the secretive one remained: he would tell no one, not even Bohemund whom he loved more than his younger son, disappointingly weedy by nature, given the size of both his parents. Not even Sichelgaita was made privy to his thinking. No one must get an inkling of what he was about, lest the defenders of Bari find out.

The time came to march and Robert looked over the thousands he had gathered outside Melfi. This was Apulia united, the army that would finally kick Byzantium out of Italy. They marched south to Venosa, to the new-built church of Santissima Trinitá were lay the remains of his family. There was a sarcophagus now, a walled tomb with painted angels and trumpets to welcome the de Hautevilles to heaven, backed by the blue and white chequer of his house. There he knelt and said prayers to his god and his deceased brothers, asking for intercession from both for what he was about to do.

They knew he was coming: Bisanzio had men working on the defences even if they were, to most minds, impossible to breach. He knew the cunning of the man he faced, was conscious he was weaker than hitherto and that there were people in Bari, even Greeks, who saw the endless conflict as a curse; men whose fortunes had diminished as the Norman advance had cut them off from the interior trade which had once made them rich. They could betray the cause of their own people: gold always appealed to some souls more than race or fealty.

The Bariots had seen the Normans outside their walls many times but never in such numbers, a cause of enough anxiety to have Masses said in every church, so the priests of the Orthodox faith could remind them it was not just stones and hearth they were defending but the way they practised their faith. Let the Normans in and they would bring Rome with them: celibate priests cut off from those to whom they administered, unleavened bread in Communion, a Holy Ghost who ranked equal with God the Father and God the Son.

As another boost to morale, Bisanzio ordered all the treasures of the city be taken onto the ramparts, where the citizens let the sunlight flash and reflect on the gold and silver plate, on religious objects of priceless value. They even dropped gold *solidi* and invited the toiling Normans to come and get them. This was aimed at Robert, of course, and he emerged from his tent to watch this spectacle designed to mock his pretensions. An accomplished master of the jest himself, a man rarely lost for words, he was not that now. Soon he was within calling distance.

'Citizens of Bari,' he shouted, 'I thank you for taking good care of my possessions. I bid you guard them carefully.'

Now it was Normans, Lombards and Italians, who were laughing; the treasures disappeared, but it was not long before a jeering crowd was back on the walls, bolstered by their faith, exchanging insults with those in earshot. The sight of a fleet of ships, dozens, then a hundred plus, first confused, then it made the Bariots laugh. They were the seafarers, and the promontory on which their city stood would always find access to the Adriatic: history told them it was too long a shoreline to be blockaded – it never had been in millennia and besides, the Normans were not sailors. Was Bisanzio the only one to worry, the only one to recall the mind with which he was in competition?

The first ship was anchored to the northern shore, to a strong jetty – one of two that had made the besieged curious when they observed them being built – the next right alongside it, then another and another. They watched as planks were laid from vessel to vessel, watched as the floating pontoon stretched out to sea then curved round to the south, each with a bridge of planking from one to the next. Still ships came to drop anchor, each one taking station in a line that began to come back to land, until the very last one tied up to the south shore and the second jetty.

Robert *Guiscard* demonstrated to the defenders what he had planned and in doing so also showed his own army, all those warriors who had been wondering what he was up to. With Bohemund at his side, to loud cheers from his whole army, he walked from ship to ship, never failing, when he could, to look at the walls before him, right round the city, to tell them inside that, for the first time in history, Bari was wholly besieged. There would be no supplies coming in to keep them from starvation, no reinforcements from the east to sustain their resolve.

If Bisanzio knew there were those inclined to surrender, so did the Duke of Apulia and he was a man who knew how to bribe. The first voices raised in Bari were of fear – this was something unknown to them – the next, talk of reassurance as the fighting men reminded them how stout were the walls. But the whispering had started in some quarters that, when Robert de Hauteville offered terms, they would be best accepted if they did not all want to die.

And then he was at the land gate, his herald calling for them to be opened. Bisanzio declined the offer to surrender. The siege of Bari was on.

# CHAPTER TWENTY-FIVE

Roger de Hauteville had one guiding principle: never to fight on a field he had not chosen – preferably one in a mountainous landscape where he could narrow the field of battle to suit his numbers, nullifying the advantage his enemies enjoyed in that area. For a long time Ayub had played cat and mouse, seeming to seek the Normans out, then, if he thought the circumstances unfavourable, withdrawing out of harm's way. So it came as a surprise, while Roger was manoeuvring on the far side of the mountain range protecting Palermo, to find the Saracen army coming forward to meet him. He knew what had tempted the emir to act: he had split his forces to range and raid over a wider area, one part under Serlo, another given to Jordan with Ralph de Boeuf alongside to ensure he was not too rash. Ayub thought he had caught him with only his own contingent of lances, a third of his strength. What the emir could not grasp – he thought as a commander of a foot-bound army – was how quickly the Normans could concentrate.

His stated aim was to destroy the Roman Christians: not to kick them out of Sicily but to annihilate them on the field of battle. Given he had spent so much time without fulfilling that boast his authority was being weakened while his army was becoming disgruntled – and that made him impulsive. So much time and endless marching had been devoted to seeking advantage that a battle he wished to fight on his terms became one he had to fight to keep his authority. Getting to grips with the Count of Sicily moved from being an aspiration to a necessity.

He chose to make good his boast near a small town called Misilmeri, unaware that the system Roger had set up to keep communications with his son and nephew meant he could gather together his entire force in the space of one day, something he had not bargained for. Ayub never grasped that the Norman raiding horses were not the destriers with which they engaged in battle, so they could still be fresh. Also, Roger was leading men who had become battle-hardened by years of warfare and had beaten the Saracens so many times they held them in contempt. That had nothing to do with individual bravery – they had met and slaughtered many heroic men; it was in the mass they were poor, lacking in both training and leadership.

The latter was paramount: no Saracen general stood in battle with his men: always they sought to direct matters from a position of personal safety and they relied on numbers, not skill. No Norman leader who behaved in that way would have lasted a day. He trained with his men, rode with them, ate the same food and suffered the same privations. When they fought, the man who led exercised close control and if the fight was to be lost the choice was his whether to stand and die rather than flee.

When contact was made, what Ayub saw was that which he expected: a hundred lances in what seemed an exposed position and no foot soldiers on a wide, open field of his choosing, with no river or broken ground on the flanks, so for once he had a chance to overlap their line, sure in the knowledge that Norman strength lay in close-order fighting. Behind them the ground fell away sharply; drive them back a short distance and they would be trying to hold on a downward slope. Emir Ayub was also sure they could not be reinforced: he had scouts out on swift horses who, if they sighted the other sections of Roger's force, would ride back to warn him so he would be given the choice of accepting battle or breaking off the engagement.

Ayub failed to consider his enemies would anticipate such a move or that they would ensure whatever tactics they would ultimately employ would be kept hidden from him. To track cavalry you must work at their pace and, if you cannot keep them in view, it was essential to follow the dust they created and evidence on the ground of their passing: hoof prints and dung piles. The former becomes a problem in rocky terrain – a scout becomes less sure of numbers, doubly so if those being observed are aware of being under scrutiny. When you do not want to be seen, the first act to create obscurity is to ambush and kill those spying on your movements.

So, when Emir Ayub, second son of the Zirid sultan and a proud prince, drew up his forces for the battle he had waited so long to bring on, he was unaware that the bones of his fast-riding scouts were being picked over by vultures, unaware that on the reverse slopes of his chosen battlefield, behind Roger de Hauteville, sat another two hundred lances he was sure were elsewhere. He expected the Normans to stay on the defensive and arranged his troops to meet that contingency; this time his numbers, with room to deploy, would encircle and crush these heathens.

His first shock, when he set his army in motion, was to find them immediately attacked by a line of Norman lances under the banner of the Count of Sicily, the real blow the point at which he realised that to either side of that line of lances came two more *batailles* of a similar size. If he had possessed any ability, he would have known that security lay in allowing the two elements to meet, then, in as orderly a way as possible, by sacrificing his leading elements, to disengage the remainder and seek to retire in good order, which he had time to organise. The very worst thing to do was to seek to break off the battle immediately.

In the confusion of horns blowing, conflicting, shouted orders, some men moving forward while others sought to retire, Ayub created maximum confusion. Messengers rode forward to deliver his commands, but he lacked the soldiers who would comprehend and, if they did do so, swiftly obey. Roger led his men into a milling mass of confusion, visiting upon the Saracen levies a slaughter greater than any so far committed. It was almost as if, with no one to tell them what to do, they decided to welcome death. As was customary, when it came to flight, their leaders were in the vanguard. It took half a day to complete the killing.

'It seems not to matter what they give up to us,' Serlo said, surveying yet another set of Saracen tents crammed with booty. 'They always have more.'

While his confrères were ogling the valuables, Jordan was eyeing cages full of pigeons, several dozen in number. Reaching in, he gently lifted out a bird, handling it as he would a very young falcon; they were clearly tame. He then joined Roger at the mouth of the tent where he was discussing with Ralph de Boeuf what this victory would mean for the future.

'We could test our hawks with these, Father.'

With that Jordan let the bird go and it rose into the sky, circled once or twice, then headed quite deliberately north-west at speed, which had Roger watching it intently until it disappeared.

'Fetch out another.'

Jordan did so and let it go, only to observe a repeat of the actions of that first pigeon: a couple of circles followed by the choice of a deliberate course on the same path of flight. Roger came to look at the birdcages, then he examined an open chest beside them, one that had been ignored given it held nothing valuable, taking from it small capsules made of parchment, each with delicate ties.

'Another bird, Jordan, and hold it this time.' With gentle hands another pigeon was presented and this time Roger laced the small parchment tube to its leg. 'Now let it go.'

Jordan did so, saying as it flew off, 'There must be a rich source of food wherever they are headed.'

'They are going to Palermo,' Roger replied.

'Why?'

It was Serlo who answered. 'Carrier pigeons, of which I have heard, but never till this day seen – a way of sending messages over long distances.'

'Had Ayub destroyed us this day, these would have carried news of his victory to the citizens of Palermo.'

'Then can we not use them to send news of his defeat?' asked Jordan.

It was an idea: Roger had with him men who had enough Arabic and writing skill to compose the message, but would it be believed? An image of the men so recently slaughtered came to him, Sicilian Saracens in their various-coloured garb; yellows, reds, every shade in between and, of course, the black of Ayub's own North Africans. Right now the locals would be scavenging the battlefield stripping them of everything, garments included.

'Serlo, Jordan, get amongst the dead. I want strips of every kind of clothing they are wearing, all the colours.'

'Why?' asked Jordan.

For once his father was not in the mood to indulge him and his response was sharp. 'Just do as I ask!' As they departed, Serlo amused and Jordan chastened, Roger called after them, 'And dip parts of the cloth in their blood.'

The first two pigeons coming into their home loft with no message was put down to error, probably poor handling, but when the rest came in with tiny bloodstained strips of cloth attached to their legs, all in different colours, there could be no doubt what the message portended. It told the citizens of Palermo that the army they had hoped would drive away the Normans had failed, and implied what was only later found out to be true. Emir Ayub had not just suffered a reverse: he had lost the last hope the city had of their enemies being beaten away from their walls.

His authority shattered, Ayub fled back to Africa, taking what remained of his forces with him, while the Sicilians Saracens had scattered. When no Norman army appeared to besiege them they were confused, but they could not see into the mind of Roger de Hauteville, did not know he was aware of his limitations and had a strong memory of another city he had supposed was at his mercy. Yes, he had broken Saracen resistance – there would still be fights but there would be no more pitched battles – but until he had a proper army he would merely contain Palermo and keep the city on edge, while making sure by constant raiding that his enemies could not re-form again. Then, when his brother was free, when Bari had fallen, then Robert would come and, together this time, Palermo would be theirs.

'But when will that be, Father?' Jordan pleaded.

'When the summons comes from Apulia, boy.'

'You are sure he will send for you?'

'Certain,' Roger snapped. 'Robert will not want Bari to fall without I should be there as witness.'

Already over a year in duration, the siege of Bari was seemingly going nowhere. Robert was frustrated and irritable, his nature would allow of no other mood, but he still kept himself in a positive frame of mind, even if, at this moment, he was trying to cheer up Bohemund, a favourite son mired in deep gloom. Inside Bari he had support, also he had methods by which information and bribes were passed to and fro, so he knew the exact state of the city storerooms and could thus calculate the time it would take to starve the defenders out. He also knew that opinion within the Greek community was moving in his direction: the rise of the Normans had been so inexorable and over so many years that many now believed their supremacy to be inevitable. Better to make peace than face a bloody end fighting what could not be gainsaid.

Set against that, Bisanzio had managed to slip out of Bari and Robert suspected he was on his way to Constantinople to seek reinforcements. Even if he doubted he would succeed he had put some ships out in deeper water to watch the approaches, with orders to intercept any vessel making for the port.

'They ridiculed me, bringing up their most precious treasures of gold and silver onto the ramparts and waving them.' Robert laughed then, a deep rumble. 'They do not do that now, do they, so what does that tell you?'

Bohemund had another concern: how they were ever going to

get a siege tower close to the walls without it being burnt? Ten had been built, ten had trundled forward and ten had been set alight by jets of Greek fire and there was no other way to surmount the walls, given their height.

'I want to try to sap,' he said.

Robert looked hard at him, thinking Bohemund was not a jolly companion, he was too concentrated on fighting to enjoy a jest and he was a mass of impatience, this being his first siege.

'The city is built on rock.'

'There must be soft earth somewhere.'

'Yes there is,' Robert growled, 'and you are likely to be buried in it.'

'I am sick of doing nothing or building towers so that the Bariots can warm their arses.'

'How many times have I told you not to fret, time is our friend, not our enemy.'

'I'll be a greybeard before I see inside that damned city.'

Robert's heir, Roger, came bursting in, as enthusiastic as a boy of his age should be, soon followed by his doting mother. Sichelgaita exchanged a sour look with Bohemund, one that the father of both boys, even as he allowed Roger to jump on him, could not avoid observing.

'I take it,' Sichelgaita said, 'the great general is still trying to tell you that you know nothing about how to fight a war?'

'I would not dream of usurping your position,' Bohemund spat.

'Can I have some money, Papa,' Roger cried, 'for my purse?'

Sichelgaita had been glaring at Bohemund with loathing, but that changed to a maternal beam as she looked at Roger: she doted on the child and was, with a motherly mote to cloud her vision, looking forward to a day when he was a match in height and build for his disenfranchised sibling. Robert was fond of Roger, whom he had nicknamed Borsa for his love of money, not the possession of it but his habit of endlessly counting coins. However, it took no great genius to see if there was an inheritance in his blood it came from his wife's family rather than his own: Roger Borsa looked like Sichelgaita's brother, Gisulf – thin, with dull, fair hair and no glint in his eye of anything martial.

'You always think my coffers are full, Borsa.'

'Are they not, Papa?'

'Maybe, I do not know, for I have to go to them often to pay my spies.'

'Then you must let me tally them for you.'

'And, my little Lombard, pocket a few,' Bohemund sneered.

'If he does,' Sichelgaita hissed, 'it is only because he has a right to it! And if you mock, it is because you have not.'

'Enough, wife,' Robert sighed.

The Duke of Apulia could silence most people, but not his wife.

'Enough!' she cried. 'You let this popinjay insult your heir and say and do nothing.'

'It was naught but a jest.'

'It was a slur.'

'That it most certainly was,' Bohemund added gaily: Sichelgaita upset was one of the few things that made him happy. Roger Borsa had turned to look at him and if, in the boy's eyes, was a kind of pleading affection, it was not returned. His half-brother was looking at him as a fox looks at a caged chicken, a stare that was broken by one of Robert's servants entering the main tent.

'Sire, a messenger from Geoffrey Ridel.'

Robert nodded, put his son on the floor, glared at both his wife and Bohemund and turned to face the man who had come in to tell him that a fleet of ships had been sighted heading for Bari, and Geoffrey Ridel suspected, by their lack of flags, they were from Constantinople.

'Thank the good Jesus Christ,' Robert boomed, which got him a hard look from Sichelgaita, who did not like the Lord's name taken in vain when her son was in earshot. He hauled himself upright. 'I have an enemy to fight that I can deal with.'

Bohemund, ever keen for a scrap, had gone before the messenger had finished his delivery, as if to be on the shore was to see this approaching hazard, which must be many leagues away in the open sea; Ridel, in command, had sent in a small, swift boat to carry the news.

'You must curb that swine,' Sichelgaita growled. 'He is too free with his tongue.'

Robert looked at her wearily: if Bohemund was too free with that, he was not alone. 'Right now I am concerned that Bisanzio is returning to Bari and if he is doing so in a fleet that means he has brought reinforcements. That I must deal with – and now.'

'And Bohemund?'

'Is my flesh and blood, just like little Borsa.'

'Whom he hates. I have asked you before and I ask you again, send Bohemund away.'

'Where?'

'To Sicily, to Normandy or to England. Let him make his way in another land, not here.'

'He will not harm our child, Sichelgaita,' he said in a tired fashion, given it was something he was called upon to repeat often. 'And before you ask how I know, I will see to it.'

'And if you do not, will his Uncle Roger?'

'He has told me he will. More than that I cannot do. Now please help me fight my enemies, not my family.'

Bisanzio was the first to admit he was no soldier – which had hampered his efforts to contain the *Guiscard*. Always having to rely on others for military advice he was never sure if the steps being taken were correct. His plea to the Empress Eudoxia for more troops – her husband was away fighting the Turks – was only part of his submission: the defenders of Bari needed a soldier, a man they could respect to take charge of thwarting the siege.

Stephen Paternos was that man, highly regarded and a proven success, so when he suggested splitting the relief force in two, separating the grain convoy from the ships carrying the fighting men, Bisanzio was happy to agree. Thus, as he approached his city and the Norman barrier, on a strong following wind, he was unaware that the grain ships had been intercepted; all he knew was what he could see, an endless stream of fighting men crossing those plank gangways from ship to ship, forming up in its defence. On the Byzantine decks, the warriors were crowding up from below, likewise preparing for battle.

'Steer straight for them,' Paternos ordered, 'All sail set.'

'They are stout bottoms, Excellency,' the captain of the lead vessel replied – his ship was hired and thus he was more careful of its preservation than if it had been an imperial war vessel.

'Not the ships, fool,' Paternos barked, 'the planks joining one to the other.'

'The other vessels?' Bisanzio asked, though softly: he did not want to be seen to question the military tactics and so undermine Paternos.

'Will follow in our wake, that is if the dolts in command of them have a brain.'

The Catapan had met many military men in his time and it seemed they all talked in that fashion, an abrupt delivery that took no regard of the pride of the person being addressed, not something he, being in essence a politician, could do. He had to persuade and cajole, and often he found himself employing such wiles with people he knew were considering betraying the empire. Would there be more now than when he had left for Constantinople? Would the sight of reinforcements, always assuming they could break through, still those seditious voices?

The *Guiscard* knew the weakest part of his defence line was where the ships were joined, so he had placed them so close that for a vessel to ram its way through would so damage it as to perhaps have it sink in the attempt. Having done that, it would have been wise to also acknowledge that another eye examining the problem might come up with a viable solution.

The captain of the vessel was clearly in a state of some distress: he could see the gap he was being asked to sail into at full speed and he knew he would not get through without massive damage. More by hand signal than spoken order he was having the sails eased so they were not drawing as tight as they might, thus reducing the way on the ship and the potential destruction. That Stephen Paternos spotted this surprised him, but not as much as what he did next.

'Tell me, Captain, who would you ask to command the ship if you were suddenly indisposed?' Seeing the man wondering at the question, he added, 'We are about to go into a fight, Captain, and I am no sailor. I need to know for the safety of us all.'

'My mate, the fellow on the tiller.'

'Call him to us.'

That the captain did, and as soon as his mate joined them, Paternos whipped out his sword and swung it high and hard, to cleave the captain's head from his body, speaking before the skull had stopped rolling into the scantlings and the decapitated cadaver had fallen over, spouting foaming blood through the open trunk.

'Set the sails properly,' he barked at the terrified mate. 'Do as I command, or you will suffer the same fate.'

His next order, given in a raised voice as the ship picked up speed, was for a division of his forces to be undertaken just before they struck. His men were evenly distributed on each side of the companionway that led below; this he wished to change.

'This vessel may founder, so we need another, and the Norman barbarians have kindly provided them. Just before we make contact I want half of one division to join me on whichever side of the ship I am on, the rest to remain to defend the other side. Our task is to take one of the Normans' vessels so quickly we will stop help coming aboard, then detach it from its fellows and create a gap for the rest of our vessels to follow. Now, everyone out of the prow.'

His enemies could not doubt as to what he intended, and they likewise began to ship men from positions in which they would be exposed, denuding the prow of one ship and the stern of another. Paternos, looking at the other vessels in his flotilla, could be content: his junior commanders, good soldiers and long servants of the empire, were implementing the plan he had discussed the last time they were on land. The grain ships might have evaded the Normans' fleet at sea but, if not, they had drawn them away from where they were really needed: soldiers were more important in this siege than loaves of bread.

'Brace yourselves,' he shouted, grabbing a transfixed Bisanzio and forcing him to take hold of a cleat, this as he moved to one side, the men he had ordered to follow doing so just in time to grab at a steadying rope.

The crunch was deafening, the prow of the Byzantine ship rising up like a rearing horse as it ploughed into the planks, brought to halt, timber shattering and splinters flying. By the time it settled Paternos was already on the stern of the vessel he wanted to take, aware and pleased that the second of his ships, without specific orders, had sheared contact with the next ship in line. The Norman tactic did not place many men on each vessel, the idea being that once the point of assault was established they could concentrate; Paternos, by his tactics, had nullified their numerical advantage where it mattered.

Those standing next to Robert de Hauteville heard him swear and it took the loudest shout he could muster to stop Bohemund rushing into what he knew would be a losing battle. He knew, too, there was no need to seal the limits of the Byzantine attack: they did not want to destroy his defence, merely to get through. It was as hard to watch his men go down as much as to see his line ripped open, but, good as they were, they were outnumbered by proper soldiers and in a situation where no quarter was a necessity. Already his mind was moving on.

'Get the blacksmiths at their forges now, from here to Melfi. I want chains made, stout enough to stop this happening again.'

That, too, had to be said loudly, to carry over the cheering from the ramparts of Bari.

# CHAPTER TWENTY-SIX

For the people of Palermo the effect of having a Norman army close by was worse than being under siege: they knew Roger de Hauteville was coming, they just did not know when and, as the months stretched to years, it induced in them a feeling of increasing hopelessness. Appeals to the remaining emirs on the island fell on deaf ears: none of them were of the stature of Ibn-al-Hawas, and besides, they would not agree to elect either a leader nor, after such a string of massive defeats, to any notion of taking the field. Likewise their brethren in North Africa: they were too chastened to have any ambitions in that quarter.

Not that Sicily was at peace: the Normans raided far and wide, plundering what they could carry and destroying what they could not, taking the smaller walled towns, any fortress too formidable could watch their fields burn from their ramparts. Roger's lances grew fat from the proceeds and naturally his coffers filled with gold as the spoils of war – animals, produce and slaves – were traded for profit, all transactions done through his agent Kasa Ephraim, now reaping a fabulous reward for his earlier support.

That there were frustrations went without saying: for all Roger was acquiring in treasure from the Sicilian hinterland, it would pale in comparison to what would be gained from the richest city on the island as well as one of the wealthiest ports in the Mediterranean. There had been temptation: Pisa had offered him a fleet and an alliance, their part of the plan to blockade the port. Roger turned them down: this was to be a Norman conquest, not a shared one, and besides, a fleet was not enough – for any siege to be decisive he needed Robert's army.

He knew matters were moving his way when the summons came, the same having been sent to Mauger at Scalea. The *Guiscard* wanted every lance Roger could spare. The siege of Bari was moving to a climax.

'You see, Robert,' Roger pricked him, 'it is not so bad having Mauger serving with you as well.'

'True, brother, it gives me someone to loathe more than the family quarrels I'm exposed to. With you arrived I am doubly protected, given no one disputes with me more than you. What a family I am cursed with!'

Roger merely smiled; he had always wanted to ask his older brother questions he knew Robert would not answer, so he had therefore left them unspoken. Here he was moaning about family quarrels – in truth it was the continued griping between Sichelgaita and Bohemund – yet he had a feeling for his relations that he tried and failed to hide. He might have been begged to forgive Mauger but that weighed for nothing. Yet here he was, close to the pinnacle of everything his predecessors had sought to achieve, and he wanted those of his family who remained to be close by when success came.

Roger had come with Jordan and Serlo; Geoffrey of Loritello, looking as if death were stalking him, was present, as was Humphrey's son, Abelard, looking aggrieved, as he always did with an uncle he considered treacherous. He had called on the two rebellious sons of Beatrix to be with him, and his own child Borsa was present. Robert also sent for his daughter Emma and, most tellingly, for Mauger, whom he claimed to like the least. The Lord of Scalea had only a few lances to add to his forces, so it was sentiment, not a request for military support that had prompted the act.

'Did you want me for my lances or just to gloat?' Roger asked.

'Both,' Robert replied, honest for once. 'But I thank you most for the Calabrian ships you brought, for it is at sea this siege will be decided.'

If others saw Robert sitting idly outside Bari they had failed to discern his other moves, not least in his gathering of a powerful fleet. He had his floating barrier, but he also had vessels at sea and in strength – a part of his forces he wanted Roger to command.

'So, how do we fare overall?' was Roger's question.

There was no need for Robert to list his failures, yet he did so: assaults on the land wall that had got nowhere, the endless destruction of his siege towers, the fractious nature of many of his captains, not least his own natural son, while to his rear Apulia was groaning under the cost of maintaining such a lengthy effort. Then there was what had happened to his boats.

'You heard of Paternos and what he did?' Roger nodded. 'Well, my spies tell me that when it became known he sacrificed the grain convoy to get his troops into Bari there was much unrest.'

'Your spies?'

'I have quite a few. The one I rely on most is a fellow called Argirizzo.'

'Greek?'

'No,' Robert scoffed, rolling his eyes. 'He's an Egyptian.'

Roger held up a hand to admit it was a foolish question.

'Of course he's Greek, and a devious bastard at that. God only knows what I will do with him if I succeed and he survives, because I could never trust him.'

Roger was about to respond by saying he did not trust anyone but he held his tongue.

'I have been sending him funds to buy grain from those hoarding it and using that he spreads dissent, not hard with people being so hungry. It was he who stirred up the Bariots against the loss of that grain. Paternos is seen as a devil and one living well while others starve.'

'Then why did they assassinate Bisanzio and not him?'

An unknown assailant had cut down the Catapan in the street: even Paternos was suspected, though Robert was a better candidate.

'Bisanzio was easier to get to.'

'Did you order that?' Roger asked.

Seeing the look he was getting, Robert added querulously, 'It is settlement for William and Drogo.'

'Be careful they don't do the same to you,' Roger insisted. 'If you instigate the murder of a leader, it will tempt someone to revenge.'

'They never believed I would press the siege so long,' Robert insisted, changing an uncomfortable subject and since it was approaching three years, that was an understatement. Robert's brow clouded, making him look devilish. 'But I am here till Bari falls, Roger. I will never give this up.'

'It could be another year.'

'Then let it be that,' Robert growled, before he brightened a little. 'But, you know God is on our side, brother. He will make something happen.'

And happen it did. Argirizzo had sent word that Paternos had gone himself to Constantinople to plead for support and news soon came back that he had been successful. An army was marching to Durazzo on the Dalmatian coast, a couple of days' sailing from Bari. The prince of that Byzantine fief had given sanctuary to the traitorous Joscelin of Molfetta, who was also raising malcontents in Robert's own domains, making it a genuine threat. Roger was sent to sea to keep watch, though he was soon back on shore.

'You cannot just keep ships at sea, Robert. If you do, they will suffer such wear they will be useless when they are truly needed.'

'Why do you never do what I command you to do?' Robert yelled.

'Let me take charge, Father,' Bohemund demanded.

'You?' Roger scoffed. 'You are barely breeched.'

'I am as good a soldier as you.'

'Which is damned useless when what is needed is a sailor.' Turning back to Robert, Roger continued, ignoring the black looks he was getting from Bohemund. 'And before you say it, neither am I. But Geoffrey Ridel is and I am taking his advice.'

'There's an army coming and I need to stop it before it tries to land.'

'Then we must find a way to tell when.'

'How?'

'Try your spies.'

In the end, it was the people of Bari who gave the answer. The populace, even the most loyal, were getting desperate: everyone knew this was the last throw of the dice. If Paternos came back with an army, Bari would hold out, if not, it might not submit immediately but fall it would. The idea was that the fleet of ships would seek to make their landfall on a moonless cloudy night, so the Normans would be blind. That the relieving force would also be blind was to be solved by the Bariots lining their sea walls with torches.

The intention was that those torches would number just enough to do what was required, but the citizens, in their enthusiasm, crowded the ramparts in their hundreds, setting up a blaze of light and that alerted Roger. He manned his ships and went to single anchors, until he received a signal of his own from a piquet boat he had left out in deep water. The enemy had been sighted and he was at sea within half a glass of sand, sailing out at the head of thirty warrior-laden ships to where he suspected his enemy must be. Soon he saw what they had to have aloft to avoid colliding with each other, lanterns at their mastheads.

'Light the ship,' Roger ordered, 'let them see what they face.'

Men ran to carry out that command, one that was repeated on every vessel Roger led, each turning from a ghostly shadow to a lit deck, which showed their strength.

'Double lights on one mast,' Ridel said, pointing ahead, 'I'll wager it's the lead vessel and that will be carrying Paternos.'

'Close with it,' Roger shouted, before picking up a speaking trumpet and passing the same command over the water to the other captains. Capture the enemy command ship and the rest should succumb.

The tragedy that followed could not have been foreseen. It was brought on by an excess of zeal, though some felt, in retrospect, it was more to do with a lack of caution from warriors unaccustomed to fighting at sea. On one deck every man rushed to the side to catch a view of the vessel Roger had indicated. With horror he watched its own lights dip towards the water as the weight produced a list. Yet it did not stop and correct itself, it carried on until it hit the sea, lanterns fizzing out as the vessel capsized, throwing in excess of a hundred fighting men, all in heavy mail, into the water. Even if they could swim, and few would be able to, their mail must weigh them down; they would all drown.

Roger had to turn away and he also had to put out of his mind any thought of rescue, not that it would have been easy. There was a battle to fight and winning that was paramount, notwithstanding he had to shout to stop those on his own deck from rushing to view the loss and bringing about another disaster. Thankfully the gap was closing fast, so his men could see where their duty lay.

'Grappling irons,' he yelled, as their movement restored the trim of the ship.

He ran to the prow so that he could control the time of contact, using a set of hand signals he had worked out with Geoffrey Ridel that would bring his vessel alongside the enemy to best advantage. All along the bulwarks men were waiting for his signal to throw the triple-hooked grappling irons, and when he gave the command they snaked out to clatter aboard the opposite deck, to then be hauled hard so they would grip. Not all held, some were cut, but three dug into timber and were pulled taut.

Hauling hard, the Normans pulled themselves towards their enemies and they, seeking to defend their ship, erred in rushing to one side, causing it to list, not as badly as the vessel which had capsized but enough to ensure when the two vessels came together the Normans, standing on their bulwarks, had height on their opponents and were thus able to jump on top of them to engage, the weight of the fall the first thing to gain them an advantage and room to fight. The sound of crashing timber was soon replaced by that of clashing metal, as swords and axes were employed by both sides in a melee that compacted men into the constricted fighting space of the ship's deck.

As ever, Norman skill told here: they knew to form a wall of shields without instructions, knew what steps to take to protect their neighbouring warrior to the left, knew to use their shields to block any blows from that quarter. With Roger in the centre they kept that line, inching forward against opponents giving ground, a strake at a time, small amounts but significant, for to be retreating was to be losing.

By the great tiller Roger could see a man he knew well, Joscelin of Molfetta, and the sight of that ingrate, who had been granted so much by his brother, urged on his arm and that alone added force to the battering the men defending the ship were receiving. The Normans were obliged to step over the bodies of the slain, careful to avoid slipping on their blood. A fellow Roger did not know, but one dressed in fine armour, stepped into the fray, jostling forward and seeking him out.

That he was a soldier and a good one was obvious: he was a man who fought with his eyes, knowing his arms and feet would obey the commands sent to them by his brain, and he was strong. No orders were given but it was soon obvious that this contest was to be decided between these two and their swords. They swung them against each other time and again in a tattoo of clashing metal, came together then fell apart with a collision of shields, the only thing still their heads as, eyes locked, they sought that one blink or wrong signal that would present an opening.

Stephen Paternos had never fought a Norman in single combat:

that he might have coped with, but he had never engaged with a de Hauteville. Roger was in his element: he could have been back at Hauteville le Guichard with old Tancred's shouted instructions in his ears and it had been the same as every fight since, a reliance on the strong arm and quick brain that were his family birthright.

Paternos moved his round buckler just enough for Roger to get his teardrop shield inside it and fix its position for no more than a blink. But it was enough: Stephen Paternos needed to correct it, his chest was exposed, needed to use extra pressure to free his own shield from the way Roger was holding it. In pushing to his right, his sword arm opened up enough for the hilt of Roger's weapon to get through his guard and take him on the upper chest – not in itself a telling blow, but one that created both the time and the opening for that blade to be raised and fall on the Byzantine's helmet with stunning force.

As he reeled back it was the following blow that killed him, a round-armed sweep that took his neck just below where his helmet ended, with a blade so sharp that it could slice through a single horse hair. The light went out in those eyes, with Roger aware that he had been a worthy opponent who never once wavered in his concentration, even when he knew he was probably doomed. Apart from the sound of his own heavy breathing, Roger now heard only the sound of dropping weapons, then, shortly and all around, coming from other ships, cries of loud cheering.

They landed with the enemy ships, bar one, under tow; that last one had broken through to Bari. On the journey back Roger had made Joscelin dress as a high-ranking Greek, in the non-fighting clothes of the man he had slain, whose name he now knew. It was a great pleasure to present Joscelin as a gift to his brother and to hear the wretch plead for his life, but there was little time to gloat.

Word came almost at once that a party of Greeks, having seen that relief was not at hand, in despair and encouraged by Robert's agent Argirizzo, had seized one of the twin towers on the land wall, calling for Normans to reinforce them. Yet another siege tower, built but yet to be employed, was quickly pushed forward to finally rest against the ramparts. Robert's best warriors, led by Bohemund, with Jordan and Serlo on his heels, flooded up over the now undefended ramparts and once in possession of that corner tower the city was doomed: at dawn, word came asking for terms.

Robert was lenient: he could afford to be. What soldiers of Byzantium remained, and any Greeks who wished to depart, he let sail away. The Duke of Apulia had what he wanted, absolute control of his domains. The Eastern Empire no longer had a toehold in Italy: on the Saturday before Palm Sunday, banners that had flown over the city since the time of the Emperor Justinian, five hundred years before, were hauled down for the last time to the sound of a Latin Mass being celebrated in the great cathedral.

Palermo suspected the de Hautevilles were coming and they knew that this time the Normans had a powerful navy. Every Byzantine satrap, from the Dalmatian coast to the Bosphorus, was busy strengthening their defences in fear of that fleet appearing off their shores. Yet Palermo had strong walls and surely, after a three-year siege these warriors would want some respite. Not so: the *Guiscard,* with that power to inspire which was the hallmark of his leadership, had his army enthused and marching to Reggio within a month, Roger insisting there was one task to perform on the way to Palermo. If there was one area where he felt outshone by Robert it was in his cunning – hence his soubriquet – a fact well known to the older brother, so it was with some amusement the *Guiscard* listened to his younger brother as he outlined his plans and reasons for taking Catania.

'For all al-Tinnah is long dead we are still well thought of there, and it would not surprise them to have me request some men to aid us in taking Palermo.'

'You think they will respond?' Robert asked.

'I doubt they will welcome the notion. Their late emir might have dangled possession of Sicily in front of us but I never thought he really believed in it. But if I sail into the harbour they will not dare refuse me permission to land. I will then request they allow you to enter with the fleet to pick up their contingent...'

Roger did not finish, leaving his brother ruminating. Even with Palermo, the rest of Sicily was not going to be easy to conquer. It was mountainous, had many elevated and redoubtable fortresses, the Greeks were not universally friendly, and while the natives were not openly hostile, the Saracens, numerous and religion-inspired, were. The problems lay in securing the big ports, Catania being one, as well as Agrigento on the south coast, which would need to be secured to stop incursions from North Africa. But biggest of all was Syracuse, the gateway to Sicily since ancient times. To hold that was to deny the island to a resurgent Byzantium; that the Eastern Empire was weak now did not mean it would always be so and Catania was not far up the same coast.

'If they resist?' Robert asked.

'I don't doubt they will, but they will succumb because we will be inside their walls.'

And so it proved: Roger was welcomed, not with open arms but with grace, and the Catanians were not so foolish as to deny the request he made, for was not the Count of Sicily known to be an honourable man, unlike his brother? They were still unsuspecting when Robert led his fleet into their harbour. His soldiers landed and fanned out through the town, the scales only falling from the Catanian eyes when they found their strong points being occupied and Normans manning the city gates. They fought but it was futile, within a week, Catania had been re-fortified and had a Norman garrison. The brothers who had deceived them were on their way to Palermo, Roger leading the army via Troina, Robert taking his fleet north to round Cape Faro.

Robert made several landings on the way to overawe the coastal settlements, so Roger arrived first and set up his camp to the east of the port on a fertile plain cut with a good river, a place of palaces and summer residences surrounded by orange and lemon groves where the rich traders of Palermo were wont to escape the stink of a crowded city, a teeming metropolis with a population reckoned to be a quarter of a million. All were abandoned, their owners now inside the walls, so the Norman host were free to accommodate themselves in much comfort in houses made of cool marble, escaping the summer heat.

There was a fort called the Castle of Yahya at the point where the river met the sea, running into a good bay, a perfect place in which to anchor Robert's fleet and disembark his army – the shape of Palermo harbour, lying as it did in a deep gulf, precluded the same tactic he had used to blockade Bari. Taking the castle looked simple, but the Saracens, expected to surrender against hopeless odds, instead came out to fight and suffered much for their bravery. Roger did not realise it, Robert did not know, but this presaged much of what was to come. Those men had fought for their faith as much as for their island and that was to be replicated in the city itself, for there was not a citizen who did not know that what they were fighting for was the honour of the Prophet and the future of Islam in Sicily.

On landing his warriors Robert ordered that a Mass be said, so that all could confess, that to be followed by an immediate assault, the hope being they could take Palermo by a *coup de main*. Robert sailed his ships round Cape Zafferano and into the great bight on which Palermo stood, while Roger led the army towards the walls to let them see the size of the force they now faced, made up of Normans and Greeks, Apulians, Calabrians and even men from Bari. Those they were intent on subduing had been waiting years for this moment: they had worked on their fortifications and even walled up several of the city gates, gathered arms and trained with them. A hail of stones and arrows met Roger, while the sheer number of vessels that emerged to meet and fight him thwarted Robert. The attack failed both on land and at sea.

Was there a soul in Palermo who thought they could repulse the men who had conquered so much? Did they, in their darker moments, wonder at a race like the Normans, and at a family, the eldest of whom had only arrived in Italy thirty-five years previously and with nothing: bare-arsed knights, as they described themselves? By sheer ability with sword, shield, horse and lance, guile, cunning, political ability and a strong dose of good fortune, they had risen to consort with kings and popes, had come to make emperors fearful. Did they reflect that in the past invasions of these lands it had been an overwhelming force of numbers that had triumphed, yet these de Hautevilles were few, and the men they led never were large in numbers? If they did think such thoughts, it seemed they knew they were doomed, yet they fought, not with despair, but with faith that when they died, all the promises of Paradise made to them would be theirs.

The Greeks of Bari had stayed behind their walls, but the Saracens of Palermo came out to fight and, if they paid a high price for their courage, they extorted a fair one in exchange, for they matched the men Roger led in sheer brio. They applied cunning too, opening gates to entice their besiegers forward, then coming out to fight in massive numbers, falling back to heavily manned walls from which their companions could inflict casualties with boiling oil, fire, rocks and arrows while their fellows slipped back into the city.

Nor were they shy at sea: a combined Sicilian and African galley fleet appeared off the Gulf of Palermo intent on destroying Robert's ships, each one with a thick awning over its deck to protect the rowers from crossbow bolts and lances, each vessel full to capacity with men so willing to die that if they lacked leadership it mattered little. A battle begun near dawn was still raging as the sun began to dip, and it took that long for the *Guiscard*'s ships to gain the upper hand. In the end, though, such stalwart resistance contributed to their undoing.

Finally breaking off the action and fleeing for safety, with their exhausted oarsmen collapsing over their sticks, the Saracen fleet made for the harbour. Pursued by Robert's ship they sought to secure the entrance with a great chain, a device that had kept them safe for decades, only to fail to secure it in enough time to stop him breaking through. Once in the confined space of the harbour, and using fire to set light to those protective awnings, the destruction of the Saracen galleys was total.

Now Robert had what he wanted, a city cut off from supplies and he also sent men to secure the mountain passes that led to Palermo, so no relief could come from the landward side. Famine was his weapon; it had aided him before and it must do so now. Yet there was hope for the besieged: news came from Apulia of yet another revolt, this time backed by Robert's powerful brother-in-law, Richard of Aversa, Prince of Capua, who had made common cause with that miserable slug, Gisulf of Salerno.

Would Robert scuttle back to the mainland, as he had been obliged to do so many times previously, to suppress such puissant enemies, taking with him most of his army? For days they waited for the sign of his departure, but they waited in vain. Robert knew he would never have such a chance again, but it was obvious to the Saracens and Normans alike that any decision, for him, must be a swift one. Palermian hopes rose: would one more hard fight convince the *Guiscard* that time was against him?

The key to the city was the walled section called the Al-Qasr, the old town full of mosques and souks, with its own fortifications and a wall long enough to require a total of nine gates. It was a fact obvious to besieger and besieged alike, and the inhabitants were not content to just let their enemies attack. They sallied forth in desperation, employing much of their remaining strength, and in taking on Roger's *milities,* showed themselves more than equal, driving them back.

Yet once again a measure of success was their undoing: they pushed too far and left themselves vulnerable to the Normans, now mounted and thus at their most effective. No Saracen horde, however brave and fired by religious fervour, had ever stood against Norman cavalry and this time was no different. They broke at the first charge, running for the gate by which they had emerged, only to have their fearful compatriots, seeing the fast-riding Normans in amongst them, shut it in their face, leaving them to be slaughtered against the walls, till not a man was left standing.

Robert, given a weakened defence, seized his chance: the great siege towers, seven in number, which had been waiting for such an opportunity, were trundled forward, though memories of Bari made many reluctant to climb them. It was, for a second time that year, left to the younger de Hautevilles, Serlo, Jordan and Bohemund, to lead the way. Swords and shields in hand, they rushed to the top and as they hit the walls began to fight with a degree of ferocity rare even for their race: they and the men they led knew that to do otherwise was to die.

Despite such efforts, Al-Qasr remained unconquered. Robert, good general that he was, had seen that with the defence before his family so strong, and given the recent Saracen losses, other parts of the walls must have been denuded. Telling Roger to press home the attack to pin the defenders, he led three hundred Norman lances to another part of the walls, hard by the port and his instinct proved right: they were undefended. Ladders were sent up and the ramparts scaled; soon the Normans were on the ground rushing to open the gates and allow Roger's main body entry to the streets of the city.

Still the defenders fought on, but when night fell it was obvious the defence was broken. It was time for Palermo to seek terms.

# EPILOGUE

The formal entrance of Robert de Hauteville into the city had to be ceremonial and it was so: he came dressed in a golden cloak and mounted on a magnificent horse. Followed by his family, with Roger near level to his brother, the Duke of Apulia and Calabria came to claim the last fief granted him by the Pope: he was truly now Duke of Sicily as well. Roger, who would henceforth be known as the Great Count of Sicily, had the satisfaction of knowing that in this conquest he had been the engine and he suspected that with the endemic revolts in Apulia, plus Robert's desire to take Constantinople, the future conquest of the rest of the island was likely to fall to him. Robert would also have to deal with Richard of Capua, a contest too long delayed, as well as Salerno: miserable Gisulf would require to be chastised. But first, having listened to the oaths of future fealty, Robert had to address his new subjects.

That his words were coloured by his difficulties on the mainland did not detract from the significance; he had shown leniency at Brindisi and Bari, now it was time to do the same in Palermo. If the people conquered by the de Hautevilles had wondered how so few now held sway over so many, it was in a legacy that came down from their Viking forebears. Conquest was one thing, to hold that which you had gained and prosper from it another. William had known it, so had Drogo and Humphrey in their turn: be cruel if you must, but be light of touch where you needed to be.

'Know this,' Robert called from the steps of the emir's palace. 'No man shall suffer for what has happened here, no property save that which comes to me as your lord and master will be confiscated, and all I ask is that you pay me annually the tribute due to me as your suzerain. No one will bear any burden for their religious belief, no follower of the Prophet will be asked to convert, no mosque, save those which were originally Christian churches will be touched, the latter to be re-consecrated in the faith we hold to our hearts, and we will request to Rome for the appointment of an archbishop of this, the Pope's new diocese. I desire only that we live together in peace and harmony and that you, my subjects, will abide by what laws that can make that a reality. My brother, the Great Count of Sicily, Roger de Hauteville, will be my supporter in this, and it is he who will hold for me these possessions. In all things, when he speaks, he does so with my authority.'

Roger was called forward to take a vow to uphold his brother's commands, then Robert de Hauteville held up his hand as the priests began, for the first time in two hundred years, and under that gifted papal banner, to say the words of a Christian Mass in Palermo, this time in the Roman rite. To the men Robert and Roger led, kneeling and listening to the Latin liturgy, this was truly ordained by God, for the conquest of Southern Italy was complete.

# AUTHOR'S NOTE

In writing the Conquest trilogy my admiration for the family at the centre of the story has grown and grown: has there ever been, in history, a brood like the de Hautevilles? I cannot think of one that managed to be so consistently successful, that with such meagre resources to begin with, conquered so much and rose to such heights. I am also amazed that in my searches I have not found this to be a story previously told in English fiction.

What I have written so far is only half their story – they went on to greater things, and because of their tolerance helped to create a court, centred in Palermo, which became the source from which sprang the Renaissance. There, Arab scholars worked alongside their European brethren in mathematics and science; there the lost ideas of Greece, which had been preserved in the East, were reintroduced to a civilisation emerging from what is known as the Dark Ages, making their way to the rich cities of Lombardy.

Yet how dark was it really? Evidence is plentiful of much travel – certainly pilgrims in their thousands traversed the highways of Europe, trade spanned the known world and there was an exchange of ideas that impacted on different cultures. Duke William of Normandy learnt from Italy and his confrères how to transport horses across water, information without which he might not have won the Battle of Hastings.

The reconquest of Sicily was possibly the first crusade, specifically blessed as such by the reigning pope to regain from Islam what had once been a Christian, albeit Orthodox, province. If there is a pity in what we know historically as THE Crusades, it is that the men who invaded the Holy Land did not have the compassion to follow the lead set by Robert de Hauteville in his capture of Palermo.

If they had, even the world we live in today would be a very different place. The Normans were Roman Christians, and some succeeding generations of the de Hautevilles cannot escape blame for their actions as crusaders: they did not follow the example of their sires. Not that those I have written about were saints, far from it. They lived in a cruel world and it would be incomprehensible to us to live like them, an existence where war, conquest and, if that was not to be had, destruction of the means of life were the sole occupation of a whole class of people.

The Normans were a warrior race, dedicated to conquest. The de Hauteville brothers campaigned ceaselessly both as mercenaries and lords in their own right, they were bloody and pitiless with their enemies, yet I cannot help but see a grandeur in their achievements, for they left behind something wholly unique. For all their faith in their Christian God, the sons of Tancred de Hauteville were not bigots.

I have plundered many a near contemporary informant to tell this story and invented as much besides, where no accounts exist. And it has to be remembered that those who wrote about the period did so when it was over and added to their tale the political needs they were determined to serve: some flattered, many did the opposite to a race and family they saw as agents of the Lord of Misrule.

For me, the tale of the sons of Tancred de Hauteville became the greatest story of war and conquest never told. I hope I have helped to correct that!

David Donachie

Deal, 2010.